Love is
a time of enchantment:
in it all days are fair and all fields
green. Youth is blest by it,
old age made benign: the eyes of love see
roses blooming in December,
and sunshine through rain. Verily
is the time of true-love
a time of enchantment — and
Oh! how eager is woman
to be bewitched!

SELL OUT

Poppaea Palmer, valuer in the Books and Pictures department of Trenton's auction house and in love with it's chairman Giles de Vere Trenton, is catapulted into a competition for the biggest prize of all: Deputy at Trenton's. Whilst Poppy is unearthing fabulous treasures her rival is not above dirty tricks, but she is helped by Nick Coles, who has more than a professional interest in her. Poppy has one ace: a priceless heirloom which belongs to her impoverished family. Should Poppy sell out and succeed, or hold out and forfeit her chances with Trenton's . . . and Giles?

HENRIETTE CHARLES

SELL OUT

Complete and Unabridged

ULVERSCROFT
Leicester

First published in Great Britain in 1990 by
Simon & Schuster Limited
London

First Large Print Edition
published May 1991
by arrangement with
Simon & Schuster Limited
London

British Library CIP Data

Charles, Henriette
    Sell out. — Large print ed. —
Ulverscroft large print series: romance
I. Title
813.54 [F]

ISBN 0–7089–2426–3

Published by
F. A. Thorpe (Publishing) Ltd.
Anstey, Leicestershire
Set by Words & Graphics Ltd.
Anstey, Leicestershire
Printed and bound in Great Britain by
T. J. Press (Padstow) Ltd., Padstow, Cornwall

To Georgie, Lou, and Vicky
friends

1

DAMN, damn, damn! Why don't they ever make alarm clocks loud enough? Poppy had to be at Trenton's at nine-thirty. She'd meant to get up at seven, wash her hair, make herself immaculately efficient-looking, have a proper breakfast so that she wouldn't have to nip out for a doughnut mid-morning, and arrive at the office in a cloud of cool, unhurried efficiency. Just once it would have been nice.

Reality was quite different. She had decided last night on the navy skirt. Privately she rocked with laughter whenever she saw a navy skirt; it was *the* auction house cliché, the uniform of all the Amandas, Selinas and Georgies who thought themselves tremendously lucky to be given a typing job in the auction world at a fifth of the salary they could command anywhere else. Most of this shifting shoal of nice, interchangeable girls failed to stick the course. After six months or so of little pay, no promotion prospects and being walked all over by their Heads of Department, they would get dispirited and leave. The quantum leap from secretary to valuer was practically impossible to make. Poppy was one of the few who had managed it.

So today was to be the day of the navy skirt but she did not own the regulation Hilditch & Key nice white blouse with the choirboy frill to complete the outfit.

She'd meant to iron the skirt last night but it had slipped her mind, as domestic chores had a habit of doing. She dug it out now and discovered that something white and furry had decided to moult very long hairs all over it. They absolutely refused to be brushed off, indeed they clung with such tenacity that they might have been glued on. Goodbye the navy skirt, hello the dear old favourite red. Poppy pulled, her tummy in to check herself in the mirror; true, the red had rather seated and, strictly speaking, it showed too much leg to convey an impression of studious efficiency but, on the other hand, the shorter skirt was absolute magic for her legs. The bit above the legs wasn't bad either.

Nobody could call Poppy tall. She had

once been referred to as a 'pocket Venus' and had been infuriated by the patronising phrase. In fact it was quite accurate: her figure was curvy without being fat, but it was her face and colouring that made her truly remarkable. To call her a redhead would be as unimaginative as to call the sky blue. Poppy was crowned with a cloud of glorious red-gold hair, the colour of honey with copper lights; her eyes were large and pansy brown with long silky lashes and her skin was warm cream, like a magnolia petal newly unfurled. Her skin hated makeup, within sniffing distance of a cosmetic counter it protested in hyper-allergenic rashes. This saved her a lot of time in the mornings.

She was aware that she'd left her room a tip. Thank God Suzie was away! Tomorrow and all the mornings after, Poppy told herself, she would wake up on time with the alarm clock, leap into action like the Genie of the Lamp and make the place gleam; it was only today that was different. People had been trying to instil a sense of proper tidiness in Poppy all her life and so far nobody had succeeded.

She was lucky with the bus. Trenton's

was a short quarter of an hour's walk from the flat in Redcliffe Gardens, but today she did not have a spare quarter hour.

Her spirits always lifted when she passed through the great double door under the sign that emblazoned the name of the saleroom in goldleaf on a sober green background: 'Trenton's Fine Art Valuer and Auctioneer. Established 1878'.

Sarah Cavendish was doing duty at the front desk: immaculate blonde hair tied back, executive earrings firmly clipped and, as Poppy bent to check under the desk, the navy skirt. Poppy grinned.

"Hi, Sarah. Good weekend?"

It didn't look like it, Sarah's face was overcast as a thundery sky and Poppy knew why. Sarah thought it beneath her dignity to be sitting behind the front desk, even for a brief half hour. Her real job was secretary to the Chairman, Giles de Vere Trenton, but the auction house was such a small firm that one of the absolute qualifications of working there was that you had to be prepared to jump into any rôle at the drop of a hat. Poppy always enjoyed this aspect of the company, Sarah Cavendish did not. Not only was she the Chairman's secretary she was also an Honourable and, on both counts, it really was preposterous that she should be dealing with any Tom, Dick or Harry who came in off the street.

"Poppaea, at last!" she looked at the Cartier watch on her wrist and raised her eyebrows. "You can take over here."

Sarah Cavendish was one of the few people who always called Poppaea by her full name, another had been her headmistress at school; Poppy often felt that the two of them had a certain amount in common.

"Can't stop, Sarah," she waved a sheaf of papers she had brought in with her, "I've got to go straight in to Giles. There's a flap on the Chinese bronzes. The press published the sale date a week early so we've got to move it all forward accordingly. I proof-read the catalogue at home over the weekend and now I'm just okaying it with Giles to take it to the printer." She swept into the Chairman's office leaving Sarah to gather the shreds of her dignity about her behind the humiliating desk.

Giles de Vere Trenton always made Poppy go weak at the knees. Maybe it was just because he was her boss. She kept

5

reading that power was a great aphrodisiac. Only last week the magazines had been full of a poll that told the world that sixty-three per cent of female employees were in love with their bosses. It never told her what she longed to know: who were the other thirty-seven per cent in love with? Poor darlings, they couldn't have a boss like Giles de Vere Trenton.

Giles was a descendant of the founder of Trenton's but that was not the reason he was Chairman of the auction house today. He was a very capable businessman indeed with a hard financial head and a remarkable flair for auctioneering that must have been built into his genes. His path up to the Chairman's seat had not been a straightforward one. On the way he had eliminated rivals ruthlessly and, once or twice, he had taken great commercial risks which, thanks to his uncanny understanding of the business, had paid off and left him in charge of what the press was now calling 'the most exciting small House in the field and still on the way up.'

He was on the telephone as Poppy came in. Waving his hand towards a chair he continued to talk into the phone while she sat down and organised her papers. His hazel eyes looked at her unseeingly while he concentrated his whole attention on what was being said. The conversation was clearly going to go on for some time but Poppy didn't mind waiting; it gave her a rare opportunity to study Giles in his office.

God, he was handsome! But that wasn't the whole story. Poppy decided that if she was to choose one word to describe Giles in his setting, it would be 'expensive'. The office was large but not ostentatiously so; there was enough wall space for portraits of the three generations of Trentons who had gone before him, all of whom had had the good sense to commission the best artist of their day. Giles's desk and chair were, of course, Chippendale and you didn't need even a second glance to be absolutely sure they were absolutely genuine.

The man himself continued this theme of 'only the best'. Giles always wore a suit, conservative in colour and perfect in cut. His shirts were sometimes white, more often a pale sky blue that warmed the olive of his skin, his ties came from Hermes, his mirror-bright shoes from Trickers. In all, it was the complete uniform of the successful City gentleman. Seeing him in the street you would guess he was a banker or financier, something of that sort, and you would be quite sure that he was at the top of his profession. The only touch of individualism he allowed himself was in his cufflinks of which he had a fabulous collection. Today he wore rare gold coins bearing the head of Alexander the Great. They would have fetched a fortune in the saleroom but instead he had chosen to lessen their commercial value by adapting them to fasten his cuffs. It was a stylish conceit.

Giles's hazel eyes now stared unseeingly at the Augustus John of his father as he concentrated every scrap of attention on the conversation in progress. Poppy noticed that he was getting one or two silver hairs in among the very dark brown. He was thirty-seven she knew and, as yet, had escaped marriage.

At last the conversation was concluded.

"Done the bronzes?" he fired at her, too busy to waste time on preliminaries. She nodded and indicated the papers.

"Good girl." His eyes came to rest on her knees. She wished the skirt had been longer but it wouldn't do to wiggle it down. "We're in a bit of a jam," he got up to stretch his long legs, "I'm afraid you'll be getting a lot of extra work from now on. How are you fixed? No holiday coming up, nothing too demanding at home?"

She shook her head.

"Good girl," he said again, his eyes sliding back to her knees. He laughed suddenly and she looked at him enquiringly.

"Sorry, Poppy, you must think I'm quite imbecile today. I've had rather a shock over the weekend. Poor old Maurice had a heart attack so it's a question of thinking fast on my feet and trying to apportion the workload."

"How is he?" Poppy was fond of Maurice, Deputy Chairman and father figure to them all.

"Oh, he's okay. The health insurance scheme seems to be paying for unlimited champagne and pretty nurses in one of those small clinics. Maurice is in his element by all accounts, I've not been to see him . . . maybe you could do that this evening or some time soon? Try and have a chat with the nurses, better still his doctor. Women are good at that sort of thing. Then you could tell me when they think he might be able to come back.

"You've been doing a lot of work with the old boy lately," he went on. She nodded. "Right. Well, I've got a list here of his work, current and prospective. Sales on this sheet, house visits for valuation on this sheet, and speculative social contacts here; people with valuable collections who might want to pop the odd thing and who should be reminded that we exist. Maurice's old pals act. I'd like you to tick the items on each sheet that you would be able to take over from him."

"Is this promotion?" she couldn't help but ask.

Giles gave one of his rare and charming smiles.

"I wouldn't call it that, not just yet. Let's call it very hard work for now. I'll up your salary by five hundred but you'll still be just plain Assistant Director with special responsibility for — what is it now?"

"Pictures, prints, books and manuscripts."

"It's grown a bit since you first began,"

Giles commented.

"Maurice kept handing me more."

"Well, if he thinks you're capable, that's fine. You'll have to find a bit of a secretary to share. You might ask Amanda, I don't think Francis is keeping her very busy. You certainly won't have time any more for donkey work. No more filling out the result forms after your sales." His smile warmed his eyes.

"Thank God for that!"

Result forms were a terrible chore. They had to be filled out in triplicate on computer, card index and flimsies for the convenience of hundreds of people who lived in the woodwork of the art world and had nothing better to do than produce endless graphs of price predictions.

There was silence in the office for a while as Poppy concentrated on ticking the items on the various lists; anything that she had any special knowledge of received a tick, as well as any particular client or sale that Maurice had discussed with her over the last weeks. It came to about half the list. She handed the papers back to Giles who scanned them quickly then looked up at her.

"It's quite a load. Sure you can take them all?"

"I can try."

"We must find time to talk further. I think we should discuss how you see your long term rôle in the company. If you're to play a larger part I think you should come to dinner to meet some of the influential people who might help you. I'll get Sarah to check with you on dates." It had the ring of dismissal.

"Do you want to look over these?" She indicated her weekend's homework on the Chinese bronzes.

"No point!" Again he smiled his crooked, charming smile. "If you can't make a decent job of a catalogue by now, you shouldn't still be here."

She got up to go.

"I'll see Maurice tonight then?"

"Send Francis in, will you?"

She nodded but Giles didn't see. He had already picked up his telephone and was dialling the first three digits that would enable him to speak to New York.

More responsibility and an invitation to Giles' house! Poppy was smiling as she made her way to Furniture, the lair of Francis Dernholm. She never liked Furniture, and it was not only because there was a rivalry between herself and Francis that was not always friendly. Furniture was the one department she found depressing. There was something really sad about large numbers of mediocre pieces of furniture huddled together anyhow with a door missing here, a leg broken there, or a great burn mark in the middle of a lovely veneer. Of all the pieces waiting for sale it was the furniture that constantly reminded you of the transience of personal possessions. 'We belonged to someone once,' the pieces mutely cried, 'we were part of a home.' Poppy couldn't come into Furniture without thinking gloomily of death, domestic breakup and financial need.

Amanda Wright was the one bright spot there. Poppy liked her a lot. Amanda was not one of the graduate girls who grudged their apprenticeship at the typewriter; she was wholeheartedly happy as a secretary, and she was a very good one. Poppy was delighted she'd have a share of Amanda's time; her own secretarial skills were sketchy and as slow as two-fingered typing must always be. Life would look up a lot with someone else to mind the Remington.

When Poppy came into Furniture she found Amanda and Francis dodging over and under tables and desks, pulling out drawers to examine dovetailing and shining torches inside sideboards to note the composition of the carcase. Francis was cataloguing while Amanda took his words down in shorthand.

"More woodworm in here than ants in an anthill!" rang out from inside a large Victorian wardrobe. "Thank God both my legs are my own, darling. Anyone with a peg-leg would be lucky to get out of here alive. We'll be bloody fortunate if this wardrobe isn't just a heap of dust by the date of the sale." Francis Dernholm uncoiled himself from inside the vast piece of furniture. He wore the bright red boiler suit that he always affected on these occasions. It was sloganned with advertising strips for Mobil, Marlboro and several lesser companies. Francis always hinted that it had been a personal gift from a dear friend, a racing driver too famous to mention.

It was normal practice for Directors

examining furniture to wear the same green baize aprons that the porters wore to protect their clothing. The aprons were very smart indeed with the Trenton's logo discreetly embroidered in gold. Poppy had decided that the only reason Francis wore the dreadful boiler suit was that he was such a snob, he would have been wounded to the quick if a viewing punter had mistaken him for a porter. Poppy and the others were always being asked to shift this here and that there so the public could see things better, they took it in good part, but if it ever happened to Francis he would purse his lips in anger and wordessly point to the nearest porter.

Amanda was following him around with her shorthand pad. Quick as an eel, Francis had transferred his attention to the next item and was now lying on his back under a table, Amanda bending over it to catch the pearls of wisdom as they floated up from floor level. She waved at Poppy and mouthed "Hello", careful not to talk over Francis in full flow.

" . . . provenance uncertain. Signed with the initials GB. Possibly George Bullock. Full stop." And then he went on in a more casual voice, "And if they believe that, Amanda, they'll believe anything."

He straightened up from under the table and caught sight of Poppy. "Ah! It's the little Winchendon heiress." He gave a sharklike smile. "How's the Hoarde? You know Giles only took you on to get his sticky hands on it?"

This was Francis's constant taunt. The Hoarde belonged in Winchendon Hall, the Palmers' Devon house which stood, stone-built and solid, on the edge of Dartmoor. Once grand, the house was now suffering noticeably from Henry Palmer's chronic inability to make millions. It would take hundreds of thousands at least to provide the new roof it needed, the central heating, and the countless other things an old house required by tyrannical right.

Poppy always thought that Hoarde was a singularly inappropriate name for Winchendon's historical relic. 'Hoarde' conjured up precious jewels guarded by fire-breathing dragons. There was no dragon associated with this Hoarde, only one great emerald and that of very doubtful quality.

An ancestor at the time of the Armada

had managed to capture a Spanish galleon. This was the version recorded in his own diary still preserved in the Library at Winchendon, and certainly it read as a very noble tale of derring-do. In fact two other contemporary accounts told in no uncertain terms how the Spanish vessel had been wrecked by the time-honoured West Country method of luring it on to the rocks with false signals from ashore. The looting that followed had been just as ruthless as such looting and pillaging had been for generations before and since on the stretch of coast around Devon and Cornwall. Whatever the truth of the conflicting accounts, one concrete and inescapable fact had emerged: an Armada Chest.

Every noble Spaniard engaged in the cause of bringing England and good Queen Bess to their respective knees, had come equipped with such a chest. It held what was referred to as 'His Personal Necessaries', objects not particularly valuable in themselves; no 'roppes of pearle each large as a good man's thum naile', no 'rubyes large as pigeones egge'. Instead the Chest was a personal possession, a wooden box containing what any soldier in the seventeenth century, or indeed the twentieth, would take with him to war. There was of course a pewter plate, his flask, his pewter mug and eating irons. Then his golden seal containing a South American emerald (much flawed) into which had been cut his coat of arms. The interest lay not in the intrinsic value of the emerald which, though large, was of very poor quality, but in the fact that it must have been one of the first such stones brought back from the New World. There were also two black anonymous sticks which were far too decayed to be reliably analysed as anything at all but which had been dignified over time as two sticks of sealing wax with which to impress the emerald's crest. No one would ever know for sure if this was the case, the two sticks being far too important historically ever to be melted by a match. Sealing wax time had dubbed them, and sealing wax they would remain.

There were various other necessary articles but the centrepiece of the collection, the one thing which made the whole hotchpotch of things unbearably poignant for Poppy, was the little miniature of the

Spaniard's family.

The soldier had commissioned the picture knowing he would be going to war but had obviously not realised that the fleet would set sail so soon and so, although his wife had been painted in meticulous detail on the tiny square of ivory, and one child also was substantially blocked in, the last, not much more than a dark cherubic baby, was indicated by the slightest wispiest strokes of the miniaturist's single-stranded squirrelhair brush. The unfinished image always conjured up to Poppy a hasty leave-taking; the young father in such a hurry, so proud to be off to capture this haughty, stubborn island of England and lay it at the feet of the noble King of Spain; so eager to return to his beautiful young wife with the shy, downcast dark eyes and tell her how easy it was, how noble his deeds, how natural for any Spanish noble to conquer the small insignificant country.

For all it was a dim ancestor who had lured the Spaniard to his death, and indeed for all this small deception had contributed its share to the ultimate defeat of the Armada and the salvation of England's independence, Poppy could not help but feel uncomfortable and ashamed at the treachery her ancestor had perpetrated in the name of war.

She decided to ignore Francis's taunt. "Giles would like to see you in his office," she said.

Francis looked like the cat that got the cream. He started to climb out of his boiler suit, hung it carefully on its special hanger so that it should not rumple, and resumed his jacket. Quite unashamed in front of the girls, he went to stand before the mirrored door of one of the sale cupboards and took his time combing his hair, adjusting his bow tie and generally making sure that he would not disappoint his adoring public. By the time he had finished he looked like the sleek, self-satisfied, rather overfed twenty-eight-year-old Etonian he was.

"No slacking," he warned Amanda. "Now I don't want you coffee-housing with my secretary and keeping her away from my work," he said to Poppy, and his voice held no hint that he was joking.

"My secretary too now!" she said pertly. Francis gave her a very sour look.

"It was Giles's suggestion," Poppy said sweetly. She knew this was the only way

Francis would give her any ground. "I'll have a chat with Amanda while you're with the Chairman; we can talk about how best to divide her time."

For once Francis was stuck for a really good exit line.

"We'll see about this," was all he could manage in a petulant tone as he stalked off to Giles's office.

Amanda and Poppy looked at each other and giggled.

"Pompous ass!" Amanda grinned. "What's all this then, boss?"

"I don't have time to fill you in now — " the Chinese bronzes were pressing — "what if we stick the company for lunch while I brief you? I should think the expenses could run to tagliatelle at Mama Rosa's."

"One o'clock?"

It was agreed.

Poppy came across Francis Dernholm a second time that day. It was an unexpected meeting that took her by surprise.

Despite very long hours indeed at work, she had not forgotten about visiting old Maurice Blessingham. It was after eight o'clock when she eventually got away but she had the St John's Wood address of the clinic and, as it was private, she knew they'd be quite elastic about visiting hours. She bought some pink roses with long stiff stems from the florist at the tube station. They were really more suitable for someone who'd just given birth to a baby girl but chrysanths were the only other choice and they always reminded her of funerals.

"I believe Mr Blessingham has another visitor at present." The pretty nurse in the starched cap looked down her list and rang the room to check. "His visitor has just left," she said, smiling professionally. "Do go up, Miss Palmer."

Poppy crossed the hall to the lift and waited as the little light descended. When the door slid open there stood Francis. For a moment he looked as surprised as she but he recovered first.

"Come to view the body, darling?" He stepped out and stood deliberately in front of her so that she had to stretch around him to press the button once more to open the doors.

"Excuse me, Francis." She squeezed round him and into the lift. "How is he?"

"Not dead yet." He jammed his foot in the door so it could not close. "I should like to see you in my office tomorrow. Shall we say eight-thirty? We need to reapportion Amanda's hours."

"She seemed quite happy with the arrangement we made together over lunch." Poppy smiled sweetly, shoved Francis's foot out of the way with her own, and sailed up to the third floor.

Maurice was sitting up in bed with what looked suspiciously like a tartan bedjacket draped around his shoulders.

"Darling girl, wonderful to see you! And roses too. Oh, lovely lovely, just the pink of those delicious cherubs' bottoms floating around cinquecento ceilings. Terrible long cruel stems . . . they're quite clueless these florists. How can they imagine we want all that stalk, those horrible thorns, and just the tiny heads sticking up on top, like the knob on a park railing? Be an angel with the secateurs, will you? Just over there by the little wash basin thing. Terrible colour isn't it, darling? I believe it's what's known as an Avocado suite. You have to pay extra for the colours, too, when white is so much more hygienic. You can't ever see if the

Avocado is really clean."

Poppy was at the little basin which, she saw, held no fewer than three bottles of disinfectant; Maurice was clearly taking no chances with germy Avocado.

"Now, a diagonal cut and then give the stems a good hard bruising with the handles. I know it seems cruel but it's kindness really, they couldn't take up the water otherwise."

Poppy did as she was told.

"You forget, Maurice, I live in the country. I'm always doing flowers." She arranged them in a very humble hospital vase and put them on the only space in the room that was not occupied by magazines, pills, lotions, or very, very expensive flower arrangements. Her few pink roses were flanked by banks of orchids and gardenias from Pulbrook & Gould.

"Sweet simplicity." Maurice was contemplating them with his head to one side.

"Small and cheap you mean," she said, ashamed of her last minute tube station token.

"No, my dear," a little frown crossed his old man's brow, "I don't mean that at all. I remember being twenty-four and

24

struggling for money in a world that thinks you should be content with prestige. Your flowers touch me. Thank you."

It would have been impossibly awkward to kiss him with the hospital table across his bed so she picked up his hand and carried it to her cheek.

"Dear Maurice. Are you all right?"

"How do I look?" He held up his hand. "No, please don't answer that. I know your terrible predeliction for truth, Poppaea Palmer. Just tell me I look wonderful and then we'll both be happy!"

She laughed. "It obviously hasn't affected your mind. I was terrified what I might find, if you want the truth. Heart attacks haven't come into my orbit before." She studied him closely. "You know, you look exactly the same." Which was almost the truth. There was an odd colour about him and a look as if suddenly the skin on his face had been pulled in a different direction but, compared to the zombie she had been expecting, he really looked very good indeed.

"We must have a good long gossip, Poppy, but not tonight. I'm tired now. That little vulture Francis came sniffing and tried to grill me on all my important sales. He didn't get much, only the few red herrings I threw him." Maurice sank weakly back into the pillows but his smile held relish at the remembrance of his trickery.

"He tired me more than I realised," he continued in a thin voice. "Take care, Poppaea. Francis is after my job and you must stand in his way. If it comes to a competition, I want you to win; I haven't consolidated my position all these years to have it taken over by a second-rate poodle." He closed his eyes and there was silence for a while but he had evidently not finished. Poppy sat still and quiet in the visitor's chair until Maurice's eyes opened again.

"Still here?" There was rare affection in his gaze. "The Millington sale is the one you must concentrate on.

"No-one has realised that the large oil in the dining room is probably a Rubens, one of his best paysages." He fell silent again, his eyelids drooping. "Here's the key to my flat," he said finally, after fumbling inside the bedjacket. "You will find the folder on the sale in the Boulle desk, the little drawer on the right. I have started researching the picture but you must follow the threads which lead to Antwerp; if you can authenticate the picture by the sale date in June you will have a spectacular coup on your hands."

Awestruck, Poppy took the key.

"One more thing," he went on. "Will you take my *cymbidiums* home with you? My daily simply doesn't understand about orchids. She will water them from the top."

"Help!" Poppy grinned. "Now that's a real responsibility. I don't know which I'm more nervous about — the Rubens or the orchids!"

He summoned up a smile. "Kill the plants and I transfer my support to the Dernholm camp."

And with a weak wave of the hand, he dismissed her.

2

TRENTON'S was to hold its first ever evening sale.

The air crackled with nervous excitement, like the atmosphere before a teenager's first party: this was the start of something big. Evening sales were quite a new event even in the exalted realms of Sotheby's and Christie's. An evening auction was always a glittering black tie affair reserved for the really Big Number; it didn't need spelling out that if tonight went off at half-cock it would be a very public failure in Trenton's bid to join the big boys in the upper section of the market.

Preparations had been started months ago. Every well-connected secretary who had ever worked at Trenton's was personally charmed by Giles over the telephone into producing the name and address of every wealthy, titled or famous relative, godparent or friend she had. Dethroned foreign Royals who were known to attend such things for money or a nice little diamond keepsake were booked in advance. The Press were not forgotten: Betty Kenward, gossip columnist for *Harpers & Queen* from time immemorial, and Peter Townend, her arch-rival from the *Tatler*, were both invited and each given the exclusive promise that he or she would be the only columnist there. A girl was allotted to each of them with instructions to keep them in different rooms on pain of death. Giles had even hired a television camera crew in case it was a slow news evening (with his luck it would be) and a world record price could be slipped into the last slot of 'News at Ten'.

Everyone was ready in place at least an hour beforehand. Tonight the van Niri collection of Important and Magnificent Jewels was to go under the hammer, along with some other pieces from here and there to pad out the sale. If he was really going for it, Giles had been known to sell a hundred lots in an hour; tonight there were a hundred and sixty lots which meant that at worst the sale would be over in a short one hour, forty. That was allowing for the most pessimistic scenario:

the whole sale falling flat with little or no competitive bidding. However, if things went as Giles hoped, the sale might really catch fire in which case it would fill two good hours, the maximum tolerance time for the punters' bottoms on the small gilt chairs. Giles, as usual, had foreseen every eventuality.

The girls were to model the jewels in the time between the guests arriving and the sale beginning. There had been a restrained riot in the boardroom when Giles had suggested such an unconventional proceeding. His fellow board directors were unanimous in vetoing the idea as a security impossibility. Whilst in their care, the collection was valued at over three million. How could it be protected in a crowded room? Half the thieves in London would come if they got to hear. After all, you only had to snatch one girl and hold her to ransom. You couldn't seriously suggest frisking all your guests as they came in, the offence caused would be incalculable.

"Don't think I haven't thought of all those things." Giles was at his iron-smoothest. "I know as well as you do the additional security costs involved, but think for a moment." He looked around his board. "We're breaking into a new league, right?" They nodded. "The van Niri collection is good, some of it's very good indeed." Again the affirmative nods. "But let's not kid ourselves that it's any better than the four or five top jewellery sales that will come up in London and Geneva over the next twelve months, right? So what we need are the big prices, the record set for pieces in certain categories."

"Punters have no imagination — " it was one of Giles's favourite maxims — "show them a diamond necklace on a piece of velvet all locked up in a case, and what do they see? Purely an investment." More nods. "Show it on a beautiful bosom and immediately you're selling them a dream. People will pay almost anything for a dream. We've got a lot of firm young bosoms on the staff — let's use them."

There wasn't a vote against him.

Poppy had thought long and hard about what to wear. She'd discussed it with her flatmate, Suzie, over the phone and had been urged to borrow "my very good new black Jean Muir". Poppy knew you couldn't go wrong in a very good new black Jean Muir but when she put it on she knew she couldn't go very far right in it either. The image in the mirror said 'safe choice' but it thrilled her not at all. She went downstairs to ask the advice of Suzie's boyfriend, Ned, who lived in the flat below.

"Where's the funeral, Pops?" was his comment as he opened the door to her.

"Oh dear, is it that bad? It's the new expensive one of Suzie's. She said to borrow it."

"Oh, is it that one? I thought it looked familiar." He put his head to one side. "Funny, she looks really marvellous in it. You look like a dirge."

"Thanks."

"You wanted the truth."

"I suppose so." She shrugged ruefully. "It's a confidence crisis, Ned." She told him about modelling jewellery among the fleet of sleek saleroom girls.

"Tell you what, Poppy," Ned's eyes caught light with excitement, "will you let me be your art director tonight? I've got an idea. I think I know exactly how to make you shine like the only

32

star in the heavens amongst that lot of well-bred, longnosed racehorses. I bet they'll all wear sensible beige tights and comfortable shoes with medium heels. Let's do something different. Glamour is the watchword, okay?"

And up they went to raid Poppy's wardrobe like two excited children.

Like everyone else working in the auction world, she had fallen under the spell of collecting: buying and selling in the saleroom on her own account. The only trouble was she seemed to do more buying than selling because her absolute passion was for really beautiful old clothes, the *robes du style* of the twenties, thirties, forties and fifties. They would have been incomplete without the jewellery that went with them so she collected that too. It was definitely not the sort of jewellery that got into the Important category, like the van Niri collection to be sold tonight, just the bits that were thrown in at the end of a Vintage Couture sale to make up a complete lot.

Once she had got over her initial nervousness of putting up her hand at her first Vintage Couture auction, the hand seemed to develop an uncontrollable urge of its own to spring into the air whenever it came within sounding distance of an Auctioneer's gavel.

Poppy's fastidious eye for a well-cut dress had inevitably led her to the monthly sales at Christie's in South Kensington. After her first visit she was ensnared. She saw and coveted a shocking pink Schiaparelli dress (accompanied by a photograph of Elsa Maxwell wearing it to a gala ball in Venice), and was thrilled to buy it at a fraction of the price of a new dress.

The Schiaparelli was only the start. It hooked Poppy on fabulous fabrics and craftsman cutting. Her next acquisition had been a Dior New Look afternoon dress with hundreds of yards of swishing taffetta and stiff net underskirts, as worn by well-bred debutantes being presented at Court. After that there was no stopping her. On she went to a Worth slipper-satin wedding dress, steamily redolent of Jean Harlow. Each new dress she bought conjured up a different personality. When she was buying, Poppy had two golden rules which she never violated: the garment must be made by one of the top designers of its period, and whatever she bought must not be so fragile that it was likely to disintegrate at the dry cleaner's. She always sent the clothes to be professionally cleaned; it was the only way to get rid of their musty smell. After three years of collecting, Poppy had quite a railful of these elaborate and exquisite creations. She simply enjoyed owning them, taking them out to look at from time to time, the occasions when they could actually be worn being very rare.

"It's a terrible thing," Ned mused as he held up a steel grey beaded Paquin sheath from a Vintage Couture sale, "only gays are meant to like doing this sort of thing, yet I can think of nothing sexier than creating my own woman for the evening. I don't think there's even the vaguest suspicion about my gender — " Poppy shook her head with a little smile — "but I know Suzie would look at me very oddly if she knew what we were up to. Don't tell on me, will you, Poppy?"

"She might not think it odd at all, you know," Poppy said. "I'd never thought about it before but it could be really sensuous being turned into something by a man. It puts a new slant on dreary old *My Fair Lady*, I must say. I thought it was all about elocution lessons but really it's sexy as hell!"

"Darling, am I turning you on?" Ned dropped the dress to reach out but Poppy had already twisted out of reach.

"Down, boy! We haven't the time. I've got to be there by six, remember?"

"God, you're a hard woman, my darling! Come on then, I think I've got it. The Rita Hayworth look. Did you ever see *Gilda*?"

Poppy had seen the film, and when Ned held up the red dress she remembered the dance sequence and realised exactly what he had in mind. The dress was a strapless silk satin sheath *pour le cocktail*, Paris circa 1950. When she had bought it she was sure it had never been worn at all, it was still in silk tissue paper with little lavender bags embroidered with the designer's signature pinned to the padded satin hanger. The original tissue paper, crinkled up, mounded out the shaping of the bust.

"I understand," she said, and went off

to the bathroom to lock the door between herself and Ned while she poured herself into the sheath.

"See if you can find the gloves," she called through the door, hoping the occupational therapy would distract him from lustful thoughts, "elbow-length."

Finally looking in the mirror, she was very pleased with herself. She bent over till her head almost touched her knees and gave her abundant hair a hundred strokes with the hairbrush. When she straightened up again her face was framed in a luminescent cloud of red-gold, while the pleasure of knowing that she looked wonderful lent a glow to her skin that could never be achieved by makeup.

"Ready?" she called to Ned, and without waiting for the answer, out she came.

When he caught sight of her his face froze in astonishment and the hand that was holding the pair of gloves fell to his side.

"My God," he said, "I had no idea."

Poppy didn't say anything, Ned's reaction was good enough.

"Will you promise me one thing?" he said, recovering. "Promise you'll let me take you out to dinner when you're wearing that frock?"

"*À trois,* when Suzie comes back." Poppy smoothed on the long gloves he had handed her. She couldn't manage the little pearl buttons so held out her arms to Ned for help. For once, he was struck too dumb to take advantage of the situation: the buttons were fastened without even a token caress. It was almost as if he were embarrassed by the blatant beauty of the new Poppy.

"You can't possibly walk down the street in that," he said, thinking clearly at last, "you'd never get there alive."

"Oh my lord! I hadn't thought. It's far too late to phone for a taxi; even dear old Charley the cab would take twenty minutes to get here." Charley the cab was the girls' favourite mini cab driver. When they were broke, he never minded being paid the next time.

"Oh, Ned, I'm going to be late. How terrible." Poppy could feel the prickle of tears starting behind her eyes. Typical to concentrate on the frills and forget about the essentials, she chided herself.

"Don't worry," Ned saw her distress, "I'll get you there. Come on." He put his arm around her shoulders and swept her downstairs.

Ned's usual means of transport was a bike because it was environmentally friendly. However, cycling had its drawbacks, chiefly that it was really not very fast. When he needed to get somewhere in a hurry Ned would hustle along on his very large motorbike. The bike was his pride and joy and the second love of his life after Suzie and all the rest of womankind.

It was a 1950s Triumph Bonneville 750cc; one motorbike was much the same as another to Poppy but from long acquaintance with Ned she understood that this gleaming monster was the last of the old brigade made in England in the days when bikes really *were* bikes.

There was no way she could climb on the back without revealing all to the whole of London so she perched sidesaddle and told Ned for God's sake to go easy round the corners.

"Here we go," he said, and the bike gave a healthy growl. The five-minute journey from the flat to Trenton's was accomplished to a background music of extremely loud wolf whistles and appreciative but unrepeatable catcalls. Poppy's arrival at Trenton's door was not inconspicuous.

"Do I look okay?" she asked Ned, wondering what the wind had done to her hair.

"Darling, okay is the understatement of the year." He blew her a kiss. "Enjoy!" And with a deep roar of the bike's pedigree engine he was gone, to make way for the fleet of chauffeur-driven limousines drawing up to debouch their exalted occupants.

Poppy hurried through the doors.

"Loved the bike rider, darling. What a handsome hunk — you must introduce me one day. Couldn't you afford to arrive properly in a taxi?" Francis hissed at her.

She had no time to exchange pleasantries. It was off to the strongroom and the extra Security Chief who was always hired for the occasions they had a lot of jewels on the premises. He had the schedule of who was to wear what, and when it was to be clocked in again. Poppy felt quite weak as, quite matter-of-factly, he loaded her with a quarter of a million pounds' worth of diamonds. A necklace of round-cut *rivière* diamonds filled the space above her cleavage, long earrings dangled almost to her shoulders, and round each satin-gloved wrist there was a blaze of twin diamond Cartier bracelets.

The Security Chief pretended to shield his eyes against the blaze of jewels. "Well, darlin', if *you* can't get rid of this lot, nobody will."

Poppy ventured out of the quiet strongroom into the hubbub of the main reception. The noise and buzz of excitement was so strong it felt almost like a physical blow. For a moment she was very frightened and wanted to run back again into the quiet. Then she caught sight of Giles, only his tall backview moving away from her, but it gave her all the incentive she needed to face the crowd. The guests were drinking but she, like the other girls modelling jewellery, held in her hand a card bearing her lot numbers instead of a champagne glass.

Threading through the mass of people she made her way towards Giles by a roundabout route, stopping here and there to answer questions. His eyes widened fractionally when he saw her and then, in a moment, his face resumed its normal impassive expression. He beckoned her over.

"Do you know the Earl of Ilchester?"

"Only from the gossip columns," was Poppy's honest reply, out before she could check herself.

"Believe it all." The Earl was obviously amused by her reply. "I'm absolutely wicked." He reached out to touch the diamonds around her neck, running his finger along underneath the necklace to make the stones sparkle in the light; while he was doing this the back of his hand was coinciding with Poppy's cleavage.

"If I buy the necklace, you come with it?" he asked.

"Not for sale," she said, softening her rejection with a smile.

The Earl was a colourful Irishman with one castle, three ex-wives, and very many girlfriends whom he ran simultaneously,as anyone who read a newspaper couldn't help but know. In real life he was just as handsome as his photographs and had something you could not see in black and white: the most seductive blue, blue eyes. You could drown in the depth of their colour; they also shone with an innocence that would have fooled the unwary.

"Giles, where do you find them?" It was plain he was not talking about the diamonds.

"Freddy, old man, stop monopolising the bait. Poppy's job tonight is to get the best price for all that ice. All the world knows you haven't got a bean.

"Poppy, will you go over to that couple?" Giles pointed to a very ancient man and a younger woman who might or might not be his daughter. "Dr Hindermitt is one of the stronger contenders for the necklace. Hands off, Freddy!" And, reluctantly, the Earl finally did stop his fingering.

"Just a moment more, Giles," he pleaded. "My reputation would crumble if I parted with a beautiful girl so soon. You must bring her to dinner. Bully him if he forgets, will you, darling?"

"Of course." As though she spent her life bullying Giles. At last, Poppy could escape.

She turned to chat up Dr Hindermitt. His was another name she knew well from the newspapers but this time from the business pages. He was an industrialist and

43

philanthropist with an illustrious present but a very well-concealed past. There had been rumours of a Nazi background and lots of plastic surgery.

Conversation with the industrialist was heavy going. Technical stuff with caratage of each stone and the date of settings. The careful doctor even made her take the necklace and Cartier bracelets off so he could inspect the back for damage or repairs. The instant her hands went to the clasp at the back of her neck, two security guards materialised at her side.

Poppy could only relax when the actual sale began and she and all the other girls were stripped of their jewels which were then carried in by porters, item by item, as their turn came to be sold. Giles had been quite right. The pieces looked immaculate on their velvet cushions, each accompanied by two armed and Perspex-masked security guards, but what they gained by perfect display they lost in the magical life imbued by adorning human faces and bodies.

Sales were always theatrical. The chief and only actor was Giles the Auctioneer. Subservient to him were the bidders who took temporary starring parts but their rôle was always silent, confined to the showing of a hand or the discreet nod of a head. It was not often that the drama of a full-blown duel developed between bidders.

The entire Trenton's staff stood at the back of the room with their attention focused on Giles. He was like a conductor, Poppy thought, standing on the podium in his dinner jacket, the centre and motivator of it all. Auctioneering was very like conducting, a lonely and demanding pinnacle, providing a centre point from which both players and audience were manipulated. You could not have an auctioneer with no personality, there would be no soul to a sale. Giles's presence certainly had something to do with his height and his dark and definite good looks but there was more to it than that; personality was what it came down to, that indefinible something that can never be precisely defined but is as obvious as the sun's shining. Giles had the commanding presence to hold the whole evening together and to invest it with an almost unbearable level of anticipatory excitement: a feeling that this was where the action was. Anyone not here tonight was missing the buzz at the centre of the universe.

Bidding was brisk, right from the start the prices were good. There were two theories as to how to conduct a sale: either you broke your bidders in gently with moderate lots and got them used to quite high prices from which things could only go up, or you took the gamble.

Tonight Giles had taken the gamble. Reversing the order printed in the catalogue, he started by selling a great sapphire known as the Star of Rajputan by reason of a sentimental and completely unauthenticated story linking the stone to a legend of the undying love between a Maharajah and a (female) snakecharmer in the fifteenth century. Giles's reason for this change in the running order was that he knew that he had a buyer determined to secure the stone at all costs. An Australian collector had been foolish enough to express in print the fact that he had 'the biggest bloody ruby, the biggest bloody emerald and now he was going for the tote treble. He bloody wanted the biggest bloody sapphire that money could buy.'

The Australian was a big fish advertising

his interest in advance; Giles just had to reel him in.

There were several telephone bidders from abroad, each of whom would have expressed an interest before the sale and booked a telephone line direct to the saleroom for the duration of the sale.

Telephone bids always made sales much more exciting. Sale-room staff would be on the end of each line, relaying the instructions to Giles. Francis, Sarah Cavendish, and two others were manning the telephone bids tonight. They sat in a line to Giles's immediate right, each with a black telephone in front of them. Flavia, one-man-band of Textiles & Photographs, was manning the Australian 'phone. At first the Australian was bidding against a client on the floor, a well-known London jeweller, but as the bids started to go up in tens of thousands the London bidder dropped out and he was bidding against the house. This meant that Giles either had, or was pretending that he had, a client who had left a written limit up to which he was prepared to pay for the sapphire.

"Forty-five thousand," Flavia relayed from the telephone.

"Forty-eight." Giles was quick, with not a second's hesitation.

Flavia's consultations were getting longer. She murmured into the telephone, listened, raised her hand a fraction. The silence was palpable. Everyone wanted the stone to reach the fifty. Flavia spoke more urgently, her hand over the receiver hiding the conversation.

Giles raised the ivory gavel.

If the Australian did not cap him, and if Giles was inventing the bids from the house, Trenton's would get stuck with a large sapphire in the vaults and a lot of egg on its face.

"Going at forty-eight thousand pounds, ladies and gentlemen, the sapphire known as the Star of Rajputan. Going once," he knocked the ivory gavel on the desk, "going twice . . . "

Flavia was speaking urgently into her mouthpiece. All the eyes in the house went from her to Giles like spectators at a Wimbledon tennis match.

"Fifty thousand," she said at last. The Australian had come good, and the room released its tension in a collective sigh.

From then on the tone of the sale was

set. Whether the Australian had won the sapphire against a real opponent or against the auctioneer's iron nerve, only Giles would ever know. The excitement of the first high price generated auction fever in the room. Elbows shot in the air as though the bidders had St Vitus' Dance. The van Niri sale was going to go down in legend; pieces bought from it would have a value-enhancing name on their pedigree. Giles had done what he set out to do: he'd got the adrenalin going in the jaded veins of the super-rich. From here on in he could take a more relaxed stance. Doing his job efficiently would be enough.

Bidding was brisk from the floor, and as if that were not enough, it was further spiced by the remaining telephone bidders; there were two New York collectors, one in Tokyo. A minion from the Japanese Embassy had been drafted in to cope with the Japanese language problem. When it came to mega-Yen it was important to have an accurate knowledge of the language: mispronounce a vowel and you could be misplacing millions. The two American lines were being manned by Francis, who was taking his bids coolly, and Sarah

Cavendish who, Poppy could see, was getting flustered as the numbers got higher. Once she had to be sharply corrected by Giles when she said 'a thousand' instead of 'ten thousand'.

Last time she gets that job, Poppy thought, and wondered what on earth had made Giles imagine Sarah was up to it in the first place. She smiled to see that the Honourable Sarah was wearing an evening version of the auction house uniform. This time the frilly-necked blouse was made of silk.

"She's got the IQ of a fish," Amanda Wright whispered to Poppy.

"A small fish," Poppy hissed back.

"The Honourable Sarah Fish-Cavendish," Amanda replied. It was a small and feeble joke but in the tense atmosphere it gave them both a bad attack of the giggles. Francis shot them a cyanide look.

Lot sixty-three.

Poppy felt a little pang as 'her' diamond necklace came up for sale. She felt responsible somehow: its price would reflect on her salesmanship. Giles started it off at its top estimate, a breathtaking price and quite a gamble, but he had gauged the atmosphere well. The Earl of Ilchester put in a little bid early on. Giles widened his eyes very slightly in warning to his friend who then obediently left the bidding to the serious contenders.

Quite soon the grave-faced Doctor Hindermitt was duelling against the Japanese on the telephone. Unconsciously Poppy put a hand to her neck. It had been good to feel the diamonds there. She looked at Hindermitt's blonde companion; for all the ball gown she was wearing had cost thousands of pounds from a French couturier (probably St Laurent, said Poppy's practised eye), the girl looked cheap and flashy. Poppy hoped the necklace wouldn't end up around her neck. She'd rather imagine it gracing the neck of a pale, modest Japanese.

"Two hundred and sixty thousand pounds." Giles had taken the bid from Tokyo. "Come, Doctor, you must save the necklace for the nation!" There was a ripple of laughter and the tycoon fell for the bait.

"Tree hundret thousand and hev done with it!" he boomed magniloquently.

This was enough to secure the necklace;

the price was twice its top estimate and indeed more than it was worth in cold commerce. There was a small ripple of applause. Freddy Ilchester turned theatrically in his chair and directed his applause at Poppy.

"I didn't know you knew *him*," Amanda said, impressed.

"Tell you later." Giles had already moved on to the next lot.

Suddenly Poppy was tired. The hot bright glare of the television arc lights had given her a mighty headache; she wondered that Giles, the focus of their beams, seemed as quietly cool as ever. Ever the consummate professional, not so much as a drop of sweat glinted on his forehead. She longed to leave the room and find a quiet place to sit down but she knew that even if her head were to split open she must stay in place. Giles would think anyone who left now either mad or disloyal.

Eventually the last lot was reached, the last sum bid, and suddenly the room emptied as though the people were a snow-drift and the spring had brought bright sun.

Poppy had thought that after the sale would be rather like the post-mortem after a party; everyone companionably mucking in with the tidying up, flopping in heaps on the floor and discussing the evening. In fact it was nothing like that at all. Giles marshalled all the staff in front of him and gave them an 'Eve of Agincourt' speech while armies of professionals cleared and cleaned.

"We can all congratulate ourselves," he said. "Tonight depended upon every single one of you and it's because you each and every one worked so hard that we managed such a resounding success.

"I'm well aware," his dark eyes beamed round the staff like twin black searchlights, "that you all take the back seat while I'm the only visible part of the iceberg up there on that podium, and I get an undeserved proportion of the glory." He paused modestly for their denials and applause.

"Thanks," he said, and there was real warmth in his eyes. "What I really want to say now is that we can't relax. Tomorrow is going to be the busiest day of your working lives at Trenton's so what I want you all to do now is forget about celebrating, go home, go to bed and be sharper in the morning than you ever have been before. Goodnight." And he swept out, with Sarah Cavendish and Francis Dernholm hard on his heels.

It said much for his influence over them that the room was cleared in ten minutes. Poppy was offered a blissful lift home by Flavia, but even so the climb up the stairs to her flat had never had so many steps in it before. Her silk Ferragamo pumps felt like lead wellingtons.

When Ned, who had obviously been listening for her, put his head round his door for a chat, she was too tired.

"Ovaltine would be ambrosia, Ned, but if I come in I'll never make the stairs up to my bed."

"The best reason for coming in."

"The best reason for not! I'll tell you all about it in the morning." Step by step she forced her feet upward.

"Suzie rang," he called after her.

She leaned over the banisters to hear more.

"She's going on to Caracas. Checking out a couple of companies that want to

54

be quoted on the Stock Exchange. She won't be back for at least a week, probably longer."

"Thank God! Gives me time to catch up on the housework."

"Oh, and I had some good news that I wanted to tell you."

Poppy plumped down on the stairs; however tired she was it would be unforgivable to ignore Ned's news.

"I've won quite a decent sized little contract in Putney." Ned was a garden designer but more often than not was frustrated in his ambitions. There were more people in the world who wanted their chaotic gardens tamed and maintained than rich patrons willing to pay thousands to have their half acres redesigned from scratch. Force of circumstance had led Ned into being more of a glorified gardener than a Capability Brown.

"Wonderful!" Poppy was immediately enthused and, though she didn't stop to realise it, her leaden headache instantly dissolved as the focus of her attention shifted outside herself.

They drank companionable cups of Ovaltine on the stairs while he told her all about his plans for paths and arbours, patios and ponds. The detail washed over her and all she heard was the excitement in his voice, and then she didn't even hear that. She had gone to sleep huddled on the stairs in all her finery and Ned was trying to prise the mug from her fingers as gently as he could.

3

THE morning after the sale, Trenton's was redhot. Just as Giles had urged, by the dot of ten every desk and every telephone was manned; if most of the staff had bags under their eyes the size of large portmanteaux, that was nothing to quibble at. Hangovers had to take second place to an over-excited press corps and a queue of hopefuls at the front counter with a remarkably diverse selection of objects under their arms which, they blithely hoped, might make them a fortune.

Silently Poppy offered up a prayer of gratitude that she was not stuck with a stint on the front desk this morning. If the retired Major with the elephant's foot cunningly converted into an umbrella stand, and the dizzy girl unwilling to believe that Mummy's marcasites were not diamonds of the first water, were anything to go by, Francis was going to have a tough morning. She winked at him as she passed the counter and he rolled his eyes heavenward in despair.

"The best course would be to hang on to it for a few years. Empire ephemera is not fetching a large price. For some reason the bottom really has dropped out of elephants' feet." He was giving the Major a stock reply. "Yes, it certainly does seem strange that an object of such interest and rarity should not be in demand. No, we really don't get many." Francis did not utter the obvious 'Thank God'.

"Keep an eye on the trends and bring it back in five years or so." Hopefully in five years' time the old boy would be in no condition to hump the appalling object along to Trenton's; either that or the beastly thing would have disintegrated all by itself.

Front desking was tiresome and time-consuming. Everyone who brought their treasure was secretly hoping that Trenton's would see pure gold in it, even if they and their families had seen only dross for the past hundred years. Chances were very slim indeed of anything rich and rare suddenly coming to light but you had to placate the customers and take care to let them down so gently that they did not feel insulted by your opinion of their tawdry wares. Each bearer of dross might, just might, have something exquisite, valuable and quite unrecognised in their attic and, if they did, you wanted them to bring it back here not take it to the opposition. Diplomacy was all.

Poppy knew she had a deskful of paperwork to deal with today, and hoped the telephone would behave itself and keep quiet. She took advantage of Francis's being otherwise engaged to monopolise Amanda. Having a secretary was a revelation, by the end of the day they had whizzed through deskwork that otherwise would have taken Poppy a week.

She planned to leave the office a little early this evening in order to get to Maurice's flat, pick up the file on the possible Rubens and take custody of the precious *Cymbidium* orchids. Just as she was leaving the office, Sarah Cavendish put her head round the door.

"Leaving?" She checked the Cartier wristwatch and raised her eyebrows.

Poppy saw no reason to owe the Hon Sarah explanations for anything.

"Anything special?" she asked.

"Giles would like you to dine at his house tonight." Sarah gave the strong impression of issuing an order to an underling. "Eight o'clock. He needs to discuss strategy with you."

Poppy bent to consult her diary. She knew she had nothing planned, and even if the Queen had invited her to dine at Buckingham Palace tonight she would have cancelled it for Giles, but there was no earthly need for Sarah to know it too.

"That'll be fine," she said, the matter-of-factness in her voice belying the swoop in her stomach.

She'd never had dinner with Giles before, never even been to his house although she knew all about it by reputation and the odd photograph which usually accompanied interviews with him in glossy magazines. She knew that he had bought a large run-down Georgian mansion in Spitalfields for a song and had since spent a considerable fortune in restoring it meticulously to the heyday of its former glory; every detail was correct from the authentic paint colours on the walls to the carved mahogany overmantels and door surrounds. Photographs of Giles were often taken in the Red Dining Room, a warm cave of gilded splendour, or the Library, all panelling and marble busts.

Help!

Thoughts of the Red Dining Room made Poppy realise that she had not asked what she was expected to wear. Remembering her conversation with Giles earlier in the week, she thought it might easily be a large party for him to introduce her to the influential contacts he had mentioned. Dinner party clothes, she estimated, but dearly wished she had thought to ask Sarah.

The prospect of the evening to come kept intruding on the more immediate prospect, her trip to Maurice's flat. She had not been looking forward to going into someone else's home all alone when they were away in hospital; somehow it all seemed sad and rather redolent of vulture-like picking of bones. The evening's invitation had put temptation in her way for a moment. Why not blow the spare two hours in a hairdresser, boost her confidence and leave work till tomorrow? A day's delay couldn't hurt too much, could it?

Sometimes a conscience could be a curse.

Her bus sailed on through a Knightsbridge that today seemed to contain more hairdressers than ever before, all of them open and beckoning her with their bright lights and large photographs of unbelievably svelte heads.

Poppy stayed firmly in her seat however. She had promised Maurice. Besides, the Millington sale was the end of June. It was now the end of April and Poppy knew that every single day would count if there was foreign research to be done on the picture. With a sigh she disembarked at Prince's Gate and dutifully walked down Ennismore Gardens to the tall narrow white house where Maurice's flat occupied a tiny portion of the top storey. 'My little Crow's Nest' as he sometimes called it. Inside, she did not feel so bad as she had expected. The air did not smell stale, windows had been opened. She knew that Maurice had a devoted daily who came and 'did'. She was referred to by him as 'Darling Dust' or 'my divine dusterette'.

Darling Dust had done her stuff. The Boulle desk was immaculate. There was, nevertheless, a sneaky and underhand feeling about going through someone else's drawers; ringing the old boy first might make Poppy feel better about it.

"Treasure girl! I was dying to hear all the gossip about last night. Glorious and glittering, according to all reports. Did you enjoy it?"

"Maurice, I loved every minute."

"Good, I'm very pleased. The *on dit* has it you looked good enough to eat. Green eyes all round."

Poppy smiled. She was pleased to hear of the widespread envy, and heartened too by the new strength in Maurice's voice.

"Don't be a silly, of course you must go into my desk! No scruples, it couldn't be less like rape. A drawer is merely a drawer, and permission has been given."

His ebullient flow stopped for a pause when she told him that Giles had asked her to dinner.

"Hmm. Report back tomorrow, will you, darling? I've known Giles for many a year, and his father before him. I know how they *think*. Now do get down to work, Poppy. I can't chatter on any longer, a delicious little nurse has just arrived with lots of pretty pills on a little tray with a doily. Private medicine — heaven! Byee."

The biggest mistake of the evening lay in trying to go back by bus with all the orchids. Five large potplants and one file were too much for any journey. A taxi would have been the answer but she'd have to take one all the way to Spitalfields Square tonight, that would not be cheap from South Ken; and, unless she got a lucky lift, it'd be a taxi back too. Economy had to start somewhere.

When at last, Poppy found herself and the plants on home ground it was, to her horror, ten minutes to eight; she was exhausted and her tights had lost the battle with the terracotta pots and were in shreds. Gone was the dream of the prolongued perfumed bath; a flannel under the armpits was about all she had time for. Frantic rummaging brought no new tights to light: she'd have to go barelegged and hope to find a late night shop on the way. Working at double speed she telephoned the cab company and turned her cupboard inside out in a frenzy of indecision. She still hadn't made up her mind what to wear when the cab company phoned up to say the vehicle was outside in the street and waiting for her.

In a last minute panic her hand went for the blue, a forties crêpe de chine. It was a dress she could imagine Katherine Hepburn wearing at the start of a movie when she was being the tough and business-like heroine, before someone like Humphrey Bogart told her to 'Take off your glasses, Miss Murgatroyd, and live!' in a masterful way.

The dress allowed ample hints of Miss Murgatroyd's cleavage; Poppy felt understated but glamorous.

"Charley!" she greeted the familiar cabbie. "Thank God it's you."

"You know I always try and get the job when you phone up. Now calm down, Poppy luv. Where am I taking you, and what's the flap?"

"Charley darling, it's a smart party, I'm going to be late and all my tights are laddered. Could you find somewhere on the way?" She gave him the address.

"No problems," came the calm reassurance. "The Europa food store sells tights till one o'clock in the morning if you want them, and we'll whistle our way to Spitalfields. There's no traffic." Nothing was any problem to Charley, he knew London like the back of his hand. Had she asked him where she could buy a steamroller at that time of night, he would probably have come up with something.

He kept up a flow of goodnatured conversation which relaxed her throughout the journey. The only real problem was trying to wriggle into the new pair of tights in the moving taxi. She knew she could trust Charley not to sneak looks in the mirror but he couldn't be responsible for the parallel Saab Turbo driver, on whom the sight of Poppy doing what looked like a cancan in the back of the cab had a predictably disturbing effect.

"Give us a ring when you need to go back, luv," were Charley's parting words.

"Thanks." Poppy took a deep gulp of air before facing the front door.

Suddenly she was hit by a violent surge of stage fright. Even the door was daunting. The well-proportioned carved stone portico, supported by Corinthian pillars, framed a heavy, imposing mahogany door, slightly oversized and intended to impress by dwarfing the visitor. Poppy needed no such Georgian artifices to put her at a disadvantage. She was plain terrified. Her hand went up to press the bell but, as in all the best Transylvanian mansions, the door opened silently before her hand had made contact.

"Miss Palmer." It was a statement, not a question. "Follow me." And that was a command.

Poppy followed the old man in the black suit whom she supposed to be the butler. Their footsteps sounded very sharp on the endless squares of black and white marble. They reached a large pair of double doors, carved, pannelled and again made of mahogany. These were flung open, Poppy was announced and the doors were then closed behind her, leaving her to gather her wits inside what she recognised as the Little Drawing Room. It was called 'Little' only by comparison with the Large Drawing Room which, she knew, took up most of the floor above this.

There was only one other person in the room: Giles himself. He had obviously been reading and put down some papers to get to his feet as Poppy came into the room. He was still dressed in the suit he had been wearing to work that day, she noticed, and was pleased that she had not changed into anything too flamboyant; tonight was to be no dinner jacket affair.

"Thank you, Scrum." He dismissed the butler. "Extremely good of you to come at such very short notice, Poppy. I have a rather delicious old bottle of *Piesporter Goldtropper,* too fragile to drink with food. I thought we might try it. I hope you don't hate German wine."

"I love it," she said faintly, thrilled to be given a clue; *Piesporter Goldtropper* had meant nothing at all to her. As far as German wines went, she expected them to be called nothing more complicated than Hock or Moselle.

Carefully Giles poured the straw-coloured wine from the slim green bottle into a pair of perfect, thin, long-stemmed wine glasses. He handed one to her and wordlessly, standing close, their eyes locked, they drank a silent toast. Poppy felt a blush creeping upward over her neck and face. She could not take too much of Giles's eyes at close quarters.

"Give me the date and origin," he said unexpectedly.

"About seventeen sixty by the shape." Quickly she mustered her wits and scrutinised the glass in her hand. "Certainly after the glass tax was levied in 1746 — a penny per pound weight, wasn't it?" He nodded.

"To save on weight they made glasses with a very thin bowl — " she was going to dazzle him with her knowledge, — "too thin for cutting. The stem had to be slightly thicker and so did the foot to support the weight, so they put all the ornament on the stem and foot. Maybe a London maker." She twisted the glass in her hand to look for clues. "Or perhaps Nailsea, just outside Bristol?"

"Very good evaluation, Nailsea is right. Glass is out of your province isn't it?"

"Yes, but I try to pick up as much as I can from all the Departments. It helps no end when you're thinking on your feet at the front desk." They shared laughter at the mention of the front desk.

"I'm glad you've got a wide range of interest." He took a sip of wine. "I must apologise for testing you; it's a question of reassuring myself that you are up to the burden of expectation I am putting on your shoulders. You're still very young, Poppaea, the board say too young to be considered for what I am recommending. They want me to bring in an outside administrator to take Maurice's place but I'm reluctant to do that."

She raised her eyebrows in enquiry. Giles had sat down again in the chair he had formerly been occupying. By the light of the reading lamp she could see that his face looked tired, careworn after a long and no doubt stressful day. She felt unexpectedly protective, wishing she knew him well enough to cross the room, ease off his jacket, and massage the tension out of his shoulders and neck.

Something of her thoughts must have shown in her eyes. His voice tailed off as he looked across at her and his look spoke unmistakably of other interests besides business.

"Where was I?" he asked.

"You don't want to bring in an outsider?" she reminded him.

"For a moment you distracted me." His expression left her in no doubt of his meaning. "Business first, distractions after dinner."

How could she possibly concentrate with such a promise hanging in the air?

70

Giles turned his eyes to study the fine glass in his hand as though finding it difficult to look at her while speaking of matters so dry and dusty as jobs. It gave her the excellent chance to marvel again at the length and blackness of his lashes against the fine olive skin.

"Maurice wasn't going to last forever, of course, but had he continued in good health for another five years I would have had the time to train you up at leisure instead of plunging you in to ordeal by fire. Pity this all had to blow up now. Most unlike Maurice to get his timing wrong."

Poppy dared not say a word. Was Giles trying to tell her he was appointing her Deputy to himself and second in command at Trenton's?

The old butler knocked on the door, bowed, and led them wordlessly into the dining room. Giles's hand on her elbow guided her with formal politeness but the correctness of the gesture was belied by his eyes, which shone with a conspirator's complicity: 'Were we alone . . . ' they seemed to say.

The Red Dining Room was quite magnificent. It took its name from the old Spitalfields silk that lined the walls. The curtains were of the same heavy sumptuous material, draped and swagged with gold silk tassels. Poppy looked up to check if the ceiling was really as grand as the photographs made it out to be. Carved and coffered, it was further enriched with gilding and married to the walls by an elaborately carved and gilded cornice.

Poppy allowed herself to be seated by the butler. Acres of polished wood and silver stretched between her and Giles. There was no chance of hand dallying with hand.

"I bought it all back." Giles's words cut through her thoughts. "I knew the original panelling still existed, it had been sold up when the family fell on hard times. It took about two years before I eventually ran it to ground, in Munich of all places. I'd combed the world."

"How did you manage to buy it back?"

He laughed. "I promised I would replace it with something better, and the family who lived in the Munich house said they really preferred French Baroque anyway. They wanted a steep price for it, they were bright enough to realise that I would have paid almost anything. At first they said they wanted a complete room out of Versailles. Imagine! When at last I persuaded them that Versailles was quite impossible even for me to pillage, they settled for a lesser château. What I wanted was to get the room exactly back to what it was, not just some rough historical approximation."

Poppy nodded. That was typical of Giles. "You were lucky."

"I often am." There was no complacency, it was simply a statement of the truth. He lifted the glass of champagne that was to accompany the first course, held her eyes, and welcomed her to all that was to be between them in the promise of his long, languid look.

Scrum offered *Fonds d'artichaut,* each surmounted by a tiny heap of creamy scrambled egg and topped with a pretty pink curl of smoked salmon.

"I propose to put you on trial for six months. I want you to see how much business you can bring in for Trenton's over that period." Giles looked hard at her as he raised the little *bonne bouche* to his mouth and relished the mingling of the salty salmon with the smooth creamy egg and thin crisp artichoke.

"I don't know what to say!" Her eyes were shining with excitement.

"Don't say anything yet, you've not heard the entire plan. I shall be making the same offer to Francis Dernholm. I am, in effect, setting up a competition between the two of you. Whichever one brings in the most business between now and, let us say, December 31st, will take over Maurice Blessingham's job as Deputy Chairman of Trenton's."

Poppy felt so frightened at the prospect of the next six months that she seriously feared she might not be able to swallow a single tiny mouthful. She might as well give up before she started. There was no way she was in the same league as Giles and Maurice, the main business-getters, she decided depressingly.

But the thought of Maurice gave her a sudden surge of hope. She remembered the Millington file, now neatly tucked away at the bottom of her underwear drawer. It would take a burglar of some imagination and stamina to delve his way down through the writhing mass of entangled tights to unearth the potentially priceless secret that lay beneath, waiting to be unlocked. She remembered too that Maurice had pledged her his support; maybe he had a notion that something like this was in the wind.

"Does Maurice know about this?" she asked.

"He suggested it," was Giles's reply.

"Well, I'm not terribly confident." Why did she always feel the burning need for total honesty? "But I'll do my best. You know the Millington collection?"

"I recollect the name. It's one you've taken on from Maurice?"

"Exactly." She told him about the suspected Rubens.

Giles was all attention.

"And you think you'll be able to tie it up in time? The sale's scheduled for early June. It'd put the whole sequence of summer sales out if we had to move it, but obviously . . ."

"I think I can do it in time." She'd make quite sure she did.

"And you said you doubted your own abilities!" His eyes were warm and teasing. "Poppaea Palmer, I think you have everything it takes." He left the compliment hanging in the air as Scrum cleared away the gilded Royal Worcester which had done its duty for the first course. Its place was taken by *Sèvres* and prettily arranged little collops of venison.

"I shall be doing a lot of travelling between now and the summer," Giles continued. "Trenton's is ready to take a greater rôle on the international stage. There are a lot of potential buyers and sellers to woo. I need to raise my profile on the international curator circuit. But if the picture turns out to be a genuine Rubens, I shall make quite sure I'm in the country so I can auction it myself; it's not the sort of thing I'd like to leave to anybody else. I may not be around to organise build-up so that'll be entirely up to you. All right?"

She nodded.

"I shall watch with interest." He raised his glass to her again, this time studying her with the gleam of professional interest still in his eye. "I wondered if your father had any further thoughts on selling the Winchendon Hoarde?"

"I didn't know it had ever crossed his mind." The question had come as a bombshell. "It's been in the family so long." She remembered Francis's taunt and felt her back stiffening. "Surely it's not very valuable? Just the paraphernalia of a soldier long-dead?"

"More than that, my dear Poppaea." Giles was testing the firmness of a perfect little pyramid of *chèvre*; his tone held a hint of rebuke. "The articles aren't valuable in themselves, I agree, but you must be aware that this is an absolutely unique collection. Most of the Fleet was sunk. It can be stated absolutely categorically that there is no such soldier's box existing from the Armada period anywhere else in the world.

"I know of a dozen aristocratic Spanish families who would give a large proportion of their fortune to get the Winchendon Hoarde back on to Spanish soil and preferably back into their own castle. And then there are the big museums: it's a question of national pride. That doesn't take into account the South Americans who feel they have an historical stake, quite spurious of course; and the North Americans who will buy anything with a pedigree. I should say," he speared the creamy *chèvre* and took his eyes from hers for a moment as he tested its balance and pungency on his tongue, "I should say you could sell it for more or less whatever you wanted for it."

"Good Lord."

"It would give your father ample funds for the restoration of the house. I know the state of the fabric has been worrying him for some time."

Surely there was concern there, friendly concern for Poppy and her father's finances? Why did Francis's spiteful little barb come back: 'You know Giles only took you on so he could get his hands on the Hoarde'?

"You look thoughtful." Giles rose from his chair. "Don't let the Hoarde cloud your brow."

She had risen too and now they faced each other, close. He lifted his hand and ran it lightly along her forehead as though to smooth the worry.

"You know you're very special to me," he said. "It's not going to be easy promoting you when I feel like this about you."

"Casting couch?"

"Exactly. Can you keep us secret, Poppy?"

"Try me."

"I might just do that." His finger moved down her face till it was against her lips in the eternal gesture of secrecy. They stood still for a moment, sealing the pact.

"Are you ready for coffee?" he asked finally. "I believe Scrum has left it in the Gothick Saloon."

Putting his arm around her waist, he guided her as though to make quite sure she did not get lost between here and their destination. The feel of his hand resting on her hip, and his face so very close to hers, robbed Poppy of the ability to speak. It did not seem to matter, Giles was not speaking either. Interlocked they ascended a flight of the broad staircase. Had Giles opened the door to his bedroom at that moment he would have met with no resistance. Nevertheless it was in some ways a relief when he opened a door into what was obviously a very small library and workroom with, on the low central table, a heavy silver tray from which came the heavy and deliciously bitter scent of coffee.

"My office," he said. "This is where I really live, not where I am photographed." He smiled. "I think we must have coffee by candlelight." He lit the candles in their silver sticks and went to the old silver wall sconces which had not been converted to electricity but still held candles as the Georgians who made them had originally intended. When fifteen or so candles were lit Giles turned off the electric lights.

At first the room assumed an incredible blackness out of which shone the small points of light, but quite soon — it might have been her eyes adjusting or it might have been the candles getting hold — all around her was a soft, mysterious glow and the smell of real wax mingled with the deliciously contrasting smell of the coffee.

"Come." He sat on the pretty low dove, grey *chaise longue* and patted the place beside him. "Come here."

He poured coffee for them both. It was extremely hot; so hot that a sip had her gasping. Her breathlessness was compounded by the fact that though Giles had poured a cup for himself, he did not touch it. Instead he merely sat watching, his eyes steadily and unambiguously fixed on her. Suddenly she didn't know what to do with the cup, her face, her hands or anything. He reached out and took the tiny fragile cup and saucer from her, setting them gently down on the tray.

"You're very beautiful," he said. "Look at me."

Meeting his eyes was impossible. Poppy found herself blushing again and staring down at the pattern of the dove grey silk. Had she had an exam on its weave six months later, she would have passed with a hundred per cent.

He traced the shape of her face with a forefinger, lightly following the line of her forehead, her temples; his touch gentle as a falling feather across the lids of her downcast eyes, and finally soft as soft against her lips. Then, very slowly and deliberately, he bend forward and his lips just brushed hers. He took them away but no more than a hand's breadth. Everything seemed to be happening in slow motion. He raised a hand to her hair and stroked it.

"You should have lived a hundred years ago, Poppaea Palmer," he said softly, almost to himself, "every Pre-Raphaelite would have committed murder to paint you. Wonderful hair, like clouds of amber, and glowing coals for eyes."

He shifted a little on the *chaise longue*

so that he could pick up an object from the coffee tray. Poppy had not looked very closely at the tray and all its paraphernalia but now she noticed one object that struck a slightly incongruous note: a silver-backed hairbrush. Like everything else in this house, it was evidently old and valuable; its back heavily chased and ornamented with *repoussée* curlicues, flowers and cherubs.

"I want to brush your beautiful hair," Giles said. "I want to see it light up the room."

He bent forward to pick up the brush and came round to stand behind her. At first he was silent as the hairbrush slowly and gently did its work. Poppy found his actions almost hypnotic. As Giles brushed her hair she went into a trance-like state, her body feeling like jelly from the sheer bliss of it. If he brushed for much longer, she would melt.

"Nice?" he asked.

"Wonderful."

"People are very unimaginative about erogenous zones." He went on brushing. "The Edwardians knew about brushing hair. I found a whole cabinet of erotica in one of the great houses; we were selling the entire contents before it was turned into a Nursing Home. You wouldn't remember, it was just before you came to Trenton's."

As he talked he continued the steady, hypnotising rhythm of his strokes.

"There was a secret drawer in a desk and inside I found old sepia photographs. There was sequence of a woman preparing for bed. She's very beautiful and very richly dressed: highnecked lace with strands and strands of pearls. She and her husband are in a very elaborate bedroom, he in his white tie and, at first, still with his after dinner cigar. She takes off her dress and sits at the dressing table in her corsets; you can see her body reflected three times in the triple mirror. She takes down her hair and it's very long, to her waist. She gives the hairbrush to her husband who starts to brush it; they did in those days, you know, it was an invariable preliminary to Edwardian lovemaking. A young man comes in, he must be a footman from the livery. The husband still stands behind her, brushing, and the footman undresses her, piece by piece, kneeling and kissing each new part of her body as it's revealed: her arms, her thighs and her breasts . . . The maddening thing is that it stops there. I'm not sure if it would end with them all three making love or the husband watching while the young stud services her. I'd give anything to discover the last photographs."

Poppy was both shocked and excited by the description. When Giles stopped brushing and came round to kiss her she was as fierce as he, crushing him to her, feeling the hardness of his lips exploring her face, her throat, his body pressing hers down against the *chaise longue* until she was pinned like a butterfly underneath his length, while his hands explored her body as though the clothes between did not exist.

"Let's go upstairs now." His voice was hoarse. "Groping on sofas is all very well for teenagers, but we've no parents to find us out."

Dimly, an edge of her mind heard a telephone ringing. Giles heard it too and surprisingly broke off.

"Damn!" he said. "I'd better answer it. I'm expecting an urgent call."

He only spoke a short time on the

telephone, and the conversation seemed mainly to concern percentages. When the call was finished he stayed jotting figures for a while. The absorption in his face quite shut out Poppy and made her wonder if he had forgotten her presence altogether. She longed for him to kiss her again but somehow could not bring herself to go to him and put her arms around him. Despite the unexpected passion he had shown tonight she was still very aware that Giles was her employer; he must make the moves. Giles was frighteningly single-minded; she dared not come between him and business.

"I'm going to have to send you home." His eyes had focused on her at last.

"That was Japan. I'm sure you've heard rumours that Mitshogun want to buy us out. I'm fighting them off with a counterproposal and they've just come up with a solution that might be profitable to both of us."

There was a knock at the door.

"A gentleman downstairs to see you, Sir." Scrum was imperturbable. This might happen every midnight. "Documents for you to scrutinise, I believe."

"Thank you, Scrum. I'll be down straight away." The butler left, shutting the door behind him.

Giles smiled disarmingly. "I'm afraid I shall have to spend the night crunching numbers." He was already dialling the number to order her a taxi.

"I'm sorry, my sweet." He had come over to her now and was standing against her, looking down into her eyes. "We'll save it, shall we? Anticipation sharpens enjoyment."

"Let's not anticipate too long." Which was politer than saying, "I want you now, dammit!"

"Let's not," he agreed. "That's the taxi." He came downstairs with punctilious politeness, but it obviously wouldn't do to be seen kissing goodnight.

"Take the morning off," he called as the vehicle pulled away. Poppy's mind was in a turmoil as she was driven home. When a few coherent thoughts emerged from the maelstrom of emotions she fastened on the idea that he was offering her a considerable promotion; she reasoned that he wouldn't be playing around with someone who might become his number two. No, Giles wanted to work with her and start a serious affair. If only they could have started tonight.

"Damn all Japanese," she muttered furiously as she climbed her stairs, almost colliding with a wheelbarrow and very muddy pair of Wellington boots which Ned had thoughtfully left parked outside his door. The door was ajar so she poked her head round to tell him what she thought of his notion of passage furniture

"What are you trying to do?" she called. "Break my neck?"

"Sorry," Ned's voice called, and she definitely heard female giggles, hastily suppressed. Poppy checked her watch. It was two o'clock. No wonder Giles had given her the morning off.

"I'm going in late tomorrow," she called in the general direction of the giggles. "Wake me at ten and I'll give you breakfast."

Ned always was a sucker for whatever was on offer.

4

"IT'S not really morning," Poppy groaned. "You're joking, Ned."

"Come on, Pops, you promised me breakfast. Some of us in this world have to get to work, remember? Anyway, you said ten o'clock."

She yawned, stretched, tried to chase the waves of sleep out of her brain but knew that unless she sat up now, this minute, she'd go straight back to sleep before he had even left the room.

"Pull the curtains, will you?" she asked muzzily.

Not only did Ned pull the curtains, he also pulled the duvet back to the bottom of her bed and let out a long whistle.

"Cream satin pyjamas. Very strokable." To her surprise he didn't stay to try, just said he'd fetch the croissants and be back in twenty minutes.

When he did come back Poppy was dressed, and the reason for Ned's lack of attempted stroking was quite clear.

"My name is Solveg, how do you do?" came in a sing-song accent from a stunning shampoo-advertisement of a girl. She must have been the giggler from last night.

"Hi, Solveg, come and have some breakfast. Do you like coffee? If not I've got some tea." The invitation met with a dazzling smile but absolutely no intellectual response.

"She doesn't understand a lot," Ned explained.

Poppy felt this was possibly an understatement.

She mimed toast, tried eggs, madly shaking an imaginary frying pan in the air and making sizzling noises; she even attempted bacon, giving full-throated pig-like grunts she had thought she would be incapable of that early in the day. If Solveg thought her hostess was mad she hid it very politely behind a smile of perfect small white teeth and said lots of 'Ja's' and 'Thank you's'. Solveg had immaculate manners; she even washed up.

"Where did she come from?" Poppy eventually asked Ned when she had made quite certain that the girl understood not a word they were saying.

"She's the *au pair* in the new land-scaping job. I really couldn't find it in my heart to resist her." He grinned ruefully.

"It must have been a hard struggle," Poppy said drily. "Teaching her English, are you?"

"We'll get round to that eventually."

A bright idea struck her. "I don't suppose she speaks Dutch?"

"Solveg's Norwegian so I doubt it, but we can always ask."

"How?"

If the simple choice of coffee or tea met with a blank, it seemed unlikely they would get very far with the abstract issue of language.

"Hang on a sec," said Ned, and returned, panting, with a pocket dictionary from downstairs.

"*Du snakker Hollandsk*," they came up with eventually which mystified poor Solveg. The dictionary did not run to putting questions and so they were in fact telling her in statement form that she spoke Dutch. She frowned and acted puzzlement most convincingly, and eventually shook her head with a very definite: "*Nei, nei, nei.*"

"I don't think she's imitating a horse," said Ned, "I think she's saying no."

"Snap."

Solveg was clearly not going to be a great help in Poppy's Dutch research which was a pity because she felt very nervous indeed of ringing up Holland cold with just as much Dutch at her disposal as Solveg had English. But she knew it must be done and it must be done from the flat; undercover detective work from the office would be about as discreet and secret as telling it to the press.

"I've got to throw you out now. Work calls."

"Thanks for breakfast, Poppy, you're a love," said Ned, and kissed her on the cheek.

"*Tusen takk, delig frokost,*" the perfect smile beamed, and politely Solveg shook hands like a well-mannered little girl. Surprisingly she then turned to Ned and engaged him in a completely unselfconscious passionate kiss.

"Enjoy your work," Poppy said ironically. "Now run along and have a nice day."

"I can't help it," his voice floated up the

91

stairwell, "she's a child of nature." Poppy heard Ned's door close and doubted it would open again for a long time yet. One day Suzie would find out about his occasional Solvegs and Chantals, meanwhile he merely laughed off Poppy's remonstrances.

"What's a red-blooded male to do when his girl lives on Concorde?"

Ned was incorrigible.

She settled down to study Maurice's file on the Rubens. The painting dated from 1620 and was one of several large canvases painted to decorate the Jesuit Church in Antwerp. The church itself had been destroyed by fire in 1718 and, as far as art history was concerned, only the altarpiece had been saved from the blazing horror. However, Rubens' sketches for the large Millington canvas existed in some of the artist's notebooks, variously locked up in the archives of the town of Antwerp and in several Jesuit archives in the Netherlands, Rome and Paris.

From what could be gathered from these sketches and from contemporary descriptions the painting, named the 'Flight into Egypt', was really an excuse for a great and glorious sweep of landscape painting such as Rubens enjoyed above all things but seldom had the opportunity to indulge in. The artist's important landscapes were very rare.

There was then, as now, more money in painting people, and Rubens was a very human artist, fond of money and all it could buy, including a sixteen-year-old wife when he himself was fifty-three. So this painting, if it really was the missing 'Flight into Egypt', would be worth a very large sum indeed; over a million pounds was by no means out of the question.

As she went through the fat file, Poppy developed a deep respect for Maurice's Dutch researcher. He might be saddled with the rather comic name of Joost van Mompert but clearly the man was no fool, and leaving stones unturned was not his style. For a ridiculously small research fee he had visited every archive, photocopied sketches and deciphered archaic writings.

He had traced the painting definitely from the fire, and unearthed a hitherto unknown manuscript: a firsthand description of an Antwerp wool merchant saving the 'Flight' dramatically from the fire by cutting it out of its frame while the flames licked closer and closer. The public-spirited wool merchant had not salted it away in his own home, but had gone on to do the decent thing and immediately taken it to the Town Hall where it had hung until Rubens went out of style and the large canvas was replaced by a huge and pompous group portrait of the Town Council.

The picture's missing days had then begun and it disappeared completely from view, evading even the zealous detective work of Joost van Mompert, until it was brought back to England some hundred years later from the continent, one of many souvenirs of an English Milord's Grand Tour. At this time there had been no clue of its connection with the famous artist, and it had simply been catalogued as 'Large Dutch Landscape'.

Thus titled, it had joined the Millington Collection from Christie's in the 1920s for the princely sum of fifteen guineas. It had hung in the vast caverns of the Millington family's gloomy dining room ever since, uncleaned, unlit and underinsured. Only

Maurice's expert eye had seen its possibilities when he went to value the house contents for sale.

Poppy must pluck up her courage and pick up the telephone. How did one pronounce Joost?

Listening to the foreign dialling tone, she felt sick with nerves. To her relief the voice at the other end turned out to belong to Joost himself and his English was shamingly fluent with just a trace of thickness around the consonants giving the clue that he was not a native. He was at first very suspicious of Poppy; his research was confidential, it was for Maurice Blessingham alone, and he would not divulge anything to another person.

This was said with considerable charm but also with considerable firmness; Poppy was impressed by his integrity. She explained about Maurice and who she was but Joost, careful detective that he was, would still not trust her with his latest findings until she had given him the number of the Nursing Home, and he himself had spoken with Maurice.

When he came back to her he could not have been more helpful. Her spirits soared; they were very close indeed to the final proof.

The telephone rang the moment she had put it down. It was Maurice.

"Darling, you must come straight round on your way to the office."

"What do you mean, on my way? It's a five-mile detour!"

"Never mind, my loveliness. I want to make absolutely sure you've grasped all the important points on the painting and, far more important, I want to know all the gossip. I'm starved of thrills here and you're the only one who bothers to come and see me. Jump into a taxi this minute."

She did.

She brought no humble flowers this time but stopped on the way at a wickedly expensive St John's Wood greengrocer for the most costly bunch of Belgian hothouse grapes she had ever encountered. They had a bloom on them like jade velvet, and where the stem had been cut from the vine there still adhered a perfect leaf.

It was small payment for what looked like a genuine saleroom discovery.

Maurice was looking less strained, the

colour in his face more natural, though in his hair rather less. She was pleased to see that it had resumed its normal beautiful rich brown, a colour that owed nothing to nature and everything to one of the little bottles round about the Avocado basin. If Maurice was up to touching up his hair he must be well on the road to recovery.

"Thank you, darling. Beautiful bunch, too pretty to eat." Nevertheless he tore off a cluster and ate them with gourmet's enjoyment.

"Now, tell," he commanded.

She told.

There was one thing she was very anxious indeed to get straight. If Giles was offering her Maurice's job, she wanted to be one hundred per cent sure that her friend was not planning to come back to it when he was better. To sabotage Maurice would not only be an act of betrayal, it would also be suicidally foolhardy.

Poppy knew quite well that if it came to a battle of wits over working politics, Maurice would beat her with one hand tied behind his back and a dicky ticker to boot. His age, experience, and sheer smartness left her standing.

"Sweet girl, how typical of you to ask. No, my dear, I've had a good run at Trenton's. I've had time to think, lying here these long days," Maurice savoured a grape, "and I have decided that at this point in my life there is only one sensible thing for me to do, and that is indulge myself. I turn my back on ambition; now is the time for fun! It's now or never for my dream."

"What's that?" Poppy was enthralled, she loved people's secret dreams.

"You won't laugh?"

"Promise. And I won't tell either."

"An Opera shop!" he said unexpectedly. "I adore Opera as you know and it has always struck me as quite lamentable that there is no shop in London devoted to Opera memorabilia: a place where you could go and buy playbills and props. Callas's rhinestones, Nijinsky's codpiece – well, maybe not quite, my darling – Venetian masks, Erté's costumes, Cecil Beaton's hats!" His voice had a dreamy quality. "Imagine a little shop in Covent Garden, just round the corner from the Opera House, and imagine tracking down all the wonderful bits and pieces. Now that could be a very pleasant occupation for the last days of a decaying old man."

"Decadent maybe, decaying never!"

The sidelong look he gave her was gratified.

"It's a most wonderful idea." Poppy's enthusiasm was entirely genuine. "There's only one problem. I think your retirement might turn out to be busier than your working life."

"I think so too," Maurice purred with satisfaction. "I've had long enough to work it out. You can see now why I don't want Trenton's any more. You must go for my job, Poppy," the old man's voice had lost all dreaminess, "go for it as your life depends. You can do it, you know, and you will most certainly never get a chance like this again."

He was uncharacteristically silent for a while. They sat companionably, each thinking round these large issues.

"Did Giles make a pass?" he referred back to her report on last evening. She had left out that bit. "No, you don't need to tell me, I can see that he did. Are you committed?" he asked.

"Do you mean, did I sleep with him?"

"I wasn't actually going to put it as indelicately as that but it was the general gist of my question."

"No," she said, and then added in a burst of honesty, "but it wasn't because I didn't want to."

"Spare me, darling, spare me!" Maurice put up a hand as if to stop her. "Heart patients aren't allowed too much excitement." He shifted his attention to the tray over his lap and took a great deal of trouble arranging the objects upon it into a pleasing and symmetrical pattern.

"You must remember that Giles is first and foremost a businessman," he said in a measured tone that carried no trace of his usual banter. "When he says you must prove yourself over the next six months that will have nothing whatsoever to do with who you are having dinner with, or even whether or not you are sleeping with him. Forgive me if I sound vulgar but I use your own unambiguous phrase. It's as well to understand exactly what we're talking about. You may think that you're entering into a halcyon period in your life but this won't be the case by any manner of means. I can't drop Rubens canvases in your lap every week, like plums in autumn."

The smile crept back into his voice.

"Also, of course, you must not discount jealousy and rivalry from Francis Dernholm; he for one will not let you rise unchallenged to the top of the heap. Madam Francis will sabotage you sure as eggs are eggs — and believe me, Poppy, he is a very, very tough cookie. You'll have to sharpen up a lot before you get the better of him."

She felt subdued. It was the truth but she didn't enjoy hearing it.

"Tell me more about Francis," she said. "I only know what I see at work. He camps it up a bit, is he really gay? Whoops!" She put her hand over her mouth, remembering she was talking to Maurice, queen of queens. He laughed indulgently.

"Certainly he is. So now I suppose you're wondering why I'm supporting you, and trying to sabotage one of my own kind? The gay mafia is supposed to stick together, yes?"

She nodded. Poppy was extremely fond of Maurice and couldn't give two figs about his sexual inclinations.

"I introduced Francis to the company,

a fact that you may or may not know."

Everyone had said at the time that Maurice was introducing one of his lovers, but the company rumour had faded fast as people saw no emotional connection between the two men.

"Little snake!" Maurice went on with sudden venom in his voice. "He stayed faithful to me for all of his first three weeks in the job, and then ripped headlong into a roaring affair with an Algerian hairdresser named Hercules."

"*Hercules!*" Poppy shrieked.

"Scout's honour." Maurice's amusement faded quickly as he remembered Francis's treachery. "Few people get the better of me, but at the time I really thought we were in love. He fooled me completely." He paused, theatrically. "Hercules didn't last long. He was none too clean, I believe, and gave Francis a rather uncomfortable complaint. He tried to make it up after that, joked about our affair, and indeed by then I could laugh about it too. But what I could not laugh about, and what I shall never forgive, is the way he betrayed me and simply used me to sleep his way into Trenton's. After that we were enemies."

"I noticed," Poppy murmured.

"He has forged a new alliance since then. Giles likes him, he can see that Francis is very good indeed at his job." The old man fell silent. Poppy didn't feel the need to say anything as she turned this new information over in her mind.

"I'd better get to the office and tell Amanda to mind my back. Thank God for her!"

She bent to kiss Maurice and turned to leave.

"One last thing," he called her back, "I almost forgot. I'm sending you my Divine Duster, do you mind? I know these daily women — nothing is more boring for them than an empty house. She'd brood in my lonely flat, dusting my things over and over again, and then succumb to a higher offer. You don't already have a daily whose feathers she'd ruffle? Good. Just while I'm in hospital, you understand. I don't imagine your flat is dull. Those sorts of young people's menageries never are. It'll keep her entertained and out of mischief until I'm released and get home to boss her about; I'm looking forward to being a tyrannical invalid. I'll continue to pay her just as usual, of course, you don't have to worry about that."

"You wonderful fairy godmother!"

"Well, darling, I've been called many things . . . " He gave her a quizzical look and they both laughed.

"Where have you been?" Amanda was holding fort in Poppy's office and greeted her with palpable relief.

"I'd no idea I'd even be missed," Poppy said. "I'm flattered."

"Well, the telephone's gone quite a bit. I can cope with the business end but it's the gossip I need you for. I'm bursting with news and there's no-one I can tell."

Poppy was immediately all attention; nobody had such a good nose for gossip as Amanda. By some mysterious process she always knew exactly what was going on.

"Sarah Cavendish has taken down her ghastly pussy-cats-with-bows calendar and put up a frightfully dull one from the National Arts Collection Fund. Not much, you may say," the lack of interest in Poppy's eyes at this fascinating fact could be spotted by a first-time amateur detective, "well, you'd be wrong. The calendar is only a *symptom*. Sarah's going intellectual. She's trying to better herself." Poppy looked sceptical.

"Oh, not socially of course, that would be quite impossible. She's fed up being smart but a secretary and wants to become Something in a Department, so she's taking a correspondence course."

"*A correspondence course?*" Poppy wailed.

"I knew you'd love it eventually. Surrounded by all the *objets* and all the expertise in the world, our Hon Sarah is Learning About Art from a place that calls itself a College in Clapham. She's also thrown away her contact lenses and is wearing a pair of glasses signed by Dior in the corner and with just a hint of glitter on the frame. She's very selfconscious about them and keeps taking them on and off."

"I must go and see her at once. Your absolute priority as my secretary is to find me an excuse."

"That's not all." Amanda's voice was thick with news. "Giles is going to Japan at the drop of a hat; rumour's flying on the old takeover story." What Poppy knew about that she would keep to herself. "He also steamed in and commanded Francis to have lunch with him. Francis was lunching a client but was ordered to drop whoever it might be. Giles was so masterful." Amanda lapsed into a half-comical stage swoon. "Was he masterful last night, Poppy? You must tell me all about it, fair do's."

"I will, I will. Finish about Francis first." There were several rules sacred in the auction world, but one was paramount at Trenton's just as in any other public service business: Never Offend A Client. That meant that a client could cancel lunch with you at the drop of a hat or even the feather from that hat. You never cancelled on a client.

"Well, Francis cancelled, and went off with Giles looking like a large cat who was both sleek and hungry. That can't make sense but you know the look?"

"Francis in his dangerous mood. Exactly."

"That's all really except that they haven't yet come back from lunch yet and the table was at the Ritz."

"Amanda, my darling, you are a dream. Promise me you'll always be there and never ever think of bettering yourself and becoming Something in a Department."

"Poppy, I'd die of boredom. Seccing is wonderful, I was born for it."

"Amanda!" The voice belonged to Francis and sounded more than usually petulant. "What are you doing in Poppy's office? I won't have you working for other people all the time."

The cross voice was followed by the equally cross presence of the man himself. His cheeks had a high pink colour induced either by his mood or the lunchtime encounter with the Ritz Grill.

"Frankie dear, you must take care." Poppy had just thought of this new name for him. Judging by his expression it annoyed him as much as she hoped. "I don't think at your weight you can afford to get too over-wrought after lunch," she said sweetly. "Would you like a seat?"

"I'm not staying. I only looked in to pick up my secretary and I'll thank you to find another to share. I've just had lunch with the Chairman and he is promoting me to take over from Maurice."

"Really? Are you absolutely sure?" Either Francis was lying or she had dreamed her talk with Giles.

"Well, it's a six-month probationary

period while I prove that I can draw the business but that's no problem with *my* connections. You can take it as read, you two, that I shall be confirmed as Deputy Chairman of Trenton's in six months' time. Come, Amanda!"

She rose to go obediently at this autocratic command, throwing an apologetic glance behind her. Poppy stopped her with a hand on the arm.

"Poor Frankie!" she called after him. "Didn't Giles tell you? I too had a meal with our Chairman — in fact, I had dinner with him last night at his house. He made the same offer to me. Didn't he tell you it was a two-horse race?"

Francis deflated like a balloon. He took refuge in bluster.

"Of course he told me. I simply discounted your chances. Come, Amanda, we must drum up new business. Your first job every morning as you come in to work will be to scan the Obituary columns for rich deaths." Amanda rolled her eyes at Poppy in horror. "Any good deaths you will make a note of. I want the note on my desk by ten when I personally shall ring the relatives. People are often strapped for cash when they're newly bereaved, particularly widows. I want to get them before they have time to start being sensible about their money. Poppy, you are not to copy my idea. If I find you have been doing the same, I shall call Amanda as my witness that I thought of it first."

"Frankie dear, I wouldn't dream of doing such a thing, believe me. It's all right, Amanda," she smiled at her friend, "run along. I've got no work for you till tomorrow at eleven, as we all agreed."

"Oh, gosh!" Amanda exclaimed. "I didn't have time to give you a message, it slipped my mind with so much else."

Poppy raised her eyebrows in query.

"The Earl of Ilchester rang. In fact he kept ringing. He said how urgent it was and it was work but he could only speak to you."

"Wasn't he the one with his hand in your cleavage the other night?" Francis asked smoothly. "I should think you'd better ring him back quickly, Poppy dear. It sounds like absolutely vital work to me."

He led the way out of the office, followed by Amanda who turned to give Poppy a look which said exactly with which boss her loyalties lay.

"Death columns," she mouthed.

"What fun!" Poppy mouthed back.

She laughed out loud at the thought of the Obituary scheme, she rather liked the idea of that; it would take up a great deal of Francis's time every day and it would cause a great deal of offence. She must tell Amanda really to pile on the names. If Francis spent an hour or two each morning tracking down the bereaved, it would be time away from more useful work.

When he'd been at it a few weeks she might drop a word in the ear of a friendly gossip columnist; it would do Francis no good at all to be known in print as 'The Saleroom Vulture'.

Meanwhile she must busy herself with more useful schemes and the obvious place to start was Maurice's list.

All was going smoothly when she received the telephone call she dreaded.

"Freddy here."

"Oh."

"Freddy Ilchester. Remember me? You wore diamonds, I wore the lecherous look."

Despite herself, she laughed.

"That's better," he went on, "I thought we were into permafrost just there. How are you, lovely girl?"

"I'm very well indeed, thank you, Your Lordship, but I'm also really appallingly busy."

"Not the moment for flirts and gossips?"

"You have it exactly."

"Well, look, two things then. Firstly, I'll think you're my parlourmaid if you Lordship me. Freddy will do. Secondly, I've got something to sell. I tried to get on to Giles this morning but that unfriendly blockhead of a secretary said he was in meetings all morning and Japan all afternoon. Tiring life, what?"

"Tough at the top."

"So I thought of you, you see. I remembered you extremely well from the other evening. Oops, you said no flirts. I asked the chill secretary for you. She passed me on to your secretary. Your secretary is much nicer, by the way."

"I know, that's why I have her."

"Is she pretty?"

"Well, I think so." Poppy thought a moment. "But I don't know if you would.

Men and women have such different opinions on these things."

"Dead right, darling. And vice versa of course. You should have seen the little squirt my second wife left me for."

"I hate to hurry you, Freddy," she said, "but things press. You said you had something to sell?"

"Look, I have a proposition." It was as if he could hear her heart sinking. "No, not that sort, you foolish girl! I wouldn't dare proposition you . . . at least not while you're in the office and sounding so frightening. There's something I want to sell, but it's not at all the conventional sort of something that you can wrap up in brown paper and tote along on the bus for an opinion. I really need to talk about it and then possibly I shall need to fly you to Ireland to view it, but the first step is the talk. Can we have dinner soon?"

All roads lead to Rome. From the minute Amanda had given her the message from the Earl, Poppy had been quite certain that a dinner invitation would not be far behind.

"Well," she said speaking her thoughts

112

aloud, "that was the most elaborate lead up that I have ever heard. It deserves to succeed. Friday?"

"I shall come and fetch you."

She gave him the address.

5

IT was late when Poppy got home that evening and she was pleased with herself. The nose had been kept to the grindstone for longer than she had thought humanly possible and Maurice's leads, all super-efficiently organised, were composed of a great deal more than hot air and hopes.

The long and concentrated session had also taught her quite a bit about how to go about generating her own business; the possibility of just riding on Maurice's coattails had worried her. A small germ of self-confidence was starting to grow.

She realised that she'd not had time for lunch today. That and the late night before it had made her suddenly ravenously hungry; tiredness always had that effect. She splurged in the South Ken Late Nite supermarket and climbed the stairs with plastic grocery bags hanging from her like decorations on a Christmas tree.

Ned's door was firmly shut, she noticed,

the wheelbarrow was still there and who knew about the wordy Solveg? As she turned the corner to climb the last two half lights between Ned and the top flat she noticed that the glass panel over her door was showing light. Someone must be in there; maybe Ned had come upstairs?

"Hello?" she called as she kicked the door shut behind her with her foot, but there was no reply. "Ned?" she called again.

Looking around at the spotless kitchen, light dawned. Maurice's Divine Mrs Dust!

The room gleamed as it never did unless it was Suzie's turn to do the housework. The windows were smear-free, the cooker showroom-bright and the floor would have done as a practice rink for skaters out of ice. There was a note on the kitchen table. In carefully formed capitals it told her:

Dear Miss Poppy, The lady who says she owns this flat is coming home today. I hope this does not mean you will have to move. Yours cordially, Dorothea. P.S. Vim and floor polish please.

So Suzie was coming home early. To

people who knew them both, it was quite surprising that Poppy Palmer should be sharing a flat with Suzie Cryer. Outwardly they had little in common but had met on and off during Poppy's Art History days at Bristol. Suzie was not at the University, it would have been entirely uncharacteristic of her to be wasting time as a student when she could be out earning money. She had at that time been working for the small Bristol offshoot of a large multinational stockbrokers and to Poppy, a penniless student, Suzie had seemed the height of sophistication. The two girls used to be invited to the same Bristol parties. Once or twice they had helped each other out of sticky corners and so, somehow, a friendship had sprung up.

'Dogsbody in the Boondocks' was how Suzie had described herself then, but dogsbody she could never have been for long, nor did she tolerate the boondocks a moment longer than she had to. Before Poppy had completed her three-year course, Suzie had moved onwards and upwards and now her daytimes were spent in pinstriped suits high up in the Stock Exchange building in the heart of the City of

London. Either there or its interchangeable equivalent in any corner of the world.

"How I envy you the travel," Poppy had once confessed.

But Suzie had told her that wherever she went, be it Turkey or Chile, all she really saw on these trips were the identical banks of IBM machines and identical hotel rooms.

"But why don't you stop and sightsee?" Poppy asked. "Build some interest into the trips?"

"And miss reporting back with the facts fresh in my mind?" Suzie had looked at her as if she were a lunatic.

Quite early on in her commercial life, Suzie was earning enough to get a good mortgage deal through the firm on the flat in Redcliffe Gardens. When she heard that Poppy had qualified and was coming to London to work for Trenton's, she had suggested renting a room to her. For Poppy the offer was heavensent and they were now entering their third year together.

On the whole, for two such dissimilar characters, it worked well. From time to time Poppy's unstructured life style (what Suzie referred to as her mess) would lead to a row. From time to time Suzie's dedicated seriousness would lead her into depression and then Poppy, with her gift for laughter and warmth, would cheer her up and help put the world back into perspective.

One of their chief areas of disagreement was clothes.

Poppy had a built-in resistance to all things marketed as 'the latest'. Suzie, however, suffered a serious lapse in self-confidence if she was not absolutely sure that she was wearing the very, very latest. Her high-flying high-profile life had reduced the art of shopping to the absolute boring minimum: Suzie had a little lady who came.

She came to visit in the City office where she showed Suzie a video of the latest collections. The lady had Suzie's lifestyle, figure and taste on computer: every three months she would be there with the latest from Saint Laurent, Lagerfeld and Chanel on her little machine, and Suzie would choose.

Poppy thought it was a seriously boring way to shop. She also thought that Suzie spent far too much on her clothes.

Suzie thought that Poppy was quite mad wearing such eccentric clothes. She dissaproved of what she called 'your jumble', though she did admit, grudgingly, that Poppy looked absolutely marvellous in them.

Many of Suzie's expensive clothes were hardly worn six times before she replaced them. She'd hand them on to Poppy with an exasperated: "For God's sake, wear something decent for once!" Quite recently there had been a really nice Chanel suit.

For two such disparate characters, they rubbed along very well together.

Poppy went to Suzie's bedroom to check that everything was in order and found that it was, with the significant exception that in the bed, fully dressed and sobbing, lay Suzie herself.

"What is it?" Poppy exclaimed. "Are you all right?"

"No, I'm not," Suzie sniffled. "Bloody Ned! I hate him. How long has this been going on?"

Damn! What was she going to say? "Come on. Let's get you some food. I bet you've not had anything except that filthy airline stuff. You'll soon feel better," Poppy stalled.

She managed to winkle Suzie out of bed, sat her down on the lid of the loo — the only place to sit if you were two in that tiny bathroom — and then for once it was Poppy's turn to be motherly with cool flannels and dabs of cologne.

"Darling, you look much better now. No! Don't risk a look in the mirror — not *that* much better. Come on, there's lots of glorious food."

"And lots of glorious Duty Free," Suzie muttered, a heartening sign. "The kitchen looks wonderful, Pops. Who's Dorothea?"

"It's a long story."

And Dorothea, alias the Divine Duster, was explained, as well as everything else that had been happening to Poppy lately — or almost everything. Breakfast with Ned and Solveg was judiciously left out. Poppy was feeling quite confident until they moved to the more comfortable sofas in the little living room with their coffee, the last remnant of the bottle of duty free red and its brother the brandy, with two large balloons just in case it turned into a long night.

"You can tell me now," Suzie said. "I'm so full of food I couldn't possibly cry. Best meal I've had since I left. Thank you."

"Well, you did me handsomely that Sunday night when you left for the trip and the fridge was full of your smoked salmon. I simply had to eat it, Suzie, you know it doesn't keep."

"Oh yes, the romantic meal I was meant to have with Ned." Stiffness washed back over Suzie's face. "What's been going on, Pops? It was just such a shock walking in on them downstairs this evening. I decided to go straight in to surprise him, and there were female's clothes strewn all over the carpet for all the world like clues in a paper chase. And then I heard this terrible scuffling behind the bedroom door."

"What next?"

"Well, I had to open the bedroom door. I was sort of committed by then, wasn't I? Pathetic! The two of them scrabbling the bedclothes up to their chins. I don't know what I called Ned. I certainly called *her* a bitch and, would you believe, she didn't even alter her expression? Just kept on this awful toothpastey smile as if she was gloating."

"She wouldn't have understood a word." Poppy explained it all.

"I really don't know if it makes me feel better or worse that he cheats on me with some dumb bimbo." Suzie opened the brandy.

"Hey, you're not meant to *fill* these huge glasses!"

"*Prosit!*" was the pithy reply.

Poppy's hangover was not a terrific asset on her first morning spent seriously trying to outwit Francis. She tottered through the first two hours of her working day, jumping whenever a telephone rang and shielding her eyes from the sunshine. Today was May 1st, her calendar told her, a day when maidens should be fresh as the cherry blossoms in Hyde Park. She felt more like the muddy duck-churned murk at the bottom of the Serpentine.

Amanda took one look when Francis released her to work for Poppy. "Good grief!" she said. "We'd better have a drink."

It was the most sense anyone had made all day and in honour of the date they declared it the first day of summer (a little prematurely) and celebrated with Pimms in the Goat in Boots.

Amanda was all sympathy when she heard about poor Suzie and, being the utterly reliable friend she was, did not stop there.

"Tell you what, Poppy, I've been invited to a party on Friday. A friend of mine in an advertising agency said to come along. What if you and Suzie came too? I'm sure Marcus wouldn't mind, he's a lamb. Shall I ask him?"

"Wonderful!" But Poppy's face clouded as she remembered her date that night with the Earl; she still couldn't think of him as Freddy.

"No probs. You won't be spending all night with him, will you?"

"I'm not planning to succumb instantly to his blueblooded charms!"

"Well then, I'll give you the address. Those agency parties go on late, and this one should be quite fun. I went to their thrash last year and it was about the best party I've ever been to. String quartet, fortune teller in a booth, endless champagne."

"If anything can cheer up Suzie, endless champagne will. Amanda, call your friend." The prospect of Friday night shone like the light at the end of a dark tunnel. A week of yoghurt eaten at the desk, endless phone calls, the usual round of cataloguing and lotting up ' . . . in magnificent condition and fitted with the original Bramah locks . . . ' hard and detailed grind. Poppy must deal with several press notices of sale, and make sure the ends were tied up on one sale before another took its place. Among the extra duties imposed by Giles' absence in Japan was the supervision of Porterage.

The moving and insuring of articles on their way to the saleroom was a very important job: more money was lost by damage and pilfering on these journeys than after the articles were safely stowed away on the premises. Trenton's always used the same firm of carriers for the jobs but even a well-established and reliable firm was only as good as its weakest link. Last year there had been a horror story which, had it got into the papers, would have cost the house a lot of business.

A crooked packer had infiltrated the carriers, a specialist in the field as it turned out, a man whose days as an antique dealer were brought to a halt by a conviction for fencing and a spell in Wormwood Scrubs. His little trick was to note the good articles as he packed them up. A Meissen teapot, say, he would simply itemise 'teapot' on the packer's note, and substitute one of far inferior quality which was then unpacked at the other end.

The net result was a very small price fetched by the teapot, a puzzled seller and an embarrassed saleroom left trying to explain why the article they had given such a high valuation had sold for so much less.

Like all small criminals, the crooked packer underestimated the wit of his opponents. Giles had become suspicious quite quickly and had baited a trap. The carriers received a particularly fine piece of Chelsea porcelain. Besides the red anchor it bore other security markings visible only through ultra violet. Very soon after that the crook had once more entered Wormwood Scrubs and, thanks to Giles's powerhousing, the carriers' insurance had compensated the cheated sellers more than handsomely, on condition they never told.

With this in mind, Poppy took the supervision of the Porterage very seriously indeed. She wished the job had been entirely allocated to Francis but Giles, impartial as Solomon, had declared that they must split it into two exactly equal halves. Poppy knew this meant her list of losses and breakages over the six months would be compared with Francis's.

The road to the top was not entirely carpeted in Aubusson, she reflected.

Because of the importance of this job there was a great deal of meticulous paperwork that went with it. Blue flimsies, yellow dockets . . . each transaction needed a number of signatures that would have made an autograph-hunter proud.

"Amanda?" Poppy looked up from her desk. "Have you ever thought this could be done more efficiently? It seems a hell of a sweat to have to fill out all these cards and have people hanging around to get them signed."

"Pre-industrial revolution."

"Could we get it all done on fax? The insurance company has a fax machine, the movers must too. Are you any good at systems? D'you think it's possible?"

Amanda's eyes gleamed. "I'd love to have a shot. Think of all the lovely time I'd have for wasting if I managed to cut this donkeywork in half."

"Do you think you could think it out and put forward a proposal that we could present to Giles as a joint venture?"

"Not a word to dear Francis?"

"How did you guess?"

"Brownie points with Giles."

"The thought had crossed my mind."

"Right, Boss."

Another cause for concern that week had been her flatmate. In Poppy's opinion Suzie and Ned went together like Marks with Spencer, and Saint with Laurent. He'd been around ever since Poppy had come to London to share with Suzie; they'd had their ups and downs, their periods when even an outsider could see that habit, not passion, kept them in each other's company. Ned had always flirted, Suzie had swatted his flirts away like flies.

Poppy had a secret theory that Ned needed to flirt to compensate for Suzie's terrifying success and competence in the world of high finance. He must earn a tenth of what she did in a year; she paid for the holidays, the meals, the weekends at country hotels when she was exhausted by her job and simply could not find the energy to broke another stock.

Sometimes it had surprised Poppy that her friend had never felt the need for a more high flying boyfriend but, listening to Suzie's accounts of life in her office, her daily life was peopled with high fliers, all of whom seemed to have low flying principles. Maybe Ned's appeal lay in the transparency of his easygoing, good-humoured laziness.

Since catching him in bed with Solveg, Suzie had absolutely refused to see Ned. He had taken to lying in wait to ambush Poppy on the stairs, begging her to plead his case. Staying late at the office to get the job done was a positive pleasure these days.

Suzie was hiding her heartbreak briskly; the latest business trip, at least, had been a bright spot in her life. She had come back from Caracas fired up with enthusiasm for the exotic glamour of South American women and Poppy was rather pleased to see that the Latin influence had brightened up her friend's style considerably. Suzie had brought back some wonderfully jungly silk dresses, designed to dazzle, not to lull; worn with one of the couture jackets, they looked spectacular and must have knocked her business colleagues spinning. She had also lightened her hair into honey blonde with sun-faded streaks; the net effect gave the impression of a lady in London by accident, her real life spent on a very expensive yacht or beach.

Poppy admired, approved, and said so.

"Darling, I'm going to make him bite his pillow, missing me."

Poppy had planned carefully for the Friday date. She made Suzie promise to stay with her from the first second Freddy Ilchester set foot in the flat. This was the moment of danger, they reckoned, *à deux* in Redcliffe Gardens; anything that came after that could be handled by Poppy solo. The taxi ride to the restaurant would be of limited duration and the meal itself must be quite grope-proof; comparing notes on their considerable combined experiences in the field, they both agreed that even the most desperately oversexed never actually leapt at you over the candlelight and flowers.

There had been the usual swinging on

cupboard doors while they decided which was to be the lucky dress tonight. The plan was that Suzie would eat at home or, if her hair had behaved first go, she'd grab something at the Goat in Boots. Poppy would make her excuses to Freddy some time between ten and ten-thirty, she'd ring Suzie from wherever she happened to be and they would go to the party together: so much more fun than braving it alone.

The last thing Poppy wanted was to inflame the Earl so she chose a dress with a modest high neck. Made of burgundy *panné* velvet, it might have been worn in the afternoon by an Edwardian lady of leisure. She was congratulating herself on such restrained elegance when there flashed across her mind the last time an Edwardian lady of leisure had brushed her consciousness.

Giles's photographs.

She blushed deeply and kept her thoughts to herself. She hoped Giles would come back soon; the thought of him had set up a hollow yearning so strong that she thought it must be telepathic. For a moment she shut her eyes and concentrated hard on willing the telephone to ring.

"Calisthenics?" Suzie came into the bathroom just then.

Poppy looked at her blankly.

"Exercises for the face, darling," Suzie patiently explained. "The theory is that nothing ages if it gets enough exercise. People screw their faces up in all sorts of contortions. I thought that was what you were doing."

"No. I was willing Giles to come back."

"Well, don't will with a screwed up face — he won't like you wrinkly. I say, that's a dull dress for a party."

"Think it'll turn off the noble Earl?"

"If anything can."

"I don't mind being dull at the party after. I'm saving myself for Giles," she said in swooning heroine's tones.

"Well, I'm not going to spare the male population of the advertising world an ounce of my charms. What do you think?"

"I think you're very brave."

"Caracas Couture. An absolute steal compared with London. Rather fun, don't you think?"

Rather fun indeed. The red silk hid just enough of Suzie's top to make it decent by a cat's whisker, the skirt was quite modest until she moved or danced when a courageously long slit up the side gave tantalising glimpses of lots of black-stockinged leg.

"Down with Ned!" they said in chorus. It had become a battle cry.

A head appeared round the bathroom door.

"I couldn't make anyone hear," said Freddy Ilchester.

"Lucky we were both decent," said Poppy.

"Lucky?" Standing in the doorway he blocked their way out of the tiny space.

"Pretty Poppy." He raised her hand to his lips, kissed it and handed her out of the bathroom. "And you?" he asked. Suzie gave him her name, and she in turn was kissed and released.

"Have I got a double date? Life looks wonderful again." He turned the pale blue batteries of his eyes full force on Suzie. "Say you're not doing anything else in that beautiful dress. Please?"

Poppy held her breath. Taking Suzie along as chaperone was the best idea she'd heard yet.

"That would be simply divine." She cooed in what Poppy knew was her best Marilyn Monroe imitation. "I'm going on to a wonderful party later on but nobody was going to feed me first. Freddy, you saved me from a lonesome Ryvita."

"A fate much worse than death," he agreed.

Freddy was in his element with two pretty girls ornamenting the worn leather seats of his ancient midnight blue Lagonda.

"Where are we eating?" Poppy asked.

"Wait and see."

They turned into the Strand entrance of the Savoy, Freddy threw the keys to a waiting doorman and the three of them swept through the double doors.

A volley of respectful Good evening, Your Lordships accompanied them down the great wide steps into the Thames foyer. A piano player was gently coaxing a silky version of 'As Time Goes By' from the grand piano which dominated the centre of the room under its elegant little mock-bandstand. Light from the chandeliers sparkled off myriad mirrors and found smaller rainbow echoes in the diamonds on throats and breasts.

"The usual, Your Lordship?" The head waiter was deferential.

"Times three. And I want to change my table reservation; we'll be three tonight. Can you manage that?"

"Of course, Your Lordship."

The drinks arrived in a flash, tall and pink-tinged with bubbles, served in champagne glasses. Not pink champagne, Poppy surmised as she rolled her first sip round her tongue.

"Kir royale!" Suzie purred. "Yum."

"You obviously went to the right school; they taught you all the important things."

"I never met a Kir royale at school, more's the pity."

Freddy and Suzie were getting on like a house on fire, and Poppy felt rather left out as she gazed about her at the super-elegant taking their ease. Freddy was nothing if not an expert on women and he very quickly picked up the rather subdued vibrations emanating from Poppy's *faux* bamboo chair.

"Suzie, you must excuse us. I have some business to discuss with the prettiest member of staff at Trenton's. Shall we talk about it now, Poppy, get it over before the food? Can't concentrate on two important things at once."

The Earl could be extremely fluent when he wanted to and extremely clear-thinking. The nub of his scheme was this: his castle in southern Ireland was, as most castles are, ancient and in dire need of funds. There was nothing left to sell.

"The last four generations went down the selling road at a gallop. We started nibbling at the assets piece by piece. First the jewels went, then my great-grandfather sold the silver, Grandpa hocked the van Dykes and poor old Dad, not to be outdone, sold the Chippendale to an American collector and grinned all the way to the bank because it had fetched three thou. Where were you then, Poppy my love?"

"I think we'd have got a little more for it than that even twenty years ago."

"*O tempora! O denarii!* Never mind. Now my job in all this is to sell, but to sell something so absolutely wonderfully valuable that it's not just staving off the next dose of fuel bills. What I want to do is make enough so that the cash can shore up the old foundations but at the same time leave a spot over for a touch of enterprise.

I'm bored of money only going one way when it meets with my pockets."

"You're not thinking of selling the castle?" Poppy suggested. It was the only thing she could think of that might generate a large enough sum of cash. Even so, decrepit castles often fetched less than sensible mansions in Weybridge. And surely, if that were the case, he'd be dining the prettiest estate agent in London, not an auction house representative?

"Couldn't do that. Nothing for the heir to inherit, if I ever get around to breeding, that is. No, no, I've a much cleverer idea than that but it's a touch unconventional, which is why I needed to talk it over."

Though the castle itself was of great antiquity, he explained, there was a modern bit that always fussed the historians. Purist scholars of Irish architectural history tut-tutted away whenever they mentioned the Adam Ballroom at Ballynally. It had been added by Robert Adam in 1762.

"Not so *very* modern," Poppy interjected.

"All things are comparative, particularly to medievalists! The Ilchester of the time," he went on, "fed up with giving parties in gloomy halls, and having a little cash in hand for a change, decided to splurge it on a ballroom. Sensible chap. Have you seen pictures of it?"

Poppy nodded her head, Suzie shook hers.

"Quite pretty isn't it, Poppy? But more to the point, it's saleable."

The little building was completely self-contained, he explained, it was joined only to the main portion of the castle by an arched covered walkway most of which had fallen down and the remainder of which was known as Murder Alley.

"The best way to kill a pal. Send him down the colonnade to the ballroom. Absolutely bound to be decapitated by a huge bit of masonry falling on him before he reaches the end."

The absolute essence of the question was that if Freddy sold the Adam ballroom lock stock and barrel, brick by brick as it were, would Trenton's handle the sale?

"It's not an everyday request." Poppy's mind was racing with the enormity of the scheme. She began to plan aloud.

"You're absolutely right, I'd have to come over to Ireland to see it for myself, but unless the whole thing is so fragile that it is going to disintegrate when the buyer tries to move it, the condition of the ballroom is almost immaterial. Restoration's very competent these days; even we have difficulty telling sometimes." She thought for a moment. "I take it the original decorations are still intact; none of your ancestors popped the panels during a lean spell?"

"Believe it or not, dear heart, they didn't. No, there's quite a lot to raise the dibs on: the panels were all by Angelica Kauffman so they're the real McCoy. The plasterwork is the usual Adam stuff, eggs-and-darts by the yard. You can't move for swags and urns all over the place. When Adam went out of style we must have been too lazy to do anything about it so all the furniture's there too: two socking great sideboards in rosewood, inlaid. Wine coolers, wine jugs, pier glasses, knife boxes, vases on pedestals, wall sconces and chandeliers: all designed by Robert."

With a jolt of excitement, Poppy was beginning to realise what this could mean. "I don't think a complete Adam room has ever been sold before. We'd have to market it worldwide before the sale.

Make a brilliant video and send it out to the world's richest men. The Ballynally Ballroom . . . We could market it as the ultimate status symbol — an entire room, shipped anywhere."

She envisaged the perfect little Georgian gem bodily transported to the Côte d'Azur, Florida, Venice . . . Wherever the millionaire with the most cash happened to live, it could be re-erected.

"Oh no!" she said, struck by a blighting thought. "What about the Heritage Lobby? We'd never get an export licence."

"Heritage lobby? Export licence?" the Earl echoed. "Darling girl, we're talking Ireland now. We've none of that nonsense about us there. The nearest we get to Heritage hysterics are the medievalists, and they would simply sing and rejoice that I'd restored the purity of line to the old place. As for export licences, I should think when the *Dial* hear about it they'll make sure to rush through a little law imposing a swingeing tax on all exported ballrooms. They won't murmur as long as I warn them far enough in advance for them to set up their little cut." He caught the head waiter's eye and held out an arm to each girl.

The three of them followed the head waiter as he led them from the Thames Foyer down to the River Room. They were shepherded to a table in the window and when the chairs had been organised, the water glasses filled and the napkins draped across their laps to the entire satisfaction of the hotel staff, Poppy had time to look about her.

Looking through the large window and down the stretch of the great river, Poppy registered the beauty of the London nightscape. For all the sumptuousness of the food that evening and the lusciousness of the wine, the glamour of the people and the wonderful buzz of enjoyment taken with the seriousness it deserved, Poppy spent the meal in a detached dream. Vaguely she registered the rip-roaring flirtation that was being conducted between Freddy and Suzie. The *foie gras* with the *Château Yquem,* the *suprême de canard et son petit farci de chou truffée,* the *soufflé suissesse,* all melted away as in a dream. Vaguely she regretted not being able to give them more attention; a meal like this would not come her way again in a hurry, but no amount of determination could turn her mind from the fairytale opportunity that had just been put on a plate before her by dear, dear Freddy.

The pianist started a gentle tinkle and people got up to dance. Freddy, perfect manners to the fore, danced first with Suzie and then with Poppy.

She felt she owed him an explanation. "Sorry I've been bad company. I can't stop thinking about Ballynally. The more I think, the more ideas I have."

"It's a business dinner, remember? You're not being rude, simply earning your corn."

"Excellent corn, by the way."

"I'm glad." He paused in the dance and drew back his head to look her levelly in the eyes. "Now, what was all this about a party?"

6

FREDDY wanted to go by boat so they left the Lagonda with the delighted attendant at the Savoy garage.

"Not often we get a real thoroughbred like this, Your Lordship. May I give it a good old-fashioned waxing?"

"Good man. Love you to. But don't leave any fingerprints, for God's sake, or the chauffeur will have me up for car-abuse."

"Odd how people get their kicks," he said as they emerged from the garage onto the Embankment. "Imagine actually *wanting* to polish a car. Now come on, you two, step lively — we've got a yuppie-bus to catch." And he marched them down to the Thames Line stop.

Freddy could not be faulted on matters of style. Going to the party in a boat was infinitely more exciting than arriving by car, even if the car was a rather sleek number. They had the Thames Line boat to themselves which meant that they could pretend that it was their own private motor launch.

Once they had arrived at Wapping pier they simply had to find the warehouse in which the party was being held. The task was not Herculean. The agency had thoughtfully provided signs.

The warehouse was large and spare. Although there were many people in it, the main impression given was one of space. Everything was absolutely bang up to the minute, the tomorrow of now. There were lighting effects that Poppy hadn't even read about.

A lot of people made a lot of conversation and took up a lot of space but they were dwarfed by the monumental sculptures disposed about the place; it felt rather like a party in Stonehenge.

The party was being given by The Agency, an advertising and PR company which over the past few years had taken the steepest and most spectacular route to the top. Ian Agen was the brave mountaineer who had led this dizzy climb and some of his success had to be due to the name he gave his company: The Agency. Not only did it incorporate his own name but it had such universal appeal that whenever anyone referred to any other advertising agency without actually mentioning it by name, people assumed they meant The Agency. So its name spread like lightning, and the work it did was good. Good enough to finance Agen's insatiable appetite for gigantic sculptures and very modern paintings.

Looking about the room for a friendly face, Poppy once again regretted her plain dress. It stood out like frost in June against the brilliantly feathered parrots of both sexes: seldom had she seen such an avant-garde display of the very latest, from cleverly coiffed heads to Manolo Blahnik pumps. It was as if the pages of *Vogue* had come to life. She caught sight of Amanda and thankfully weaved her way through the crowds to reach her.

"I'd almost given up on you," Amanda said. "Did you manage to shake the libidinous Earl?"

"He's here, too, dancing." Poppy indicated the end of the room where the more energetic part of the party was going on.

"Poppy, meet Marcus. And this is Nick Coles. Marcus wangled us the invitations

144

and Nick is an art director at The Agency. Isn't that right, Nick?" He nodded. It was easier than trying to make yourself heard.

"Come on," Marcus was pulling at Amanda's arm, "let's dance. I want to show you my snakehips."

Poppy was left alone with Nick Coles and not much to say. He was not typical of the men in the place, most of whom wore their fashionable clothes like flags of intention.

While he could never be mistaken for a City man, there were differences in his dress. Nick Coles was no slave to fashion. He wore a very well-cut suit, admittedly an offbeat one of cream gaberdine, a dandy suit worn with casual elegance and surprising touches. His hair was short, cut sculpturally close to his head, and he looked like a man at ease with himself; playing the trendy agency game but not taking it very seriously. Poppy guessed he was no older than herself.

"Do you feel as awkward as you look?" he asked her.

Her chin went up.

"Sorry I don't fit in with all the hi tech," she said. "If it offends you, do move on.

The only reason I came to this party was to see the sculptures anyway." And she swept off, feeling extremely angry.

Her excuse led her to the nearest monolith which she stood and looked at. She walked around it, treading on a few toes as she rubbernecked, and then moved on to the next. She had evolved a plan in her mind. One by one she would look at the huge sculptures between herself and the door: if she got to the last without anything interesting happening on the way, she would simply melt into the street, find a phone box and call Charley the cab to come and rescue her. With this satisfactory agenda in mind, she was quite happy to devote her attention to art.

So it was another disappointing party — surely she was old enough by now to know that every party did not produce a Prince Charming?

"Do you like it?" said a voice behind her.

"I think it would be better displayed on a vast hillside where you could see it from half a mile away. Even in this huge room, it's rather sad; like a noble lion caged in a zoo." She turned. It was Nick Coles who had asked the question.

"I didn't mean to insult you, you know," he said. "I was just surprised to see real beauty — unadorned and completely pre-Raphaelite — in a roomful of New Brutalists all tricked up to look unisex and frightening. Put it down to art director suffering from aesthetic shock, will you?"

"My fault," she said, "oversensitivity induced by overwork. Sorry."

He put out his hand, and solemnly they shook. She noticed his even teeth, strong jaw and air of relaxed self-confidence. In the absence of Giles, there were worse ways of spending an evening, she decided.

"Do you want to tell me about the overwork or is it the last thing you want to talk about?"

"The very last thing. Tell me about you instead. Tell me what it's like to work here."

He did, and it seemed from his narrative that an art director's life was not a great deal simpler than that of a department head at Trenton's. Life in an advertising agency, it seemed, was stuffed full of assertive ladies jockeying hard for the star places in a competitive world and not caring too much who they screwed up on the way.

His life was also bugged by a creative director who was always presenting Nick's ideas as his own, and a TV buyer not literate enough to make sense of the schedules who invariably made sure that the life assurance ads were slotted into morning programmes for under-10s, while the toy marketing campaigns would show up during the breaks in heavy current affairs programmes. Clients were not a smooth ride either: life with them was a tightrope dance. On the one hand they wanted the artwork of a Leonardo and the intellectual input of an Einstein. On the other they really didn't want to pay the prices that would ensure them the fruits of genius.

"You've succeeded," Poppy laughed. "Trenton's is like a Teddy Bear's picnic in comparison. I feel much better."

"Good." And for the first time she noticed he had a very nice smile, one that crinkled his grey eyes and made her want to smile back.

"I happen to know that in about a quarter of an hour there is going to be a tremendous firework display. I love fireworks, don't you?" She nodded. "If we grab a drink and go up to my office, we'll see it better than anybody else. Shall we?"

"Lead on, Macduff."

A wooden slatted balcony in beautiful teak ran round the great central space of the warehouse, like a minstrel's gallery. They paused for a moment to look down on the chattering, dancing mob.

Nick's office had a panoramic view of the Thames as it curved down to the dotty gothic of Tower Bridge. Everywhere lights were moving, dancing and doubled by their reflections.

"I'd find it difficult to get my head down to work in here."

"I spent the first week raising the art of boat-spotting to unprecedented heights. Then I realised that the only sensible thing to do was move my desk so I had my back to the window. Pity to waste one of the great views of the world but I've never been very good when it came to temptation."

"So you got yourself a swivel chair," she said, sitting and spinning herself dizzy.

"That helps."

The office had three desks in it. Nick explained that his team at The Agency consisted of a writer, a typographer and himself; they reported to the creative director (the villain of intellectual thievery) who was responsible for the whole agency's artistic output. On the sidelines were a planner, who made sure that everything was running to time, and an account director who presented the clients' view and kept a very tight hold on the finances. Above them all, like God, was Ian Agen whom Nick liked and respected a great deal.

"If only it was as simple as working for Ian himself," he said, "things would get done in quarter the time and I'd be enjoying my work. As it is I'm starting to resent the time wasted on office politics and in-fighting. Even at a very good salary, I'm wondering if it's worth it."

"But what would you do?" she asked. "Join another agency?"

"More of the same?" He shook his head. "No. There'd be no point; we're the best. I would hate to trade down, even if it meant a bigger job. No, what I'd really like to do is paint."

"Paint?"

"I know that every art director thinks

he's an artist but I just have a notion that I am; and if I don't stop all this airbrushing around I'll be looking back over my life at the age of sixty, wishing I'd had the courage to give up everything and paint for my life."

"Curious," she said. "I had a very similar conversation with a much older man, just this week. It took a heart attack to get him out of his established career and starting up what he'd always dreamed of doing. He's really excited about it." She smiled gently as she thought of Maurice.

"It would be dreadful to leave it so late," he commented.

"Maybe," she mused. "Or maybe it's realistic. It would be tragic to give it all up for painting if you weren't good enough. Not many are. Are you?" She looked up at him candidly.

"That's the heart of the matter, Poppy. Do you always ask the perceptive question?" He was adjusting the parallel motion on his drawing board now, she had an idea he was doing it to avoid her eyes. "I suppose the real answer is that I don't know," he said at last. "I think I'm good, the College thought I was very good; tears were shed and teeth were gnashed when I said I was going into this game. My teachers spoke about waste of talent. That's as maybe." He laughed lightly against himself.

"I suppose the real answer is that I'm tormented by the fact that I'm not spending all my time painting. I paint in the evenings at home but that's not the same thing. You work at a canvas for three or four hours maximum and then you just have to stop and go to sleep if you're to be any good at the agency in the morning. It's cheating on both. I've been gradually realising over the last few months that I've come to some sort of crisis. Quite soon I must decide which way I'm going to jump. Oh, look!" he said as the first firework blossomed pink against the midnight sky.

They stood side by side and silent, watching the magical coloured sparks form and reform into patterns, ascending halfway to heaven to flower for brief seconds, rest, fade and die; leaving only an after-image on the retina: a memory of momentary glory.

"I love them," she said quietly. "They just exist for pure pleasure."

His arm tightened around her shoulders and, unexpectedly, he bent his head to kiss her very gently on the mouth, an exploration. It was nice; fireworks outside, fireworks inside. Suddenly she remembered Giles and broke off. Nick looked puzzled but he didn't probe.

"Do you have a car?" he asked. "I've got to leave soon, there's a shoot in the morning so I must get up at seven. You'd have no chance getting a taxi out here."

She explained how she'd arrived with the others on the boat. They went downstairs to find Freddy and Suzie entwined on the dance floor, obviously with little intention of going home right away.

"See you later," Suzie called around Freddy's embrace.

Nick drove a small, nippy Golf GTI. He drove it very fast and very competently, it did not take long to get through the quiet midnight streets to South Kensington. Even now the streets were swarming with foreigners of every nationality. There were still some shops opportunistically open.

"I love this area," Poppy said. "It's such a polyglot mixture. There's a lovely Frenchman I see quite often: very dapper

153

in his bowler hat. If he had spats, I'd think he was Poirot."

"I live in Tite Street," Nick told her, "not far away. I was lucky enough to get one of those Victorian studios with a huge North light."

He didn't invite her to come and see his paintings, and so she didn't ask to, though she would have been interested. She couldn't quite fathom his lack of pushiness. They got on well together but maybe he just didn't like her enough to try and take it further. Pity, she would have liked to see the pictures; judge for herself.

He parked the car and insisted on seeing her up all the steps to the door of the top flat.

"Don't bother. You'll get little enough sleep as it is before you have to get to work. I must say it's rather tough having to be there at seven on a Saturday morning."

He shrugged. "Schedules wait for no man. I'll see you up the stairs, make sure you're safe."

At the door, he put his hand on her arm.

"What was it earlier?"

"Confusion."

"Is there somebody else?"

"Do you read minds?"

"It was the only possible explanation when we were getting along so well." He turned quickly to go back down the stairs but she had seen the disappointment on his face.

"Nick?" Poppy hated the idea of him walking out of her life as suddenly as he'd appeared. "I'd like to see your paintings," she said impulsively. "May I?"

"Shall I call you?" He'd turned and was examining her face carefully from a lower step, looking for more than one answer.

She felt a pang of guilt. This was a beginning with Nick, she couldn't pretend it wasn't dangerous. She ought to tell him she'd changed her mind, didn't want to see him again. What about Giles? And then Nick's hair flopped forward, he tossed it back in a way he had and stood quite still, looking at her with clear grey eyes.

"I'm on Trenton's central number."

Either her words or her look had told him enough.

"I'll call." He grinned and bounced downstairs.

7

POPPY had long promised herself a weekend at home. She was quite convinced her skin would turn grey like the London buildings if she didn't touch base for good long draughts of Devon air. Besides, there was much she needed to discuss with her father, and she must check he was not being bullied by his latest housekeeper.

By the time her Saturday chores were done it was late afternoon but that didn't bother her; she'd take the night train from Paddington. It always had a special excitement for her. There was no earthly reason why it should. Just like every other train it had harsh neon lighting, the floors were none too clean and the seats could have been more comfortable. But it was the night train, and night trains meant adventure.

Even at that late hour the train was crowded, which only added to the excitement. Despite the people, Poppy was lucky and managed to find a window seat. The journey would have been quite spoiled if she couldn't look out of the window at the lights whizzing past. And later, as they got beyond Reading and into more countrified areas, there were the massy shapes of oak trees against the sky, and the faint white glow of moonlight reflected on fleecy sheep.

Finally the contours changed. The landscape became like a child's model: miniature hills and valleys with hedges poured along them, following their natural lines. The little folded valleys of Devon. And then she was getting out into the colder, softer air, looking for a taxi. Thank Heaven they never seemed to run short in Exeter. It would be no fun to have to sleep on a station bench.

In no time the taxi had brought her to Winchendon.

Winchendon Hall nestled into its Devon hillside as though it had been there forever, which it very nearly had as the money to turn it from modest farmhouse into a Hall had come from Armada plunder.

It boasted a Tudor Gallery which had been invaluable for roller skating on the long rainy days in Poppy's childhood. There was also an eighteenth-century Gothic Library, noted in guidebooks for its fine decorative plasterwork. Poppy herself thought the abundance of gothic plaster crockets, finials and general curlicues really right over the top but, when roller skating eventually lost its fascination, the Library had become her haunt on those long days when the Devon rain gave the impression that God had a limitless supply of it and was never going to tire of pouring it down.

No-one had studied the dusty old books for generations. Poppy's interest, born at first of boredom, had become a real and absorbing passion. There were any number of long days to fill after her mother had died; her father had engaged a succession of housekeepers, friendly but too busy about their jobs to take time keeping the little girl company. Henry Palmer was trying to put meaning in his lonely life by busying himself about the farm. So day after day Poppy had kept company with the books until she started to love them with a real bibliophile's passion: she loved their slightly fusty smell, the feel of the old ridged handmade paper under her fingers, the smooth bindings of Vellum and gold-tooled Morocco.

Little had she known it then, but these books had given her an extra education through their early woodcuts, strange spellings and odd notions of what lay beyond the edge of the world. So that when she left school and went to Bristol to study Art History, she had had a distinct edge on her peers.

Henry Palmer had a very good brain but it was not a commercial one and what Winchendon needed at this precise point in its history was lots of money. If history had been kind it would have made him a great financier but in fact his greatness lay in meticulous and useless inventions. Nothing delighted him more than a problem with the flow of water through the antique guttering system: entire days would be spent with the fierce gleam of enthusiasm in his eyes worrying that problem until it was satisfactorily solved. Most things he did took absolutely ages and never, ever earned him any money; the farm was kept ticking over with the help of a non-communicative farm manager and an understanding bank manager.

As a matter of fact, Henry Palmer was not entirely convinced that money was the answer to his problems. He had once invented a small, but helpful device to speed sheep through the dip. Such a success had it been amongst local farmers that he had been persuaded to market it. The ensuing money was used to instal central heating and this had been a dire mistake. The delicious heat, so necessary to the comfort of all in the Hall, was the absolute death-knell to the house itself. Outbreak after outbreak of dry rot ensued, and the expense of continually cutting out rotten timber and renewing it was quite simply a bottomless pit down which Henry poured money that he increasingly did not have.

Poppy paid off the taxi and pushed open the heavy oak door that led straight into the large central hall. The stone fireplace held huge smouldering oak limbs, dying down now and warming the grateful backs of van Cleef and Arpels who gave her the affectionate welcome that only golden labradors can. She took them out for a last airing and then they exchanged mutually affectionate goodnights. The rest of the house had gone to bed but the lights were left that she would need to see her up to bed.

She loved her room. The flowers on the wallpaper were so old that only she knew that they were really a cherry pink, the curtains had faded just as badly and their leading edges were frayed like the carpet; its bald patch was a memorial to the spot her feet always hit first thing in the morning.

One day she'd take down the photographs of the tennis player she had worshipped for three long Wimbledon summers, one day the gymkhana rosettes would simply fall to pieces with age. Till then, not a thing was to be changed. She turned her eyes to the photograph that sat on her dressing table in its silver frame.

"Goodnight, Mummy," she said as she always did in this room, last thing before she got into bed.

Her feet had the pleasant sensation of meeting a hot water bottle, and the darned sheets were well-aired; no cold clamminess here. Poppy thought kindly of her father's new housekeeper. Old Bridget would

161

never even have dreamed of such an indulgence as a hot water bottle, the Good Lord would have been outraged. She composed herself for sleep in the narrow, familiar bed.

She was woken, ten minutes later it seemed, by an almighty crash. Her eyes flew open, her hands reached for her watch, and she saw with surprise that it was in fact already half-past eight.

A head came round the door. It belonged either to a small boy with long hair or a small girl with short hair.

"I'm really sorry," it said. "They told me not to wake you up but the football hit the big bronze gong. The one the butler used to hit for meals. You won't tell them I woke you up, will you? I didn't mean to, and I have said sorry."

Poppy decided it was a boy. Only boys could have such knees.

"What's your name?" she asked him.

"Terry," he said, and whizzed out making aeroplane noises and forgetting to shut the door behind him.

Poppy went down to the dining room for breakfast but there was no sign of it. Bridget used to lay it out every morning on the long mahogany table: two cups, two plates and quantities of silver. So Victorian was Winchendon in layout that the scrambled eggs had always had a repellant congealed look by the time they had made the long journey to the dining room. Poppy swore this added to Bridget's Puritan satisfaction.

No luck in the dining room. She might as well explore in the kitchen.

In Bridget's day the kitchen had been forbidden territory. Raid the fridge for a piece of celery and you would be sniffed at for a week and the rice pudding would be all swimming in milk as a punishment.

Under the new regime, the kitchen looked lived-in and a lot more cheerful. 'Untidy', Bridget would have called it. She would not have approved at all of the practical plastic cloth, a riot of blowsy roses, which now covered the scrubbed deal table. Nor would she have liked the beaten up old sofa that had been moved from some room or other and now sat in a recess, strewn with today's papers and odd bits of darning thread. Poppy immediately gravitated to the comfort of the sofa with her cup of coffee. This was a great improvement, she decided as she lounged and read, it beat stiff formality in the dining room any day.

Perfection never lasts long in this world. This particular patch of it was shattered by the entrance of Terry, still being an aeroplane.

He looked at her and she looked up at him, and for one blissful moment he switched off his noisy engines.

"I know I asked you before," Poppy said, "but who are you?"

"I'm Terry, like I told you, and I live here."

"I live here too." She paused. "At least I did. I live in London sometimes now. I'm Poppy."

Recognition lit his face like sun after clouds.

"Oh! you're her," he said. It wasn't much of a lead.

"So will you tell me all about living here and what you do?"

He told her at length about the best places for playing football, the best trees to climb, the best places to go if you wanted to stalk rabbits. Stalking rabbits made his eyes go all shiny with dreams; his ultimate ambition was to sneak up behind one so quietly that he would be able to 'leap down and strangle it', a feat never accomplished even by the most experienced gamekeeper telling his tallest stories in the pub.

"I've got to get a bit quicker yet," he said disarmingly, "look." And quick as a flash he had rolled up his shirtsleeve to display a very creditable bicep for a nine year old.

Poppy gave up trying to make any sense of Terry at all. Clearly his and her notions of the essentials of life were on parallel paths that would never meet. Who his parents were and what he was actually doing at Winchendon Hall were issues of such supreme unimportance in his life that he simply disregarded them.

"Shall we go and see the horses?" he soon suggested.

Poppy complied with alacrity. To her certain knowledge there were no horses round about the place. Terry was probably going to lead her to some imaginary animals but she was game for anything.

Hand in trusting hand they went together to the stables where, to Poppy's amazement, there actually was a rather sweet strawberry roan head looking intelligently over one of the stable doors. Two of the other boxes had fresh straw on the floor and, indeed, more obvious evidence that horses had recently been in occupation.

"Tell me about the horses," she said, leading Terry to sit beside her on the old mounting block.

"We got three," he said. "They're lent from the Fowler-Watts." This made sense indeed. The Fowler-Watts owned the local riding stables and often boarded out surplus horses during term time when there were fewer horse-mad schoolgirls hanging about for lessons and helping with the mucking out.

"This one here's called Trigger," Terry went on. "When he came here he was called Cindy but I couldn't ride one called Cindy, could I?" Solemnly she agreed. "Then there's Makehaste — he's a big chestnut devil, your dad rides him — and Feathers, 'cause she's grey. That's for my Mum."

As if on cue, the two horses and two riders came round the corner of the farm drive; Henry Palmer and Terry's mum were having an animated conversation that absorbed the majority of their attention so they did not see Terry and Poppy until they were almost upon them.

"Hello, Poppy darling." Her father dismounted and held the head of his companion's horse while she swung her foot over and neatly got down. He took both sets of reins in one hand and led the two mounts towards his daughter, stopping to exchange a kiss of greeting.

"Poppy, this is Lorraine, who looks after me now, and Terry her son whom I can see you've already met."

Lorraine came up from behind the horses and shook hands.

"Pleased to meet you," she said, and blushed.

So this was the new housekeeper! Things were falling into place. Old dour Bridget had been replaced by a vivacious bottle blonde.

"Thank you for my lovely hot water bottle last night," Poppy said.

"Well, I hate a cold bed myself," said Lorraine. "Did you find the breakfast? We thought you might sleep on. Terry didn't wake you, did he?"

Poppy did not look to see but she

could feel the little boy's eyes fixed on her beseechingly.

"Terry? Oh, certainly not. I'm in the habit of waking early these days."

"Things must have changed," snorted her father.

"Henry," said the relieved urchin, "can I clean the saddles and stuff? Mum says I got the hang of the saddlesoap."

"It's called tack, remember? Course you can if your mother says so but, remember, go easy on the saddlesoap or you'll have more bubbles than a laundrette on amateur night." He loaded up the little boy with the two heavy saddles and laid the bridles carefully across them so the reins would not drag on the ground and trip him up. Thus overburdened but blissful, Terry went off to be busy in the tack room.

"That'll keep him quiet for a bit," Lorraine said. "We usually have another coffee after our ride. Would you like that, Poppy?"

For a moment she was taken aback, the housekeeper usually called her 'Miss Poppy'. But, looking at Lorraine, this form of address would have been absurd from her. For all she was probably forty,

Lorraine seemed young, more of Poppy's generation than her father's; she wore jeans for riding today and an old shirt under which were very creditable bosoms. Under the bright hair was a pleasant, pretty face which would have been much the better for less powder and less colour about the eyes and lips. Her makeup was more suitable for a cocktail party than a country ride; Poppy guessed she was one of those women who felt undressed without it and probably put it on first thing in the morning when she got out of bed.

The weather was so beautiful that Henry Palmer suggested they had their coffee on the terrace. He and Poppy sat and drank in the view to the south, content to be quiet until Lorraine appeared with very good filter coffee and hazelnut biscuits which would have broken anybody's diet.

"That's a new coffee machine," Poppy commented.

"Well, your silly father put up with rotten coffee all these years. D'you know, Poppy, he said he never dared ask any of the other housekeepers if they'd make him proper coffee! I can't see the point of having people work for you and not getting them to do as you like. I love the filter too, so that's easy, and I told your father that if there's anything else he likes and didn't dare ask for, or if there's anything I do wrong, he's to tell me straight away and I'll be much happier. Right, Henry?"

"Right, Lorraine." He looked a bit sheepish.

"It sounds like a recipe for contentment." Poppy held out her cup for more of the excellent coffee. Not only was it good, but there was enough of it.

"I'm glad you think so." Lorraine's first truly natural smile came through. "I was a bit frightened of meeting you. I thought you might not approve of me and Terry moving in and changing things."

"As long as Daddy's happy."

Henry Palmer did indeed seem happy and more full of energy than his daughter had ever known. Had she remembered him as a young man in the days before her mother died she would have recognised his natural optimism and vitality.

Henry and Lorraine were having a spirited discussion about the vital subject of the work for the day. Ordinarily Henry would be concerned with the farm work which he and the employed manager would apportion between them at the start of the week. Both of them would go about the farm's business, quietly getting things done that had to be done, an efficient but joyless routine.

Lorraine's plans for the day did not seem to include farm work at all. The rest of the morning the three of them were to spend clearing the bit of garden that led from the terrace down to the top pond. A considerable amount of this jungle had been cleared already. Brambles and bracken had been pulled up and burned, nettles poisoned, the old gravelled path treated with weedkiller, and this top part of the wild garden was looking once more like romantic woodland.

"Poppy and I can do the jungle-bashing, Henry. Why don't you start on the duck enclosure?" Lorraine suggested.

They worked like slaves all morning and when he had finished cleaning the tack, young Terry joined in, designating himself wheelbarrow pusher.

"Vroom!" He pushed the barrow piled high with brambles.

"Take care on the corner!" Lorraine was

anxious not to have to reload the prickly brambles twice after a spill.

"It's a Formula One wheelbarrow. It's brilliant through the chicanes." But Terry had overestimated the cornering of his racer and they ended up picking up the load and starting again.

Over an excellent home-produced ham at lunch, Lorraine explained that she and Henry had plans to get the whole of Winchendon working again as it used to.

"It was that depressing when I came," she said, "your poor father rattling around in all the gloom and glory, and anything that wasn't the farm was just falling to pieces. It seemed a crime, the lovely garden and all. So we're cleaning it all up gradually, outside and in. Doing what we can with our own hands. We've applied for some grants too but it takes forever with all that paperwork so we're not waiting for handouts. Whether we get the money or not we're going to go for it, aren't we, Henry?"

"When we get the garden looking respectable, we're putting in a wildfowl reserve," her father joined in the explanation. "The duck pen I was building this morning is the start of it; people love to see animals in their natural surroundings. You see, we thought if we got it all tidy we could open the garden again like we used to in the old days, except this time it won't be for charity, it'll be for us."

"And it's not stopping there." Lorraine's blue eyes were alive with enthusiasm. "I've always loved animals, so we're starting on a few rare breeds, Gloucester Old Spot pigs and Jacob's sheep, and I'm setting up a tea room in the old dining room. It's no good having a dining room the size of a railway buffet any more these days. You wouldn't want to sit down twenty to dinner, even if you had the help."

Looking at her father's face, Poppy decided that all this activity was doing him all the good in the world. His face looked pinker, he'd shed some weight, and he simply seemed more alive. Heaven knew if these ideas to turn Winchendon into a moneymaking venture were based on sound common sense or cloud-cuckoo optimism; she just hoped they worked.

The afternoon continued as busy as the morning. Henry continued to construct the duck enclosure, aided and abetted by the enthusiastic Terry. Lorraine took Poppy to the old walled garden where there were early peas to be picked and frozen, lettuces to be cut and packed for sale at Winchendon market, and tall blue delphinium spires to be picked and hung upside down carefully in the Long Gallery for drying, because: "People pay the earth for really good dried flowers."

"Where did you get your business instincts, Lorraine?" Poppy wanted to know. "It seems you just have to look at something to think of a way of making money from it. I'm impressed."

"Where I grew up there was so little of it, you spent all your time thinking about it," she said honestly.

In the unlikely setting of the Tudor Long Gallery, she told Poppy all about her life as the two of them sat on the floor, carefully sorting the flowers and fastening them to the beams in little bunches to hang upside down and dry in the constant drafts that made the gallery cool and airy at any time of year. Terry dotted in and out, running errands for them.

Lorraine, it seemed, had grown up piecemeal, the youngest of a family of five, in and around London. Her father had been a builder. She dimly remembered his glory days when there had been a marvellous shiny red Rolls Royce. The Rolls had lasted all of a week and then it had been repossessed; it was unpaid for, as was almost everything else in her father's life.

"It wasn't that he was a crook," Lorraine explained, "just an eternal optimist."

Her mother was obviously a respectable woman, trying hard to make a decent life for her children but fighting a losing battle against a stream of repossessions, and her husband's relentless inability to tell her the truth about their finances. Eventually it had worn her down and she had died. The lesson that the children had learned from all this was that the minute they were old enough to go out and earn, they were on their own.

Lorraine herself had done, "Just about everything. From receptionist at a property developer's in Park Lane; that one didn't last long, they went up the spout for millions!" She laughed cheerfully. She'd also been a Bunny Girl. "Not fun and games all the way, I can tell you. You have to report in every morning before you go on duty and if you've broken a fingernail or you've forgotten to shave your legs they fine you, take it out of your pay. Real dragons they are."

"You'll be wanting to know about Terry's dad," she went on, and she was right; it was only delicacy that had stopped Poppy asking. "A real sod he was. I didn't marry him, thank God." Lorraine was silent for a moment, her customary ebullience evaporating at the thought of him. "I didn't want him to know that Terry was on the way even, but one of my dear girlfriends thought it was her duty to tell him I was in the family way. He turns up with hard luck stories every now and then. Says he wants to take care of Terry, but all he really wants is a handout. I pay him what I can on condition he leaves me alone; it usually works. I've been very careful coming down here, hidden my tracks. Jo's not too bright, it wouldn't occur to him I might have hidden myself in the middle of nowhere."

They'd finished the careful tying of the flowers.

"Thanks, Lorraine," Poppy said.

"For what?"

"You didn't have to tell me all that."

"If I didn't tell you then somebody else would make it their business to, wouldn't they?"

"You seem to have caught the hang of village life pretty quickly."

"Oh, it doesn't only happen in villages."

Poppy's visit that weekend had a very specific purpose but it was supper time on Sunday evening before she asked the question.

"When I first started work at Trenton's, Giles came down to see you, didn't he, Daddy?"

"Before you started actually, if we're to be burningly accurate."

"Hmm. Did he say anything about the Hoarde?"

"Yes indeed!" Henry broke into a deep, rumbling laugh. "He read me a great lecture on how important it was — I've forgotten the details. He seemed to think it was immensely valuable, too. I showed it to him, funny little bits and pieces, but even after he'd seen it he semed to think it was worth an inordinate amount."

"He told me that too."

Silence fell. It seemed that nothing more would be forthcoming unless she asked the direct question, the one to which she dreaded the answer.

"There was no condition attached to giving me the job, was there?" Her father looked at her uncomprehendingly. "Nothing like promising that Trenton's could have the sale of the Hoarde if I got the job?"

"Oh, I see. Who's been trying to sap your confidence? That Francis fellow you talk about?"

"Well, sort of."

"What a rat!" Lorraine was deeply on Poppy's side.

"Clever rat," said Henry. "Clever enough to incorporate a grain of truth. Of course, if I decided to sell the Hoarde I should sell it through Trenton's. That was unspoken between me and Giles but clearly understood."

Poppy's heart was not far above her boots.

"But," her father went on, "it certainly wasn't a condition of your getting the job. Maybe I'll sell and maybe I won't, Giles knows that. I'm absolutely free to decide for myself."

Henry Palmer's honest answer was intended to reassure, but still Francis's taunt rang in her mind.

The meal over, Poppy went to look at this immensely valuable treasure that was important to her in so many ways. If it were really so valuable then Henry must be made to secure it more efficiently. Certainly there were locks on the Library windows, but these were themselves so old and rotten it wouldn't take much of a burglar simply to push in the old frames.

It was difficult to look at an object you had known all your life and suddenly see it as a piece of world history, worth a fortune in anyone's language. She picked up the leather purse containing the old gold coins, and remembered playing shops with them in her girlhood. She looked at the vellum-bound Spanish Bible, the handwritten prayer to Sant Iago, complete with a translation into English by Poppy's grandmother. All the little familiar objects. There was no logic to it but she felt that Winchendon would somehow be diminished by the loss of this little iron-nailed chest.

Best go to bed. She'd have to catch the

milk train to get her to work on Monday morning.

Climbing the stairs she caught a glimpse of a flowered dressing gown whisking quickly into her father's bedroom. So Lorraine . . . well, well. No wonder Winchendon had such a fizz and crackle about it!

8

THE Millington sale dominated the media on Monday morning with the predictable result that Francis was in Poppy's office not long after the morning post.

"Well, this is a how-d'you-do! I hope you know what you're up to, Poppy dear. Trenton's name will be mud if you've not done your homework properly. We're quite sure it's a genuine Peter-Paul, are we?" His plump face was pink over the bow tie.

"Joost van Mompert has no doubt whatever. Nor does the Curator of the Riiksmuseum. I think I'd be foolish to doubt the opinion of either of them. I don't know if you saw Geraldine Norman's column this morning?" Poppy said sweetly.

Geraldine Norman had long been the most respected writer on saleroom matters in the London press.

"She condenses the evidence very well for the average reader with only a few minutes to spend. I commend her to you,"

Poppy said sweetly.

"I suppose it's one of Maurice's discoveries," Francis said with deadly accuracy. "*You* certainly wouldn't be up to a piece of heavyweight detection like this."

Poppy merely looked at him and silently thanked the instinct that had made her wear Suzie's cast-off Chanel suit today. It was surprising what confidence she gained from the businesslike costume.

"I fancy *I'm* doing rather well too. Of course my strategy doesn't rely on single coups, however brilliant they may be individually. I've gone for the more steady, persistent assaults on the marketplace. My Social Calendar Sales will spread the profit throughout the year while introducing the collecting habit to an entirely new sector of the market: uppercrust philistines with plenty of money."

Francis lifted the bulk of the pinstriped bottom he had been resting on Poppy's leathered desktop; he was preparing to make a move but Francis would not have been Francis if it had been unaccompanied by a sweet little barbed adieu.

"Giles is terribly pleased with the idea.

Sent a message specially via Sarah this morning. Has he rung to wish you luck with the Rubens?"

Truth or fantasy? Poppy wondered.

"I do so hope it turns out to be a real Peter-Paul, darling. You could do with a little success."

"Thank you so much, Frankie dear. It looks as if I might be lucky today. I've got about a hundred press enquiries to answer." She indicated the telephones whose lights were flashing, to show the number of callers waiting. But her mind wasn't in the game of trumping Francis's sweet sentiments; it was already hard at work unravelling the clue about the Social Calendar Sales.

Amanda would know what he was up to. Poppy called her in and asked.

"Oh, it's quite clever really," she said. "The little snake's got brains. He's taking the dates of all the Season's events and having a sale to match, so to speak. Yards of Munnings horse portraits in Ascot week, Polo trophies on Smith's Lawn (Royal attendance guaranteed if something's done for charity), Cricket paintings, historic bats and I daresay sweaty jockstraps too, coinciding with the Ashes at Lords. Eton memorabilia on the Fourth of June. Need I go on?"

"I get the picture. I suppose it'll work," Poppy said gloomily.

"Bread-and-butter sales." Amanda put her head to one side. "All of them put together would be pushed to give a clear profit of a million. We should get that on your Rubens in one fell swoop or all the analysts have got their price predictions badly in a twist."

"Amanda, my love, you cheer a girl up wonderfully." But Poppy's face clouded over again, belying the cheerfulness of her words. "Francis guessed it was one of Maurice's discoveries, you know. It's one of the things he handed over to me. I don't really deserve any of the credit at all."

"Count your blessings. The next one will be all your own work . . . didn't you say the lecherous Earl had made a very interesting proposition?"

"Oh, the Ballynally Ballroom. I really need to speak to Giles about that. I do hope he comes back soon."

Amanda could see she had drawn no smile from Poppy; more drastic treatment was called for.

"Come on, I'll show you something to cheer you up."

"I really haven't time . . . " Poppy was in no mood for frivolity but Amanda pulled her up by the arm and dragged her along to the Holy of Holies, the Dragon's Lair: the office of the Honourable Sarah Cavendish.

"I just needed some more yellow dockets," Amanda had her excuse off pat but she did not need it.

Giles's secretary sat at her desk with earphones firmly clamped to her head, listening to the pearls of wisdom pouring down her cochleas. The Hon Sarah was doing her art course, frowning a little as she concentrated on the difficult lesson, and concentrating through the diamanté glasses on a volume called *The World's Art. A History from the Cave Paintings at Lascaux to the Impressionists.* This learned and detailed book was proposing to unlock all the secrets of Western Art to Sarah in the space of a hundred and twenty pages with many garishly coloured reproductions.

Amanda looked at Poppy with raised eyebrows. "Bettering herself." They giggled.

Sarah shifted the headphones so they sat behind her ears. "Will you be long?" she asked. "I'm in the middle of a rather complicated tutorial." She radiated self-importance.

"Just run out of these." Amanda waved the yellow flimsies that she'd just picked up.

"Right." Sarah was already tuning into the headset; nothing must come between her and higher education.

Amanda and Poppy spent the rest of the day shoulder to shoulder dealing with an overexcited world press. It was not often that major paintings by major artists were discovered. Apart from the London ratpack, the Europeans were here in force but it was the arrival of the American art press that really brought home to Poppy the magnitude of what she had set in motion.

They were all keen to examine the picture and every scrap of evidence supporting the claim. Joost had flown over, a rangy loose-limbed Dutchman with fading pale hair, old-fashioned gold-framed spectacles, a beard and a friendly old tweed jacket.

He and Poppy held an impromptu joint press conference in the Red Room where the picture would be sold. They sat before the huge canvas which would now be flanked by security guards day and night until it was sold and had safely left the premises.

It was Poppy's first press conference. At first she found it extremely disconcerting to be faced by a mob of strangers, all screaming at her at once and popping dreadful blinding flashes from their cameras.

"I'm not sure I can cope with this," she muttered to Joost.

"It is like the driving at night," he said sensibly. "Do not look at the lights."

Her fear evaporated after the first twenty minutes and then she found it all rather enjoyable. The firm presence of Joost at her side, fielding the scholarly questions, was no end of help.

At last the journalists started to ask the same questions they had already asked at the beginning of the conference. Poppy evaluated this as a sign that they had finally run out of steam and it was time to break up the happy party.

"I think that's all, gentlemen," she said. "The only thing I really do want to emphasise is that the discovery was originally made by Maurice Blessingham. Some of you will know about Maurice but for those who don't I'd like to explain that he is recovering from a heart attack, which is why he is not here today to take the credit for himself. I was merely fortunate enough to inherit his mantle, so please don't give me too much praise — it rightly belongs to Maurice."

This unselfish sentiment brought a round of scattered applause from the journalists. No one knew better than the cynical press how rare it was to encounter generosity of spirit in the public arena. Poppy's honest tribute had won her their goodwill; an asset that was to prove invaluable.

Over tea in her office afterwards, she rubbed her eyes.

"I hadn't realised how tired I was," she said to Joost, whose endlessly long frame seemed to sprawl the entire length of the room.

"It is always tiring, such a thing," he said, "but it went well."

"You think so? I'm glad."

"Ja." He nodded slowly and little reflections from the goldrimmed glasses danced up and down with the movements of his head. Like a miniature marionette theatre, she thought, and idly wondered if she could ask him to sit here nodding so she could see the end of the story.

Suddenly she felt weak with needing Giles. All the uncertainties floated about Poppy's head: the battle with Francis, the Hoarde, the Ballynally Ballroom — brilliant coup or wild folly? Nick, too, how did he fit into her life? Why, oh why, couldn't Giles come back and sort out the pieces?

She must be very tired indeed to be thinking such thoughts.

Flavia poking her head round the door disturbed their peace.

"Awfully sorry to disturb you, Poppy, but I'm doing front desk and there's a chap turned up who says he's got a Titian to sell and won't go away until he's spoken to you. We tried awfully hard, we really did, but he absolutely insisted. I thought Francis was going to get a slipped disc he was bowing and scraping so much. He even invited the chap to tea at the Ritz to discuss it." This sounded dangerous. "But not even Frankie's famous charm . . . "

"Sorry, Joost, sounds as if I'll have to go."

"Let me know if you need verification for the Titian!" It was the nearest she had heard the solemn Dutchman get to a joke.

"Are you all right for getting to the airport and everything?"

"I am going first to see my old friend Maurice."

"How right you are. He'll want you to relive the whole thing for him, word for word. Give him lots and lots of love, will you? Coming, Flavia."

She went out into the reception area. It now being considerably after five o'clock, there was none of the normal milling crowd of staff going about their business and hopeful clients waiting for valuations or appointments. Only one figure sat in a large leather Porter's chair close to the door.

The back of the chair was tall and shaped like a niche to protect the porter from drafts as he sat on his long vigils. The chair's high superstructure prevented her seeing much above the occupant's waist. All she could see of the mystery Titian-seller was a pair of long legs in cream linen trousers; at the end of each long outstretched limb

190

was a perfectly polished brown and white leather co-respondent shoe. Today was the era of the tall man with endless legs. By his trappings it looked as if this one might be an old-fashioned millionaire with a penchant for golf.

Poppy's heels made a clacking as she walked across Trenton's empty front hall. One definite fact about the stranger in the Porter's chair revealed itself: he was not deaf.

Hearing her tread he uncrossed the long legs and, still ten feet from him, she saw him bending forward at the waist, preparatory to getting up. The cream linen trousers were the bottom half of a suit, she noted. There was also a very distinguished old-fashioned laced clove carnation in his buttonhole, a soft bow tie in floppy navy crêpe de Chine, and a panama hat with a navy silk ribbon. The brim of the hat shaded his face.

Under his left arm there was a Titian-shaped package, from which plastic bubble-packing showed under good old-fashioned brown paper and string. Poppy registered the protection with some relief; it was wholly inadequate for a precious painting but it was better than nothing. Few people realised how frightfully fragile old canvases were.

The hand not occupied with the precious parcel was raised to remove the panama hat in a timeless gesture of gentlemanly politeness.

"Hello," said Nick Coles.

Poppy was speechless. Exhausted by a long and difficult day, she simply didn't know how to deal with this. She surprised both herself and Nick considerably by bursting into tears.

Simultaneously he dropped the hat and the package and slid across the floorboards to put his arms around her.

"There," he said, "there. It's all right."

Their conversation continued on this high intellectual plain until Poppy had got over her first storm of weeping. By that time Nick's extremely elegant foulard silk handkerchief had been whipped out of his top pocket to do duty for noseblowing, eyewiping and other mundane tasks that it had never been designed for.

"I'm sorry," she snuffled at last.

"No, *I'm* sorry. I suppose it was a silly trick. I thought it would make you laugh, but I didn't get it quite right, eh?" He looked down at her with the crinkled corners of his eyes radiating sympathy and understanding. Now he had jettisoned the hat, a long lock of hair had flopped forwards over his forehead. She pushed it back into place.

"I think I'd better get you out of here before I get you the sack. Would you like strong drink or a fortifying cup of tea?"

"Do you know, I'd really love some tea."

"I was hoping you'd say that. Come on. I've got a favourite place."

Nick, Poppy, hat and package all crammed into the GTI that he had left on the double yellow straight outside Trenton's door.

He drove with the verve she remembered and parked again on a double yellow line round the corner from South Kensington tube station. He walked her to Daquise, the small restaurant run by Poles in exile.

"Do you know, this was the first place I found when I came to Redcliffe Gardens?" she told him as they settled at their little table in the window. "It's one of my favourites, too. Daddy told me about it. It's been here forever, even he said that. Nobody makes such marvellous cakes. I've always thought it was full of spies."

"And sad exiles in moustaches plotting to go back," he interjected. "It's a good place to go if you're alone. I love to sit listening to the language — so full of mystery and darkness. Poppy, I'm sorry about the picture. I thought you'd laugh."

"You must think I'm very dull. I don't usually break down and cry with disappointment if people give me surprises."

"Hard day?"

"And some!"

Nick himself had spent his time finishing off the campaign shoot so he had been blissfully removed from radio, television or anything that might have blared Poppy's name and Trenton's at him.

"You mean I'm tea-ing with a celeb?" he asked when she told him about it. "Hang on."

He nipped out of the door and she wondered if he'd changed his mind about the foolish double yellow. No such thing. When he came back it was apparent he had covered the hundred yards up to the newsvendor outside South Ken tube station and bought himself an evening paper.

"There you are," he said as he sat down. "Page one, no less."

The photograph showed rather more of her legs than it did of the painting behind her.

Nick raised his long glass in which was suspended a teabag on a string and a slice of lemon; Daquise served tea the Polish way. They toasted each other.

"Cover girls are allowed to be a little overwrought," he said. "Do you want to tell me all about it? The *Standard* only says that you're twenty-four, which is very useful in itself, and that your eyes are brown while your hair is red. They're not quite right there, by the way. I should say that red was a very inadequate word for the colour of your hair." He looked back at the paper on the table, "Oh yes, it also says something about a painting?"

Poppy couldn't help but laugh.

She found herself telling him all about her duel with Francis; the frantic competition that must exist between them for six long months before the power struggle could be decided.

"I wonder if I might help you there," Nick mused.

"Help me get ahead of Francis?" It seemed unlikely he could sway the balance either way.

"It's just an idea. I'd need to do a certain amount of research into Fine Arts marketing first. Could we spend an evening on it?"

"I'd need to get the Millington sale behind me first. It's absorbing every working moment."

"Tell me something Poppy." His voice had changed; the excitement at a new scheme had given way to thoughtfulness. "What drives you so hard?"

She told him how important it was for her not only to make a go of her career but to make a financial success so that she could shore up the failing finances of her family and prevent her father's having to sell the house or its only remaining treasure. She told him about Giles's references to selling the Winchendon Hoarde; she even confided the terrible germ of suspicion that had been planted in her brain by Francis: that the Chairman had only employed her to get his hands on the Hoarde.

Nick listened. He let her talk unchecked,

sipping his tea quietly with his eyes fixed on her face and a thoughtful expression on his.

"You know, you'd make a perfect shrink," she said at the end. "I've never known anyone listen like you. Not even Suzie knows all this. It's such a relief to be able to tell somebody."

"You're pretty impressed by this guy Giles, aren't you?" he asked.

"He's the most marvellous man." The shine in Poppy's eyes told him all he feared but needed to know. His own eyes dropped down to the tablecloth momentarily until he could be sure they would not give him away.

9

IT was the week of the Millington sale, and Trenton's was buzzing. Poppy's office was at the centre of things and she was thriving on the excitement. London echoed the party mood; the city was in its midsummer glory, the sun shone and the birdsong was deafening.

As Poppy came in from the street, Amanda gave her a wicked grin. She raised her eyebrows interrogatively but Amanda merely winked in reply.

Businesslike, Poppy went straight to her own office; it was going to be the hub of the week's busy wheel. When she opened the door a heavenly cloud of cool fresh scent billowed on the air to meet her. Her eyes were drawn straight to the desk which was entirely swamped by a huge basket brimming with rare blooms: exotic tuberoses, waxy stephanotis, fragrant cream freesias and huge green lilies ramped and rioted in luxuriant profusion. Never had she received such an extravagant display.

Frantically, Poppy hunted for the card.

Darling, The course of true love never did run smooth. Today we'll smooth its path far from the telephone's shrill summons. Lunch? The car will pick you up at twelve.

There was no need for a signature: Giles had written the message on his visiting card in his distinctive Blancpain pen.

"Amanda, you hold the fort. I'm going straight back home to change."

Oh, the joys of having a secretary!

Poppy looked up and down the vintage couture rail. Today she didn't need Ned to help her choose. Her hand went unerringly to a Balenciaga corded silk grosgrain in gunmetal grey. The skirt moved with her body, the jacket would have been cruel on a waist carrying an inch of fat; but Poppy went in where the jacket went in, and where it went out, she did too. Under this was a whisper of a cream silk chiffon shirt. She added some high grey suede shoes and her panther earrings that had been copied in frank imitation of the Duchess of Windsor's famous Cartier suite.

She growled at herself in the mirror. A very grown-up tiger growled back.

The morning went all too quickly. There was no time to savour the prospect of lunch. At twelve, Front Desk rang up to say there was a taxi waiting and by twelve-twenty she had been whisked over Battersea bridge, down the river and on to Westland heliport.

The moment she was strapped in her seat, the helicopter took off. Where was Giles? She asked the pilot but he shrugged and told her that he had been told to expect only one passenger. There wasn't much conversation after that, the noise of the rotors didn't encourage it, and besides, Poppy was too entranced looking out of the window and feeling excited.

She could have stayed in the air for hours, flying over Toytown, following the big broad bends in the river. The pretty riverside houses at Kew and Chiswick; the great royal palace of Hampton Court with its gardens so geometric, they were just as a child would build them out of Lego blocks and cotton wool blob trees. Then Windsor castle and Eton College chapel in their grey stony masses, and the water meadows and playing fields of the great school: cricket under the poplars, sculling on the water.

The helicopter started to turn and lose height. Poppy was sad because it meant they wouldn't be going on to overfly Blenheim and Oxford but the sadness was more than cancelled out by the fact that a descent meant Giles.

Down they swerved. She thought they were going to land in the Thames. Did they make amphibious choppers? With a lurch and a bump they landed. The window on her side looked out on to a landing stage and the river. The narrowness of the green inches between gave her a great respect for the pilot's accuracy. He had already unstrapped and was holding the door open for her. He pushed her head down as she got out and when she straightened up she had the greatest difficulty in the world not uttering a wild whoop of joy. There, sure enough, was Giles, looking absolutely wonderful in his customary suit: navy today, and pinstriped. He'd picked up a tan on his trip, it could not all have been meetings in offices and hotel rooms, and the darker olive of his skin made his eyes and the dark hair more intense. He stood on a green lawn, waiting for her.

Poppy was very disciplined, she didn't let herself run. Eyes locked, they walked towards each other. When they met, their arms twined round each other compulsively. He kissed her mouth and she stayed, eyes closed, and held the moment.

"Darling," Giles said, "it's been forever."

She opened her eyes and nodded. She couldn't speak, her mouth was dry and she was having great difficulty breathing.

"I could kiss you again and again," he said, "but not here."

"We must have an audience of hundreds," she agreed.

"Come on up to the hotel."

Arms around each other's waists, they strolled languorously up the lawn towards the Riverside Inn, a pretty beamed house, washed creamy white. There were green-and white-striped awnings stretching over the lawns, shading little groups of chairs and tables with fresh bright flowers. A tall man in a white chef's jacket came up to them, politely hoped that she had had a good flight, and wondered what she and Monsieur Trenton would like to drink? His face was familiar from a hundred cookery book jackets and the sort of television programmes that made a perfect *roulade* look like child's play.

"No drinks just yet, thanks, Michel. I think we'll just go up to the room to freshen up first. Mademoiselle feels a little dusty after the journey."

"Of course, M'sieu."

They could hardly keep their hands off each other going up the stairs. The moment the door closed behind them they kissed as they had wanted to kiss from the moment their eyes had met, down on the lawn. He kissed her as if he wanted everything at once and she revelled in his urgency. At last he broke off.

"I've been waiting for that ever since I got that blasted telephone call," he said. "Damned Japanese! It's been too long."

"Mmm," was all she could manage.

"Now come here." Giles pulled her over to the fourposter bed. Another time she would have stopped to marvel at the pretty chintz hangings. He sat and pulled her down beside him.

"I don't want to scrumple you," he said, and raising a hand he ran one finger lightly down the edge of her silk jacket; only the very tip touched her flesh through the thin silk chiffon blouse. The feather touch made her shiver.

"I've booked us a table for one-thirty." He checked his gold Patek Phillipe. "Have you ever eaten here before?"

She shook her head.

"Good. The food's the best in the world. This afternoon is going to be the most sensuous of your life. We're going to eat a long, long lunch and we're going to drink some good wines. And all the time we're eating, we'll know that we have this to look forward to." The pupils of his eyes had narrowed to pinpoints. "Would you like that?"

Mesmerised, she nodded.

"Good. I've got you a little present," he said, and handed her a shiny black oblong box, giftwrapped with silk ribbon. In the corner was a dragonfly motif and the name Janet Reger.

"Put it on," he said. "I'm going downstairs now. You'll find me at the bar, thinking of you."

After he had gone, Poppy was quite incapable of movement for a long moment. The warmth of Giles's attention had completely stunned her.

She looked around the bedroom and decided it must be the prettiest in the world. All pink and green and white, it was as fresh as the garden and from the window you could see the river. There was a deep windowseat with lots of pretty cushions in the same Colefax and Fowler chintz as the bedhangings. The fourposter itself was immense, with beautifully turned cornerposts carved with cherubs and swags of flowers. Its roof was tented so that when you lay on the bed, as Poppy was doing now, you gazed at a pretty little gilded cherub who seemed to be gathering up the festoons of fabric and ribbons above your head. She grinned a wicked little grin. The next time she lay here, and it wouldn't be too long now, she would not be concentrating on the cherub.

She sat up and turned her attention to the box; she did not want to keep Giles waiting. Slowly she pulled the ribbon ends and undid the knots, making it last. Then she took off the lid and found white silkpaper, sealed with a little round gold seal with the dragonfly emblem again. She broke the seal, unfolded the paper and took out of the box a black basque, made of lace, black silk, ribbons, and tiny red rosebuds.

She started to take off her jacket. Giles had told her to put it on, so put it on she must.

Quite soon she discovered that this was easier said than done. The basque did up at the back with extremely pretty black ribbon lacing. Unless you had a ladies maid it was quite impossible to do yourself. For one mad minute she thought of ringing the bell to summon someone, but her courage failed her. She went to the bathroom. There were mirrors on three walls above the level of the bath and basin. Looking over her shoulder, she tried to lace herself up by following the reflection of her backview.

This was even more complicated than doing it by feel.

She would have to do it up at the front, hold herself in to make herself as small as possible, and then swivel the garment round her body so the lacing was at the back.

A hundred sexy reflections leapt out at her from the bathroom mirrors. She saw herself front view, backview and sideview and from each angle she looked like something from Paris in the nineties, and a very naughty bit of Paris at that.

How could such a fragile garment completely change her body? The lace and ribbon cups lifted her breasts and gave them a deeper cleavage, their patterns making her body look like the prettiest Christmas parcel. The basque ended in a flutter of black net around her *derrière* with four little ruched ribbon suspenders.

Oh dear, she had been wearing tights! Please God he had bought her some stockings too. Scrabbling and hoping fervently, she investigated the bottom of the box. The stockings were lying in a piece of paper that she had discarded. *100% Soie*, the label read.

Silk stockings felt utterly different, rather slithery, and they shone. Suspenders were not a doddle to do up, one kept popping. Not all jam, being a courtesan, she reflected, smiled a huge smile at herself in the mirror, and then hurried herself back into her clothes. Suddenly she could not wait to see Giles again.

She rushed across the room and then remembered that she had forgotten to brush her hair. She made herself walk slowly back to the bathroom, brushed her hair a hundred times, leaning forward so it would cloud out when she stood upright again. Then she picked up the leopard earrings that she'd left by the basin in the first flush of excitement. Suddenly icy cool, she checked every detail and only then allowed herself to go downstairs.

Giles's eyes were fixed on the door. He stood up when he saw her.

"You're wearing it," he said, and only the lift of his eyebrows made the statement into a question.

She merely looked the answer.

"Good." He took her by the elbow. "Come, they've put our drinks in the gazebo."

Leaving a distinct and tantalising gap between them, he led her out of the bar and across the lawn, threading through the tables and their happy occupants eating, drinking and talking. At the bottom of the lawn, just on the edge of the water, was a pretty little *Chinoiserie* pavilion: octagonal in shape, no more than ten feet across, and with a little pitched roof pointed like a Coolie's hat. There were two chairs, flowers spilling everywhere, and a table on which stood a bottle of Vintage Dom Perignon Rosé.

"This is magical," she said.

"We can see and yet we are invisible. Thank you, Charles." He waved away the waiter who had been waiting to pour their champagne. Charles disappeared.

"Look." He led her to a little pointed window. "From here you can see the river traffic, and from here — " he led her by the hand — "you can spy on the people as they eat. Do you like being invisible, Poppy?"

Again, she could only nod.

"I should like to ravish you here, while nobody knew we were doing it, but we shall have to save that for another time. For today we must wait and restrain ourselves like good children, so I shan't even kiss you. While we eat you will tell me all about business and what has been happening at Trenton's in my absence. Come, sit down."

Poppy was barely capable of coherent thought but Giles had seated himself at the other little chair opposite her and was wearing his business face. She must somehow pull herself out of this maelstrom of longing for him and report on Trenton's business.

Charles reappeared with two plates bearing the prettiest little lobster mousses, exquisitely arranged. His presence helped restore Poppy's presence of mind and she was relieved to find herself reporting quite coherently on the latest developments.

The lobster mousses were followed by *éventail de selle d'agneau poêlée minute.* Each arrived under a silver dome and was unveiled with due solemnity. With this they drank a Lafitte Rothschild which was absolutely the most delicious wine that Poppy had ever drunk but Giles put his hand over her glass so she should not have a third. His eyes reminded her of what his voice would not before the waiter. The paradisical bottle went back half full, which she thought was a terrible waste, but when the last course arrived it was accompanied by a new wine.

"Château d'Yquem '75," Giles said, holding the straw-coloured liquid up to the light. "Remember the taste on your tongue, my love. You won't meet it often again."

Solemnly, they both drank.

And then, when the waiter had left them

alone for the third time and the *soufflé chaud aux framboises* was in front of them, he took her hand in his, raised it to his lips and ran his tongue along the palm of her hand.

"Shall we leave the soufflé?" he asked. "I don't think I can wait for you a minute longer."

She looked at him, wanting to fix his face in her mind forever, the way he looked just at this minute. Every detail suddenly seemed crystal clear: his dark hair brushed back over his forehead, the few silver hairs shining in contrast to the dark brown. The arched eyebrows, slightly raised in question over the deep-set hazel eyes that had now darkened with passion. The clearly etched line of his lips that had been kissing her such a short time ago.

She stood up as if to leave. "Thank you for lunch," she said mischievously.

But Giles was bent on other things and had no time for small flirtatious jokes. He got up too and snatched her so roughly towards him that it hurt. Holding her hard with their bodies pressed together, he simply looked down at her. His eyes were unfathomable, they asked a question which she did not understand and which she did not know if she could answer. A thought crossed her mind that they were deeply troubled eyes, which seemed absurd in the circumstances, but before she could stop herself she reached out to stroke his face in a gesture that had everything to do with tenderness and nothing with lust.

"Giles?" she asked him quietly.

"Poppy." His voice was hoarse.

They left the little pavilion hand in hand, the longing and the anticipation tangible between them. She could never remember afterwards how they made their way across that lawn under the public gaze and all the way up those long flights of stairs that led to bed. She remembered every detail of what came after Giles had shut the door to enclose them in their own little world. There was a long silence between them as they looked at each other, savouring the last moment before their bodies would come together.

"Take your clothes off." His voice was soft and quite controlled. "Slowly."

Hypnotised, she undid buttons, slid out of silks, unclipped the panthers from her ears — still with his eyes fixed upon her.

She heard his sharp intake of breath as she reached the black underwear.

"Stop." It was a command. "Now, come here and undress me."

He didn't help her, just stood as she coped with cufflinks, shirt studs, all the complicated Savile Row details. Under his scrutiny, she felt acutely aware of her body. Self-conscious but proud too, proud that her body was exciting him so much. When finally she had got the last of his clothes off him and the cream silk boxer shorts were down on the floor about his ankles she was left kneeling before him.

The fourposter bed was wasted on them. Giles had no patience for such refinements. He took her immediately, suddenly, on the floor and it was only after his first violent need was satisfied that he carried her up to lie under the gilded cherub to take his pleasure at greater ease. There were no words between them, just endless sweeping sensations and afterwards a long, sated silence.

"Giles?"

But he was asleep.

As she lay there, Poppy wondered why

she felt a little cheap, a little cheated? She frowned as she tried to understand it and, looking down at her body in the black lace underwear, felt suddenly absurd. She'd go to the bathroom now and take it off. When he woke up they'd make love skin to skin. That would put it right.

Dallying with her hair in the bathroom she heard the telephone and sped in to save Giles from being woken. Too late, he was already speaking.

"Thank you," he said crisply. "Ten minutes to quarter of an hour."

He was out of bed before the receiver was back in place.

"Can you make yourself respectable in ten minutes?" Already he was pulling on his shirt. "That was my alarm call, the chopper's back to pick us up. We'll just get back to the office in time for the wrap on the day's developments."

He looked her up and down in the hastily assumed clothes, adjusted the sit of a lapel and then opened the door to let her go first. Poppy felt quite breathless. There were so many things she had planned to say to him afterwards and now suddenly there was no afterwards, just a snatched dash to a noisy helicopter where there'd be no chance of talking.

They hurried across the bar and towards the door.

"Giles de Vere Trenton!" a determined American drawl stopped their progress.

"Why, Mrs Box!" Giles dropped Poppy's hand as if it was a red hot poker. "How perfectly charming to see you and how absolutely wonderful you look!"

This last was plainly a barefaced lie. The ancient crone who had greeted Giles was overweight, overage and overdone. Her cascade of blonde curls tumbled improbably over a face which had certainly seen sixty summers, maybe more. The sables that swathed her were neither suitable for high summer nor for the English countryside. The pearls that hung from her neck and ears like Christmas baubles were undeniably real and of a size and lustre that simply didn't come off the production line.

While Giles flattered, Poppy gawped.

"Mrs Box, this is Miss Palmer who works for me at Trenton's."

A brief nod acknowledged the introduction. Mrs Box plainly didn't waste any words on anyone below Chairman level.

"Giles dear, didn't you always call me Phyllida in New York? What have I done to deserve this terrible formal 'Mrs Box'? Let me know my sin and I'll atone!" she twinkled archly, squeezing his arm.

"Phyllida, my dear, I didn't like to presume . . . "

"Oh, you formal English! Now you must come and have some coffee and we'll have a good long chat. I've got something very important I want to tell you about. It must have been the Good Lord that brought us together here today. You know I was on my way to Christie's to see that good-looking Auctioneer of theirs — and, well, here *you* are! My late husband, Henry Box III, would have said to me: 'Phyl,' he would have said, 'this is a sign sent from Above. It's a sign that the Lord wants Trenton's to sell your bronzes.' That's what Henry Box III would have said and so that is exactly what I am going to do. Come sit down here and talk with me, right now!"

She fluttered the long black nylon lashes at him in a caricature of seduction.

For one moment his face was completely blank and Poppy could tell that his mind was assessing the chances of the good-looking Auctioneer from Christie's if Mrs Henry Box III was deterred from speaking to Giles 'right now'.

"Phyllida, my sweet," he put all his charm into his voice and his hand on her arm, "we'll do better than that. Let's talk it over in my helicopter while I fly you back to London. I haven't much time before I need to be back in town for some meetings. Miss Palmer here is the clever girl who discovered that the Millington Rubens *was* a Rubens. We sell it tomorrow and she has a lot of work to do as well. Could you fly up to London with us?"

"Why, Giles," the pink tongue licked the heavily glossed lips, "that would be just wonderful! I must just organise my chauffeur to take the car and the dogs up to the Connaught without me. Starch!" She let out a yell that would have been heard over miles of rolling prairie.

In reply to her summons a grey-liveried chauffeur appeared, pulled by the intertwined leads of four fat, disagreeable-looking pekineses.

"Starch, you must take my darlings up to London without me. Now you're to make sure that they get a good walk first, and when they arrive at the Connaught they have their usual suite. Check that their baskets are aired and that Chang has no feather cushions." She turned to Giles. "An allergy, you know. Milk at blood-heat with a tablespoon of codliver oil," this to Starch, "and I want the hairdresser in my room at seven. I'm due at the Embassy at eight-thirty."

"Very well, madam." He showed not a trace of surprise at the orders and took the four reluctant Chinamen off for their exercise.

Giles was already striding across the lawn, supporting the tottering swathes of sable on his arm. If Poppy had a blowpipe handy, she would have pierced Mrs Box's ample derrière with a curare-tipped dart and thrown herself on the mercy of twelve good men and true.

As Giles handed her aboard the helicopter he gave her one snatched private look, and when he was quite sure Mrs Box was absorbed in arranging her curls to their best advantage, mouthed, "Sorry darling." Then he got into the pilot's seat and smoothly lifted them off.

So, thought Poppy without surprise, he's the perfect pilot too. Had they been returning to London unaccompanied she would have delighted in this new discovery, but relegated to the third seat behind the pilot and his principal passenger, she felt like a second-class citizen.

Her mood on departure was quite different from that of happy anticipation that had marked her arrival at the Riverside Inn earlier in the day. Poppy couldn't hear much of what was passing between Giles and Mrs Box, it could hardly have been a sparkling conversation on account of the noise, but she had obviously managed to make clear her request that Giles should fly over some of the famous London landmarks. Mrs Box was clearly too important to be denied.

Giles made the machine swoop and turn and soar like a demented seagull. One last glissade over the Houses of Parliament and at last he touched them down at Battersea Heliport.

When he handed out a delighted Mrs Box, she was pink and flushed and skittish from the ride. "Well, that was just wonderful! You know, back home we'd never be allowed to overfly the White House, just in case we had a bomb on board. Isn't it just typical of your quaint and sleepy little country that nobody even dreams of such things?"

"Well, actually," said Giles, "we're not either. I was watching for Police helicopters all the time but we got away with it today. Our markings are quite similar to the choppers that carry the Royal family about, so I reckoned we stood a good chance."

"Why, Giles, you naughty boy!" She grasped his arm possessively. "You know what we were talking about before? Well, you've just secured yourself the sale of the Henry Box III collection of Fine and Important Bronzes. Now how about that!" She stood very close to Giles and breathed up into his face in her best little-girl manner.

Something gallant was obviously expected of him. He lifted the cerise-taloned hand to his lips and said with great solemnity, "Madam, Trenton's are honoured."

Giles had gambled and won.

He now organised the three of them into a taxi; Poppy, of course, got the uncomfortable fold down seat with the back to the driver. She had to strap-hang on the corners. The only consolation was that the cramped little seat let her mix up her knees and legs shamelessly with Giles's. Their nether regions kept up a dialogue of flirtation while Giles's best patrician accents kept up a Fine Arts conversation with Mrs Box.

"And what are you thinking of doing with the money when you sell up the collection?" he asked.

"Well, I have just the most thrilling idea!" Her eyes shone like a child's in a sweetshop. "I am going to make an Oriental Palace for my boys!" She looked at him and waited breathlessly for him to gasp and grovel in excitement at the idea, but Giles was for the moment nonplussed. Clearly he had no idea at all what Mrs Henry Box III was talking about.

Poppy, who had summed up the woman's mental capacity as being approximately that of a pea-hen, knew exactly.

"Her dogs," she mouthed at him, and watched in breathless admiration as he turned back to Mrs Box without a flicker of astonishment on his face.

"Why Phyllida, what a completely

absorbing idea! Tell me all about your plans."

Both Poppy and Giles were silent for the rest ot the journey while they listened in wonder to the plans for the disposal of the Henry Box III fortune.

The merry widow had, it seemed, recently taken a trip to Japan where she had fallen in love with every aspect of life there. She had decided to make the next stage in her life as completely Japanese at it could possibly be. Overlooking the fact that Pekinese were a Chinese breed ('Well, they're all much the same over there — small, yellow and foreign'), she had bought a lakeside property in upstate New York, was building her lacquer pavilions with a will and, when they were erected, was going to fill them with oriental artefacts to make her dogs feel at home.

"And just think of the wonderful Japanese party I can have, my pagoda-warming, so to speak. It just thrills me to think of it. New York won't have seen a party like it since Truman Capote passed to the Other Side."

When they arrived at Trenton's it was apparent that Mrs Box was still enjoying herself hugely and had no plans to rush off to her hotel. Giles invited her in to see behind the scenes, an invitation she accepted with alacrity. He also included the suggestion that Poppy show her round: "It might be a good idea if you got to know Miss Palmer better. She will be handling the disposal of your collection."

But Mrs Box wasn't having any of that.

"I thought you said Miss Palmer was busy with this big deal tomorrow? Why don't *you* show me round, Giles dear? It would be thrilling to peek into your office!"

How could he refuse?

Francis was behind the front counter as they went in. He was talking animatedly on the telephone while keeping a small queue of six or eight waiting for his professional opinion on their assorted offerings. The minute he saw his Chairman come in he slammed down the telephone smartly without even a goodbye and, when his eyes had registered Mrs Box, sailed out from behind the desk, leaving the queue to yet another interminable period in limbo.

"Phyllida!" His pink face glowed with the excitement of greeting an important acquaintance. "We've not met since the Americas Cup Ball. I see you're still wearing those fabulous pearls. You look quite ravishing, darling — and you've changed your hair. It suits you beautifully, makes you look even younger. You must tell me what diet you're on, or is it vitamins?"

"My dear, can I leave you in Francis's very capable hands?" Giles asked Mrs Box. "He'll give you a much more amusing tour than I will."

She graciously consented, and Giles and Poppy made their getaways. There was a great deal of work for her to do on tomorrow's Millington sale. She had been mad to leave the office today; it might well mean working most of the night to catch up.

The arrangements for the sale were unusual in that the Millington family were selling some, but not all, of the contents of their house. It was a question of raising enough money to cover death duties so that the family could continue to live there.

Usually a country house sale involved selling everything which made the operation quite straightforward however large the house and numerous the contents: there was an established pattern to follow.

In this particular case Poppy had decided, on Maurice Blessingham's advice, that the items to be sold would be best viewed in the house itself, rather than being brought up to London for viewing and disposal at Trenton's.

"Quite frankly, darling, some of the pieces they're getting rid of are a bit iffy. Show 'em off in the clear light of day and we'd get peanuts for them," Maurice had said. "But if we keep them together in the context of all that brocaded grandeur, the reflected splendour will draw much better prices. We can't fool the dealers, of course, nothing can fool the dealers; but a big house sale always attracts the tourists, and they're the ones we *can* fool."

So the contents had remained in the house while the tolerant family hid in the servants' quarters, leaving Trenton's staff and security men to play host to buyers and sightseers curious enough to pay £25 for the catalogue which secured them admission to view.

The job in hand now was to assemble all the pieces to be sold in small marquees adjoining the large Sale Marquee in the garden, so that the porters could carry a smooth flow of objects in sequential catalogue order before the high desk as they were auctioned. The sale was broken up into categories: furniture, silver, porcelain, paintings, books, bibelots and jewellery. One porter was in charge of each category and the Head Porter, Henry Ablethwaite, was in overall charge.

Henry had come to Trenton's from the Fraud Squad: security was a dream with him in charge but there was more to running Porterage than making sure that things didn't get nicked. Before the sale it was Henry's responsibility to see each item displayed to the best possible advantage: his department got through gallons of Goddard's Long Term Silver Polish in a month. They also made up their own beeswax and turpentine furniture restoration cream that was the only thing Poppy knew that would make wood shine like a mirror. If you were especially favoured, Henry would let you have the recipe on pain of secrecy or death: Francis had wasted much money buying Henry lunch in hopes of being let in on the secret but no amount of Native Oysters would change Henry's opinion of Francis Dernholm.

Henry's duties did not end once he had presented the objects looking their best. After the sale they would then have to be loaded carefully on to trolleys and taken as quickly as possible to the delivery area for impatient purchasers to pay for and take home. Or, in the case of large objects or goods to be sent abroad, the necessary paperwork and transport arrangements all came under Henry's umbrella.

"How goes it, Hen?" Poppy had taken another taxi direct to Millington House, tied a green baize apron over the Balenciaga suit, and with the new apparel her mind had switched from all the day's triumphs and absurdities. She had entered completely into working mode. This big house sale was the only thing in the world that could have taken her out of herself and, for the moment, made her forget completely about Giles.

Somehow the marquees had been delivered with one too few floors. Either the Refreshment tent or Silver (the smallest category to be sold) would have to be pitched directly on to the lawn. The arguments for each side were brought to Poppy: like King Solomon she must sit in judgement.

"Well, it seems perfectly plain to me that neither of you can do without a floor at all," she said. "We can't have silver porters holding precious objects aloft with white-gloved hands and thickly-muddied feet. It wouldn't impress the punters at all." The catering tent started to object but Poppy held up a hand to silence their complaint.

"Equally," she said, "it won't help loosen the pursestrings if the punters are up to their ankles in mud all over their best *Guccis* while eating their lunch. Leave it to me. I'll make sure that by tomorrow you each have a good wooden floor to walk on — and the quicker you let me alone with my telephone, the quicker it arrives. Okay?"

The supplier of marquees had a very feeble excuse indeed. The floor for Trenton's had gone with another order to North Wales where a dance would be given tomorrow night by a surprised hostess with double the floor capacity she expected. Miss Palmer must accept the manager's apologies. There was a new supervisor at the depot who was taking his time getting used to the jobs and one or two little mistakes were inevitable in the circumstances . . . He was sure Miss Palmer would understand.

"Indeed I do," she said, sweetly and firmly. "I understand that you have employed a complete incompetent. Now, I passed a circus packing up its tents on the way here — " this was true but the train of thought it started had only just flashed into her mind. "If you don't ring back in one hour's time and tell me when you are delivering the floor tonight, I shall negotiate for the circus tents and send all of yours back to you without paying a penny of your hire charge."

The marquee man gulped and Poppy put down the phone rather astonished at her own aggression. Normally she would have taken this set-back lying down and muddled along one floor short. Maybe it was the last lash of an angry tail at Mrs Henry Box III; maybe it was just sheer anxiety that this large sale, of which she was in charge, should work perfectly. She knew in her heart that it wouldn't be the end of the world if the silver porters had muddy boots, but an angry impulse had made her determined not to be pushed around.

She was considerably relieved when the telephone rang within twenty minutes reporting the marvellous and coincidental finding of a floor of exactly the right size in the London warehouse. "It must have been overlooked."

Poppy was most grateful to be spared tricky negotiations with a circus master.

Tonight was not destined to be a calm one. She had hoped just to nip in and out, check that all was in place and go home to bed. It was not to be.

Henry came in with a long face which boded ill. It took quite a lot to rattle Henry Ablethwaite.

"Don't worry, Miss," he started, "it's not the Rubens." Something was seriously wrong when Henry called her Miss. It signalled formal business.

Poppy raised her eyebrows in enquiry.

"What is it, Hen? Tell me quickly."

"Two of the lads, Miss, they were getting the big picture down over the stairwell and their ladder slipped."

"Did it . . . ?"

"Yes, I'm afraid so, Miss. There's a shocking great tear in the canvas. It's the Victorian still life."

"Glasses of wine and fruit and such. I remember. Well, Henry, it was in a bugger of a place, I'm surprised they managed to get a ladder up to reach it at all. Are the lads okay?"

He nodded.

"Good. Get on with the patching then. I'll see if I can track down Julian."

Mishaps of this sort were not unknown, although they didn't happen very often, and as long as they didn't happen to anything absolutely priceless it was just one of the incidentals on the debit side that cropped up from time to time: nobody's fault, and get on with the rescue operation was Poppy's policy.

Francis in the same circumstances would have punished the porters by docking some pay. All he achieved by his mean little revenge was their undying resentment and less cooperative service.

Poppy's first thought was to get hold of Julian Barrow. While the telephone rang out she prayed he hadn't gone out to a dinner party or off on a painting jaunt to the High Himalayas. If he were out, there were others who would do, but Julian was top of Trenton's list. An artist in his own right, he had been taught by Annigoni in Florence and as a result had an excellent groundwork in classical techniques. Although his paintings sold well, he was not in such deep funds that he felt insulted by the standard fee of five hundred pounds for a spot of speedy rescue work. Besides, he always rather enjoyed the challenge.

"Hello, Julian, thank God you're in. Can you get up to Middlesex?"

"Tonight?"

"ASAP."

When Poppy had explained, he told her it was all systems go and who was the artist?

"Paoletti."

"That's a bit downmarket for an expensive repair job, isn't it?"

"If it was in London we'd just withdraw the canvas pro tem, but the family will be here; I think it's better to be seen to be trying and lose a bit on your fee. With luck the Rubens will fetch such a good

232

price that nobody's going to worry about a few hundreds here or there on a Paoletti. The family don't like the picture anyway so it's simply a question of getting rid."

"Right, Poppy. I'll bring my lights and my Commercial Italian Artist With Very Little Taste pigments. Expect me soon."

"Julian, you're a wonder."

It was time to do the rounds. Inventory in hand, she checked every place in the house where a lot to be sold had hung. There were brighter squares on the wall where pictures had prevented the paper from fading; there were bare electric wires sticking out of the walls either side of mantlepieces where girandoles had hung. In alcoves there were niches bereft of statues, but none of this made Poppy sad. She had seen the designs the family had commissioned for rocketing the house into the twentieth century, and they were exciting.

Having checked the rooms, she went down to do the grand tour with Henry. Category by category they went through the catalogue together. Each item in its glass-fronted safe cabinet carried a clear label with its lot number and, such was the expertise of the porters' display technique, Henry and Poppy had no difficulty in checking the numbers speedily without even having to open the cabinets, which saved a lot of time.

"You've done brilliantly on this one," Poppy said. Henry grinned.

"Mr Barrow has arrived."

Receiving the message, they went to make sure that he had everything he required. He had wasted no time on arrival and was already in his working smock, with the damaged canvas on a large easel in front of him. Three anglepoise lamps were doing their best to compensate for the lack of natural light; Julian had already started to squeeze the colours from the tubes on to his large wooden palette. Some artists these days used disposable palettes. You could buy a block of kidney-shaped papers, complete with thumbhole, on which you could mix your colours. At the end of the day you did not have to clean off the muddled pigments but simply tore away the top sheet from the paper palette block and the clean one underneath was ready for tomorrow's work.

Poppy was glad that Julian still used the

old-fashioned sort; it seemed much more fitting.

"Got everything you need?" she asked.

He tossed the long brown forelock out of his eyes in a very characteristic gesture. She often wondered if it wouldn't be less bother simply to have it cut.

"Piece of cake," he said. "Hardly a sophisticated technician."

"I'll bring you some coffee later if I can squeeze it out of Catering. Meanwhile I must see if I can organise five hundred slips declaring the damage to the picture. I hope to God I can get hold of my secretary at this time of night; she could organise it in no time on her machine but eight hours would hardly be enough if I had to type them all."

"Mmm." Julian had stopped listening after the offer of coffee. For all it was a doddle, he knew the restoration of the canvas could not be accomplished in a minute.

Poppy knew what she must do next and she very much hoped that Amanda, too, would be at home. It would be the third lucky strike, after the marquee floor and Julian. She checked her watch: ten forty-five. With luck, with luck . . .

"Amanda, who was that?" A man had answered the telephone.

"Never you mind."

"And I thought I might be disturbing your sleep! Listen, my love, I'm really sorry but I'm at the Millington sale and there's been a problem. One of the porters was doing death-defying things on the top of a ladder getting a picture down and you can guess what happened."

"And now you want me to produce six million declaration of damage slips to insert into the catalogues and give out at the door?"

"Amanda, you read my mind."

"And I don't suppose the Millingtons happen to have a secretary and a state-of-the-art photocopier up in that Gothic Mansion of theirs?"

"Well, no, actually."

"You know, Poppy, I'm beginning to wish I'd never answered this telephone call! Marcus is looking extremely sad at the thought of being sent home in a taxi. When do I need to get them to you?"

"Eight o'clock?"

"Only because you're a friend."

"And, Amanda . . ."

"What?"

"If you're going to be up at crack of dawn, do you think you could do something else for me? I didn't have time to go home and it looks as if I'm going to be sleeping the night here on one of those black iron beds they had for the servants. I'm going to look a wreck tomorrow."

"What do you need?"

"My Chanel suit? Suzie's cast-off, the one I gave the press conference in. I feel it's lucky for this sale. And the odd toothbrush, that sort of thing."

"Right, no probs. Now I shall kick Marcus back to his own home and get on with some work. D'you know what, Poppy?"

"What's that?"

"I certainly wouldn't do this for Francis."

10

GOD bless Amanda! First thing the next morning Poppy was in her lucky suit, and all the extra paperwork was not only there, but professionally presented, centred and justified.

The two of them were sharing breakfast: croissants and paper cups of coffee begged from the Catering tent, eaten standing up in front of the latest Barrow masterpiece.

"Julian, you're brilliant!"

He smiled his soft shy smile and tossed back his hair "It won't be dry for a bit."

"Oh, that's okay. The porters always carry them by their frames with the canvas facing outwards; it's the only way they're allowed to, wet paint or dry. That way you can be sure not to put your knee through the canvas if you trip up."

"You know what I'd like?" he said.

"Another croissant?"

"Well, that too. But what I'd *really* like is for one of your chaps to damage a Holbein. He's always struck me as the

238

most difficult painter, with those smooth flat expanses . . . "

"We'll see what we can do."

"You're right about the picture in the dining room, by the way," Julian went on. "There's no mistaking that technique. It's a very good Rubens, too. I should say he did all of it himself; it's not like his later work when he got so successful that the assistants did the paintings and he just filled in the eyes and mouths."

"I'm glad you think so. However much of Joost's archive work we have supporting its history, there's nothing like a painter's opinion on the actual brushstrokes. Particularly confidence-giving when Francis keeps trying to sabotage it all the time."

The crowd was starting to arrive now and the marquee filling. It was extremely exciting; this was the moment when the sale became real and, seeing the crowds, Poppy was suddenly daunted. What if someone stood up to denounce the Rubens at the last moment, as she always half-expected people to do at weddings when the priest told you to 'speak now or forever hold your peace'?

There were a lot of punters from the Low

Countries: Holland and Belgium were both keen to claim Sir Peter-Paul as their very own. You could tell the Dutch; overgrown and with a fondness for Burberry macs worn long and untidy, like their hair. You would not have thought they had a penny to rub between them but you would have been very wrong.

The quality Belgian dealers had come in force, and Poppy's heart lifted high as she recognised one or two important American collectors. She could relax now. With the big boys in place, the big prices would not be far behind.

She saw Francis arrive with Mrs Box on his arm and a pink rose in his buttonhole; he was to do telephone duty again. The Hon Sarah had been taken off telephones after her *bêtise* at the jewellery sale. Her job today was more suited to her capacity: noting down the buyer and price against each lot number as it was sold. She ought to be up to that. Now the staff were in place, all the gilt chairs filled, and the overspill jostling for the best vantage points.

The room had not yet settled, it was busy with movement and chatter, and then Giles made his entrance. An uncanny silence fell.

He took his stand at the tall desk, picked up the ivory gavel and stood motionless, raking them all with his dark eyes. He was taking in every detail of the room, reading it so he could make full use of what he saw. His eyes passed over Poppy and on. She knew he could give her no secret signal but hoped he had seen the message in her eyes.

"Ladies and Gentlemen." Giles began.

The sale was ready to roll.

It was time for Poppy to vanish behind the scenes; her duty today was with the porters, and she looked forward to it.

"Morning, Miss Poppy, the repair's first class," said Henry Ablethwaite, a note of new respect in his voice.

She had never been allowed behind the scenes before: there was no room for idle spectators in narrow spaces with objects being carried to and fro at high speed. Good porterage made a sale run smoothly: bad porterage could ruin it. Giles chose the speed and the porters kept up the impetus. The balance between speed and care was crucial and that was what good portering was all about. Teamwork was absolutely essential, teamwork and a system.

Henry compared his porters to a regiment; Poppy thought they were not unlike a chorus line, though she would never share this sacrilegious thought with him. Like chorus girls they were graded by height: you couldn't have a picture presented lopsided on account of one chap's arms being longer than the other. Then there were the sacred rules of how to handle the breakables. Each category had its own right and wrong. China must always be carried with two hands and on no account must it ever be carried by its handles. Even a jug must be supported underneath in case the handle had been repaired at some time: the auction house could look foolish if the hot lights melted the old glue and left the porter with nothing but a handle in his hand. The 'both hands' rule also applied for single plates, but a set might be carried in stacks of four with one hand underneath, and one at the side to steady them. Chairs must never be carried by the arms or back, they were a weak point and might snap, so a chair was always lifted by its seat. Tables must always be lifted, never dragged; quite apart from the excruciating noise, table legs could be snapped and damaged by dragging.

Thus, in their white gloves, observing all the rules as if by second nature, Henry's team moved between the smaller marquees and the large, with the discipline of a regiment at great speed; such was their expertise that when they appeared under Giles's tall desk, displaying objects high for all the room to see, their gloves were still a perfect white and not one of them showed even a trace of a huff or a puff from his exertions.

Poppy was busy taking down the prices and customers from Sarah. This served two purposes: a double check for safety, and a speedy collection for the customers. Once the objects had been sold they were carefully put on a succession of trolleys by the porters. Poppy filled in a flimsy for each object, stating the floor-price paid, and then she added on the additional percentage of the buyer's premium. Then she noted the paddle number by the side and looked up in her list to find what name corresponded to what paddle number.

Gone were the days when bids were made in guineas and signified by nods and winks. Those were the days when an inadvertent sneeze could cost you a million pounds! That old, charming, amateurish system had been superceded after one or two punters had taken advantage of it to try and wriggle out of bids they regretted. Nowadays anyone intending to buy applied for a paddle at the start of the sale. Each paddle was numbered, and in exchange for it you gave your name and address. If you were unknown to the saleroom and looked not quite the part, you might be asked for further proof of identity. Nothing made sellers more cross than thinking their object was sold for a good price and then finding that the phantom buyer had melted back into the night, having had the kick of pretending to buy. The paddle system was the best devised so far to prevent fraudulent bidding.

Once a trolleyload was finished it was wheeled off to Dispatch, where cheques changed hands and transport arrangements were made. So busy was Poppy with her paperwork that she had no time to watch how the sale was going but the list of good prices passing in front of her gave her the encouraging feeling that there was a lot of money floating about in the room just waiting to be spent. She was completely absorbed in her clerical task. Henry's tap on her shoulder startled her into a jump.

"It's your picture now," he said. "I thought you might like to watch."

"Bless you, Hen." She got up to stand in the doorway. It gave her a sideways view as from the wings of a stage.

Four porters were needed to carry the large landscape, and when they showed it there was a sudden silence. Giles held the silence as long as he saw fit, and once again Poppy was lost in admiration for his skills as an auctioneer. It took courage to milk a silence, as every great actor must know.

Suddenly there came a shrill telephone ring. On his television link, the first foreign bidder had seen the painting carried in and was eager not to miss the bidding. From then on it was fast and furious. Francis was kept busy on his telephone but not so busy he couldn't pout at the press and twinkle at Mrs Box from time to time. His bidder dropped out at 2.5 million. The press had forecast a price of 3.2, a world record. The successful bidder went to 3.2, one of the nondescript Dutchmen in a mac.

At the third and final knock of Giles's gavel, an overexcited Texan in the audience gave a gleeful "Yee-ha!" and punched the air; flamboyant behaviour more usual at the hoedown than the saleroom, but it echoed the feelings of a lot of other people who were too restrained actually to whoop.

Poppy felt nothing but approval for the Texan and could well have imitated him. She looked up at Giles who showed absolutely no emotion. It was vital to the theatre of the occasion that he should give the impression that selling a painting for a world record price was nothing out of the ordinary to him. He was, however, allowing himself the luxury of watching as the porters carried the painting out the way it had come. He knew he could relax thus far; he would get no attention until the painting had left the room. The picture's journey took it past Poppy. Giles's eyes caught hers for a brief moment and he sketched the very smallest suggestion of a wink.

The rest of the sale was unremarkable except for the public's disinclination to leave. Even the millionaires of the art world get excited by successful sales; none of them had wanted to break up the party that had taken place impromptu after the last lot had been sold. They were finally driven away by the simple expedient of the Catering tent's running out of champagne. Now only the Trenton's staff were left congratulating themselves over paper cups of coffee.

"Lovely, dear, well done." Francis complimented Poppy with the right words but a world of sarcasm in his tone, "We'll have to see if we can do even better with the Box bronzes. I believe there's a Rodin in Phyllida's collection that might reach the three."

"I *shall* be busy!"

"Not you dear — me." He put his head to one side and smiled a little purse-mouthed smile. "Phyl wants me to handle it as I'm such an old friend. She's told Giles. It's all fixed. Toodle-oo, Pops dear. I've got a date at the Connaught and I really mustn't be late."

She felt an arm round her waist and looked up into the eyes of Freddy Ilchester.

"Nobody should be frowning after the Ball."

"Freddy! How lovely." She gave him a smacking great kiss on the cheek which he returned with enthusiasm. Looking over his shoulder she saw, as expected, Suzie.

"You didn't tell me you were coming."

"We tried but you haven't been the easiest person to get hold of these last few days. We thought you might feel flat after all this and in need of taking out to dinner."

"What an absolutely splendid idea. May I just check with Giles? Make sure I can be let off the leash?"

Poppy knew perfectly well that her duties were over but she did want to find out if he had any other plans for her this evening. When she eventually caught up with him he was getting into the Bentley Mulsanne Turbo with the Hon Sarah as his passenger. Giles pressed the button that rolled down the window.

"No, of course you've no more work to do. Go to dinner with Freddy, have a good time. And do some work on that ballroom idea; he ought to be keen as mustard to sell through us after today."

"Okay." She suddenly felt very flat.

"Sarah and I have to do some more work

on the Japanese," he said in explanation, and then added, "You know what Henry Ablethwaite said about you today?"

She shook her head.

"'Miss Poppy is one brilliant girl.' It's a sentiment I echo entirely. Will you let me take you out for lunch one day next week to thank you properly? There's a rather special place I know on the river." He winked at her out of the car window and turned his head so that Sarah would not see him blow Poppy a kiss.

"Goodnight, Giles." Poppy was happy again.

She was too tired to spend a long evening with Suzie and Freddy but too touched by their kindness to bow out of it altogether. So she contributed her share to the champagne drunk and the simple fillet steaks eaten, but bowed out when Freddy suggested: "Let's see if there's anyone fun at Annie's. You know, Poppy, it's a whole twenty-four hours since Suzie and I last had a dance."

"Have a good time." She waved them off cheerfully.

"You bet!" Suzie sparkled.

Who'd have believed the change in her

stockbroking friend?

Nick came to pick Poppy up from work the following day.

"Look, no Titian." He held his arms wide to show how innocently empty they were.

She hadn't expected him, and her surprise must have shown on her face.

"I said I'd come, remember? I said I'd have something to show you, and you said not until after the big sale?"

"Of course, Nick, I'm being stupid. I've felt shell-shocked ever since."

"Well," he put his head to one side, his eyes full of laughter, "I suppose we can let a few million turn you into a zombie for a day or two but no longer. It's only money. Come on, we're going to play football."

"Football?" she wailed.

"I'm going to play and you're going to go all goggle-eyed at the sight of my manly knees." He was bundling her into the Golf GTI and waving quite charmingly to a traffic warden who ought to have dieted for speed.

In no time at all he had found a jammed meter in Chelsea Bridge Road and was slinging a canvas sports bag out of the boot. He grabbed her hand to run across the road under the nose of a speeding taxi.

"Are you mad?" she panted.

"Good training." Quickly, he kissed her. "Come on." He vaulted over the railings into Ranelagh Gardens while she sedately walked to the more conventional entrance via the gate.

"We're playing the Green jackets today," he explained, stripping off his workshirt. The glimpse she got of his body looked rather good but it was soon covered by an ancient All Black rugger shirt.

"I don't know much about football but aren't the All Blacks the wrong sport?"

"Well spotted. You sound like an absolute expert on ball-games. The shirt dates from my footloose and fancyfree days in Rotorua but there's no time to tell you about them now." He was pulling a pair of football shorts over some very fancy boxer shorts ornamented with characters from the Flintstones.

"Fred and Wilma!" she recognised with glee.

"And Barney in his brontosaurusmobile

on my left hip. But I'll give you the full tour of my sophisticated underwear after the game, if you'd care to see." And he was off.

Poppy hadn't watched a football match for ages. Sometimes she'd stop and catch a quarter hour or so of the local derby in Winchendon of a Saturday afternoon. She knew the rules roughly but subtleties like the off-side trap passed her by.

She was one of many campfollowers on the sidelines and the camaraderie of the game spilt over to encompass the spectators. A tall blonde with bubble curls turned out to be The Agency cook. She took it upon herself to explain to Poppy.

"Our team doesn't take itself seriously but it's actually quite good. Nick plays midfield so you won't necessarily see him do anything spectacular unless a piece of luck comes his way. We're playing the very, very worst team of the TA. The Duke of Yorks Barracks — " she indicated a vast stone building modelled roughly on the lines of a Greek temple — "is their HQ. They're all so fit that they really only do this for a laugh, but they're a good lot. Somehow it's become an annual event.

Come on the Agents," she ended in an encouraging roar.

Poppy volunteered to be waitress at half time. Her new friend the cook took care of the home team and Poppy was sent to refresh the soldiers with her two plates. She was amused to see that while one plate contained the traditional half-time oranges, the other was crammed with beautifully arranged smoked salmon pinwheels. It was never like that at school.

Welcoming and suggestive remarks greeted both Poppy and her edibles but once she'd handed over the plates she was chased away with brisk efficiency lest she overhear any half-time demon tactics.

She lost all her reserve during the second half, cheering her team as though her life depended on it, and when the Agents actually managed to get a goal she found herself hugging the complete stranger next to her and jumping up and down with excitement.

The final score was 3–1. The Agents, as Nick told her, had managed a lot better this time than on many occasions. Last year the army had wiped the floor with them.

He didn't bother to get out of his football gear.

"I'll shower and change at home."

Two minutes along the Embankment and they turned up into Tite Street whose high narrow Victorian houses had originally been built for artists like Whistler and Walter Crane. Most of the buildings still had studios with large North-facing windows for a constant light.

"I don't suppose artists need lifts." Poppy was panting.

"Can't make the garret too comfortable. Only three more flights."

"Three!"

"You'll have to take up football, get your lungs working." He fell in behind so he could shove her up with a hand in the small of her back. Poppy realised that Nick was not only very fit, he was strong as well.

"You must jog and things to be such a superman."

"No. But I never walk if I can run. Here we are."

He opened a small door off the narrow dark communal stairwell and let Poppy into a room which gave an overwhelming impression of spaciousness. She supposed it was because the ceiling was quite ridiculously high, it must have been twenty foot, and the North wall was simply a huge expanse of Victorian paned window. There must have been thousands and thousands of little panes in between the stone glazing bars. It gave a unique effect, rather like an absolutely enormous spider's web. The furnishings of the room were not ordinary either. There was an ancient mahogany grand piano draped with an equally ancient tigerskin, head stuffed and glassy-eyed; the teeth looked vicious.

"Would you like to sin with Eleanor Glynn on a Tiger skin?" she asked.

"Or would you prefer
to err with her
on some other fur?" he answered correctly.

"Do you play?" She indicated the baby grand.

"A little."

In a corner stood a large palm tree in a Benares brass pot. It might have strayed out of any painting by Lord Leighton. "I like to think it pleases the ghosts of the Victorian painters, they were all dotty about the East."

The juxtaposition of large disparate objects in this striking room was arresting, amusing and completely individual but above all there were huge canvases everywhere: on walls, on easels, propped up against bits of furniture and even lying on the floor.

"You told me you painted a little."

He grinned.

"I'm going to have a shower, Poppy. Can you keep yourself amused for five minutes without dying of boredom?"

"Where?"

"Ah, yes! There are two little cubby holes off the studio, you see. This one leads to bath and bed, and this to the kitchen. You could try the kitchen if you're ravenous; there are salad things in the fridge or, if you can contain yourself, we'll do that together later."

"Later. I'm lousy in other people's kitchens."

Nick disappeared into the other cubbyhole and Poppy was left with time to look round the studio. She examined each picture slowly and was surprised to find that in fact she liked them very much. Contemporary painting was not one of her great loves: much of it she found difficult and inaccessible, some of it she found crude and too obviously political. Nick's paintings came into neither category. Some were figurative and some were abstract but she could relate to all of them. Even if there was nothing recognisable in a canvas, Nick made the colours and the shapes evoke thoughts and emotions.

So absorbed was she in her tour of inspection that she only realised that Nick had come back into the room when she heard the piano behind her.

"I'm stepping out my dear
To breathe an atmosphere that simply reeks with class.
So I trust that you'll excuse my dust when I step on the gas . . . " he sang.

She joined him for a wow finish.
"You do it well," she said.
"Aw, shucks!"
He'd changed into baggy cords now. They were faded brown and looked like old friends. He hadn't bothered to do up too many buttons on his cream Oxford cotton shirt; Poppy could see that the even tan

on his face didn't stop in some dire white tidemark at collar level. This new glimpse confirmed what she had suspected on the football field: his neck and chest were a satiny gold, his skin so fine and smooth it was hard not to reach out to see if it felt as good as it looked.

She was pleased to see that the relaxed outfit didn't end in trainers. The feet on the piano pedals wore well broken-in conker brown penny loafers that he could only have bought in America.

"Well?" He swivelled round on the piano stool to look at her.

"Well?" She looked back at him unswervingly and knew that if she didn't look away he would take her in his arms.

She put temptation firmly behind her and turned back to the paintings.

"I didn't realise your work was like this."

"Meaning?"

"Meaning that you're serious about it. I thought maybe it was just a little hobby. The odd daub when there was nothing worth watching on TV — that sort of thing."

They both laughed.

"It's a bit more than that. Do you want to talk about the paintings or about my brilliant idea to put your nose ahead in the race for Trenton's?"

"The paintings," she said unhesitatingly, and to her eternal credit.

They shared the beginnings of a bottle of wine while Nick told her about art college and about the dilemma in his life ever since: it came down to balancing money against dreams, responsibility against ideals.

He'd always known that an art director's job was the logical one. What else paid a good artist good money? The trouble was that the more comfortable his life became, and the greater his success, the stronger the feeling grew that he wanted to give it all up to paint.

"And I'm really not a self-destructive person at all. Quite the opposite. I know I'd be mad to do it."

"Do you have to be so black and white about it? Can't you just sell some of these paintings as you go along, see what happens?"

"There speaks the voice of moderation! And you're absolutely right, it's exactly the course any sensible man would take, but I'm being put on the spot by a gallery owner. He's not an old mate or anything like that so he's not just being nice to me. It's Leonid. Do you know him?"

Of course Poppy knew him, or at least his face and his reputation.

An extremely successful gallery in Cork Street displayed his name over the door and he controlled a stable of controversial artists whose pictures all sold for big numbers. The general opinion was that although Leonid generally had a good eye for talent-spotting, he sometimes backed a dud, in which case he was not content to let the no-hoper quietly fade away but would, tenacious to the last, mercilessly hype that artist's work. Such was the uncertainty of modern art collectors that many were fooled by the hype. In this way Leonid made sure that he never lost out financially but over the years had acquired certain indelible stains on his reputation.

"They say there's no-one tougher with contracts when it comes to tying up his artists. I gather he makes Sam Goldwyn look like a babe in arms."

"I'd heard that too. And a lot of other

things besides. The point is that if Leonid believes in you, it means that you probably can make it. Now he won't take me on unless I guarantee him thirty finished canvases a year. I know it doesn't sound much but, believe me, it's more than I can squeeze into my spare time. For that he offers a minimum income for three years with a rising percentage as the sale prices go up. It's laughable compared to my salary at The Agency but you can see why I'm tempted."

They were standing side by side at the big window, watching the sun's reddening rays illuminating Wren's great dome over the Royal Hospital, gilding the old copper to some approximation of how it must have looked when it was first erected.

"What are you thinking?" he asked.

"Two bits of my mind were thinking two different things," she said truthfully. "I was looking at all this, and understanding the pressures you've put on yourself by following so exactly in the physical footsteps of those Victorian painters. Even to the tiger skin."

"Ouch! I didn't bargain for quite such a perceptive answer. What was the other bit thinking?"

"Simply that there must be a way of getting to paint without selling your soul to Leonid."

Nick sighed and changed the subject. "Let's get some food organised, shall we?"

In the larder she was surprised to find proper lettuces with real mud on them.

"Where do you get these?" she asked. Even Nick couldn't garden five floors up.

"A sculptor two floors down has a country cottage. He brings them up after the weekend, usually enough to last all week."

"How I hate shop carrots." Poppy had found one no thicker than a pencil and was devouring it with great pleasure.

Nick unfolded his plan for Trenton's over supper.

"Let's run this one up the flagpole." He was suddenly West Coast Advertising Man. "Trenton's wants business, right? So how does Trenton's get business? It advertises. Follow me so far?"

She nodded.

"You're a bright gal, sweetheart, go to the top of the class. Now we don't want the business to go to just any old body at the company. Right? Particularly we don't want the business to go the way of the guy with the well-manicured fists and the Pleasing Personality. Am I right or am I right? Uh huh. Well, in this corporate situation there is one very easy answer indeed. We make *you* the Trenton's girl, honey. How d'ya feel 'bout that?"

She raised her eyebrows incredulously.

"Sweetheart it's not difficult. Look."

Like a magician he produced a stack of storyboards on which he'd roughed out his ideas for an advertising campaign for Trenton's.

"I've taken very well-known images which we recreate in photographs. Look at this one: Madame Récamier reclining on her sofa. Right? Only *you* are Madame Récamier. Top of the page: pic of Madame doing her reclining bit. Caption: 'We won't guarantee you'll find this in the attic . . . ' Bottom picture: only the sofa this time, Madame's got up and only the sofa's left. Caption: 'But you might find this. Trenton's sold the sofa for £20,000.'"

Poppy whistled. "I begin to see."

"I thought you might."

"A whole campaign on those lines?" Her mind was moving fast. "A new object each month, say; encourage them to hunt for treasure high and low. What sort of figures are we talking about, Nick?" Her brow clouded and not only with the thought of the notoriously high scale of fees charged by The Agency. Had Nick gone to all this elaborate rigmarole just to get some business out of her?

"Trenton's has no advertising budget at present," she went on, "it's all business by word of mouth. I'd have to put up a good case for Giles to authorise vast sums."

"No vast sums, sweetheart. This isn't The Agency, this is me moonlighting because I want to help you. I come for free. I'm not bad at artwork, and if you okay it I've got a photograper who owes me and then some: I've managed to put a lot of business his way. That's two of the principal costs knocked out. Trenton's would have to pay the going rate for space, that's all."

Nick's generosity robbed Poppy of words; she was utterly astonished.

"You thought all this up to help me?"

"Call it a creative challenge."

"What have I done to deserve you?" She put her arms around him and embraced him with abundant gratitude, standing on tiptoes and covering his face and throat with kisses, The golden skin was just as smooth and delicious as she'd imagined, but she mustn't linger over it.

"Oh, must you stop? I thought we were just getting to the enjoyable bit."

He looked down at her teasingly but then his expression changed; he saw the shadow of Giles in her eyes.

"You're not going to show your gratitude by spending the night with me?"

"No."

"Let me know if things change, will you?"

She nodded solemnly.

"And now, like the perfect gentleman I am, I suppose I'd better drive you home. I hope that guy realises how lucky he is."

11

A CALL from Maurice reminded Poppy that she owed him an update on gossip.

"Are you still at that terrifying hospital?" she asked him.

"I'm back and pining for my *cymbidiums*. Empty *cachepots* all over the place."

"They're still alive." She looked doubtfully across at the browning leaves on her kitchen windowsill. "Truth to tell, they've not been absolutely my first concern lately."

"Small matter of selling a Rubens?"

"Exactly."

"They're very accommodating plants. Nothing they like better than a little judicious neglect. Now when are you going to bring them over, and what's the next stage in the campaign to outwit Francis? I need to know, darling. I've just reached that convalescent stage where I haven't the energy to get on with my own life so I really need to organise somebody else's."

"After work tonight? I've really missed you, Maurice. There's so much to tell."

She struggled through the day with five terracotta pots as her personal ball and chain. As she carried them up the stairs to his flat in Ennismore Gardens she vowed that in future she would choose her friends by their flats. From now on only ground storey and basement tenants need apply.

"Maurice darling, you look wonderful!" It was nearly true.

"I spent all afternoon resting with slices of cucumber on my eyes. *Vogue* told me to. Darling Dust got quite a fright when she came in, I think she imagined I'd been laid out, you know how they used to put pennies on the eyes? Well, she screeched, which made me jump, which made the cucumbers leap off. They'd probably been on long enough anyway, and I was bored of them by then." He picked up a handmirror to scrutinise his eyelids. "I think they've worked rather well."

"I'm jolly glad you're up. Visiting bed-patients inhibits me; this way I can simply imagine you're Noel Coward and it's business as usual. Your dressing gown is much more cocktails-for-two than medicine-for-one."

"Sulka always have known how to cut a *robe de lounge lizard*."

Maurice poured tea from a very pretty Queen Anne silver teapot into perfect paper-thin Spode cups. Apart from looking a little faded, he seemed quite back to normal and it made Poppy glad to see him again in place among his exquisite little collection of French furniture and rococo *objets de vertu*.

Coming to Maurice's flat always made her feel she was entering a dolls' house world. Here every single thing was, in its own way, absolutely perfect. The tasselled and fringed curtains were of the best silk brocade; the carpet a lovely faded Aubusson that must have started life in a very grand château somewhere in France. Every surface was rich with 'my little bibelots'. Wherever you looked there was another pretty object in silver, porcelain, jade or semi-precious stones.

Poppy picked up a small neophryte carving by Fabergé; it had always been one of her favourites because she loved the smooth feel of the stone in her hand. Unconsciously she kept it in her hand, rubbing it as they spoke.

"So what is Francis's answer to Millington?" Maurice wanted to know.

She told him about Deaths and Mrs Box, the Social Calendar sales and the endless stream of men with carefully preserved figures and faces who poured through Trenton's, all seeking Francis to sell their precious things.

"He's very well connected in the gay mafia, darling. The nouveau end of it, I mean. How very irritating I hadn't thought of that — you could have quite a tough one on your hands there."

He tented his fingers and thought for a moment. "The *on dit* has it that Ceddo is going to sell his Art Deco; it would go through Francis, I'm quite sure. We'll need a telephone numbers answer to that."

Poppy mentioned the Ballynally Ballroom then surprised herself by telling Maurice about Nick's campaign idea. She was still turning it over in her mind, and had almost decided against.

Much to her surprise, Maurice was extremely enthused by the idea.

"He's obviously not stupid, your young man."

"Not *my* young man."

He gave her a quizzical look.

"You know, you and Francis can go on battling for trade as long as there are collectors in the world and enough sale days to fit them in. Giles has created the most perfect setup: he just sits back and watches the turnover soar. A month ago, the clever money should have gone on Francis's winning the race. Frankly, when I gambled on you I had my doubts as to whether you had the killer instinct. Now I have no reservations at all on that score."

"I seem to have developed it rather strongly where Francis is concerned."

"That's enough," he said contentedly. "Now you must present your advertising idea to Giles as soon as you possibly can, and you must do it direct: not through Sarah Cavendish."

"Why not through Sarah? Is she rooting for Francis?"

"Let us just say that she is not waving placards saying 'Poppaea for Pope'. She has considerable influence with Giles, you know."

"But she's such a ninny."

"Ninny or not, she's rich and she's well-connected. In the larger game that Giles is playing, she has an important part."

Though inclined to take Maurice's advice in everything else, Poppy was not going to pay any attention to this. Maurice had misjudged; it was simply not possible that a nonentity like the Hon Sarah could influence Giles's judgement.

After an affectionate goodbye to Maurice, she retreated to the privacy of Redcliffe Gardens to crunch some numbers. There was all the difference in the world between presenting an idea to Giles and presenting a credible advertising campaign with production costs, print, and distribution figures at her fingertips. It looked good. The further she went into the details, the more viable it looked.

"Where are you going to get the Object of the Month?" Suzie was looking over her shoulder.

"Hey! Don't spill coffee on my beautiful balance sheet. Trentons's stock, of course, there's no shortage."

"Additional insurance?"

"Covered." Poppy waved another sheet at Suzie.

"Can't catch you out however hard I try. Okay, you'll do."

Suzie drifted off, leaving Poppy to rehearse the scene in the Chairman's office tomorrow morning. Giles behind his desk was just telling her how absolutely brilliant she was and how there was really no need to wait until the New Year to make the judgement between herself and Francis, when the telephone went and the very real Chairman himself was on the other end.

"Poppy? Is that you?"

"Mmm."

"Listen, I'm on my way to the airport."

That would account for the sound of background mechanical sighing.

"Darling, I'm ringing to tell you that I can't take you out to lunch for a few days. I'm on my way to California."

"Will you be there for long?"

"I don't know, sweetheart."

"I've rather a lot of things to talk to you about."

"Me too. But I'll spare my driver's blushes."

"It was work I wanted to talk about."

272

"Important?"

She could hear the immediate change in his voice and told him then, as clearly and concisely as she could, glancing down now and then at her papers. Giles's enthusiasm matched her own.

"Brilliant idea, Poppy. Put the details on hold; save the figures for now and give them to Sarah first thing. She can bring them when she joins me tomorrow. Oh, and of course I have to warn you formally that the costs will go on the debit side of your equation, though you hardly need bother about that. They should pretty quickly be wiped out by the additional business generated." He paused.

"How did you keep the costs so low, by the way?" Giles was never a fool with a balance sheet.

"I've an art director friend at The Agency. He'll moonlight for us, but we must keep it a secret. He'll lose his job if he's found out."

"Good girl." Giles chuckled. "Useful friends are worth their weight."

"There was something else too," she continued. "Sorry to bother you like this but I need your decision on the Ballynally

Ballroom. The sale video should be out and about as quickly as possible. We'll have to pay proper agency rates for that, but I thought we might use the same team who are freelancing on the ad campaign. Freddy is suggesting we fly over next weekend."

"That sounds a wonderful excuse to leave California. I can't promise anything, my love, but look for me in one of those castle bedrooms. I just might be there."

She laughed.

"We're going into that long and Freudian tunnel in a minute. I'll have to say goodbye. 'til Ireland."

"''til Ireland," she echoed but his voice had already faded and all she could hear was the swish of static that sounded like the sea.

Poppy sat for full ten minutes cradling the phone and feeding on his last remark. It seemed sacrilegious to use the same instrument to make a call to Sarah, but boss's orders were boss's orders. Nothing made Giles crosser than delays.

"Yes, I'm leaving tomorrow morning to join him in California. I don't think he likes the American agency girls they provide in the hotels. He says they can't

274

spell in proper English!" Sarah tittered.

As long as she was only going for her spelling.

The Irish trip gathered impetus over the week. Freddy was fired with enthusiasm and, never one to do things by half measures, had decided to charter a plane to take them over.

"We'll fill it up with a few friends, have a jolly. Maybe a little party when we get there."

Suzie was already organising her wardrobe.

The small plane proved to be a Boeing 737 which Freddy, a man with no shortage of friends, had managed to fill up quite nicely. The bar ran out of booze way before they were halfway to Dublin, and Freddy's guests spilled on to the tarmac in fine form.

The Earl had hired a charabanc, which weaved off into the wide blue yonder, trailing rousing choruses behind it like festive ribbons in the air. Freddy himself, Sarah, Poppy and Nick went in great state in the family limo: a fifties Daimler, the sort used for funeral processions and unsmart diplomats. This would be the family car until it dropped into a thousand fragments, Freddy explained solemnly; O'Rourke, the driver, had learned to drive on it way back in the mists of time and he was now far too old to learn the ways of any other.

They were heading South-west out of Dublin. Poppy had never been to Ireland before and was intrigued by how foreign it was and yet how familiar. Soon they had left all villages behind and a soft green countryside unfolded under a romantic hill mist.

"This is the home valley," Freddy said.

They were driving through a narrow defile, the first natural defence of the ancient castle; their eyes were irresistibly drawn up the valley ahead. Ballynally Castle was everything a castle ought to be. The valley was so long that at first the great stony walls might be mistaken for a great craggy outcrop among the drizzle-green hills and woods. As they drove closer towards the great grey mass, its towers and ramparts clarified. Every wind of the drive brought new detail into sharper focus as the approach followed the river with its winds and curves, through little copses and boscages.

"I say, that looked like rather a good rise." Freddy was instructing O'Rourke to stop the car.

"Freddy darling, you're not thinking of going fishing?"

"The rod's in the boot," he said eagerly.

"You really can't stop off now even if it is the largest salmon you've ever seen in Solomon's pool." Suzie was firm. "We've got eighty or so guests to dispose of once that coach gets here."

"Do you know, Poppy," Freddy's voice held only contentment, "I've never had a bossy wife. They've always been so eager to become my Countess that they'd say yes to pickled pig's trotters for breakfast. I think I shall enjoy being married to one."

"Oh, by the way." He was addressing Suzie exclusively. He fished into a deep pocket of his tweed jacket and, after some fumbling, his hand came out holding a small red Morocco leather box; it was about the size of a matchbox but rather grander. You could hardly believe so much gold tooling could be fitted on such a small area.

"I promised myself I would wait until I had you on Ilchester land before I formally proposed. We're here now, so will you make an honest man of me? I shall blaze in hell for Lust if you won't."

Suzie looked at him for a long moment. Freddy steadily returned her look, and for once his face was quite serious. Then she opened the hinged lid and looked down on a very large diamond indeed, sitting neatly on its white velvet bed. Silent, she held the open box, her eyes returned to Freddy.

"I'll not drink Guinness," she said at last, "or your filthy Irish whisky." He nodded. "And you know I'm going to organise you into a proper job?"

"I've lived off the fat of the land for far too long, my love. Now, will you put the damn thing on?"

"No. You will." And she held up her hand and smiled at him.

As O'Rourke jerked and shuddered the car to a standstill outside the castle door, the huge ring was glittering on her engagement finger.

The public proposal was the beginning of a weekend which became more unreal as it went on. The charabanc of roisterers eventually arrived, having taken a picnic on the Devilsbit Mountain by mistake, or was it Keeper Hill? Not even the coach driver knew, and it really didn't seem to matter much.

As word spread amongst his neighbours that good old Freddy was over, they turned up in entire families expecting a party. The Ilchester household was evidently used to running along these lines and a long Saturday croquet party developed, with the moat as the worst local hazard and treacherous kicks aimed at winning balls when people thought no one was looking.

Suzie was thoroughly enjoying herself. She had slid into her place at Freddy's side as if it were what nature had made her for. She wore her new rôle as naturally as she wore her new diamond, and with as little fuss; she simply wanted to meet all his friends and get to know his life as quickly as she possibly could.

Poppy, Nick and the two Agency photographers were meanwhile trying to stave off the increasing feeling of carnival and concentrate on the job of making the video that would sell the Ballynally

Ballroom as the most desirable useless object in the world.

Poppy felt rather redundant with Nick and his team hard at their jobs. She really didn't know what she could contribute but felt it would be a dereliction of duty to be leading the life of Reilly among the croquet hoops and champagne bottles when this was, after all, meant to be a working trip. So she watched as Nick suggested angles and approaches that might lift the video out of a mere pictorial record of the ballroom and into a shape that would catch the eye and imagination. David was taking the stills for the brochure, while Josh made the video. Busily they bounced lights off umbrellas, caught worlds of architectural detail reflected in the single teardrop crystal of a chandelier, and generally out-arted art.

"Well, I've photographed every acanthus leaf and swag, every inch of cherrywood veneer and dancing nymph. The pix are pretty, the lighting's beautiful. It's fine," Josh said, but his tone said quite otherwise.

"What's bugging you?" Nick was pouring the champagne which Freddy had thoughtfully sent down Murder Alley at four o'clock in the careful hands of Crust, the butler.

"The trouble is," said Josh, "it's dead."

He drank a little more champagne, looked a little glummer and thought some more.

"If we were trying to sell a museum, the film'd be up for an Oscar. But we're not."

"I think I have a glimmer." Nick held out his glass to Poppy. "The little grey cells just need some more bubbles to take them over the brink . . . I've got it!" He was suddenly excited.

The same champagne bubble had obviously burst simultaneously in Josh's brain. Like people long accustomed to working together they chorused: "You can't sell an empty ballroom!"

Poppy felt a bit left out. Nick turned to explain to her.

"It's an ancient sales concept, sweetheart, the same logic that gave birth to the fashion show: put a dress on a hanger and you're lucky if it walks out of the shop. Put it on a catwalk, you'll be fighting off the customers. You know what this means, don't you?"

"I think I'm beginning to."

"We've got to go persuade Freddy into a party! Shall I, or will you?"

"Together?"

They found Freddy and Suzie on the ramparts, fully occupied in dropping the crusts from their teatime cucumber sandwiches into the moat. The carp thought Christmas had come.

"Shall we leave it till later?" Nick suggested to Poppy. "They've hardly had a minute to themselves."

But Freddy had seen them and was already smiling and waving. Suzie came forward to Poppy.

"I'm so excited," she said, "there's just so much to talk about." She put her arm round Poppy's waist and bore her off round the ramparts to talk wedding plans.

"Of course, it's everything I've always wanted," Suzie said reflectively. "I dreamed of all these things but I could never see the face; where Prince Charming was meant to be there was always a socking great empty space. Now it's come true back-to-front! I adored Freddy from the very first moment I set eyes on him. He was Prince Charming even if nothing came with him at all. You know he gave me the impression that this — " she waved her hand " — was a ruin and all the money had gone. I didn't care, it was him I wanted. The joke of it is he was exaggerating as usual. Freddy's still a very rich man."

"So what will you do?"

"Work pretty hard, strange as it sounds. Oh, not my old job. I also think it's absolutely vital for *him* to have a proper job; he really hates having nothing to do and I'm quite sure that boredom must have been at the root of all his philandering. I'm working on the germ of an idea for the two of us to try together. I'll tell you about it when it's gelled."

"Situation under complete control?"

"I think so." Suzie allowed a squeak of excitement into her voice. "And, wow, will we ever have a wedding party!"

"A party," Freddy was saying to Nick, a hundred yards further down the ramparts. "Two minds with but a single thought. Now, you must swear not to tell the girls, but in fact the Ballynally Ballroom is being given a last run out tonight. Can't get rid of a ballroom without giving a party to mark the occasion. It will also be our engagement party; I planned it as soon as I dreamt up this weekend."

"And what if Suzie had said no?"

"I'd have needed a party to console me!"

"Freddy, you're incorrigible!"

"Let's go and break the news to the girls." The girls saw them coming and came to meet them.

"We've got a problem," he said, with a worried frown for Suzie's benefit. "Nick and the video photographer say we need to animate the ballroom, my darling. Waltzing couples, a little music, that sort of thing. Make it seem as if we're having a party."

"Well, we can organise a party in a week or two, can't we?"

"I was really thinking of something tonight," Nick said earnestly. "We need to finish the video as soon as possible. I'm really not sure we can build another week into the schedule."

"I know!" Suzie was in her element, she liked nothing better than solving a good problem. "Why don't we give our dinner party tonight in the ballroom?"

"The tables are all organised in the Great Hall," said Freddy.

"Don't worry, darling, I'll sweet talk the kitchen."

"We'll freeze to death," he said lugubriously.

"Fires." Suzie had the bit between her teeth, it would take nothing short of an Act of God to stop her now. "We were going to be sitting down eighty to dinner anyway," she said to Nick. "I know that eighty people won't absolutely fill the space but might they give you enough atmosphere for your video?"

He looked doubtfully at Freddy who seemed lost in thought.

"Would a nude party sell the ballroom better?" he asked interestedly.

Nick shook his head solemnly. "We could have a problem getting the video through Customs."

"Bang goes a good idea." Freddy was still solemn as a vicar. "But you follow my line of reasoning, light of my life?"

She followed. Her brow was clouded. For the first time she had hit a real stumbling block. "Of course," she said in dismay, "we've got nothing to wear."

"Oh dear!" Freddy heaved a deep sigh. "I think we'd better abandon the idea then."

He paused. "Though, of course, we could always have a look in the dressing up box . . . "

"Freddy, you're absolutely wonderful." Suzie's arms were round her fiancé and he was being liberally kissed.

Over the top of her gold-streaked head, Freddy winked at Nick.

The dressing up box turned out to be located in an easterly turret and resembled nothing so much as the luggage room of a large liner in the twenties.

There were dress boxes and linen presses; shoe boxes neatly stacked, rack upon rack; there were parasols and umbrellas with turned handles in exotic woods and semi-precious stones, wrought in the shape of fantastic animals' heads set with twinkling jet eyes and real little foxy teeth. There was lace in cascades: waterfalls of petticoats carelessly stacked together; swirls and eddies of little collars and fichus; tiny dresses for tiny babies now long grown-up and dead. There were gloves softer than a kitten's paw with little pearls the size of flower seeds to fasten them.

As well as the clothes there were the later additions to the Ilchester cast-offs.

The twenties and thirties must have seen the family crossing the Atlantic as a full-time occupation; only the coming of war must have signalled the abandoning of this mountain of cruise luggage. There were early Louis Vuitton trunks with their distinctive monogram, unchanged to this day. There were also numbers of less grand corded cabin trunks of wood and canvas and leather, in browns and greens, decorated with the family crest and pasted over many times with romantic little labels from long-defunct legends: the old Cunarders, *Mauretania* and *Berengeria*. The only Liner missing was the *Titanic*.

There was also a family of very sophisticated hatboxes. There was one in aubergine crocodileskin, richly crested, that Poppy could not resist. She looked inside it to find the most comprehensive collection of hatpins she had ever seen; they ranged from everyday plain, to huge ornamental bodkins suitable for stabbing an over-amorous Maharajah if you had no other means to hand.

"What about this?" Suzie had not been lingering over Poppy's sentimental time-wasters but had gone straight through the dresses with her customary efficiency. She was holding up a dress of plunging black taffeta sewn with diamonds and black pearls. "I don't want to look too bridal."

"I've just seen exactly what you need to wear with it." Poppy was already heading for the right hatbox. She held aloft a thin diamond circlet with a black egret's plume. "You'll look like that portrait in the Long Gallery. Come here." In her excitement she pulled Suzie in front of the mirror, swept up her hair and crowned her.

"That'll do." The satisfied gleam in Suzie's eyes belied the understatement of her words. "Now don't dawdle here, Poppy, will you? Remember we've got to be ready by eight-thirty, okay?" And she whisked off with a cloud of rustling black taffeta over her arm.

Poppy could have spent a week in the room, and made a mental note to sneak back in here just as soon as she had a free minute. Meanwhile she knew she was cutting things fine but there was just one more box she was going to permit herself to look into. It was plain and white and in very small black letters someone had written 'Celine's Coming Out. 1934. A happy evening.' The simplicity of the message attracted Poppy and, like Pandora, she had to see inside.

It didn't look much but when she lifted out the slither of thirties bias-cut satin, she just knew that this was her dress for the evening. It felt like a familiar friend and she hardly needed to hold it up against herself to know that it would fit.

"Thank you, Celine," she murmured and, mindful of punctuality, left the treasure trove to go and change.

Poppy knew that her own appearance was not of paramount importance tonight; it was Suzie's evening and a good friend would be a spectator, not a star. Celine's dress was lovely but not in the way that diamonds, sequins and spangles are lovely. It was lovely in its simplicity, the plain line of satin sweeping from shoulder to floor following Poppy's body quite naturally. She gathered her hair up and fastened it with a diamanté star.

Maybe it was the kind reflection from the age-spotted silvered mirror, maybe it was actually how she looked, but her face tonight looked softer, her skin glowing ivory white. Along with the dress, Celine had lent her the vulnerability of a young girl allowed a first party in her Coming Out dress. These last few weeks of strain and anxiety at Trenton's had lately lent bruised shadows under Poppy's eyes, her cheeks had grown thinner and the set of her mouth had adopted a firmness that went with executive stress. This evening she had lost all that, and she was glad.

Would Giles come tonight? He'd told her to look for him. She lost all sense of time and simply remained sitting on the tapestry stool in front of the old moon-soft mirror, willing him to appear in reflection behind her shoulder.

Suzie's knock disturbed her reverie.

"My God," Poppy said admiringly, "Freddy's not going to change his mind tonight!"

"Good." Suzie gave her a mannequin's twirl.

If Poppy looked the soul of youth and simplicity, her friend was every inch a *femme fatale*. The black taffeta skirt billowed and rustled, the fullness emphasising the slim waist and moulded bodice which glittered under their encrustation of pearls and brilliants. Suzie's blonde hair tumbled about her shoulders and the little nodding plume echoed her bubbling high spirits. Poppy thought she had never seen anyone look so completely the picture of happiness.

"Oh, do come on," Suzie begged. "If I don't get down to Freddy and the party, I shall die."

She pulled Poppy up from the stool and, arm in arm, they navigated the complicated order of passages that would bring them down to the Great Hall.

Freddy was waiting for them there, looking extremely handsome in his white tie and tails.

"Darling!" Suzie exclaimed. "You've even brushed your hair." In truth it was the first time that Poppy had ever seen him without an errant wisp taking its own eccentric direction against its companions.

"And you, my love, look wonderful. Just like Aunt Elizabeth in the Whistler picture on the stairs. Poppy, my dear." Freddy was never too absorbed to forget his manners, "you look perfectly charming, as always. Nick, come on," he said, and led the way with Suzie on his arm.

Nick, who had just come in, caught

sight of Poppy and stood quite still, looking at her.

The Earl and his Countess-elect stepped out of the castle, followed by Poppy and Nick. The sight that met their eyes stopped them in astonishment. The late evening sky was streaked and dabbed with the salmons of sunset, and under the pink sky Murder Alley had never looked less murderous. Its crumbling stone columns were festooned with drapes and swags of fresh white flowers caught up and secured with green ribbons, feathers, and great cornucopias of grapes. Scarlet-liveried footmen were placed at intervals, holding candelabra to light the guests on their way. The soft light of the candles illumined the milky mist rising off the moated river. The pretty little octagonal ballroom appeared to be floating in the air.

The colonnade seemed endless as they walked though the heavy perfumes of the jasmine and gardenia, tuberose and freesia, entwined and garlanded about the pillars.

"Look, Nick," said Poppy.

And he looked upwards as did she. Above them grapes hung down like fantastical fruit off a stone tree, and they glimpsed the sky, darkening now from pinks through that rare green moment before the night falls utterly. In it the tiny stars were set, faint as yet but present. They stood still for a long moment, looking up, and then Nick turned to her and was just starting to say something when Suzie called, "Come on, you two, we're waiting."

He shrugged, reoffered his arm and they caught up the others just as the ballroom doors were opened, and Freddy swept his Countess-to-be into the opening dance.

"Can you see the photographers about anywhere?" Nick asked.

Poppy was glad of the excuse to look about her, she could search for Giles. The crowd was surprising and fantastical. Never had she seen guests so dressed for a party. Some were in evening dress, the men in white tie. Others had let their imaginations rip. There were Maharajas with cork-blackened faces, Regency beaux, powdered and perruque'd, Venetian gondoliers, spacemen and Tarzans. Some wore masks and some wore glitter, atrocious wigs and false moustaches, pomaded kisscurls and sprayheld Mohicans.

The women, too, were living out their dreams: Gainsborough ladies rubbed shoulders with cancan dancers, Egyptian *houris* jostled fragile ballerinas or rubber and latex sex icons. Sausage curls and blue satin pompoms held animated conversations with mermaids under seaweed-draped hair. There were diamonds — tiaras, necklaces, earrings — in all the conventional places, but somehow they had managed to seep into the most unexpected locations as well. One Nubian slave sparkled from her belly button; a languid *demi-mondaine* twirled her long cigarette holder between fingernails studded with the precious stones; a sloe-eyed odalisque gave off prisms of light from her eyelids. Poppy could only stand and stare.

"It's not quite the impromptu party that Freddy would have you believe," said Nick. "He planned it weeks ago, but he wanted it to be a surprise."

"He was so sure of Suzie?"

Nick laughed. "It was going to be his consolation if she turned him down."

Poppy laughed too and then gasped as she caught sight of Josh. He had climbed a pilaster and somehow managed to dispose himself, his heavy camera and endless pieces of equipment on a narrow cornice above a window. As a balancing trick it would have gone down well at a Circus; she could only think of the dire consequences should a drum vibrate too furiously and disturb the photographer's perilous equilibrium.

"I don't think we'll risk talking to him," said Nick. "I'd hate him to ask me to come up and check an angle. Just for once his art can go undirected. Shall we dance instead?"

The long evening passed through many moods. First an air of fiesta gaiety, vast amounts of energy expended in extravagant displays on the dance floor, and then as blood sugar ran low the red-liveried candlebearers bore on food that was demolished as if the dancers had been deprived of a crust for weeks.

Poppy constantly searched the tables, looking for Giles's face, but he was not there.

After supper the party resumed but with a different feel about it. Arms were entwined about necks and tempos became slower and more languorous. Some stopped the pretence of dancing altogether and simply lapsed into lechery. A handsome satyr, bare-chested with goats' horns and goat-fleeced legs, danced close behind a silver-necklaced slavegirl, licking her back as if it were an ice-cream. Poppy felt uncomfortable and Nick understood her feeling without a word spoken between them. He had been there for her all evening, melting away when others asked her to dance but reappearing again when she needed someone to be with.

"Shall we walk?" he said, and took off his jacket to put it about her shoulders.

The footmen had left the colonnade to do their duty with the supper but their candlelabra remained behind to light the decorated tunnel, standing unsteadily on the grass with candles low and guttering into waxen stalagtites. The early morning air struck chill. Poppy pulled Nick's jacket closer round her shoulders and looked up through the trellised fruit and flowers. The stars were less mysterious now. Their clearer light pierced the heavy navy sky like little pencil torches. It was just an ordinary starry night.

"Never look back," Nick said softly.

She glanced up at him.

"Do you remember the first time I came to your studio," she asked, "and you said I went directly to the point of your thoughts?"

He nodded.

"Now I know how uncomfortable it is."

He drew her to him then, and as she looked up his face blotted out first the stars and then the flowers high up behind him until she could not even see the texture of his skin, merely feel it on hers. The warm masculine smell of his skin added astringency and warmth to the cloying clouds of fragrant flowers. He kissed her slowly, gently at first, and then because he could not help himself, with mounting passion. Each time it was harder for Poppy to resist him but eventually it was Nick who drew back.

"I keep forgetting, I'm not allowed on the grass. You'll start to think I'm a bore."

The thought had been far from her mind. Too far. What was she doing? Kissing Nick when Giles might turn up at any minute — madness!

"Just mail me a card when he's out of your life, will you?"

She put her hand tentatively on his arm.

"Here I am," he said, with some of his old lightness, "sleeping in a damn great fourposter bed for the first, and probably only, time in my life, and I shan't have you beside me to chase away the spiders as they creep out of the curtains. I don't suppose you'd come — just as a spider-swatter, you understand?"

"What's the going rate for spider-swatters these days?"

"Huge salaries. They get paid the earth."

"Raincheck?"

She yawned, suddenly overwhelmed with sleepiness.

"Come on, little one." Nick swept her up effortlessly into his arms and carried her as far as the door into the Great Hall. It was beyond him to open great doors with arms full of girl so they both dragged their weary feet up the twisting stairs and stonewalled passages that led to their rooms.

Alone in her big bed she willed Giles to materialise. Her eyes swept the darkness until the heavy lids could no longer stay open.

Sleep came, but Giles never did.

12

THE thought of the studio session ahead was making Poppy jumpy. Dave, The Agency's stills photographer, had not been notable for his restraint at the Ballynally Ball. Life was quite complicated enough already with Giles and Nick. The last thing she needed in her life was a randy photographer.

Dave had told her to come made up for photography. Poppy had no idea what this involved, so had made an appointment at the Face Place and told them what she needed.

She had not opened her eyes once during the full hour it had taken them to create a face that the camera would like.

"I want to look really natural," she kept saying as more and more things were applied to her face. "Natural, you know, not made up or anything."

In the end the girl became quite exasperated and asked if Poppy wanted to look like a washed-out ghost or someone with eyes and a good jaw?

"You've got marvellous features and wonderful skin but the camera sees things differently. What I'm doing will make you look like yourself, only more so."

"Are you sure?" The session had at last ended and Poppy was now looking into the mirror at a painted hussy who seemed purpose-made to vamp Dave.

She took a taxi to the Holland Park address for fear of spoiling this new perfection by even a bead of perspiration on her nose. Her nerves had not abated by the time she rang the bell.

"It's me under the paint."

"Great," he said, putting his hand under her chin.

She jumped as if she had been stung. Was he going to ravish her now, to loosen her up for the photograph?

"You okay?"

"Who, me?" Why had her voice gone squeaky? "Yes, quite all right."

"Would you like a drink?"

First ply them with alcohol . . .

"Well, maybe a glass of water." It might bring her voice back to normal.

"Right."

He went into the little kitchen, scarcely more than an alcove, while Poppy looked around. There was nothing in the room to calm her fears. A sort of dentist's chair: chrome, leather-padded and levered for height adjustment stood in front of a wall which could be changed from light to dark by means of roller blinds. There were endless lights trailing snakes of flex and the Récamier *chaise longue* looking horribly suggestive with what looked like the pick of a negligée catalogue draped over it. The sight held an awful fascination.

"Here." Dave was at her elbow with the water. She jumped again.

"You're sure you're okay?" She nodded.

"Maybe I'll put on some music." He went over to a state of the art black and chrome tower. "What do you like?"

"Mozart?" she ventured. Surely safe.

He put on an extremely gloomy Requiem which, if it was supposed to relax her, had no chance.

"Where's the funeral then?" A large girl with cascades of obviously dyed black curls was coming down the white-painted iron spiral staircase which led to who knew what chambers of seduction. Poppy was never so pleased to see anyone in her life.

"Any camomile going? You must be Poppy, you're dead on time." She, too, raised Poppy's chin to the light. "Marvellous skin. I'm Jane, by the way. Ready to roll?"

"Yeah. You organise Poppy, I'll get the light readings."

Poppy felt like a Cindy doll being dressed.

At last they had her organised into straw-coloured muslin, Jane taking tucks with pins and clothes pegs wherever there were gaps or bulges. A wig was arranged in the *Directoire* style and Poppy was draped along the *chaise longue.*

"Smoulder," said Dave. "Come on, smoulder."

"She can't smoulder to this rubbish." With an air of great conviction Jane changed the music from Mozart to Bros and started dancing. It didn't help at all. Poppy felt like a wooden stick being asked to perform; the more she was asked to smoulder, the less there seemed to smoulder about.

"Come on, love." There was exasperation in Dave's voice. "I can't do anything with you if you won't help. Tell you what," he said to Jane, "put on something slow. And you, Poppy, you think about Ireland on Saturday night. Remember what you were thinking when you were dancing. I saw your face then. *That* was the look."

He'd found the right trigger. Smouldering was a doddle with Nick and Giles in her mind. From that moment the photo session picked up tempo.

"Okay, Jane, we've got a wrap on that one." Dave checked his list. "Next one's Gainsborough: blonde hair, big hat, pretty pretty. I'll have some more tea. Anyone thirsty?"

But the girls were too busy to be thirsty, and now Poppy was entering into the spirit of the thing. Climbing in and out of different clothes she ran through six photo identities in one long afternoon. When they stopped, she was surprised at how tired she was.

"Now I would like some tea," she said. "I really enjoyed that, Dave."

"You're a natural, darling."

It was odd to see herself on posters and in newspaper advertisements. Until it happened Poppy had not foreseen all the implications of the advertising campaign. Suddenly she was public property. Her father rang her up from Devon.

"The *paparazzi* have got hold of the Winchendon connection."

"Sorry, Daddy."

"Well, it's okay actually. Lorraine has never been one for looking gift horses in the mouth and so she's been plying them with buns and getting advance publicity for the tea room and things. Not exactly what they expected but then Lorraine can charm anybody. There's just one thing I am keeping quiet about," her father continued, "the Hoarde. Until we can afford better security I think we'd better not mention that it's kept here, okay? I didn't exactly tell a lie but I managed to give them the idea that I keep it in the deep and doomy dungeons of the Plymouth NatWest."

"Extremely sensible, Daddy. I'll do the same." She thought for a minute. "As a matter of fact, why don't we do just that?"

"When we've got the wildfowl reserve organised, I promise it'll be the first thing I do. Just at the moment I'm up to my ears in foxproof netting and Mandarin duck eggs at incubation temperature."

"Understood."

"Lorraine sends her love and — what's that?" Poppy could hear Lorraine's voice in the background. "She says the one of you in the Gainsborough picture hat is her favourite."

"Good. Give her my love."

The Trenton's reaction to the advertising campaign was predictably mixed.

"Clever idea, Miss Poppy," said Henry Ablethwaite, "just the boost the saleroom needs to keep it in the public eye." And, rather sheepishly, he asked her to sign a copy of his favourite picture.

It was Francis's petulant fury that convinced Poppy she had a success on her hands. That and the constant stream of paper-parcellers asking for 'that girl in the picture'. She found herself increasingly delegating her desk work to Amanda and doing a great deal of front counter duty herself.

Mostly her time was taken up with tact and mollification.

"It's a really decorative piece, well worth holding on to for a few years," was a phrase she was probably repeating in her sleep these days, but just occasionally there was a happy surprise.

One particularly frantic Thursday she was confronted with an extraordinarily hideous collection of Tribal Art. The two words in conjunction were a contradiction as far as Poppy was concerned. She'd sent the proud possessor of the various skulls and grinning masks into the cubbyhole to the side of the front desk that was grandly referred to as the Valuation Room, and rung down for Flavia to give a preliminary opinion. She had come out shrugging her shoulders.

"That particular valley in the Bornean jungle has apparently only ever seen one white man in all its history: this bloke's missionary grandfather. I really haven't a clue, Pops. What price unique junk? I'd better get the Prof. along. That is if the BM's switchboard isn't on Egyptian PT this afternoon."

The switchboard of the British Museum was not known for its efficiency and still suffered in reputation from one day when Giles, exasperated at a permanently engaged tone, had leapt into his car and stormed the bowels of the Museum's telephone system. There he had found every receiver off its hook and the entire staff sleeping off the effects of their lunch.

Poppy stuck her head into the cubbyhole. "We're just trying to get in touch with the British Museum. We won't keep you a moment." She smiled reassuringly at the missionary's grandson and turned to the little old woman, next in the queue, who had been waiting patiently with a painting.

She unwrapped the pages of *Woman's Weekly* which had been doing protection duty round the canvas and was faced by a dark little beachscape of the sort that had been brilliantly painted by the Impressionists with all their light and colour. Though the subject matter was delightful — several young women taking their ease under parasols with romping children round their feet, and all this under a long horizon — the overall tone of fudge brown was simply impossibly dull.

"Where did you get it from?" Poppy asked.

"Oh, it's been in the family," the little old lady said vaguely. "It was that picture of you under the parasol that brought it to mind. I thought, I'll have that down off the wall and take it to the Trenton's girl. It looked so like the one you sold in the advertisement."

"You're absolutely right," said Poppy, "it does if you see it in black and white reproduction." She twisted the picture to catch the light, looking for brushstrokes and clues through the umber foggy gloom. "In fact, the iconography and the treatment of composition looks very much indeed like a Boudin. Honfleur landmarks too . . . the trouble is, there's no light. Oh! A signature."

Deep down in the bottom right hand corner, brown on brown, was a very indistinct scrawl.

"Anne Cox?" Poppy read aloud.

"Ooh, that would be my Aunt Annie. Well, Great Aunt really. She used to paint. So it's one of hers, is it? Well, fancy."

"Did your great aunt travel to France a lot at the end of the last century?"

"Ooh yes, every summer, and Easter too. She used to love the sea air."

"I wonder if she saw a Boudin and copied it?" Poppy said quietly to herself. The picture puzzled her, there was something that did not quite add up about it. "If it's by your great aunt, I'm sure you don't want to sell it, do you?"

"Well, my dear, I'm a pensioner, you know, and I've no family to leave it to. I've a nephew, of course, but he wouldn't be interested. Young people these days . . ."

"I don't think we could get you a great deal of money for it," Poppy warned her. "The best I can do is put it into the next British Paintings and Drawings sale with a reserve of, say, two hundred pounds. I'm sorry I can't do more."

But the mention of two hundred pounds had set Mrs Blessed's eyes alight; suddenly she was rich.

"That'll be lovely, dear. Can you sell it soon?"

Poppy moved on to the next in the queue, making a mental note to look at the little canvas one more time, maybe get another opinion on it. Meanwhile she filled in the necessary form to ensure that Mrs Blessed's picture would go into the next brown catalogue sale. Brown catalogues were reserved for the also-rans in every category.

The next item was a rather interesting and very saleable Victorian bronze and ivory group of a Knight on horseback embracing a Maiden. Typical Gothic Revival stuff and possibly by Pugin or Scott. She must do a little research but it wouldn't be difficult, and meanwhile she could with confidence promise a price of at least four to six thousand.

So the afternoon wore on and at five o'clock it was a relief to shut the doors to more comers and finish for the day.

"The ads have brought them piling in." Flavia had come with a cup of coffee. "You must be pleased, it's a great success."

Whenever anyone congratulated Poppy on her brilliant idea, she found it extremely hard not to explain that it was nothing to do with her, but Nick had said that on no account must she tell a soul so she took the credit and kept the secret even from Flavia and Amanda.

"It's brought in the punters but very little real money comes in off the street."

"True." Flavia sipped her own coffee companionably.

"There's a picture that puzzles me,"

Poppy began, "maybe you could look at it?"

Suddenly a head came round the door of the Valuation Room and the missionary's wispy grandson said in a hesitant little voice: "May I come out now?"

Poppy and Flavia looked at each other with but one thought. The poor man had been completely forgotten for two whole hours!

"I'm so sorry," said Flavia, "we have been trying to get hold of Professor Thom at the British Museum and he simply can't be found. I wonder if it might be best if you left the artefacts with us and we could get back to you when we have a proper valuation?"

"That would be splendid. Very kind, very kind." And out he pottered.

"Only an Englishman would thank us for locking him up for two hours in a tiny room and forgetting all about him."

"You can do the decent thing by all these dreadful chieftan's stools and fertility thingies." Poppy indicated a particularly imaginative piece of carving. "Take them round to the BM in the morning. The Prof.'s fragrant breath can be your penalty for forgetting our poor friend."

Flavia grinned.

Francis, meanwhile, was not lying down under Poppy's initiative. His counter-offensive took the shape of an unofficial advertising campaign: word of the fight to the death between Francis and Poppy had, without a doubt, reached every cranny of his social milieu. The Box sale had netted every bit it needed to put Francis breathing down Poppy's neck on the Grand Total race. It was galling that he'd taken over Phyllida Box. Without her he would be floundering badly.

His Social Calendar sales had not been a huge success; Poppy rubbed her hands in glee when she saw the thin catalogue proofs of the Cowes Week sale coming up shortly: the highlights seemed to be a copy of the golden Americas Cup (scaled down and very poorly executed in bronze), and a brass telescope said to have belonged to Nelson (unauthenticated).

The third prong in his offensive was to be, as Maurice predicted, the Ceddo sale.

Sales of the relics from the lives and studios of dead interior designers fell into a predictable pattern: some good stuff interspersed with many 'Decorative Pieces' and, in Ceddo's case, a whole waggonload of gayola memorabilia. The Louis Quinze *Bureau plat,* star of the show and authentically documented back to the royal study at Versailles, had been decorated by Andy Warhol when under the influence of artistic inspiration or something stronger. The priceless piece had been artlessly ornamented by the artist with sourdough flowers and acrylic paints during a famous Ceddo party.

This put a very large question mark over its saleability. Would a serious collector pay the hundreds of thousands such a piece would normally expect to fetch in its uncorrupted state? Clean off the acrylic and would the exquisite rococo marquetry underneath be completely ruined or merely badly scarred? On the other hand, would the Warhol collectors pay the premium for the expensive vehicle decorated by their hero who usually worked on an altogether cheaper canvas? Only an irredeemable optimist would expect the combined top price for the two disparate parts.

Many items in the Ceddo sale teetered on such decisions, most of the collection remaining as resistant to valuation as the personality of Ceddo himself. It was all plumes and Lalique (cracked), 1920s woodcarvings of Josephine Baker in the *style nègre,* and some notably minor Hollywood mementos: a musty coil of mousey hair that purported to be Judy Garland's pigtail, discarded with her girlhood somewhere in the Hollywood Hills; a turban decorated with a tall pyramid of wax fruit and said to have been worn by Carmen Miranda. There was also some rather repellent Dali erotica, pretty Erté costume designs and a few Beardsleys, palpably fake. Francis had got away with labelling them 'After Beardsley' in the catalogue, and this was closer to misrepresentation than usually allowed. Altogether the substance of the sale was truly not first-rate; the outcome depended on how much money was in the pockets of those who remembered Ceddo with love.

Despite rumour widely spread by Francis, the Princess of Wales did not turn up anonymously, and the crowd of those who did were more *demi-monde* than *monde bien riche* so, at the end of the day, Poppy could be well-pleased that Francis had simply produced an absurd media circus and done himself very little good financially or by reputation. The Londoner's Diary would have column inches for weeks on who turned up to the Ceddo sale in nothing but leather shorts and winged mercury boots; the saleroom reports would not be full of record prices paid.

Giles was due back from his travels next week. The full six months trial would not be up, strictly speaking, till after Christmas, but Poppy felt so confident of her achievements that surely she could ask Giles for a decision now?

Meanwhile, the advertising campaign was being such a success that they must do a special Christmas poster to take advantage of a responsive market. She intended to talk to Nick about it.

"What about this evening? Come to Tite Street and bring some food?"

It sounded like a good idea.

She was very fond of Nick, Poppy thought, as she lay in her long hot bath. She put on a favourite old cotton dress, nothing special, just one she felt comfortable with. It had been a Winchendon Market seventy-five pence special. She'd seen the material in a bundle — soft blue hydrangeas printed on cream — and had known she wanted it even if it was quite worn out and fit only for little bits of patchwork. It was the sort of print dress that had you thinking of cream on your scones and playing with kittens. Usually she only wore it at home: it was not an item of power dressing. She smiled as she put it on. It felt good to stop fighting for her life with her claws out. She went out into the street without even bothering to dry her hair properly. The late August sun would do it for her as she walked down to Chelsea.

There were all sorts of things to make her dawdle on the way; the colours in a wool shop conjured up amethyst and opaline Kaffe Fassett jumpers she would always be too busy to knit. There was a pretty young mother juggling with an impossible puppy and an even more impossible babybuggy with wheels with a will of their own. Poppy wanted neither the baby nor the way of life but it was quite therapeutic to realise that there were people in this world who didn't even know the name of Francis Dernholm.

She knew of a really good Chinese

takeaway in the King's Road, she'd go there; it was better than making a hash of burning the food in an unfamiliar kitchen. It wouldn't make her late; Nick hadn't specified a time.

"Come on in," his voice called. There was a heavy haze of turpentine and linseed oil in the air and Nick was painting in old jeans and a shirt of antique ancestry.

On the piano was a huge bowl of old-fashioned roses. Some had shed their petals which lay like scraps of velvet on the polished mahogany top; the heaviness of their scent was astonishing.

Poppy investigated the kitchen, managed to discover the secrets of the cooker far enough to turn on the oven to keep the takeaway warm, and then went back to watch Nick paint.

"You look lovely." He had at last raised his eyes from the canvas to her. "Can I paint you?"

She was so surprised she did not immediately reply. Nick took her silence for refusal.

"Quick sketch," he said. "Nothing to give you cramp sitting for hours."

"How do you want me?" Poppy asked.

"Just like that in the last golden light. Wonderful! I like you *au nature*, it suits you."

He started quickly on a new and much smaller canvas board, sketching straightaway in paints with his brush.

"Talk to me," he said. "People look like blocks of wood if they're posing with nothing going through their minds. Talk to me but don't wave your arms about, okay?"

"I'm not a great waver anyway, am I?"

"No, but it's the standard warning to models, like Government health warnings on packets of cigarettes."

Poppy remembered being told to talk as a child. It had the same effect on her now as it had then.

"If anyone tells me to talk, my mind immediately empties," she said. "Want to suggest a subject? Philately? Amphibians?"

"Sorry. I'm exactly the same. What if you tell me about the advertising, how all that's going?"

"The response is phenomenal. There can't be a piece of junk left in any attic. We're up to December with the campaign. Do you think we might do a sort of super de luxe Christmas card?"

"A Madonna?" he suggested. "Prod anyone with a Virgin and Child to bring it in?"

"Nice idea!"

"You're blocked in," he stepped back to scrutinise the canvas with narrowed eyes, "I can't paint any more now 'till it dries."

"Shall we delve into my home cooking? Bon Pang Prawn Balls!" She produced the different dishes like a magician presenting amazing surprises. "Sesame toast and seaweed!"

One by one she carried them to the table under the great long window. They would eat by the last of the late summer light seeping over the London roofscape.

"All my favourites." Nick produced chopsticks for them both. "Poppaea Palmer, you are a great cook!"

"How nice to please my public." She gave a little oriental bow.

"Very demanding public. I wouldn't be happy with just any old takeaway, you know."

They juggled with chopsticks for a while.

"Dave's away," Nick ruminated, "but I

think we can manage without him. I know which end of a camera to point, and the downstairs neighbour with the vegetables and prolific rose garden has a baby as well. It's a kind of essential prop."

"Oh my lord!" Poppy laughed. "I've never seen a Virgin with a baby in nappies."

"We'll have to be very quick about the photographs and take our chances."

They looked at each other and burst into laughter.

"Everyone keeps congratulating me on the campaign," she said. "I'm finding it very hard taking credit for your idea."

"Darling, you'd sink in the advertising business. People do nothing else."

"It's brought a huge amount of customers through the door, and the media love it. The *Evening Standard* want to interview me. I even had an offer to appear on Wogan but I said I didn't have the time. I think I'd be shy on television. Giles is so much better at that sort of thing, I'd just go blank."

"Yes. I'm afraid the campaign's been too successful from my point of view. It's attracted a lot of attention. *Campaign* wrote it up last week and Dave was so anxious to get his work acknowledged that he told them all about his involvement. From that it's a short step to me."

"So will you be found out?"

"Well, Ian's in Los Angeles at the moment, buying up Hockneys. I hope it will have blown over by the time he gets back. We'll make the Christmas poster the last one and hope to get away with it."

They had finished eating now. It was a quiet moment, looking out on the lights of London, some moving, some still, and some reflected in the great dark treacle Thames.

Nick was looking at Poppy with his grey eyes moving over her face as if to memorise it. She felt suddenly self-conscious under his scrutiny, as she had not felt when he was painting her for all his close attention.

"The great joy of takeaways is that there's so little to wash up," she heard herself gabbling as she started to clear the table.

"Life's too short for washing up," he agreed. "Would it be a bore if you sat for me just a little more? I'd like to get a bit further with the sketch."

So they finished the evening, quietly and companionably, speaking from time to time when there was something to say but otherwise Poppy sat silent, watching him and feeling a sensation of peace steal over her, like the scent from the old-fashioned roses on the piano.

13

GILES was back in the office but getting hold of him was quite impossible; he might just as well still have been on his travels.

"Ah, Poppaea!" Only the Hon Sarah would be wearing a pearl choker with a real sapphire clasp on a Monday morning. "I did give him your message. Maybe he has more important things to attend to."

"How's the course coming on, Sarah?" Poppy picked up a book. "Still reading *From Giotto to Cézanne*? You'll be catching up with us all in no time at all."

She thought there was scant chance her messages were getting through to Giles but, to her surprise, he telephoned her soon after and asked if she could come to his office straightaway.

When she got there she found a full-scale meeting in progress between Giles, Francis, and the Trenton's solicitor. This looked serious.

"We've got a problem," Giles said.

"Rather a big one," Francis added smugly. Whatever the problem, it wasn't bugging him too much.

"Miss Palmer," the solicitor began formally, "I wonder if you remember a lady, a Mrs — " here he peered at a paper — "Blessed, bringing you a small oil on canvas some weeks ago? A seascape, I believe?"

Poppy searched through the identity parade of front counter hopefuls.

"A little old lady?" she suggested. "A picture by her granny or something? Oh yes, I do remember now." It had suddenly come back to her. "Rather a puzzle of a picture, it didn't make absolute sense, but I ran out of time to get to the bottom of it."

"You recommended putting it in a British Paintings and Drawings sale, I believe, with a reserve of — " and here again the lawyer seemed to need the paper to jog his memory — "two hundred pounds?"

The way he said 'two hundred pounds' he could have been reading out a death sentence; Laurence Olivier could not have wrung more menace out of the vowels.

"I think that's right." Poppy could feel herself becoming extremely hot. She was quite sure her cheeks were scarlet.

"She *thinks* that's right," Francis mocked. Both Giles and the lawyer gave him a withering look that would have crushed anyone else.

"Do you have anything more to say about it?" Giles asked. And in his manner there was everything about being her boss and nothing about being her lover.

"Well, not really," she said. "I ran out of time as I said. It was by Annie Cox." The name had suddenly come back to her as well. "She had obviously copied a Boudin."

"Annie Cox *was* a Boudin," Giles said and, although she did not yet fully understand the sentence, Poppy knew she was in deep trouble. She looked at him enquiringly but he gestured towards Francis.

"Let him tell you. The seller rang this morning and Francis took the call."

He had obviously decided that he could not increase Poppy's embarrassment by camping up his delivery so he gave it to her unusually straight.

"The picture fetched two hundred and

fifty pounds when we sold it on July 2nd. The buyer saw at a glance that the painting was a Boudin. Honfleur *plage*, circa 1880, classic picture, absolutely the artist at his best. The buyer, a dealer, reoffered the painting for sale and displayed it as the centrepiece of his window in Bond Street within a fortnight, with a price tag of five hundred thousand. You can guess the rest."

She raised her eyebrows at Francis, asking him mutely to finish the recital of horror.

"Little old Mrs Blessed took a toddle down Bond Street one sunny morning and saw her picture in the window with this huge price tag on it," Francis went on, "so she couldn't resist going in and asking the gallery if this was her picture and if everything was quite right. Well, Poppy dear, imagine her surprise."

"Cut the crap, Francis," Giles's voice was harsh, "the story's bad enough if you tell it straight."

"Sorry," he fluttered, and his campery gave Poppy heart. She would not show him how utterly humiliated she was. Her chin went up, courage seeping back.

"Go on."

"That's it really." Francis was alert to the subtle change in Poppy's attitude. He hurried through to the end of the story as though he knew he could not wring more drama out of it.

"Little Mrs Blessed went straight to her solicitor, who's one of the good ones by the way," here the lawyer nodded in gloomy agreement, "and Trenton's are being sued for 'failing to exercise sufficient care in valuing a painting worth five hundred thousand pounds'."

"Forgive my simplicity," said Poppy, "but could our insurers not pay the five hundred thousand and be done with it? Giles, I'm sorry I failed to spot it, it's a big mistake but not irreparable surely?"

"My first thought too," he said, "but I'm afraid it's not as simple as that. You see our little old lady is either something of a battleaxe or she is rather too well advised by her solicitor." He got up to stretch his legs.

Poppy watched him walking round the Chippendale desk, pausing to straighten the corner of a picture frame. There was silence until he had the tiny Turner sketch hanging absolutely straight.

"If our liability stopped at the half million, I would simply write it off and clock it up on the debit side of your performance, Poppy. Unfortunately Mrs Blessed is threatening two things: first, she says she will take us to court where she would quite possibly be awarded damages over and above the value of the painting. Judges enjoy punishing 'experts' who mislead little old widows. There would also be the associated press coverage which would, of course, be very damaging." He paused to let the implications sink in. "Her second threat in so many words is a demand for a million pounds hush-money: she guarantees not to go to Court or to the papers if we 'compensate her adequately for her loss and distress'."

"Can she do that?" Poppy asked.

"Don't you realise?" Giles's voice had a hard edge. "She can do what she damn well wants!"

Poppy cowered at his tone. It was one she'd not often heard, and never it to herself. It made her utterly miserable.

She had longed to see him again, but none of the reunions she'd envisaged were anything like this one. The room blurred.

She wanted to cut and run. Then Poppy caught sight of Francis; she stiffened her back. She wasn't going down without a fight.

"And our insurance doesn't cover us for this sort of thing?" She was thinking aloud. The moment she voiced this thought she knew it was a silly question. Francis was down on her like a gleeful avenging angel.

"Your expertise," he drew out the word for emphasis, "is meant to be our insurance against this sort of thing, Poppaea."

She ignored him.

"So do we give in to the blackmail?" she asked Giles.

He indicated the lawyer.

"We make a few moves but we're floundering like a fish on the hook. To answer your question, yes, basically we do give in to blackmail, though it goes against the grain."

"It makes no difference that another signature had been imposed on the painting at a later date?"

"Poppy, my dear," Giles's voice was impatient, "you must know that we never go by signatures. They can be the most misleading part of any work of art."

She acknowledged this absolutely basic truth of art dealing.

"You should have seen past the signature to the quality of the painting, I'm afraid. That's the painful truth of it all."

"All that front desking," Francis couldn't resist, "the Trenton's girl . . . Well, if you'd paid more attention and not let your head be turned by so much publicity, you might have kept your eye on the ball."

"I don't think Poppy needs a sermon," Giles said crushingly.

Poppy and Francis were dismissed while the lawyer remained behind to discuss the finer points with Giles. As they passed Sarah Cavendish's desk she smiled up at them, one of her rare and perfectly happy smiles, and Poppy wondered how much she knew. She had realised that by raising her profile, going for the big prizes and featuring in the ad. campaign, she had made many jealous enemies for herself, but this was the first time she fully understood that Francis and Sarah hated her so much that they rejoiced in her downfall, whatever the price to Trenton's.

"I'm meeting some chums at Fortnum's

for a Lobsterburger and a glass of non-fattening Chablis," Francis said. "Care to come? I think it might turn into a little celebration."

"Celebration?"

"Well, let's face it. You've scuppered your chances. Apart from the money, it's the sheer professional incompetence. Thinking a Boudin was an Annie Cox! I've a feeling I can safely count on having a new job to celebrate quite soon."

She'd give anything to puncture his self-satisfaction, but her mind was fresh out of clever replies.

Francis was going to treasure his sweet moment. He grasped her arm so she couldn't get away.

"Do you know, I've really enjoyed watching the Trenton's girl floundering in the mire of her own incompetence. It was a good campaign, by the way. I might take it up when I'm Deputy. A new series of ads featuring me: The Man From Trenton's Knows The Price of Everything."

"And the value of nothing," she put in.

"What's that?" Francis was momentarily distracted from his glorious pipedream.

"Lady Windermere."

"Oh, well. It's not important. Coming to Fortnum's, dear, or going back to your desk to rough out your resignation?"

"I'm going back to my desk," she let him have a delicious moment of satisfaction, "to discuss my new computerised system of transport and storage with Henry Ablethwaite. I believe it's working rather well."

At last she managed to disengage her arm, and walked to her office with her head high. It was only after she shut the door behind her that she disintegrated into a shivering wreck.

Amanda was there with tea and sympathy and everything a friend could offer. Poppy gave a row with Francis as the reason for her tears and Amanda, who had herself been reduced to tears by him on several occasions, took this at face value.

"Why don't you go home, Poppy? I'll cover for you this afternoon."

"Saddle up and remount," she managed between sniffles. "If I went home now I don't think I'd ever have the courage to come back again. I might as well write my bloody resignation for Francis to post on the door. No, we'll have our meeting with Henry. That's what's on the agenda."

Henry Ablethwaite had not worked in Trenton's for the last four years without learning to use his eyes.

"Are you all right, Miss Poppy?" he asked her in a fatherly way.

"I'm fine, Hen. Just a little hiccup with Francis, that's all." She did her best to smile.

"Unpleasant piece of work." It was not often Henry offered an opinion. "He's got his knife into you, right enough. Jealous of your success, and your being a girl. But you don't need me to tell you that. Yes, another cup of tea would be fine, Amanda." Henry settled comfortably into the visitor's chair in Poppy's office. "There's one or two things he's been doing lately which are not altogether straight. I've kept my peace because it's not my place to comment on such things but maybe I could see my way to. It concerns Trenton's good name, and when that is at stake it ought to be the business of every member of staff, high or low, expert or porter."

Poppy offered another iced bun and kept quiet. Asking for things was not the way to get information out of Henry Ablethwaite. If he had something to tell her, he would tell her in his own time and when he was good and ready.

"One case in point." With some skill Henry found the point of balance necessary to keep the huge bun on the tiny rim of his saucer. "That set of chairs, back in May. I wonder if you remember there was a good set of Chinese Chippendale diners, nice quality carving, said to have been made for Harewood House originally."

"I remember them," Poppy said, "they were lovely."

"Well, you may or may not remember also that our Mr Francis had a customer who was keen as mustard to buy them. Francis had kept him on the boil for about a year. A dozen Chips was on the client's shopping list to furnish his home, but it had to be a dozen, mind. Our Francis told him he'd got just the thing, see. Showed the punter the ten chairs and said the other two was being repaired in the workshop: fair wear and tear after two hundred and fifty years' use. Right?"

Poppy and Amanda nodded in unison.

"Right," they agreed.

"Well, the punter bought the ten at the sale for a price that would include the other two and then he got all excited about the restoration job. Said he'd like to see the pair of chairs being worked on: 'new craftsmen reviving old skill', all that kind of guff. You know how some of them go overboard for that sort of thing?"

They did indeed. Again they nodded.

Henry paused for some more tea and a monster bite of bun. He was enjoying milking his audience.

"Well," he continued, "Master Francis took him on the grand tour, showed him the workshop where one of his friends was doing the work, and the punter got all pleased because one of the chairs was finished, so he might as well take it home to join the other ten already sitting in his dining room. Want to know the punchline?"

It was an unnecessary question.

"He couldn't get the chair through the door." Henry paused for effect. "That chair hadn't been *repaired* in the workshop, it had been *made* there."

Poppy whistled.

"I think it might be time for our Chairman to learn about those chairs, and one or two other little things our Mr Francis has been up to. A saleroom exists on its reputation; that's the first rule of this business. Once people think you might not be straight, you may as well pack your bags. The punters won't touch you with a bargepole."

"That's true, Henry," Poppy said. "We exist by our probity. It's the first and only commandment in this game."

The three of them nodded. It was an axiom drummed into every employee of every saleroom of reputation. Deviate one whisker from the straight and narrow and you rendered yourself, at a stroke, worthless in the eyes of your public, buyers or sellers.

"Henry, you've cheered me up no end. The next time Francis is a beast, I shall think of Chippendale chairs and take heart."

"Thanks for the tea, Miss Poppy." The big gnarled hand replaced the cup with unexpected delicacy and precision. "And if you'll forgive the language: don't let the bastard grind you down!"

336

"Bless you, Hen." Her laughter was almost unforced.

She felt much better after she had spoken to Henry. Not that his little tale of the jiggery pokery fakery meant a huge amount against her own Boudin blunder; just the fact of such loyalty and support from a member of staff who, in his own unassuming way, was one of the mainstays of Trenton's.

She sat quietly for a while after the Head Porter had left her office. Henry's words had woken a small germ of optimism. She must try and see things with a balanced eye. It might be optimism or it might be sheer wishful thinking, but the story of the chairs had reminded her that the auction house world was full of frauds and fakers. A little old lady . . . a valuable painting with a strange signature superimposed . . . Didn't it carry the whiff of a set-up? Might someone be working a rather elaborate scam to get a lot of money out of Trenton's? It had been done before.

She made a resolution. It was worth investigating, but she'd do it secretly; not even Amanda should know. Poppy felt much better with a definite course of action before her. She settled happily to her busy afternoon's schedule.

First there was a heavy session with the shipping agents who were transporting a large and valuable Meissen dinner service to the German Embassy in Istanbul. Poppy took great pride that the Germans had needed to buy their native china in London; she must be absolutely sure it reached its destination without even a minor chip or hairline crack.

Then there was a catalogue to check for the Fine and Important Paintings sale coming up, and a special viewing room to be arranged for two absolutely delicious little Renoirs which had come Trenton's way much to the chagrin of Christie's and Sotheby's. They were darlings, full of light and the love of apple orchards and pretty women. More important, and to everyone's satisfaction, they were very tangible evidence that Trenton's was indeed shooting up in the ranks of Fine Arts Auctioneers. A year ago it would have been unthinkable that two such priceless pearls should come their way.

It was well past six o'clock when Poppy

ran out of her allotted work. She went along the passage from her office to Records, and found the department deserted, as she'd hoped. She checked some files, ran some discs through the computer, and made a few brief notes. Then she walked home, full of thought. She had the information she wanted. Now: how best to use it?

Curses on all long flights of stairs! Poppy could hear the telephone ringing in the flat as she rounded the last bend. Immediately her fingers turned to thick fat sausages, hopelessly incompetent at finding the bunch of keys and tackling the whole complicated affair of trying to unlock the door. Three Chubb and Yale locks later and she thought she'd fall flat on her face rushing to pick up the receiver.

"Hello?" She must have sounded like FloJo after a world record.

"Poppy?" It was Giles. "Darling, are you all right?"

"Yes." More frantic pants, she must explain them. "You see, there are so many stairs."

"So I deduce." He chuckled. "Do you always run up them all? Is this the secret of the great Poppaea Palmer two-handspan waist?"

"One day I'll afford an apartment with a lift."

"Not asking me for a rise, are you?"

"Not after today . . . " Suddenly all the joy had gone out of this conversation.

"Make it up to me later. Are you alone tonight?"

"Yes."

"I'm on my way."

Poppy dithered. She wanted to make the flat look organised and herself ravishing and knew she had about twenty minutes to do it. Never had twenty minutes been so short.

Before he had even crossed the threshold, Giles crushed her to him in a long and passionate kiss. It was as if the time lapse since their lovemaking at the Riverside Inn had never existed.

"Giles, I'm so sorry about the Boudin . . . " she began.

"Hush. I don't want to talk, we're always talking. Where's your bedroom?"

He undressed her impatiently and took her hastily. She was left breathless. It was like being caught up in a whirlwind.

Lying beside his strong, well-proportioned body, Poppy reflected that he lost none of his presence when he discarded his expensive clothes. Giles de Vere Trenton was impressive through and through. Even the intimacy of love making hadn't completely dissipated her awe of him.

"You're just as good as I remembered." He smiled lasciviously. "Now vamp me. Do you have any boots?"

But her mood did not match his. Until they'd talked, she knew she wouldn't be able to vamp to save her life.

"I'm dying of thirst," she said. "Shall I get us a bottle of wine?"

She brought it back to the bed where Giles was lying looking handsome and contented. It seemed extraordinary that he should just have made love to her and yet be so utterly unaware of the turmoil in her mind.

"The Boudin . . . " she began.

"Bloody silly," he said shortly, "I'm surprised you were taken in. I thought your eye was better than that."

Poppy felt small. She wasn't going to plead the busyness of that day as an excuse.

"You do realise, don't you, that whatever we have to pay out to this little old lady is debited to you? The job will have to go to Francis now, I can't see any other way. You can still have the rest of the six months to try and pull yourself up but you'll need more than a wing and a prayer. There's always the Hoarde, of course . . . If you could persuade your father to sell, it would add a sizeable chunk to your credit."

Why did she feel so reluctant to tackle her father when Giles made it sound so sensible, such an everyday thing to do?

She decided not to mention her pathetic little gleams of optimism over the Boudin; it would sound like excuses and wishful thinking.

"How did you get on in America?"

"Between you and me, extremely well. There's more international interest in us than I'd realised." Giles had finished his glass of wine and refused another, holding his hand over the top and studying her speculatively.

"You know, you talk too much, Poppy. You've reminded me of calls I have to make, work I have to do. Run me a bath, will you?"

After he'd kissed her and left she blamed herself. She'd struck the wrong note. If only she'd taken it at his pace, been content to make love and leave the talking for later. Then maybe the love would have been a healing, rather than a deepening of her humiliation.

She decided to use the long night before her; she would look into art scams and forgeries, study the mechanics of van Megeren and Tom Keeting. She had one chance to unravel this knot: she'd better get it right!

Poppy was heavy-eyed when she hit the office next morning. Heavy-eyed but hopeful. She tackled her desk and met two welcome surprises. Nick had sent her the proofs of the Madonna poster; they were good. Of course they might never see the light of day if the scheme she had dreamed up last night didn't work. She'd know quite soon.

The other surprise was also from Nick: a bulky package in brown paper. It came with no note but there was no need for that. The oil sketch of herself in the Tite Street studio could only have come from one source. It was a lovely picture, giving an overwhelming impression of light: the lights in her hair, the softer lights of the flesh tones in her face, and the creamy satiny lights on the fabric of the misty dress printed with blue hydrangea heads. Behind her, in the corner of the canvas as an incidental detail, was the brass pot with the late summer roses, overblown and falling. Poppy contemplated the canvas with a smile about the corners of her mouth. She was remembering that evening in the studio with the heavy scent of roses and turpentine mingling, and the brown column of Nick's throat, rising out of his painting shirt.

She rang down to Porterage. She loved the picture and wanted it on the wall straight away.

Trenton's was the handiest place to be if you suddenly had an overwhelming urge to put up a picture. In no time at all an aproned porter appeared with the necessary wire and hammer. All she had to do was say "Left a bit, up a bit", and it was done.

Now any visitor coming to see Poppy in her office would see her in duplicate.

She called The Agency.

"Nick? You're brilliant. I don't know

which to thank you for first."

"I thought you'd forgotten about the oil sketch. I wanted to surprise you."

"And you did. It's on the wall, I'm looking at it now. I really love it. Nick, I know it's not the time to ask you for yet another favour but I really need your help. I don't think anyone else will do."

"Good. Ask away."

The asking and explaining lasted some time.

"And you think Freddy will be my passport?" he queried.

"He stands a better chance of gaining entry than anyone else I can think of. Have you ever known anyone refuse to let in a lord?"

Nick chuckled. "Under that auburn halo there ticks a cynical brain. Leave it with us?"

"Good luck."

Now she must try and occupy her mind while Nick and Freddy decided her fate. She knew in her heart of hearts that the central issue of the Blessed Boudin was not that of the money. Francis had, in his maddening way, been right. Failure to recognise a great master when he was staring you in the face was indeed gross incompetence. Unless she could salvage her professional standing over the painting, there was no other course than to offer her resignation. It was the only way to get Trenton's out of an embarrassing situation.

Meanwhile, daily duties: she'd start off by seeing what was going on in the saleroom. One of the weekly run-of-the-mill furniture sales was taking place: 'brown' furniture, mostly late Victorian. The sale was well attended by the familiar, undistinguished faces of dealers and trade buyers. No glittering occasion this, just the trade looking for cannon-fodder to fill shop floors, or make up the volume of container lorries. If she had to leave Trenton's, she'd miss even these bread-and-butter sales.

Next stop the highest security viewing room where the Renoir pair were just starting to attract some early interest. She checked that the two bullet-proof glass screens were in place: high estimates had the habit of attracting the odd nutter.

"I'd better check over the alarm while I'm here," she told the security guard. He unlocked a panel to display a completely meaningless spread of circuitry, lights and batteries.

"Is this thing meant to be hanging down?" She pointed at a wire.

"Certainly not, Miss Palmer." The bored guard was suddenly interested. "It's been cut, I should say. I'll get Mr Ablethwaite, shall I?"

She could safely leave it with Henry.

Next she looked into Flavia's office to find her cataloguing a whole sale's worth of nineteenth-century photographs. Boxes and boxes were strewn about the room at every level, from floor to desktop. Some were even precariously balanced on top of cupboards. Flavia was scrabbling about, looking dusty and desperate. Poppy remembered just such a job in her own early days at Trenton's. At the time it had almost reduced her to handing in her resignation. Today she felt nostalgic for the impossible task.

"Is this a foot I see before me?" Flavia's nose on the floor among the photographs had met Poppy's shoes. She looked up. "Full colour and three-dimensional! What a relief. I thought the whole world was flat and sepia-toned."

Poppy smiled and reached for a spare green baize apron. "Shall I help you?"

"I'd be your slave forever. I think they're the left-overs from all the photo sales we've ever had. 'Unsolds' from everywhere! I've got to lot them into some sort of sensible subject division and box them accordingly. I've done twelve and we've got at least two hundred lots here. It's a nightmare."

"How are we doing it? By Photographer? Subject? Geography?"

"By bad, worse, and worser, I should think. Look at this one — what can we call it? 'Blurred backview of female(?) retreating down indistinct road somewhere definitely not in Africa'?"

"Let's start a sub-section." Poppy was thrilled to have something to absorb her whole mind. "This one can go into 'Historical costume'. The length of the coat is about all we can be definite about."

The afternoon sun was slanting low through the window, Poppy and Flavia were thinking about tea and starting on a new and innovative section with a working title of 'Inebriated Monks', when Giles appeared in the doorway.

"I've been looking for you everywhere, Poppy. What on earth are you doing here?" He wrinkled his nose against the dust and must of the old photographs. "I need to see you in my office."

He didn't wait but left before she had finished untying the strings of the all-protecting apron; hastily she used a corner of the green baize to remove any speck from her shoes. Organising her tumbled hair by the reflection in a windowpane, she left Flavia to the last thousand thrilling pics.

"Thanks, Poppy, you've saved me days."

"I'll come back if I've time."

There was a third figure in Giles's office. Poppy's heart swooped in fright and anticipation.

"Freddy?"

The Earl grinned at her.

"He wouldn't tell me why he was here until you arrived." Giles sounded irritated. "I hope this isn't some silly prank."

"By no means." Freddy had dropped the usual bantering tone. "It's rather serious, Giles, and it concerns your company."

The mention of his company had, as usual, focused all Giles's attention. A shaft of light caught his features, bringing the sharply modelled jaw and the long-fingered hands into clear focus; he wore large cabochon lapis lazuli cufflinks today, like great knobs of gold-veined midnight, caught and held forever.

"Tell us about it from the beginning," he said, and brought down his long-lashed lids so he could concentrate fully while evaluating Freddy's story.

"You've a clever girl here, Giles. And, in case you hadn't realised, one who takes Trenton's interests very seriously indeed."

Giles did not break his concentration by looking up at Poppy or at the speaker.

"Poppy was worried about the Boudin. She had the idea there was something fishy going on and so she had the bright idea of sending me to call on Mrs Blessed, the little old lady with the painting, in case you'd forgotten."

"I hadn't." Giles's tone was dry.

"She lives on the edges of Fulham. Poppy had done the spadework with the address. Old Mrs B. is rather like somebody's nanny fallen on hard times." Freddy ruminated a moment. "With one important exception — I didn't like her."

"You didn't like her?" Poppy prompted.

He shook his head.

"Neither did Nick," he said, "and I'd trust his judgement. You remember Nick Coles?"

"The ad. man," Giles nodded.

"My first gleam of hope came when we managed to get into her flat," Freddy went on. "There wasn't a picture about: no immortal collection of daubs by the talented Aunt Annie. Not a picture in sight. Unless you count 'Bubbles' and a cross stitch dog, home-framed.

"Well, I'd done my job by gaining entrance to the flat and getting Mrs Blessed all fluttery round the teapot. The rest was up to Nick. He'd brought some baggage in the form of two large padded envelopes. I hadn't asked him what was in them because I didn't want to spoil the surprise. He took over from me then and started to talk in a general way about the dangers and pitfalls in the art market these days. Then he got into the more specific and technical stuff about how easy it was to change the appearance of works of art by burying them in the garden, or covering them over with a thick coloured varnish to add age. He talked about scumbles and glazes and then went into very precise detail about the analysis of varnish in various recent cases, and how all materials could be dated very exactly with today's technology. Quite soon Mrs Blessed was looking just like a rabbit that's been hypnotised by a stoat."

Poppy brightened. Hope was becoming something more concrete.

"It all came out then. She'd tell us anything to save her own skin. Anything except the name of the person who put her up to it. Great Aunt Annie never existed, of course. Our Mrs Blessed swore she had received an anonymous telephone call with an offer of making five hundred pounds by doing something 'quite easy and perfectly legal'. Well, she jumped at it, of course. If the person was a stranger, he had judged her circumstances and her temperament well. Personally I think the whole business of the stranger on the end of the telephone was made up; I think she knew the instigator. Nick thinks so too, by the way, but it would have taken thumbscrews to get it out of her and I didn't think we were there for thumbscrews. Right?"

Reluctantly, Giles nodded. "Right."

"The person gave her strict instructions exactly when she was to take it round to Trenton's and exactly what she was to say. You were to be on the desk, Poppy. She was shown a photograph of you, and if anyone else was on duty she was to go away and await instructions for re-presentation of the picture."

"Trenton's girl in cock-up," Poppy muttered bitterly.

"That was not the only condition. If you showed any doubts about Great Aunt Annie, or said the painting might be worth a good sum of money, then Mrs Blessed was to take it home immediately and wait for it to be collected. She was paid in cash the day after Trenton's accepted the painting for sale, and she seems to feel that if she so much as breathes a description of the person who organised all this, she'll be got by a mixture of Mafia hit-men and Voodoo magic men."

"So what do you think?" asked Giles. He was deeply interested now and leaning forward across his desk.

"Wait!" Freddy held up his hand. "We've not finished yet, not by any manner of means. My 'technical expert' slipped a canvas out of one of his brown envelopes and, like all the best magicians, made her gasp. It was a little landscape he'd washed over with a burnt sienna scumble. He showed it to her and she said, yes, that was exactly the effect her painting had given. Nick said it was the easiest way of fogging up a perfectly good picture and of course anyone could do the signature. So we had a pretty clear case of deliberate deception. I threw the book at her then: fraud, conspiracy, intent to obtain money by deception, intent to endanger the good name of Trenton's, you name it. I'm afraid we frightened her into signing this piece of paper," he waved it at Poppy, "which as you'll see, removes any claim whatsoever on Trenton's."

"My God, Freddy, you're wonderful!"

"She won't sue, and whoever put her up to it, can't," Freddy said. "Hoist on his own petard. Why did Shakespeare always get there first with the mot juste?"

Giles was musing. "If he reclaims the picture, we take him to Court and to the cleaner's. If he doesn't he's lost an absolute packet: the picture's out of his hand and all he's got is £250. The dealer bought the picture from us; it's his rightful property now. I suppose he thought it was a small stake against such vast potential damages."

They sat in silence for a while, turning it over.

"What I don't like about it," Poppy said at last, "is being singled out as the Patsy on the front desk. I didn't think I had the worst eye in Trenton's but that's the implication."

"Not necessarily," Giles said slowly. "It could be a backhanded compliment. After all, you are Books and Pictures. If you didn't spot it, then no-one else was likely to either."

"That cheers me mightily, Giles, thanks."

He lapsed into thought again.

"I can't believe it!" Poppy had suddenly realised that her plan had worked.

Giles's heavy lidded eyes lifted. Slowly and deliberately they travelled from her head to her feet.

"Not just a pretty face." An eyebrow arched in admiration. "It looks as if you're back in the running, Poppy." The quizzical expression in his eyes gave the remark more than one meaning.

"Freddy," he stood up and shook the other man's hand, "I owe you. May I keep this?" He waved Mrs Blessed's signed renunciation. "I think I'd better get the whole thing wrapped up legally post haste." Giles picked up a telephone.

Freddy and Poppy both rose to go, he murmuring about breaking some bubbly to celebrate.

"Sorry, Freddy. She has a prior engagement."

"Later this evening then? I've found a terrific new place. Come with me and Suzie, we'll have some fun!"

"Lovely. And you know, I can't begin to thank you enough. If the plan didn't work, I knew I'd have to leave Trenton's with my tail between my legs."

Freddy beamed and left the office.

In a rare impulsive gesture Giles crossed the room to gather Poppy in his arms.

"You weren't going to leave us, were you? How could you think of it?" With his lips exploring her face and neck, she wondered too.

"I thought I'd have to, Giles. If Mrs Blessed was holding Trenton's to ransom, there was no way I could stay to be an embarrassment."

"Darling," he devoured her with his kisses, "you could never be an embarrassment."

His telephone rang.

"Let's ignore it for once."

They were so busy ignoring the phone that Sarah Cavendish had to clear her throat before they noticed her.

"I didn't hear you knock," Giles said icily.

"I don't think you heard the phone either," Sarah reproved. "If it's not working I must get the engineer."

She was dressed today as if she were going out hunting, Poppy thought. Sidesaddle, of course, in that long navy serge skirt and sensible cardigan. The white shirt had a stock tied high about her neck and fastened with a stickpin in the shape of a jockey's cap. Today's executive earrings were Hermès horses' heads. Maybe her studies had got as far as Stubbs. "This concerns you, Poppaea," Sarah was at her most schoolmistressy, "and it's no laughing matter." She had seen Poppy's smile.

"Can't it wait?" Giles was still on his feet and eyeing the door.

"I think you'll want to deal with it as soon as possible." Sarah was full of importance. "It's the Millington Rubens."

Another forgery? Poppy thought frivolously. After the relief over the Blessed Boudin, nothing could be serious.

"The Arts Minister has denied an export licence." Sarah dropped her bombshell.

"Damn!" Giles sat down with a face turned suddenly grave.

"But that doesn't make sense," said Poppy, "there was no question of an export licence being needed. The picture's got no historical connection with this country. It belongs in Holland and it's going back there. Nothing wrong in that, is there?" She looked at Giles who shook his head.

"There's no museum that wants to get its grubby mitts on it. We'd have heard before now if the National or the Tate were trying to raise money to keep it in the country. I don't understand."

"Waverley Rules," Giles said quietly.

Of course.

Under the Waverley Rules, first laid down in 1952, a painting could be brought before the Review committee with a recommendation that it should not be granted an export licence if it was worth over £30,000, closely connected with British history or of outstanding aesthetic importance.

"Outstanding aesthetic importance," Giles said.

"Undoubtedly," Poppy agreed, "but no connection with this country."

"It qualifies under the fifty year rule," he went on.

Foreign works of art were only exempt from the Waverley Rules if they had been imported during the last fifty years; the Millingtons had lived with their unrecognised Rubens for a lot longer than that.

"But who wants it?" Poppy asked. "I haven't heard a whisper."

"That puzzles me, too." Giles's tones were measured. "The new owner obviously wouldn't have brought the question before the Committee, he's under no obligation to seek an export licence. And the Millingtons didn't mind about it leaving Britain?"

Poppy shook her head. "They were just thrilled with all that lovely money!"

"If the picture can't leave these shores, the foreign buyer is quite entitled to withdraw from the sale. It looks to me," said Giles slowly, "as if someone is trying to sabotage Trenton's. This and the Boudin coming together are too much of a coincidence."

"But who?" Poppy asked. It seemed so fantastic.

"Our rivals?" Giles mused. "No, they've everything to lose themselves by a cut-throat war. Someone inside the organisation with a grudge? No such person." He was ticking the possibilities off on his fingers. Suddenly comprehension dawned in his face. "I wonder . . . " he said.

"You can't not tell." Poppy would burst with curiosity if he didn't.

"Only a thought," he said cautiously, "and the thought is absolutely not to go any further than this room." He looked at Sarah and Poppy in turn and, for once in agreement, they nodded. "I've one or two parties keen to invest in Trenton's as you know." They waited. "Well, the smaller our profits, the greater their bargaining power. Think about it.

"Finding the person who's trying these little tricks may be quite difficult but I have some influence in the Ministry for Arts; it shouldn't be impossible to ferret out a name. Forgive me, Poppy,

I've some detective work to do. It must take precedence over our celebration."

She was not to be entirely deprived of celebration.

"Put on your glad rags, girls," Freddy commanded. "We're going to the Caviar Bar."

Suzie and Poppy hurtled towards the bathroom.

"I love this cut-throat competition for the mirror." Poppy was craning to put her mascara on above Suzie's head while she was doing things with silver eyeshadow.

"God! You've pinched my Chanel moisturiser again!"

Poppy's mood of elation demanded a crazy dress. She dived into a red taffeta Balmain number with a wonderful swishy skirt on which, here and there, was embroidered a microscopic insect in the tiniest beads. She clipped a pair of Lalique wasps on her ears. She'd spotted them at a Trenton's Fine & Decorative Jewels and had shut her eyes to the price.

Suzie was looking extremely polished in a cream suit of a silk so rich and thick and delicious it looked poured from a carton. There were also some new diamonds sparkling at her ears. Poppy hadn't seen them before. It didn't take a Brain of Britain to deduce where they'd come from.

"A lot more than two minutes." Freddie checked his watch. "But who could complain at the result? Nick's joining us there. We can't go off to the Caviar Bar a gruesome threesome."

The restaurant's menu had the virtue of simplicity: Russian or Iranian? And the prices absolutely guaranteed that the eaters would be rich, and as beautiful as nature or money could make them. Poppy was pleased she had dressed up. In this crowd she was by no means overdone.

"Nick, here!" Suzie was waving across the room.

Poppy looked up and suddenly had difficulty with a butterfly that had decided to swoop around inside her ribcage. He was wearing a conventional white tie with a stick up collar and had done something about the eternally flopping hair which was now smartly disciplined. Why had she never realised he was so tall? Suddenly she felt very self-conscious. She had to stand on tiptoe to kiss him.

"What's happened?" she asked. "You've grown about a foot."

"It's the cod liver oil, Mother," he said, laughing. And "Bzzzz," he told the nearest wasp.

The dinner jacketed and brilliantined quartet were playing a tango.

"Shall we?" Nick asked.

"I can't!"

"Course you can, anyone can. Come on."

His tugging hand would brook no refusal. Poppy found her nose at shirt-stud level.

"I've so much to thank you for," she began.

"Not now, we're coming up to a good bit." And he flung her, very expertly, so she was entirely horizontal and about six inches off the parquet. Just as she was quite sure she was going to be knocked out, his other hand expertly scooped her up and off they went into another swooping dive across the floor.

"Why does everybody know how to do this dance except me?"

"What were you doing last summer? It was all the rage. A wonderful old trout we discovered in Sloane Street used to give us lessons on a Saturday afternoon. She wore flame-coloured teagowns. I found her in the local paper."

Poppy didn't care to ask who 'we' was, but she wondered.

"I can see our food arriving."

"Part two on a full stomach," he laughed, and pulled her back to the table.

For a while they were completely absorbed in Bollinger and Beluga. There were toasts and thanks and mutual congratulations on the day's triumph, and when at last every detail had been exhausted, Poppy asked, "How's Ballynally?"

"Alas, poor Crust!" Freddy was lugubrious. "He thinks his knees will be worn out altogether if he has to show more tiny people round."

"Tiny people? Leprechauns?"

"I think there's a secret tunnel leading direct from Tokyo. We're flavour of the month out East."

"One small Korean wanted to buy the whole estate and turn it into a theme park," Suzie interrupted.

"So we've no doubt the sale is going to go?"

"With a bang. It'll keep me in earrings for life." Suzie winked.

"At last, the prospect of a straightforward sale! I was beginning to feel jinxed."

When they had eaten enough, danced enough, flirted enough, laughed enough, Nick saw them to Freddy's Lagonda but didn't accept the offer of a lift.

"I've got a dance to go to."

"Oh." Poppy was disappointed.

"You don't think I always dress up in my penguin suit when people ask me to come out and eat, do you?"

"I didn't think." She was waiting for him to invite her along to the party but he didn't.

For a girl with purely Platonic feelings, she was remarkably annoyed.

14

CHRISTMAS was coming and Giles was away again.

His detective fever had redoubled his air miles. Poppy pictured him like some avenging angel, swooping across the skies in retribution. She wouldn't like to be on the receiving end of his vengeance. They'd had a long talk, so at least she knew exactly what he was up to. He had also sent her an early Christmas present from Hermès in Paris. The large orange and brown box had contained the most sumptuous pair of crocodileskin boots, with the simple message: "All the best things come in threes. I'm waiting."

She knew exactly what he meant.

He would be absent for the annual Christmas lunch which was a great pity. It was traditionally a lovely happy occasion that every single member of staff made gigantic efforts to get to. Only sudden death qualified as a reasonable excuse for missing it.

Each year the girls decorated the big saleroom where the party was held; it was the only room big enough to hold everybody comfortably and also, as a kind of extra Christmas decoration, there lingered about the room the special atmosphere of all the echoes of the year's exciting sales with their furious flurries of competition, drama and emotion. This was a room that held very special memories for every single member of Trenton's staff.

Tradition had the room decorated by all the girls on the last official morning of work before the Christmas break, which this year happened to be Christmas Eve. Male staff were forbidden entrance under pain of death and, as a result, any lugging about that had to be done was done by the girls.

Whichever items were lucky enough to be spending Christmas at Trenton's while awaiting the sales after the holiday, had to be incorporated in the Christmas decoration, however absurd they might be: it was a house rule.

Henry Ablethwaite had been known to comment that he wondered his porters were needed at all after the year when one object awaiting sale was a huge marble fountain, so large and heavy that it had been dismantled for transport and lay in bits all over the place. The girls had dragged all the bits into the centre of the room and reassembled them with truly Herculean strength. Afterwards they had draped the whole confection with swags of greenery and bunches of ribbon, filled it with polar quantities of ice and used it as a giant winecooler for the party's champagne.

This year they were lucky enough to have a huge chandelier. Compared to the fountain, it was childsplay. They rigged it up in the centre of the ceiling, took out the thirty-five electric bulbs and put in their place thirty-five tall candles of best beeswax.

"Candlelit lunch," Flavia rejoiced. "I think that's about as far as my notions of enchantment will take me. Oh, palmy days!"

"Give me a hand with Augustus," Poppy called.

The marble Emperor, temporarily between homes, was spending Christmas with them.

"He can go at the head of the table instead of Giles," Poppy directed the moving party.

"I was going to go there," said Sarah Cavendish.

Her remark had the effect of making the statue move all the quicker towards the head of the table.

Poppy straightened up. "Were you?" she asked innocently.

"Yes. Francis was going the other end. That way we could both be Giles's representatives. After all, I am his personal assistant and Francis is really the Deputy Chairman in all but name now, isn't he?" Sarah issued the question like a challenge.

"I've already invited Maurice to head the table." Poppy hadn't, but she would as soon as she got to a telephone. "It seemed fitting that he should go there, seniority and so on. A sort of farewell Maurice party, the one nobody got around to giving him when he left."

"What a perfectly splendid idea," said Amanda, ever the loyal lieutenant, and the rest of the staff joined in a little chorus of approval.

Sarah realised that nobody was going to offer to move Augustus back to make way for her. Poppy saw her face in that instant and was extremely pleased that the two of them were not alone somewhere dark with a carving knife handy.

It crossed her mind, not for the first time, that Sarah might be behind the two attempts at sabotaging Trenton's. Giles only saw the two acts as malicious trickery directed against the auction house; Poppy, from her own particular vantage point, had not missed the fact that both strikes were directed not only at Trenton's profits but also against herself. Was it coincidence that both blows came through two of 'her' paintings?

Until now Francis had been Poppy's chief suspect. It made sense: he had everything to gain by victory over her. However, it did surprise her that he should have a valuable Boudin at his fingertips. Francis just wasn't in that league; though he might of course have an admirer rich enough to count half a million a small investment to secure his protégé's position in the firm.

Sarah, on the other hand, might well

have a spare Boudin hanging around. Her family were notoriously rich. Not wealthy, rich. There had been a grandfather in the Industrial North with absolutely *the* patent medicine for childish ailments: every mother's favourite little helper through three generations. The money and title had come to him. Sarah's father had simply sat back and enjoyed the royalties, and she was the only child of this generation, doted upon and denied nothing. She certainly had the money but why should she do it? There was no doubt that she disliked Poppy intensely. Was spite reason enough?

Such unChristmassy thoughts were swirling through Poppy's mind as she crowned Augustus Caesar with his crown of mistletoe, hung coloured glass balls as earrings on his imperial ears and, over the arm pointing commandingly towards new victories, slung a large wicker basket. The basket was the posting box for everyone's Christmas presents to each other. As none of them but Sarah was rich, and each of them prided themselves on an eye for a bargain, a little Christmas competition had built up. Presents between staff must, on pain of death, not have cost the giver more than a fiver. They must also be breathtakingly clever: unspotted auction bargains were the smart thing to give.

By midday the room looked splendid. 'Edwardian Christmas' had been the theme and the girls were very strict in interpretation. It meant the loss of party poppers and balloons, both of which would have been an anachronism, but on the other hand it meant the efforts that had gone into food and floral decoration had been redoubled. The great shaped puddings marched down the table, their wobbles crowned with sticky glacé cherries. There were whole salmons covered in aspic with their scales recreated from paper-thin cucumber; these noble fish had been brought down from Scotland as trophies by the pinstriped young men who aspired to Directorships. Each year they vied for the biggest catch on the Christmas table and their mothers, wives, or whoever could be persuaded, nursed the fish through the long autumn in the deep freeze and finally produced it as triumphant as she could possibly make it on the great day.

There were also coveys of pheasant and partridges, killed on home shoots, roasted, and arranged Edwardian-style on silver platters surrounded by black grapes, cunningly woven baskets of crisp game chips, and crowned with a flourish of their own tail feathers.

Everyone was happy. Another decorative triumph, nobody would forget the table this year.

Maurice had been forewarned and made his entrance as one who could only sit at the head of the table. He had found an Admiral's costume of the right date, and in white, gold and nodding plumes resembled no one so much as Lord Mountbatten in Colonial days.

Not everyone had dressed for the period but many of the girls had gone to great lengths. Francis, with crashing predictability, had dressed himself as a sailor and started by making a little speech to welcome all and sundry, particularly: "Our guest of honour Maurice Blessingham who served us all so well."

"I don't recall serving under you, dear heart." Maurice had no compunction in interrupting. "You were always of lesser rank, as I recall. Why look at you today — a mere bum-boatman while I have risen to

the dizzy heights of Admiral of the Fleet."
Maurice expected, and got, laughter.

Francis reddened with fury at both the reprimand and the singular choice of words but Maurice had gained control and was not letting go.

Poppy decided it was safest to cut the speeches and get everyone seated as quickly as possible: bitchiness might entertain them all but this was, after all, meant to be an occasion of goodwill to all men.

"Maurice darling, come and sit at the end here where you can gaze at Augustus." She took his arm bossily.

"Always the best-looking Emperor," he twinkled.

Francis was not one to miss the social nuances of *placement*. Despite being at daggers drawn with Maurice he sat himself quickly on the older man's right: the place of importance. After that it was more or less come as you please with some attempt to alternate the sexes though they were not exactly evenly divided. When last of all Poppy took her seat, she found there was only one place left at the table, between a trainee porter and the Honourable Sarah.

The trainee porter had come to Trenton's

on a Youth Opportunity Scheme, was called Adrian and suffered painfully from acne and blushes. Whenever any of the female staff talked to him, he reddened from the roots of his hair to his Adam's apple which bobbed uncontrollably. Such evidently agonising embarrassment brought out only kindness in the girls who had set themselves the target of curing the scarlet flushes by Easter.

As a conversationalist, however, Adrian was impossible. Poppy tried some questions about where he was going for Christmas, but it was worse than trying to engage a small child in conversation; clearly her attention was torture to him. She gave up and realised that she must spend most of the next two hours talking to the Hon Sarah. It was not what she would have wished.

"How goes the Art Course?" was an obvious beginning.

"Well actually I'm giving it up." Sarah smoothed the already immaculate blonde hair and wiped her lips fastidiously with her linen napkin.

Poppy forbore to ask if it was too difficult for her.

"I think I shall be getting married soon,"
Sarah added unexpectedly.

"Gosh, who to?" Poppy craned her neck
to see if there was a ring.

"Well, we haven't announced it yet so I
hope you don't very much mind if I don't
tell you," Sarah said primly.

Poppy didn't mind at all. The only thing
she fervently hoped was that marriage
would prove so time-consuming for Sarah
that she would have to give up working at
Trenton's.

"I should think you'll be very busy,"
she said.

"Yes." And so interested was Sarah in
the subject that she forgot to speak to
Poppy in her habitual manner, as though
addressing a naughty child, and went on
almost as one equal to another.

"I'm going to Prue Leith's cooking
classes in the evening," she confided, "just
to brush up my skills. I did the Cordon
Bleu course before I starting working here,
you know. But cooking's changing so much
all the time, you have to keep on top of
it; it really is the way to a man's heart.
Mummy's quite convinced of it, and she's
kept Daddy for ever so long. Mind you,

we have a housekeeper so Mummy only has to cook on Wednesdays and Sunday evenings."

Poor Mummy, Poppy thought, it must be a hard life.

There was something else she wanted to ask Sarah about.

"How's Giles getting on, do you know?"

"Well, I can't breach any confidences of course," only Sarah could be so pompous, "but it's no secret he's got several interested parties who want to buy into Trenton's and finance expansion. I think he's playing eeny meeny miney mo. A question of balancing the pros and cons of the different proposals."

"Will it be a foreigner, do you think?" Maybe Sarah had enough wine under her belt by now to give away some further tiny crumbs of information. Her cheeks were turning pink.

"A surprise Briton has suddenly popped up, a late entry but possible none the less."

"But isn't Giles in Australia just now?"

"He'll be back before the New Year, I expect. Look," Sarah said in a rush of confidentiality, "would you like to see what I've got him for Christmas?"

She was already groping in the big practical pocket of her big practical skirt. She was not one of those who had made an effort to dress up for the Christmas lunch. All that sort of thing was, she said crushingly, a little silly.

Sarah pulled out a little grey box and opened it with a flourish to reveal a truly awful pair of cufflinks.

"You know he collects them," she said eagerly.

"Indeed." Poppy was gazing into the eyes of badly enamelled foxes' masks in garish colours on modern gold links. "Heavens! The eyes follow you round," was the only polite thing she could find to say.

Happily, it was enough. Sarah took it as a great compliment. "Aren't they brilliant?" she asked. "I think he'll be thrilled."

"How's he getting on with finding out who's behind the Export Licence?" With Sarah in a rare giving mood, Poppy might as well find out as much as she possibly could.

"No luck." She tucked the little box back into her skirt pocket and ostentatiously consulted her Cartier watch, not for the first time. Poppy wondered if Mummy had never told her that it was rude to look at your watch more than once every ten minutes.

The conversation petered out after that, they had nothing left to talk about. As Christmas lunches went, Poppy could remember ones she had enjoyed more but nobody else seemed disappointed with the party. In fact it was going with great gusto. Maybe she was simply missing Giles.

Maurice brought things to a close with a neat little thank you speech and then Amanda presided over the present basket which Poppy didn't have a huge interest in this year; she'd taken trouble over tokens for Maurice, of course, and Amanda, and for Flavia she'd found a photograph frame.

The party was breaking up and people were drifting out. Poppy knew she must turn her thoughts to presents for her father, Lorraine and Terry. When she'd spoken to her father about coming down to Devon, he'd been full of expectation. Winchendon was going to be like the old days: they'd have a real family Christmas. Poppy couldn't get excited about it, she'd rather be in London, but the flat would be empty with Suzie in Ireland rehearsing for all those married Christmases ahead of her. She'd confessed that she was really rather terrified of it all, but with the confession came the distinct impression of excitement. Poppy was pleased for her friend. Suzie would love being queen of the castle, a role Poppy would not want for the rest of her life.

"Poppy," Celia called from Reception, "there was a call for you just now. Somebody called Nick Coles? He sounded a bit funny, asked if you could call him."

"Yes. Thanks. Of course."

She'd do it from the privacy of her own office.

The Agency switchboard was very hostile for the time of year. No, Mr Coles was not in. No, they had no idea when he would be back. Yes, certainly she could leave a message but they couldn't guarantee that he would get it. She rang the studio. No reply. She must make sure to wish him a happy Christmas before she left. Maybe she could find him a good present, she owed him that and more.

Poppy decided to do her shopping in

Covent Garden. She leapt on to a bus, squeezed in on the long seat at the end and wondered if her nose was as red as everybody else's. It had got colder in the last week and suddenly everyone was talking of a white Christmas with all the excited anticipation that children attach to snow. It was well dark now in the early afternoon and, however cynical you might be feeling, it would take a hardened misanthropist to resist the excitement of Christmas. The bus swung round the thick traffic at Hyde Park Corner and Poppy looked up Park Lane where the leafless branches of numerous tall trees had been simply decorated with hundreds of tiny pinpricks of white light. It looked as if a cluster of stars had fallen to earth and been caught in the branches.

She got out at the Strand, smiled at the Savoy all giftwrapped with fir branches and red ribbons. Her evening there with Freddy and Suzie seemed a world away. Who would have thought it would end in their engagement? Turning her back on the great Liner of a hotel, she swung up a narrow street which came out in the Covent Garden Piazza and was immediately pleased she had come. Here was all the bustle and excitement she had been looking for. It was crammed with people who'd come with Christmas shopping as an excuse, but in truth were there just to enjoy themselves.

Here and there entertainers had drawn little knots of spectators about them as they performed: tumblers, jugglers, mimes and clowns. Musicians were everywhere: violinists, kilted bagpipers, even an optimistic three-man opera company, but today nobody grudged the silver they threw into the outstretched hats. Helium balloon vendors looked as if they might be carried up to heaven any moment with their armfuls of skyward-reaching silver globes. Food sellers were offering everything a jaded shopper could possibly require for instant energy to fuel the next assault on the Christmas list. The smell of hamburgers and old-fashioned roast chestnuts mixed curiously with the waft of spicey satay on skewers, clove-sharp mulled wine and the brown-sugar smell of Creole bananas cooked by a cheerful black American wearing little but sequined shorts and body paint.

The cold sharp air had not made Poppy's

nose red. Instead it had brought pink to her cheeks, the colour that had been missing too often lately through work and anxiety. With glowing face and sparkling eyes, and her amber hair clouding out round her face in the crisp air, she had no idea how pretty she looked, remaining unaware of the admiring looks directed at her.

She would go to a little shop in a downstairs arcade that specialised in animated toys. Her father was always fascinated by such things. The shop was full of automata, hand crafted in beautiful woods and each one more ingenious than the last. How could she choose between the keeper who climbed the ladder to wash the giraffe when you put a penny in the slot, the diminutive Grace Darling who rowed her ship out to rescue the shipwrecked sailors, or the simple carousel that played a tune as the horses went round, each painted more prettily than the last? In the end she decided on a perfectly simple elephant in beautiful pearwood; he swivelled his head and trumpeted when you wound him up but, which would fascinate her father particularly, the animal did all this at the same time as appearing to be made from one solid block of wood.

Pleased with the present, she headed for the joke shop where she took a basket and filled it up with farting cushions, black soap, rubber chocolate biscuits, lifelike flies and spiders; every horrid sidesplitter she could find to delight Terry's heart.

Two down, the hardest to go. In the end she bought a large and absolutely fascinating book on all the medicinal properties of herbs and flowers, with a section that she knew Lorraine would value on how they should be harvested and stored for commercial use.

Only Nick was left now. It would be nice to surprise him with a present tonight, call in on Tite Street on the way home. She dawdled at windows but nothing was quite right. Her eyes were trying to penetrate the clutter of the dark window of a little shop wedged up tight in the corner of a narrow alley behind the Opera House when Maurice's face floated up behind the window display. He smiled and beckoned.

"Hello again!" she said, inside.

"Welcome to the Emporium!" He bowed theatrically.

"Your shop?" It was dawning slowly. "You mean, this is the Opera shop you talked about? You've got it? Oh Maurice, I'm so happy for you." They hugged but he quickly disengaged because he immediately wanted to show her everything. He darted to and fro, like the Genie of the Lamp conjuring objects from nowhere: an ostrich fan here, a *ridotto* mask there. All his little favourites came out on display in a frenzy of proprietorial pride. It was an odd sight since he had not yet changed out of his admiral's costume, merely set aside the hat. The extravagantly gold-braided costume added to Poppy's feeling that she'd fallen through a hole out of the real world, like a child in a fairy tale.

"Why didn't you tell me about this at lunch?" she chided.

"I wanted to bring you here as a surprise. I looked for you after we got up from the table but you'd vanished! I'm glad you found it this way," Maurice went on, "so much more magical. Come, you must meet Felix." He indicated a slim young man, thirty-five going on seventeen with the light behind him.

Felix gave her a hazy smile. Under a

floppy blond thatch of hair he was very pretty and also wore nautical gear. "I found him a sailorsuit from the original production of *Pineapple Poll*. He looked so wonderful in it I thought we could blur distinction between ballet and opera, don't you agree?"

Felix gave a little pirouette.

"He can lift things off the top shelves and fetch and carry things like I never will again. Were you looking for anything, Poppaea dear, when you pressed your nose to my glass in that Holly Golightly way?"

She explained.

"I know just the thing," Felix said at once and Poppy was glad. It would be wonderful if Maurice had finally found a young friend who was kind and obliging as well as pretty. She crossed her fingers for him and fervently hoped that Felix would not prove to be another Francis.

When he came back it was evident he was both thoughtful and intelligent; he'd found a stunningly appropriate present.

"It belonged to Dame Nellie Melba, believe it or not," the younger man said as he drew an artist's ivory travelling sketchbox out of a soft suede envelope.

The box was small enough to be tucked into a pocket, and when you pressed a little ivory acorn the lid flew up. Inside were were ten tiny cakes of pure watercolour pigment in blocks, two ingenious telescopic squirrelhair brushes, and a small crystal bottle with a screw-on silver lid for your water supply. The whole perfect little set carried with it the satisfaction of something that had been thoughtfully planned and 'specially made for a single purpose.

"Nick will love it," she said. And then to draw out Felix, "I never knew that Nellie Melba painted?"

"I don't think she did," he flashed his boyish smile, "but she was always being presented with things. I don't suppose she used them all."

"Is it terribly expensive?" she asked Maurice, and was so busy looking at the exquisite little box that she didn't see Felix's eyebrows shoot up as Maurice named a ridiculously small sum. The two men smiled at each other over her head and, had she seen that smile, Poppy's last fears for Maurice's future would have left her altogether. There was affection in the younger man's smile, and understanding.

"I shall take it to him straight away." Poppy's eyes were shining.

"I'll walk you to your taxi." Maurice took her arm.

Out in the street they met a man selling packets of sparklers. Poppy bought some on impulse and lit one for herself and one for Maurice; now they were part of the pageant.

"I approve of Felix." Poppy gave her friend a sideways glance.

"I do too. Vixen!"

"Some office gossip," he went on. "We didn't have a quiet moment at lunch and, as you'll see, it's hardly the thing I could have shouted at you down the table. I didn't want Felix to know either," he said. "I trust him completely, you understand, but I've lived long enough to believe that what you don't know, you can't gossip about."

Poppy nodded.

"The Blessed Boudin," he went on. "I have no direct knowledge you must understand, Poppy, but what I do have is access to the gay grapevine and a certain nose for how things work."

She was all attention.

"The painting itself used to belong to a certain happily married banker who would hate the world to know that he longs with an all-consuming longing to get into Francis's knickers. I cannot find anything more definite to go on than that but, given Francis's ruthlessness, I am inclined to let the evidence rest there. The very fact that tracks have been so carefully concealed points to the theory being right: they're two men with formidable brainpower between them. I believe they can be seen together every Thursday evening in Xenon. Maybe the banker's lady has evening classes?"

"Maurice!" Poppy gurgled. "Now it's my turn to tell you. I sat next to the Hon Sarah at lunch, you may have noticed?"

"Nought out of ten for the *placement*."

"Well, she said that Giles had got no further forward in ferreting about the Export Licence. I don't suppose you did either?" He shook his head.

"But that's not my great and glorious news. Sarah's getting married!" Poppy paused for the bombshell to sink in.

"Did she say who the lucky man is?"

"She's keeping us in suspense."

It was starting to snow as the taxi took her through the slowmoving traffic to Chelsea. The flakes were too small and infrequent to merit the compliment of windscreen wipers, but snow they were and Poppy's heart was glad.

She saw the light on in the studio window from the road before she started the long climb up the stairs. She was kept waiting such a long time outside Nick's door ringing the bell that the timer switch in the passage clicked off.

She'd never seen Nick look disorganised until tonight. His clothes were actually rather smart: Armani suit, grey shirt and tie still knotted but pulled down as though he'd started to take it off then forgotten and gone on to do something else. It was his face that looked different and, seeing it now, she realised that she'd always taken his smiling good humour for granted.

"Poppy?" he said, hardly believing the message of his eyes. "Tell me now, very slowly because I'm very drunk, you see. Is that Poppaea Palmer, straight from the Steppes of Siberia with snow on her shoulders, or is it a dream?"

To make absolutely sure, he reached out, crushed her to him and kissed her with conviction.

"You're real," he said at last, their faces still almost touching.

"Yes."

"We can't conduct our lovelife on the stairs. Come in."

He pulled her into the studio and immediately started to apologise for the mess.

"I'm afraid I can't clear it up either," he said, "I've got the most terrible roomspin." He plumped down on a chair.

"Heavy Christmas lunch?"

"You could say that." His happy expression faded. "I got the sack."

"Why?"

"Ian Agen found out I was freelancing on the Trenton's campaign. All gone. Out. Don't bother to clear your desk. Damn, damn!"

"Oh, Nick, it's all my fault. I know it's pretty pathetic and doesn't compensate in any way, but I'm so sorry."

He had closed his eyes again.

"What are you doing for Christmas, Nick?"

"Painting?" He smiled wrily. "My new career."

"But I mean Christmas, like tomorrow. Where are you going, who will you be with?"

"I don't know," he said tonelessly. "We'd rented a cottage in Wales, a group of us from work. They drove down after lunch. I couldn't face it."

"I'll call home," said Poppy, suddenly managerial, "you're spending Christmas with us."

Lorraine answered the telephone so Poppy couldn't speak to her father, who was out giving van Cleef and Arpels their evening walk. Poppy explained the situation. She couldn't come down tonight on the last train as planned, not with a sozzled Nick in tow. They'd have to drive down tomorrow in his car when he'd sobered up. They'd arrive in time for Christmas lunch.

"Oh." There was unaffected disappointment in Lorraine's voice. "Terry and I spent ages making you a lovely Christmas stocking."

"I'm sorry." Poppy was touched.

"Couldn't you come down tonight if

Nick's got a car?" Lorraine coaxed. "It would be so much nicer if we could all wake up together on Christmas morning."

"I'll see what I can do," she found herself promising.

"Your father's just come in; he says to come as soon as you can before the snow really sets in. He's heard the late forecast and thinks you might not make it through the lanes tomorrow if the weather breaks."

Nick's and a car." "Driving seemed "It would be so much ... that we could all ... up together ... Elsie was saying."

"I'll see you ..." ... Elsie and herself presuming ...

15

NICK spent most of the journey asleep curled up on the back seat. Driving through the ever-thickening squalls and swirls of snow, Poppy felt like some very heroic nurse persevering against all odds to accomplish a mission of great bravery and mercy.

The real fun started after Bristol when she ran out of Motorway. All the lanes now looked the same to her and all the signposts were covered in an icing cap of pure white. She'd freeze to death getting out and scraping off the snow; better to rely on homing instinct. No-one was more surprised than she when she found the gateposts and, turning up the drive, saw the familiar roofline against the sky.

Lights had been left on in welcome, and there was for the first time a large and cheerful holly wreath fastened to the door. The grandfather clock in the hall told her that it was now almost two o'clock; the large logs in the stone fireplace had long since given up flaming but their ash gave out a fierce and glowing heat. Nick stood in the hall and looked about.

"It's lovely," he said. "Is it really your home or have you lured me away to an isolated mansion so you can have your wicked way with me?"

"It's really home," she said, putting a log on the fire and warming her back against the resulting flames. "Would you like some hot chocolate?"

"I'm not *that* much better."

"Straight to bed?"

"It might be safest."

Poppy was leading the way upstairs.

"I didn't disgrace myself in the car, did I?" he asked.

"Apart from leaving me to the mercies of Jimmy Young, you were a model passenger."

"No snores?"

"No snores."

"I'm greatly relieved. Is this my room?"

"We call it Hell."

"That seems remarkably inappropriate."

"Only because you go down this little flight of stairs to get to it."

He sat down suddenly on the narrow fourposter.

"Oh dear, Hell seems to be rotating."

"Can you manage?"

"Are you volunteering to undress me?"

"No."

"Pity."

"I'll see you in the morning." She started towards the door.

"Poppy?"

"Yes, Nick."

"Sorry I was so bloody drunk." He looked rueful. "I wish I'd been able to help with the driving. And thanks for bringing me here."

"It was a pleasure," she said, and realised she meant it.

When she woke, she found herself looking straight into a pair of eyes fixed firmly on hers.

"I was hypnotising you awake," said Terry happily, "it worked."

"I don't think you can hypnotise people awake." She raised herself on one elbow to address this complicated problem. "I think it only works if you're sending them to sleep."

396

"Like I do to the chickens."

She widened her eyes and waited for more.

"It makes them go all giddy and run around in circles. Sometimes they fall down."

"Do they get up again?"

He nodded.

"Good."

"Aren't you going to open your stocking then?" He had lifted it off her bedpost and was shoving it under her face. "That's what I came in for."

"You want me to open it now?"

"Well, it's morning."

"Happy Christmas then, Terry."

"Yer. Happy Christmas," he mumbled, embarrassed.

The little hand that thrust the stocking at her was absolutely freezing. She wondered how long he had been standing there, hypnotising. Poppy folded back her bedclothes.

"Here," she said, "jump in. Your mum will kill me if you get a cold. Youch! Just keep those feet away from me. They're colder than two frozen fish."

"It's a good stocking." He grinned up

at her and proceeded to help her immeasurably by opening it all himself.

"Nick's stocking isn't so good," he confided, "but we had to do it at the last minute so it's got rather a lot of nuts and things to fill it up."

"I should think he'll be really pleased to have any stocking at all."

"Mum says you can't have Christmas without a stocking, it's not right. Shall we go and open Nick's?"

"I don't think so." She looked at her watch. "Do you know what a hangover is?"

He nodded.

"Well, Nick should have a monumental one this morning."

"D'you mean he'd hit us, like our dad?" Terry's face was shadowed.

"No, Terry, of course not." Horrified by this matter-of-fact reference to the little boy's frightening past, she gave the little pyjama'd figure an affectionate hug. "Nobody will ever hit you in this house."

"I like it here," he said. "I wish your dad would marry my mum and then we could always be here. You'd be like my big sister, Poppy." He looked up at her trustingly and she was lost for words at the touching little solution to the boy's insecurity.

"I gotta go." His mood had changed in an instant, he was already halfway out of bed. "I promised I'd do the 'orses this morning and if I don't, 'enry'll 'ave me guts for garters."

There was no going back to sleep so she made her way downstairs, quite sure that she'd be the first down by hours, but in the kitchen she found Lorraine, looking flustered, surrounded by jars of mincemeat and pastrycutters. A long apron protected her pink mohair jumper and matching pink tweed skirt.

"I forgot all about the mince pies," she said when they'd wished each other a Happy Christmas. "I could have killed myself when I realised! I did want to do it all so perfectly, too. You see I've never done a proper Christmas before, not one where we were in the middle of a real family and could afford to have all the proper things, instead of just some of them. Sit down and have some coffee while I get these into the Aga."

"Let's do them together and then we'll

both deserve that coffee."

But today Lorraine wasn't the relaxed and natural person she had been when Poppy had first met her.

"You mustn't worry about Christmas dinner," she guessed the source of Lorraine's anxiety, "nobody's going to mind if the mince pies don't turn out okay."

"Yup." Lorraine's smile was strained.

"And thanks for the stocking, it was lovely."

"Oh, good." This smile was more natural. "I love a stocking. You wait for it all year and it's always exciting when the moment comes."

"Terry and I opened it together. He's great."

"Do you think so?" Lorraine's face was thoughtful. "It's done him the world of good being here, and it's a good school too. They don't stand any nonsense. Trouble with those London schools is the kids are up to mischief soon as they're big enough to break a window. I wouldn't want Terry to grow up like that."

"No chance of that here," Poppy said soothingly.

"But am I doing the right thing by him?"

Lorraine stopped fitting little round pastry lids on the pies that Poppy had filled. Her hands hung idle and she looked up towards the kitchen clock, seeing not time present but the future. "We won't be here all our lives, surrounded by soft, kind people. It's a hard world out there, Terry'll have to learn to fight his corner. I'm giving him a little taste of paradise here; maybe it's better not to have it at all than to have it taken away once you've known it."

"I'm the last person to help," Poppy said. "I'm not a mother and I know I've always had it easy compared to you," she remembered Terry's glancing reference to his father's violence, "but I can't imagine that a period when you've both been happy together could do anything but good, whatever came after."

"You're right," Lorraine sighed and gave a small shake of her head, "I can't think what got into me. Come on, or these pies won't be finished before the men turn up."

Nick finally appeared at midday, looking tousled and rueful. His offers of help were firmly refused. Christmas dinner proved Lorraine's worries unfounded. The Aga had produced a perfectly moist bird and perfectly crisp potatoes. They ate in the dining room as it was a special occasion. It was quite unrecognisable from the dining room of old days. Much elbowgrease and beeswax polish had been expended on the oak panelling; where once it had given the impression of a last resting place for woodworm, it now looked shiny, decorative and cared-for.

"Well, you couldn't have a gloomy tea room," Lorraine said sensibly, "it wouldn't sell many buns."

She, Henry and Terry must have worked for a week decking the room with holly, fir boughs and giant red crêpe paper bows. Balloons hung from every light fitting, much to Terry's joy. No sooner had they sat down to the table than he produced an elastic band from the recesses of his pocket, converted his fork into a catapult and, with earsplitting accuracy, fired almonds from the fruit dish at the balloons, until threatened with instant expulsion by his mother. Nick winked at him.

"We'll have a competition after lunch."

Terry grinned back.

After lunch they gathered round the

gaudily decorated tree to open their presents, and Poppy was pleased that she'd taken so much trouble with Lorraine's. The thought behind it pleased both the recipient and her father greatly. Terry was instantly and blissfully absorbed in his horrid toys and her father was equally fascinated by his; Poppy would not like to bet how long Henry could resist taking the little pearwood elephant to pieces so he could find out exactly how it worked. She didn't give Nick his present under the tree with the others, not wanting to embarrass him when he probably had nothing to give her in return; the right moment would come.

Being convinced royalists, Henry, Lorraine, and by compulsion Terry, watched the Queen but Nick declared he would die if he didn't have a good long walk before darkness fell, so Poppy took him out.

"Are you feeling any better?"

"Fragile."

"You were going very easy on the Pomerol at lunch."

"I've never believed in the hair of the dog; the wretched animal just comes back to give you a second bite. I've got a present for you, by the way."

They were on the top terrace, ploughing through drifted snow. She stopped walking and looked up at him as he took off his thick glove to delve deep into a pocket.

"Maybe you shouldn't give it to me now. Is it the sort of thing that would get lost in a snowdrift?"

"Very much so." He had found the little packet. "You'd just better not drop it. I want to give it to you now, here. It wasn't right inside with the others."

"I'd better find a firm footing first."

Till now it had been not so much a walk as a tipsy wade through an unpredictable carpet of snow. From one step to another you could not be sure how far you would sink in, which made the whole progression both cumbersome and comical.

"We'll make for Livia's Folly, it should be out of the wind."

It was no longer snowing hard but a teasing, gusting North wind carried light but consistent swirls of flakes. From the little colonnaded building at the end of the terrace they had a magnificent view over the snowy undulations to the South and the Moor. Livia's Folly, like everything else at Winchendon, had known much better days. This particular piece of the Winchendon jigsaw had been put up by Great Grandmother Livia who, taking her distinguished Latin-derived name seriously, felt it should be commemorated with due pomp by erecting a Classical building. The stucco was peeling off the pretend-stone walls now, and there were gaps in the roof slates where birds had built and no time had been found to repair their ravages.

They scraped the snow off the stone seat that ran the length of the back wall and looked out at the view, framed between the pillars of the portico.

"It's the only time the Moor doesn't look savage, when it's hidden like this."

"I'd like to get to know it. Will you take me there?"

"Not today," she laughed, "we'd flounder and drown. Two more bodies added to its toll." Like all who lived near it, Poppy held the ancient place in awe and respect.

"I didn't realise you were so grand."

She raised her eyebrows in surprise. "Grand?" she echoed.

"All this." He indicated the view they shared from the folly. Nick's gesture included the long South Front of the house, all stone with a central pillared and pedimented portico, the doors and windows framed by moulding with blocked quoins. Winchendon Hall sat like a stone giant contemplating the grounds and landscape spread gently before it.

"Mere glimmerings and decays," she quoted. "Think of it as a millstone and you've just about got it right."

"And this is why you're so serious about your career?"

"Got it in one."

He was thoughtful and sat so still and serious, he'd forgotten all about the red-wrapped present in his hand. She held hers out for it.

"Well?" she asked with a provocative look from under her lashes but he wasn't responding. It was as if the realisation of Poppy's circumstances had placed a weight upon his shoulders.

"Till now I thought your duel with Francis was just a game. Now I see you have to be serious about it. It's more than just ambition, you really *need* the money."

"Not today," she wanted to lighten his

mood, "today I'm only serious about one thing: presents!"

"Here," he said diffidently, "it's not much."

"I love the paper, it looks Japanese." Poppy knew she was talking too much to cover the awkward moment. She didn't understand what had happened on this walk but she knew that something had taken Nick further away from her.

"Not much? It's incredible!" And there was no false enthusiasm in Poppy's voice as she looked down at a classic Lalique brooch: a girl's head in profile worked in gold, with flowing hair entwined with enamelled poppies and waving corn.

"Where did you get it?"

"One of your competitors, I'm afraid." He gave her a teasing smile and pushed back the floppy lock of hair in the way that recently had started to turn her knees to jelly.

"I'm besotted by Lalique. How did you know?"

"I remembered the wasps." He grinned again and made the little buzzing noise she remembered from the Caviar Bar. For a moment she thought he might plant a kiss on her earlobe but then the troubled mood came back. "I wish it was a grander piece with carved rubies for the flowers."

"I couldn't afford the insurance if it was," she said prosaically, "and then I'd worry about wearing it. This I shall wear every day. Will you put it on me?"

She held her face up to his like a flower and undid the thick coat that was keeping her warm. Nick pinned the brooch carefully on to the red cashmere jersey that Suzie and Freddy had given her as a Christmas present. He must take advantage of the open invitation of her breasts under the soft cashmere — couldn't he tell that they were aching to be touched as he'd touched them in Ireland? She'd stopped him then, she wouldn't stop him now. But Nick didn't read that message in her eyes. He wasn't looking into her eyes at all and she couldn't tell him to.

"I love your present, Nick," she said simply.

"You'll get cold," he said. Tenderly he pulled the coat around her and buttoned it with great care. "Let's go back now, I've an idea for a Christmas present for your family. I felt so badly that I didn't even have a box of chocolates to give them today. Come on."

He pulled her up from the stone seat quickly, with a roughness that she half expected to lead to an embrace, but again she was disappointed as he led her outside and they made their way back to the house.

"You go in," he said, "my present's out here."

And he was in such an unfathomable and contradictory mood that Poppy didn't question or disobey him, she simply went inside: thoughtful, hurt, and rather puzzled.

"Suzie telephoned." Her father was reading *Country Life,* sprawled on the kitchen sofa, while Terry played silently at his feet, totally absorbed in something mechanical and vehicular. Lorraine was back in her apron, mulling wine in a large copper saucepan big enough for a baby's bath. The smell was intoxicating.

Lorraine took a taste from the wooden spoon. "Mmm, it's wonderful," she said. "It's from the book you gave me."

Poppy was touched by the gesture. She walked the few paces across the kitchen floor to give her a kiss on the cheek.

"You're giving us a great Christmas. Thanks a lot."

"Did Suzie say where she was?" she asked her father. "I'd like to thank her for the sweater."

"Unpronounceable and Irish. I wrote the numbers down on the pad." He returned to the all-absorbing article. "Oh," addressing her retreating back, "does Nick know about the bell ringers?"

"He'll be on parade, don't worry." Poppy was on her way to the privacy of the phone in the Library.

Crust answered her call. Poppy was impressed that he did duty on Christmas Day; thus are castles run.

"I'm wearing your sweater, it's wonderful," Poppy began when her friend had been summoned.

"We love the cherry tree, darling. Can't plant it yet, the snow's thick on the ground."

"Here too. The cherry tree's the same sort as the ones in Redcliffe Gardens. It's to lure you back to the London pavements when Irish moss starts to sprout behind your ears. Are you having a good Christmas?"

"Best ever. Listen, I've got rather a lot of news." Suzie's voice was brimming with laughter.

Truly, Poppy thought, Freddy had wrought strange and wondrous changes in her friend. Gone was the pinstriped tycoon of yesteryear and in her place was a Suzie no less efficient but a lot more fun about it.

Poppy had a sudden flash of intuition. "You're not married?"

"Yesterday. In a tiny little room. There seemed no reason to wait any longer."

"Oh, Suzie." Poppy was suddenly stuck for the right words. "I wish I'd been with you. It's wonderful, I think I'm going to cry."

"Don't do that. I've far too much to talk to you about. Business."

Poppy laughed instead. Married one day, talking business the next. Suzie hadn't changed all that much!

"There's an adorable man called Alan Jervis. He's a neighbour of yours down there."

"I know who you mean."

Who in the area did not? The Devon community had been horrified when Alan

411

Jervis, the self-made property developer, had bought a very large estate indeed just on the edge of the Moor and decided to settle there. His arrival had been the cause of consternation and suspicion. Immediately he was suspected of wanting to turn the gentle landscape into oceans of rolling bricks and mortar.

The county's worst fears had gone unrealised and Alan Jervis had existed amongst them as a shadowy figure, posing no local threat, for the last ten or so years. Whenever he popped up in the local paper it was for endowing a Scout hut or growing a large vegetable marrow: if Alan Jervis was planning to swamp Devon with development and caravans he was certainly taking his time about it.

Harmless he certainly seemed to be, adorable might be overstating the case.

"Well," Suzie went on, "he's a fishing crony of Freddy's. We saw him at a party in London before Christmas and you know how you get stuck for something to talk about, and somehow the sale of the Ballroom came up. So, anyway, he asked me about Trenton's because he's got some things to sell and, of course, I said you were brilliant. The long and the short of it is that he's in Devon for a very short time over Christmas but he'd like you to come over and look at his things. I'll give you his number, he's expecting a call."

"But I can't just call Alan Jervis out of the blue!" All Poppy's telephone shyness came streaming back at the thought.

"Nonsense. He's expecting it, today."

"Christmas Day?"

"Darling, he leaves the day after Boxing Day." Executive sterness had come back into Suzie's voice. "Look, do you want to screw that bastard Francis or not? Remember the Boudin."

"Remember the Boudin!" The battle cry stiffened Poppy's sinews. She'd make the call and to hell with feeling timid.

"When will I see you, Suzie?"

"We'll be dotting in to London quite soon, I expect. I've Freddy's new career to organise." Poppy heard grumbles in the background and then a squeal.

"He says I'm to stop being bossy and to give you a big Christmas kiss. See you soon."

With Suzie's dynamic example in mind, Poppy called the Jervis number straight away and was rewarded by speaking to his private secretary, a man.

Yes, Mr Jervis had been expecting her call. He would be leaving Devon early on the morning after Boxing Day. He realised it would be an intrusion on Miss Palmer's holiday but it would be so much appreciated if she could come tomorrow. The car would be round to pick her up at four o'clock and he looked forward so much to seeing her then.

Poppy sat for a moment, stunned. She'd maybe spoken four words during the conversation. She felt as if people were simply slotting her into a large and well-oiled machine which could go forward perfectly well with or without her; her name had come up on this particular cog and if she didn't grasp the opportunity, it'd slip away for Francis or someone like him to pick up.

She wished she'd had the presence of mind to ask what sort of things were being sold. It always helped if you knew what you'd be expected to value. Please, please, let it not be Oriental Bronzes!

Full of excitement, she went back to the hall where she found her father.

The handbell ringers were due soon and preparations were being made for their reception. They always came about teatime and were rewarded with Christmas cake and tea or something stronger if they preferred. It had happened every Christmas that Poppy could remember. She looked round the Hall. Never had it been decorated so flamboyantly. As Nick had said, no-one could mistake the great fir for a designer tree. The robustness of the tinsel, multicoloured baubles and great big crêpe paper bows were the very antithesis of the sleek, chic little trees that bid magazine readers celebrate Christmas in good taste.

"I like our big vulgar tree," she said to herself, and her father gave her a quizzical look at the unexpected outburst. She told him about tomorrow's appointment.

"Alan Jervis!" She sat down with the sudden realisation. "I can't believe it."

"I'd better have a word with you now, in that case. Catch the busy executive before she flits on to matters more important." Her father sounded rather cross and decidedly sarcastic.

"Well, I couldn't miss the opportunity."

"It just seems a pity that we can't have

415

you for two days over Christmas without work interfering. And you have got a guest here, you know."

"Nick won't mind."

"That's not the point." His voice softened. "I'm not trying to row with you, darling. What I'm trying to say is not about this particular appointment. It's to do with a certain hardness creeping into you — business first, people later. Does that ring any bells?"

"Oh." Poppy felt devastated. She turned to prod the fire to hide the quick tears, but at the same time wanted to defend herself.

"It's sink or swim at Trenton's, Daddy. You're probably right, I have become tougher, but I don't see there's any other way to cope."

"I know you're having a competitive time, darling, just try not to trample people in your rush for the top, eh?" He paused. "You haven't asked about my decision on the Hoarde."

"There, I can't be such a toughie after all." She managed a small smile.

"Good girl. You can tell Giles that I've decided we're not going to sell it for the moment. You know I've always said I'd prefer to ride the storm without realising the money; though I must say, when people start talking in millions it's all more than a little tempting. Put our troubles right at a stroke and then leave us some change. But there are two things against it, to my mind. Firstly I distrust magic wands, they usually bring more trouble than benefit, and a million at a stroke would be a very large magic wand. Secondly I should be very reluctant indeed to be looked back on by future generations in Winchendon and be remembered as the man who separated the house and the Hoarde. The two belong together. I know you'll say that's sentiment but it's how I feel."

"I'm pleased."

He looked at her sharply. "You're not just saying that? I thought you were pushing me to sell."

"No. I've always loved the Hoarde and feel exactly the same about it as you. It belongs here and it ought to stay long after you and I have gone. But, after all, it's you who's trying to make ends meet. It has to be your decision, not mine."

"I think, with Lorraine's help, that we

might start to get a significant rise in income. No wall-to-wall Jacuzzis yet, you understand, but if we have an additional source of revenue that's steady, we can get some way towards paying off the overdraft and building some capital. She's a whizz with money, you know. Leaves me standing."

"It never was your strongest point."

"I know. Can't think where you got your commercial talents." He put his arm about her shoulders and she knew that peace had been made.

"Daddy, I don't want to worry you," she went on, "but from something Lorraine was saying earlier this morning, I'm not sure she's thinking of staying here very long."

She explained Lorraine's uneasiness for Terry's future.

"Thanks for telling me," he was thoughtful, "I felt she was troubled but didn't know why. To be honest I thought she was worried about you coming down. Funny thing, she had the impression that somehow you didn't like her. I told her that was absolute nonsense. I was right, wasn't I?"

"It's difficult to see someone else in Mummy's place."

"Not in your mother's place, darling. Lorraine's quite different, you know that as well as I do. But it's good to have a companion after all this time; I'm very fond of her and that little rascal Terry." He put his arm around his daughter. "I didn't suppose you might still mind after so many years."

The dogs were restless. He stooped to fondle van Cleef's ears, which made Arpels nudge his leg in a fit of doggy jealousy.

"All right, old girls," he said, "we'd better take you out before the bells arrive. They always stay so long. Coming, Poppy?"

They met a thoroughly excited Terry as they made their way to the door, swathed in snow-defying layers.

"Come and see," he panted. "Come and see what Nick's done." His eyes were shining and if he had been stronger he would have pulled Poppy over in his eagerness. "Come on, 'enry."

As they stepped through the front door into the snowy landscape they saw, in the middle of the lawn, a Christmas nativity

sculpted in snow. Lifesize white figures
rose out of the white snowfield with
a ghostly grace. A worshipping Virgin
Mary knelt at the crib while Joseph stood,
tenderly bending over his wife and the
child, with one of Henry Palmer's shepherd's
crooks in his hand. Nick had made little
niches in the figures, and placed a night-
light in each so the delicate modelling of
the hands and faces was highlighted by a
soft glow.

The landscape had suddenly been
transformed into something magical and
holy.

"It's my Christmas present to you, Sir,"
Nick said to Henry. "I'm sorry I didn't
have anything more conventional."

"I'm glad you didn't," said Henry. "There
is nothing I would rather have. Thank you,
I feel the spirit of Christmas has truly come
down here."

"I helped too." Terry was not to be
forgotten. "I got the stick and I found
the candle things and the matches," he
said, urgent with the importance of his
contribution.

"It wouldn't be the same without them,"
Henry Palmer said solemnly. "Call your

mother, Terry. I'd like her to see this now."

Lorraine came out to see and thus it was that when the handbell ringers arrived in the parish minibus, they found the whole party outside, clustered round the sculpted nativity.

There were ten ringers in all, led by Ernie Stonor, a village ancient who'd started ringing some seventy years ago when he was considered old enough for such responsibility. The full ring was a set of twelve bells so some, the more quick-witted, operated one bell in each hand. The bell was secured by a strap which could be slipped over the hand and kept round the wrist.

There was much shuffling about and clearing of throats as they disposed themselves in front of the Christmas tree.

"She'm a good tall 'un."

"Well branched." There was always a discussion of the tree.

They each stood in exactly the same place year after year, and the family disposed themselves in exactly the same chairs as they occupied year after year to hear the performance. They started as always with 'The Holly and the Ivy', and on they went from there. The old tunes, picked out in bells, had a clarity and simplicity which must have been very ancient. After all, there were bells long before pianos were invented.

Poppy looked round the little family circle and reflected that it was much diminished since her earliest Christmas memories. Surely those remembered Christmases had been filled with grand-parents, vague uncles and aunts, children who must have been related; and, of course, her mother. The candle lights on the tree blurred when she thought about her mother so she blinked hard and looked at Terry who was sure to be doing something devilish. But he was sitting at his mother's feet, still as stone, and with a look of complete wonder on his face.

Her eyes moved on to Nick who must have been watching her for some time. Her dark eyes met his grey eyes. Caught off guard she thought she saw love in his look, but it was there so briefly she might have been mistaken. Had she turned him down too often? Had she managed to kill his love? She put her hand up to the brooch. The bells had stopped ringing.

"Will you help me with the wine, Nick?" Lorraine asked, as Poppy and Terry shared the solemn task of handing round the fruitcake.

They all went outside to wave the ringers off and to press more cake on them for the journey.

"Iron rations, in case you get stuck in a snow drift," Henry boomed cheerily.

"Not with Vicar at the wheel." Ernie was full of faith in his spiritual shepherd.

The day ended with games and charades. Lorraine finally fell asleep in front of the television and Henry banished them so they should not wake her up. Terry reminded Nick that he had a promise to keep and so the three of them went off to the dining room to hold the Great Catapult Contest. Terry won hands down with twenty-one balloons to seven. Nick made Poppy have a try but she couldn't even make the almond fly in the right direction, let alone pop a balloon. This pleased Terry no end.

"Girls," he said to Nick, man to man. There was a world of condemnation in his tone.

"Girls," Nick agreed solemnly, and winked at Poppy who aimed the almond at him but his duck was too quick.

"I'll murder you later." She chased him round the dining room table but, as usual, he was too fast for her.

"Come on, Nick!" Terry was getting excited.

"Time for you to be in bed," she told the little boy.

"Spoilsport! Just 'cos you can't hit a balloon for toffee."

"Not just 'cos I can't hit a balloon," she checked her watch, "'cos it's after ten and you ought to be in bed or you'll be even more poisonous in the morning."

She and Nick conducted a pincer movement round the table, caught the little boy and Nick hoisted him up to give him a shoulder-ride up the stairs to bed. Despite his protestations that he was really not at all tired, they heard his first sleeping breaths before they had left his room.

"Shall we see what the grown-ups are doing?" Nick whispered.

Henry looked up from the kitchen sofa. Lorraine was still asleep.

"We've got Terry into bed," Poppy said, "will you let me do breakfast in the morning? Lorraine's been working so hard."

"It seems a shame to wake her," Henry replied, "but she'd be better off asleep in bed. Yes, please take over." He managed to wake her and take her upstairs.

Poppy and Nick were alone in the kitchen now with only the steady tick of the clock for company. It was gone eleven but seemed too early to think of going to bed yet. Besides, she couldn't bear the day to end.

"There's a bit of mulled wine left," she discovered, lifting the saucepan lid, "shall we finish it off?"

"It'll be no good for breakfast."

"Have you ever noticed how extra-quiet it is when you're surrounded by snow?" Carefully she handed him his mug of hot wine by the handle so he should not burn his hand.

"Thanks."

As soon as she had joined him on the sofa, the dogs came and sat on their feet.

"Fur feet-warmers — luxury," Nick sighed. "Poppy?"

"Mmm?"

"It's been the best Christmas." His free arm, lying along the back of the sofa, pulled her close to him. "Thank you and all that, you know?" His voice was drowsy, tender. He dropped a kiss on the top of her head.

"It wouldn't have been the same without you," she said truthfully.

He smiled. "Good."

She looked up at him, hoping he might drop a kiss somewhere more useful this time. At last he had tuned in to her thoughts. Slowly, very slowly and deliberately, he brought his mouth to hers and took his time kissing her — softly at first and then, as he felt her passion, the kiss changed to something more deep, more urgent and demanding.

The movement of a foot must have disturbed a dog. Van Cleef got up and started to bark.

"Ssh!" said Poppy, but the dog wouldn't hush. "She'll wake the whole house."

"Come on now, there's a good girl." Nick soothed her with ruffling motions behind one ear and whispered sweet nothings but she took her time to stop barking.

"Let me take your drink." A mug in each of their hands had considerably hampered the smooth progress of romance.

"Your snow sculptures were beautiful," she said. "I didn't realise you sculpted too."

"Neither did I 'til I did them." He smiled wryly.

"We've not had time to talk properly. Nick, I'm really sorry you lost your job."

Maybe he was blaming her, maybe that was the shadow in his eyes when he looked at her. If so, she didn't see what she could do about it. Suddenly she felt shy and awkward. She got up, fiddled about washing and drying things and putting them away. Anything rather than go back to the sofa and seem to be asking him to kiss her. If he really wanted to, he'd get up and come to her.

"What will you do now?" she asked.

"Starve in my garret."

"Not take another advertising job?"

"Definitely not. Like I said, it gets in the way of painting. I was thinking about it out there," he indicated the snowy lawn beyond the drawn curtains, "if I don't give the painting a full-blooded try now, it'll be something I'll always regret. I may be lousy or I may be good enough to make the grade; I've got enough to live off modestly, very modestly, for a year. No little jaunts to caviar bars for a bit."

"I've got your Christmas present," she said uncertainly, feeling in a pocket. "I was waiting for the right moment."

Nick waited, still lazily spread on the sofa while she stood with the drying up cloth in her hand. She felt vulnerable and unsure. What if he didn't like her present? Suddenly she wished she'd bought him something conventional and unobjectionable; if she were a magician she'd say a spell here and now to turn the little paintbox into a bottle of cologne or a pair of cufflinks.

"Well, are you going to give it to me or just tell me about it?" he said at last.

Reluctantly her hand came out of the pocket with the present in its soft suede protective bag. He pulled open the drawstring, and when he found what was inside his face changed at last and it was like sun breaking over clear water. He examined the miniature paint box with simple delight, relishing the precision of the springing lid, the neatness of the telescopic squirrelhair brush and the square blocks of pigment.

"Gamboge!" he exclaimed. "Terra sienna! All the proper old colours. Oh, Poppy!" The face he turned to her shone with a new clarity and happiness. "I wondered . . . but I was wrong. Anyone who can give me this understands me exactly, just as I am."

Van Cleef and Arpels, who had been celebrating Christmas like children by behaving badly all evening, suddenly gave tongue to a doggy chorus rivalling in volume the full peal of the departed handbells.

"They'll wake up everybody," Nick said. "I'd better give them their last run, then bed I think."

Out in the snow the dogs were unusually disobedient, running backwards and forwards, barking and disturbing the calm of the night.

"Quiet," Nick told them. "Here, girls." But his commands had absolutely no effect. The dogs yapped and hunted as if they had found the trail of the rabbit to end all rabbits.

"I'm no Barbara Woodhouse," his grin

was rueful, "here." Poppy hadn't bothered to wrap up adequately for the small matter of taking the dogs out and Nick tucked her freezing hand in his pocket.

"Maybe it's just excitement." She regarded, the disobedient pair. "Animals pick up the vibes too, they say."

At last they managed some semblance of authority and brought the two dogs indoors again.

"Poppy," he said, as they stood outside the door to Hell, "I asked you once before if you would come into my room. Have you changed your mind?"

He was holding her lightly, one hand on each shoulder as she faced him, ready to give her her freedom any moment she indicated; his grey eyes looking searchingly down into hers as he asked the question. She had the impression that the lightness of his touch was because the answer was so important to him: he didn't want her to say yes just because she was overcome by the powerful sensual spell of his body close to hers.

She looked up at him. "I was frightened you'd given up asking!"

"Banzai!"

430

Impulsively he picked her up and swung her over his shoulder as though she weighed no more than a cloud. Thus she entered his bedroom in the classical manner of Stone Age man's chosen mate. They were both laughing as he swung her down to the ground again, and then a new solemnity overtook them as they stood face to face, no barriers between them. Nick put out his hands to undo the first button.

"You do know that I love you very much, Poppy?"

"Yes."

And after that there were no more words, just their two bodies learning about each other. Nick was kind and thoughtful and tender, relishing every different stage of their loving, not rushing things, taking his pace from her. His eyes never left hers all the long while their bodies tangled and entwined in a mounting crescendo of passion.

"Mmm?" he said afterwards.

"Mmm," she agreed.

"Well, that's all right then."

16

NICK's happy affectionate nuzzlings and murmurings gradually subsided into the heavy regular breathing that signalled sleep. Poppy was happy to be awake. She lay with her eyes open, not thinking, just looking at the way his eyelashes rested on his cheek. She revelled in the past hour, totally happy about this new step in their relationship. She ventured a small stroke of his hair, the touch of her hand tender and soft lest she wake him, and then just the littlest kiss on the smoothness of his forehead.

Poppy didn't want Giles in her thoughts but he pushed his way in. How different his lovemaking was to Nick's. Now she had two lovers but she didn't feel like a scarlet woman, just a muddled one.

She knew she must get up and go to her own room but didn't want to go yet. It would be setting a new pattern in the house if she slept in any other room than her childhood bedroom. Her father and

Lorraine would probably take it in their stride if they knew she had spent the night with Nick, Terry too probably, but Poppy wasn't certain she was ready yet for quite such a public statement. She was growing drowsier and, had it not been for the dogs, might have thrown caution to the winds and yielded to the combined spell of the heaviness of her eyelids and the warmth of Nick's body.

Through the opiate drowsiness the sound of barking called her back from the lethargy washing over her; she could hear they were getting excited again. She must go down to the kitchen and quiet them.

The labradors must have heard her shut the bedroom door even though she pulled it to as quietly as she knew how; their supersonic senses picked up the small disturbance and their barking grew louder. In the kitchen she did what she could, breaking every house rule by taking the two of them up on the sofa with her and spoiling them, fondling their ears and smothering them with the affection that she felt for all the world in the afterglow of Nick.

The dogs grew calmer, but when she

tried to leave them they thought this was a very bad idea so the racket started all over again. Their water bowl was full so they weren't thirsty, and they merely sniffed the bits of turkey leg she offered, so they couldn't be hungry. They just looked up at her with four beautiful liquid brown eyes saying, politely as they could, "You're so dim, why can't you understand?" Finally she left them and made her way to the Gothic Library.

She was properly awake now and might as well use the time to good purpose.

Her visit to the Jervis Collection tomorrow had settled on her mind and was worrying her; she needed to do a little homework first. In the library she'd be able to look up the saleroom records and, with luck, they'd give her the answers to what the Jervis Collection comprised. If she could discover that then it would be no problem at all to work out some pretty accurate price predictions for him.

Quietly she turned the handle of the door and switched on the light. As ever when she came into this room, she looked first upwards at the blue dome of the ceiling with its exuberant ornamental plasterwork;

finials and crockets tumbled about each other in gay abandon and here and there a gargoyle peeped out, bulge-eyed and pretend-fierce. They always made her smile.

She took a pace or two into the room and sensed that something was wrong. Suddenly alert, she looked about her but there was nothing to be seen. Nevertheless her heart swooped in fright and she backed towards the door in sudden alarm.

"Don't be silly," she said aloud to herself. It was only night nerves.

Firmly she set her feet to cross the Library, past the big central reading desk and towards the little inlaid table in the corner that held her files and the telephone.

She should have trusted her first instinct.

As she passed the desk a man rose up behind it, and placed himself so that he was between her and the door. He seemed to have materialised abruptly in that instant, although logic told her that he must have been crouching behind the desk all the time. Poppy was absolutely frozen. She knew she must shout but nothing would come. She couldn't even manage to get her mouth open, simply stood with her hands at her breast and tried to shift the great iron door in her chest that seemed to have shut against her struggles for breath.

The man stood quite still, looking at her. The moment seemed to last forever, she felt completely paralysed. It was as if someone else's eyes watched the man crossing the room towards her, someone else's mouth was open and screaming, someone else's legs were refusing to run away. The man had reached her and was holding her in a powerful grip. She could smell his stale smell and feel the roughness of his hand as he put it up against her mouth.

"What're we going to do with you, then?" he asked himself.

Poppy could think of a lot of good answers, like 'Let me go'. She came to her senses then. The initial paralysis left her and she started to struggle and kick, trying to bring her knee up to connect with his groin.

Suddenly she saw a change in the man's gloating expression. Nick was there and pulling the man away. She saw his blessed face behind the dark intruder and the sight gave her the courage for a last kick to his shins. Annoyed, he lashed out at her with a huge blow to the head as if to swat her away like a fly before he turned to face the real threat.

The blow to her head accomplished exactly what it was meant to, disabling her so the man could concentrate uninterrupted on fighting Nick. Poppy's senses swam. Just before she lost them altogether, she saw Nick's head too take a shattering blow from the man's strong knuckles. Black hairs like wires on the back of a grimy hand closed her knowledge of the present.

When next she opened her eyes she saw her father's feet and legs in pyjama trousers. It was plainly a dream. Her eyes travelling upwards, she was quite surprised to see his head attached to the top of his body and a telephone to his ear. As yet she could hear nothing but his mouth was clearly moving in speech.

Slowly her eyes travelled sideways and the vision became even more absurd. Lorraine was there in a perfectly hideous dressing gown covered with far too many retina-shattering pink roses. Her face, as usual, was loaded with eye-enlarging blue shadow and mascara but her lips were less glossy. In her hand, the final surrealist touch, she brandished a poker. Poppy had a strong impulse to tell her that she looked silly but the words got stuck before they came out. The dogs were at Lorraine's feet, restless and milling about, just as they had been in the kitchen. The sight of them triggered her memory. Nick, how was Nick? Fearfully, she moved her head and in that movement took in two things simultaneously: the crumpled sprawl of limbs that was Nick lying on the floor, and the crouched defensive figure of her attacker held at bay by Lorraine, the poker, and the two dogs.

Henry Palmer on the telephone was giving a very precise description of the exact whereabouts of Winchendon Hall and telling someone to hurry. To Poppy's blurred mind it seemed a daft moment to be giving travel directions. Her consciousness faded then and only came back when it was invaded by the insistent noise of a siren; now the travel directions made sense.

Her most anxious moment was the ambulance ride. Lying on her side of the ambulance she could look across to Nick's motionless body. His eyes were closed, his face waxy, and he was the focus of the paramedic's ministering attentions.

"Is he all right?" she asked anxiously.

"Fine," came the hearty answer she knew she'd receive, and didn't for one moment believe.

She was checked over quite quickly. She was given a bed for the night and then the hospital were keen for her to go home and rest. Nick was to be kept in longer.

"How can I rest when he's looking so ill?" she fretted at Lorraine who came in the morning to collect her.

"They said there's nothing wrong with his head, they X-rayed it."

"I wish he could have spoken to me."

"It's okay, Poppy, he's not going to die. I know he looks terrible but that's just the shock and loss of blood."

"Oh, Lorraine, I know I'm being idiotic."

"People are, after shocks," she said kindly. "Come on, we'll make you look human again. I've got some miracle cream."

What Poppy saw in the bedroom mirror would need miracle cream. Her neck was one huge rainbow bruise.

"I'll be in polo necks for months!"

"Think yourself lucky." Lorraine's face

looked strained. "There was a knife."

"I don't know what happened after Nick came in. Thank God he did!"

"The dogs would have woken the dead!"

"Of course." Poppy was realising slowly. "That's why they wouldn't settle all evening. He must have been about for a long time. How creepy."

"Look," Lorraine said awkwardly, "I don't know if you made the connection but I got to tell you anyway. The chap who broke in last night was my ex, Terry's dad."

"So he was after you? I thought it was a burglar after the Hoarde. I could have killed Daddy for not putting it in the bank as he said he would. I'm sure I saw the purse of gold on the floor in the Library where it shouldn't have been."

"Well, Jo would never pass up an opportunity, but it's me he was after. Me and Terry. I'd had some idea that he'd found out where we were but I didn't want to believe it so I took no notice. It's my fault. I brought all this on you." Lorraine got up from the bed. "We're nothing but trouble, me and Terry. It's time to be moving on."

"But can't you stay, for Terry's sake? You must be safe now," Poppy reasoned. "Presumably the Police will keep your ex out of mischief for a bit. Breaking and entering? GBH? It certainly felt pretty grievous to me, if not worse." She wanted to coax a smile from Lorraine's serious face but she was having no success.

"Even if they put him away, he'll come out and then he'll be after us again. I can't live with the thought of bringing that on your father again. I love Henry," she said simply, "too much to bring him trouble. It's best to be going now."

"But he can't get Winchendon on its feet without you, Lorraine. Who's to get the leaflets printed, organise the organic market garden you were talking about? Who's to run the tea room and take care of the visitors?"

"Oh, *that.*" Lorraine's voice was bitter. "I don't suppose you'd have any trouble finding someone else to administer Winchendon."

"I'm not talking about the job." Poppy knew her words were inadequate.

"I know." Anger had joined Lorraine's bitterness. "It's my life, and my boy's. And a lovely life it could have been in cloud cuckoo land. Happily ever after, and just waiting for Jo to be released so he could come back again. Sorry, love," she gave a brave little regretful smile. "It's not to be. And anyway," her voice took on a new harshness, "if your father needs someone to run his commercial life, he can always raise a little finger, get his friend Giles de Vere Trenton to sell the Hoarde; then he'll be able to afford as many *housekeepers* as he wants. I know I'm as dispensable as the last one — Bridget, wasn't it? You'll talk of me in years to come like you speak of her now. Just a memory: 'Wasn't Lorraine the one who was rather good at making coffee? Didn't the filter machine date from her time?'"

"Oh, Lorraine, you know it's not like that." Poppy wanted to explain how different Lorraine was, how she'd changed Winchendon and made Henry happy.

"It's okay, Poppy," she cut in. She didn't want sympathy or explanations. "Let's go and see what we can get together for lunch, shall we? One thing I'm not having today and that's cold turkey."

Lunch was eaten in a subdued spirit. Voices were softer than usual and there was an unnatural politeness; only Terry, with the resilience of extreme youth, was right back to normal after his long sleep. He established that his father would be safely locked away for a good while yet.

"Oh well, no worries then. What's on telly?"

Soon the noise of space guns, accelerating spaceships and warring Votrons filled the kitchen.

"Let's take our coffee in the Library." Henry looked at Poppy as he made the suggestion. "If you don't remount, my darling, you'll never go in there again and that would be a pity. There's still the whole section from Q to W that needs to be dusted and have the bindings checked. Come on," he added when he saw the strain on her face, "Lorraine spent hours last night cleaning and tidying it up before she went to bed. She doesn't want her efforts wasted."

He was right, of course. Poppy had a dread of entering the room again but with her father's hand firmly under her elbow and Lorraine behind them with the coffee tray, she was simply bullied into it. Lorraine had as usual done a marvellous job and, with a stroke of genius, had taken the big flower arrangement off the dining room table and put it in the centre of the Library reading desk. The brilliant poinsettias and cyclamen were a positive gesture against the memory of violence.

Poppy smiled weakly as she sat down rather too suddenly. Her legs had just refused to do their job. She looked over to where she had last seen Nick's bloody head. A rug had been moved to cover the spot.

"You're great, Lorraine. Thanks."

"She is, isn't she?" Henry was pleased at this tribute. "And I wanted to talk to you both about something important to do with that. I hope you'll forgive me, Lorraine my dear, this isn't the conventional way of going about things but I feel I must ask you this way with Poppy here. I want you to marry me, you see.

"But when you get to our age and stage we can't just think of ourselves; I know Terry likes the idea but I need to have Poppy's blessing as well. I'd be miserably unhappy if she disapproved, and we couldn't be happy together if that happened." His usual confident humorous manner had deserted him. The importance of the issue was evident in his tentative tone of voice.

"What do you say, Poppy?"

"I say yes, of course, Daddy."

"I don't believe this!" Lorraine had gone pink, she looked quite furious.

"I'm so glad we've got Poppy's blessing," she blazed, "but what about me? I don't recall being asked anything about this. And you might as well know, Henry, I'm leaving. I told Poppy earlier."

"But," he looked bewildered, "don't you want to marry me?"

"Marry you just because you feel sorry for me and Terry? Never! And I'm not going to be your housekeeper either, so you'll have to get another one of those."

"But . . . " Henry didn't know what to say next. He took a few tentative steps towards the blazing Lorraine but, fearful of her fury, failed to complete the journey. He turned to Poppy, quite mystified.

"Daddy darling, maybe your proposal lacked a certain something? You've been wonderfully practical. Believe me, speaking for the children involved you have our blessings. But have you thought that possibly

445

you're not entirely too old for a little romance as well? Lorraine loves you, I know that."

"I don't," Lorraine snapped like a petulant child.

"She told me so herself this morning," Poppy overruled. "I don't see why you shouldn't sort it out between you if you love her too. But not with me here. Three's a crowd for proposals." She slid out of the Library.

At last she could do what she wanted: telephone the hospital. The news was reassuring. Nick could be collected later in the day if it could be guaranteed that someone would be there to nurse him for the next week or so. A concussion had been sustained and must be kept an eye on. When her father had settled his immediate business she'd take the car over to Exeter General; the weather was not letting up at all. A blessing on snowchains!

Poppy joined Terry just in time for the supersonic intergalactic megabattle. She settled down to a long wait, her eyes on the television, her thoughts in the Library, but the wait was not so long as she expected. The Alien spaceships

446

hadn't even reached Earth when Henry and Lorraine emerged, their faces telling their own story.

"Is it too early for champagne?" Henry asked.

Terry was disbelieving when handed a teaspoonful in the bottom of a grown-up glass. "All for me?" He knocked it back in a gulp before anyone could change their mind.

"I think we're drinking to you and me becoming brother and sister," Poppy said.

He was not slow in understanding.

"Okay," he said with a grin, and turned his attention back to more vital happenings in the galaxy.

The doorbell rang in the midst of this happy celebration and there, quite forgotten in the frantic activities of the last twenty-four hours, stood Alan Jervis's chauffeur in immaculately pressed grey livery, complete with cap.

"Oh my Lord!" Poppy greeted him unconventionally, her hand flying to her mouth in horror. "Can you hang on a bit while I get a coat? Have some champagne, we're celebrating."

"I'd better not drink and drive, Miss."

"Oh, of course, how silly of me. My father's just got engaged to be married. He's a widower, you see. It only happened this afternoon. The last hour, in fact."

The chauffeur seemed to be able to unscramble the essential message, and smiled.

"Congratulations, Miss. I can see that business appointments might slip your mind in the circumstances."

"I won't be a minute." And she left him to the non-alcoholic consolation of tea while she got herself organised.

The mirror paid tribute to Lorraine's miracle cream. Poppy's neck looked a great deal better, and her face almost normal now, if pale. Inevitably her eyes still bore the traces of shock; the blue-veined lids were paper-white with heavy shadowing like the edge of thin milk. She made quite sure that her jersey came right up to her chin. The snowy weather would serve as an excuse for her being less smart than she would usually have been on such an occasion.

The chauffeur handled the Range-Rover with ease along the narrow lanes. High winds had banked up tall drifts but to this car they presented no problem. Poppy had never actually seen the Jervis house though of course there had been pictures of it in the paper: a Jacobean Manor house, tall brick gables, high chimneys and stone mullions round the windows, it had all looked very grand. Photographs never give a sense of scale, however, and as she approached the house, she realised with some surprise that it was really quite small, smaller than Winchendon in fact, a tiny masterpiece. The entrance avenue of Limes gave way to garden gates and then they drove up through the ancient and famous Chess Garden that stood in front of the house. Today the topiaried chess set rose up out of a level expanse of snow but she knew that underneath the snow was a pavement laid out in giant squares of white and black Italian marble with, every so often, a square removed to give growing room for the ancient yews that had first been planted and cut into their fantastical shapes several hundred years ago.

The car stopped and Alan Jervis himself stood in the shaft of light that beamed out from the front door.

"Thank you for coming," he shook hands

formally, "it's doubly kind of you to spare the time after your troubles of last night. I was half expecting you to ring and cancel."

"How did you know about that?"

"Oh, the Chief Constable called. He felt I should be warned, special alert if there are art thieves about. I gather he didn't manage to get away with the Hoarde."

Poppy shook her head. If people thought that straightforward robbery had been the motive, then so much the better for Lorraine and her father.

"You're all right, are you now?" Alan Jervis scrutinised her with a pair of shrewd blue eyes not much above the level of her own. He too was smaller than she would have guessed from his pictures. Small but vital, he exuded energy in a way that she had often noticed in self-made successful people.

He was leading her into a small study now, lit by old Dutch brass chandeliers, warmed by a brilliant log fire and inhabited by a small pretty fair-haired woman whom Alan introduced as, "Liz, my wife."

She also enquired after their visitor's health and when Poppy said that last night had been nothing, really, the other woman looked penetratingly at her as if she knew that the truth was far different. Then Liz Jervis smiled her approval.

"I'll leave you two to talk business," she said, "I'll be packing if you need me. Not a night for driving up to London," she smiled at Poppy, "but Alan says he's got to be at his desk at eight o'clock tomorrow so needs must."

"You've got some marvellous paintings here." Poppy looked at the eight or so tiny perfect Dutch pictures glowing out under their picure lights on the wall. "Vermeer, van Goyen, Cuyp . . . I didn't realise there was a collection of this quality outside Buckingham Palace."

"Secrecy's the best security," Alan Jervis said simply.

"And you're thinking of selling these?" Poppy's mind was notching millions on to Trenton's profits for the coming year.

"That's right. Now tell me how you'd handle the sale of my collection."

She told him simply and clearly how first the suitable sale must be found to put the absolutely first-rate pictures into. You couldn't sell them alongside second raters

451

or you'd have the edge off their price; so enough first quality material had to be amassed to make a sale.

"They might be top quality pictures throughout the sale or, as I think is more likely given Trenton's position at the moment, your collection could form the paintings element in a mixed sale of smaller first-rate collections. We've got the Pekin Armorial china to dispose of. If we wanted to make up an entire sale of first-rate porcelain to keep the Pekin company, we might have to wait another six months or so which is time lost." She was ticking off the points on her fingers. "Then we have the Jesse Name collection of medieval jewels which is not large but absolutely first rate, and the Kufir Islamic collection. They'd fit together well: all small collections, making up in quality what they lack in quantity.

"I might indeed go into the logistics of shipping them all over to Ireland for auction in the Ballynally Ballroom before we sell the Ballroom itself. I should have to go into the transportation and insurance costs, of course, but I have a feeling that the Ballynally sale is going to be such a star in this year's calendar of auctions, talking on a worldwide scale, that it would be foolish not to ride as much on its back as we possibly can. I take it you'd have no objection to that?"

"It sounds like good commercial sense."

"I'd have to get Giles's approval, of course. You realise I'm only throwing ideas around."

"Tell me about your new computer system. I'd like to know what happens from first to last; from when the seller makes the first contact to when you finally sell a piece and wave it out of the door."

They seemed to be straying rather far from the purpose of her visit but, Poppy supposed, business was what made Alan Jervis tick so she shouldn't be surprised that he wanted a detailed picture of how the auction business worked. His questions were thorough, detailed and astute, and Poppy was extremely glad that she was able to answer them; she had a feeling that Alan Jervis didn't suffer fools gladly if indeed, he suffered them at all.

"And your young man was behind the

publicity campaign? You dreamed it up with him?"

"Nick Coles? He's not my young man but, yes, he dreamed it up. Actually, it was entirely his idea. I had nothing to do with it except choosing the works of art we were going to photograph, and then doing the dressing up and so on."

"And he's a painter? Is that right?"

"Yes, rather a good one I think. Not that we deal with living artists at Trenton's so I'm not really qualified to judge."

"I think it's a great pity, that," Alan said ruminatively. "A business that makes a living out of art ought to be putting something back into the profession as it exists today. If you think about it, Miss Palmer, we've got the structure all set up to help support living artists."

"We?"

"Well, Trenton's then. I was thinking in terms of the function of an auction house. It's a pity not to be making a market for living artists: completely contemporary sales with reasonable reserves, say two hundred pounds as our lowest ceiling. That's pretty cash to most collectors. A publicity campaign attached: Discover the

Hockney of tomorrow!" It might be quite a commercial proposition, as well as helping young painters along."

"I love the idea," Poppy said, her mind already moving along practical lines, "but I'm not sure it would appeal to Giles. He's quite happy within the conventional auction house pattern; I think that his plans for expansion are more in the realm of extending a nationwide network of small auction rooms round the country. Also I can think of one very mundane but very relevant obstacle: we're simply running out of enough days to hold sales as it is. Adding any more categories would, I think, necessitate extending our premises in London." She paused and allowed her thoughts to slide laterally.

"I suppose Suzie filled you in on Nick?"

"She's a good girl. Best thing that ever happened to Freddy Ilchester."

"I quite agree. But *he* is also the best thing that happened to *her*; Suzie was in danger of disappearing into her own relentless efficiency before he created a little untidiness in her life."

Liz Jervis reappeared.

"I've done now," she said. "Alan, I'm

sure you shouldn't be keeping Miss Palmer away from home on Boxing Night. Have you finished?"

He smiled. "I'm sorry, Miss Palmer. I forget that other people don't get quite as carried away talking business. I find it fascinating, you see. I hope you've not been bored."

"It's been fascinating for me, too. I wonder if I might ask you a great favour?"

"What's that?"

"Well, I know you're going up to London later but I don't think it would delay your departure. Nick's in hospital in Exeter, you see, but they said we could collect him this evening."

"And you'd like Rollins to take you there on the way home? Of course. It's not a night for you to go driving round the country by yourself, ferrying invalids about. After giving up your Boxing Day afternoon, it's the least I can do for you in return."

Alan Jervis had telephoned the hospital so Nick was ready and waiting, dressed and on a chair in Casualty. On seeing him Poppy's emotions turned somersaults and she was pleased there was an empty chair beside him, her knees having decided suddenly they didn't want to carry her any more. She took his hand, which made him wince.

"Sorry." She did her best to smile, but his pale face and bandaged head made her smile weak and her voice wobbly.

There was no time for all the things Poppy wanted to say. The chauffeur's streamlined timetable had no period marked 'loving conversation'. Before Poppy or Nick could organise their thoughts, they found themselves efficiently disposed in the Range-Rover. Nick, horizontal, took up the length of the back seat, and was made as comfortable as he could be, given his bandages and strapping. Poppy, in the front passenger seat, turned from time to time to give him loving looks, but Rollins' presence acted most effectively as a conversation inhibitor.

Everything conspired against a private talk. The moment they got home, Lorraine took over. Nick was rugged up in front of the Aga, with Terry and his mother vying to bring him any little thing his heart could possibly desire.

"I feel like a Pasha," he grinned at

Poppy, "Turkish Delight at every turn. Look! Terry's just brought me all this Lego in case I get bored."

He indicated a tray on his lap, full of bright primary-coloured bricks.

"I'll build a castle and say you did it." For a brief moment the two of them were alone. She stooped to kiss him and knelt beside him so her face was on the same level as his.

"Are you all right?" she asked.

"Never better."

"Stupid!" she laughed.

"I'm all right." His eyes clouded. "And you?"

"Never better," she gave him back in his own coin.

They looked at each other for a long moment.

"I wanted to kill him," he said, and his face took on a desolate look, "I just wasn't strong enough. Did he hurt you very much?"

"I'm glad you *didn't* kill him! Trial for manslaughter would have been tiresome."

"You didn't answer me."

"A little." She pulled down the neck of her jumper to show him. "I'm all right, really. But I wouldn't have been if you hadn't come in just then. What brought you down?"

He grinned crookedly and winced as the grin caught his bruising,

"There was a certain amount of noise. The dogs were in full cry. Also I think you did a bit of furniture moving in your struggles. Thumps and bangs and so on."

"I don't remember that. Did I ever say thank you?"

"I don't remember *that.*"

It seemed quite natural to lean forward just the little bit that was required to put her lips very gently to his and leave them there for as long as he wanted. He seemed to want quite a long time. They were getting on very nicely when Lorraine and Henry came into the kitchen. Lorraine cleared her throat.

"I was just going to offer some soup," she said, "but maybe it's not the right time?"

"No, of course it is." Poppy got to her feet, embarrassed.

"Instructions from the hospital," Lorraine explained, "something hot to drink, early to bed and no excitement!"

"I'm absolutely not excited, Lorraine,"

he said solemnly, "except about your engagement. Congratulations."

"Thanks." She blushed and asked Poppy, "How did you get on with Alan Jervis?"

"Very well indeed." Poppy told them at length about the interview, her excitement at selling the collection, and Alan's ideas on supporting living artists.

"He sounds a man after my own heart," said Nick. "If only someone with real power in the art world felt the same."

"I'm going to suggest it to Giles," Poppy told them and, because she was looking at Lorraine when she made the remark, did not see the way Nick's face closed up at the mention of Giles's name.

"I've got to go back to work tomorrow, I'm afraid," she went on. "The Jervis Collection is another thing that wants attending to ASAP. The hospital say Nick's okay at a pinch for the car journey."

"There's really no need for you to go haring home, Nick," said Lorraine. "I'd be much happier if you stayed here with us for a bit. There's no-one in the studio with you who could look after you, is there?"

"No, but I'm fine." He indicated the

bandages and strapping. "Just hospital drama."

"Look," Lorraine said firmly, "I feel badly because my one time boyfriend beat you up. He came to this house because I live here, right?"

Nick nodded.

"Well," she went on, "I'd feel a lot better about it all if you'd let me look after you while you get better. Understand?"

"I understand," he aquiesced, "it sounds lovely. Truth to tell, I don't really feel like going home right now. Coping sounds rather like hard work."

"Good," she said, "that's settled then."

"Just as long as you keep that blasted Lego away from me. It gives me a headache just looking at it." He tried a grin, and the bravery of it made Poppy long to fold him in her arms. Suddenly he was very pale under the bandages.

"Bedtime," he said briskly, and refused anybody's help in getting him up the long flights of stairs.

She had hoped she might have a long talk with him before she left in the morning, but he was still sleeping and his rest was policed by Lorraine and Terry more jealously than Cerberus guarding the gates of Hell. There was no feat of persuasion or cunning Poppy could perform to get past them.

So many things to say to him. Now she'd have to rely on the damn telephone!

17

POPPY was furious. After years of successfully avoiding the pie crust frills from Hilditch & Key, she'd have to join the high-necked blouse brigade! It wasn't fair but, scrutinizing her neck in the mirror, she realized there was nothing else to be done. The famous alabaster Palmer neck looked like nothing so much as a makeup-artist's novel experiments with the Army Camouflage Look. A look that, Poppy could confidently predict, would never catch on. The face above the neck was glum.

Then she remembered a *Vogue* shot of Brigitte Bardot in the fifties, pouting from under a printed leopardskin chiffon scarf. Poppy had just such a scarf. With chiffon leopard round her neck, mock Cartier panthers in her ears and her crocodile boots, she was ready to face any animal in the Trenton's jungle.

Not everyone had come back to the office so quickly after Christmas. Sarah was not at her desk, Poppy noticed. She must be prolonging the delights of pinstriped love in shady Bracknell.

Giles, she noticed, was. The Trenton's-green Bentley had been hastily parked and was taking up most of two spaces; someone would be cursing Giles.

Amanda was in her office, busily opening mail.

"Good Christmas?" Poppy asked her.

"Dull by your standards."

Poppy raised her eyebrows.

"'Trenton's girl in break-in drama'." Amanda indicated a *Daily Mail*.

"Damn!" Poppy was really distressed. "I'd hoped it could be kept quiet."

"Are you all right?" Amanda asked. "No, that's a silly question, I can see you are. Trust the papers to exaggerate; by this account you were practically raped and Nick left for dead."

"They never get anything right." Poppy didn't want to look at the paper, it made her feel sick. "Tell me about your Christmas, Amanda. Did you have a good time?"

"Great. Family stopped short of coming to blows and I even did a little work for you."

"'Well done thou good and faithful servant.' What sort of work?"

"I got into one of those 'Do you really work at Trenton's? I've got a picture in my attic' sort of conversations after church. Well, I needed some exercise after Christmas lunch so I bicycled over to have a look at the picture."

"At home you'd have been engulfed in a snowdrift."

"In civilized places they clear the roads with JCBs these days." It was part of Amanda's mythology that Winchendon was Sleeping Beauty's Castle, stuck in a cul-de-sac of time, never to see a twentieth-century convenience.

"Want to hear what happened?"

"I promise not to interrupt." Poppy was penitent.

"Well, the painting in the attic was practically ripped off a calendar. No good at all but it wasn't that, it was the house. Absolutely extraordinary. Full of those heavy, ornately carved oaken pieces that depress you just to look at them. 'Brown furniture' with a vengeance. The old biddy doesn't want to sell it, thank God! She thinks it's worth lots and is passing it on.

I hope the heir has sombre taste."

"Makeweight for a containerload?"

"Just that, but listen: she had a Tiffany lamp with a big domed shade. It was up in the attic and absolutely filthy. She'd no idea of what it was, told me the shade was made from the shell of an old turtle her uncle had shot in the Seychelles."

"Do you *shoot* turtles?"

"I told you she was a bit doolally. She wouldn't believe me when I told her what it was, swore blind about the ancestral turtlehunt; so I took the shade off. It weighed a ton, I was terrified of falling down the loft ladder with it. I got it to the nearest bathroom and scrubbed a hundred years of dirt off it and shone a torch behind to show her. Convinced her it was glass then, not priceless shell. Now she thinks it's no longer connected with her uncle the turtlehunter she finds it quite unbeautiful and so I've brought it up in the boot of my car with instructions to sell."

"The base is stamped underneath?"

"Yup, TIFFANY. Clear as a bell."

"Good. And the shade?"

"A rather unusual subject: magnolias."

466

"Hmmn. Offhand I can't think I've seen that before. Wistarias, yes, ten a penny. Magnolias, no. Maybe it's a one-off? I wonder what really good Tiffany lamps are fetching now? They've peaked, of course, but they're still not cheap."

"I checked on the computer. Sixty-five to eighty-five thousand dollars in New York at the moment, that's the best market."

"Well done!" Poppy beamed at Amanda. "It's great to be back at work!"

"Could be greater. I've got to go off to Francis." Amanda's voice changed to parody: "*I'm* your boss, not that bitchette in Books and Pictures, and don't you forget it, Amanda *dear*."

"Damn! I could have used you this morning."

"You know what he's like."

"If only I didn't." Poppy waved Amanda away, knowing the game wasn't worth the candle.

"Maybe we'll have time to nip down to Mama Rosa's for lunch."

Vain hope. In the event the day caught up with them both: Mama Rosa's was a non-starter.

Francis came to see Poppy in the middle

of the morning. She braced herself for complaints about Amanda-stealing.

"Still here, darling?" His little pointed teeth were nibbling round the edges of a cream doughnut.

"That won't do your diet any good." She was mesmerised by the busy little pink tongue that was flicking in and out most efficiently to hoover up every last little smudge of synthetic cream.

"'A moment on the lips, a lifetime on the hips', darling, but ooh I do love them so much! No need to worry about the *embonpoint*." He sleeked his hands down his burgeoning bulk — Poppy thought he had every need to worry — "I'll sweat it off in the gym tonight," he went on. "I've found a marvellous new place full of the most delicious young bodies."

She didn't need to ask the sex of the bodies.

"Good for you. If ever I get to the stage when I need a gym, I'll know just who to go to for advice," she said sweetly. "Was there anything special? I've got work to do."

She quickly exited from the computer program on screen in front of her which was, though Francis must not know yet, framing the first draft of the entire Jervis sale campaign: catalogue descriptions, advertising campaign, terms of sale *et al.* She had also started the laborious process of tracing the provenance of the paintings. The more that was known of the history of a painting the better, a fact which always showed in the eventual selling price. The perfect painting would be one clearly signed, referred to in the artist's account book at the original time of sale, and never lost sight of thereafter. Such paintings were rare. And, of course, with a bunch of canvasses each, on average, three hundred years old, there was a lot of history to verify. She'd be in touch as soon as she could with Joost de Mompert: more Sherlock Holmes-ing in Holland was indicated.

"Yes, there was something special, there was indeed." The rump end of the doughnut disappeared in a large gulp and Francis leaned over her desk for a tissue to clean his hands: had the computer been on, he would have had a perfect view.

"It's the day of reckoning, my darling. First of Jan. is not far off, or had you forgotten? I half-expected you not to come back after Christmas, dear." The endearment was syrup-sweet. "You know you haven't a prayer."

"I know no such thing!"

"Don't you realize when you're beaten? I've had my little calculator out over Christmas and it really doesn't take a sophisticated mathematical mind to work out that I'm miles in front." He smiled his smoothest crocodile smile, the one that made his pink cheeks plump out like a little *putto* puffing a gentle zephyr.

"I just don't see how you can work that out, Francis."

"Look at this." And he put a very efficient balance sheet in front of her.

"But you've left out whole big items." She looked up from the paper. "The Ballynally Ballroom's not here, nor's the Millington Rubens."

"There's no money in for either, yet. The accounting's at the end of the year. Monies not received don't count." He sat back with his smuggest smile.

"They've traced the blockage of the Rubens export licence to you, you know." It was now or never for her little bluff.

She had the satisfaction of seeing the smugness vanish and in its place, momentarily, was shock.

"What proof is there exactly?" He had recovered his sang froid quickly.

This was the very question she'd hoped he wouldn't ask.

"And the trick with the Boudin." Keep hammering and she might panic him into admission.

He smiled.

"That *was* a good one." He looked round to make sure the door was shut behind him and then settled into his chair. He paid a little attention to his bow tie, studied his nails for imperfections and then, comfortably crossing his ankles, looked across the desk at Poppy with a little smile.

"Darling, your guesses are spot-on. But, I know they are only guesses. There's no fun in anonymous victory so I'm admitting to those two strokes. It will make my eventual triumph even sweeter knowing that you know." He wagged a rosy, perfectly manicured finger. "I laid my trail far too cleverly to leave the smallest trace of a connection. And without proof, it is simply a question of my word against yours."

His face was a study in malicious pleasure.

"Have you decided to sell the Hoarde, darling?" he persisted like a dentist probing an aching tooth.

"My father doesn't want to."

"Oh dear. Well, there goes your job! Giles certainly won't bother to keep you on now; it was the only reason you were here in the first place. That and your *beaux yeux*. Of course, the *yeux* aren't worth much now you've been handled by the rough trade: Giles would never go for second-hand goods."

"He didn't handle me." She was trembling now, torn between equal urges to cry and to hit him.

"Oh, silly Jo. Missed his moment! Don't forget," Francis paused at the door to deliver his customary parting shaft, "you can prove absolutely nothing."

"I shouldn't bet on it, Frankie," she told his receding back. Alone, her rage evaporated and Poppy was suddenly still and thoughtful. Francis might just have given her the one piece of evidence she needed against him. She buzzed for Amanda.

"Bring me one copy of each of today's

472

papers from Publicity, will you?"

The door opened and there was Giles. "Poppy, my love, are you all right?" His hand lifted the heavy tresses off the back of her neck and he bent to kiss her nape, sending shivers down her spine.

"Happy Christmas, darling," he murmured, somewhere in the region of her ear. "God, it's wonderful to see you! I've missed you so much."

"Giles." She couldn't believe it. She felt his lips all about her. Nick, she thought, and tried not to respond but Giles's lips and hands were finding their way to places that made her shut her eyes and melt with pleasure. Nick. The thought was fainter but Giles felt her momentary hesitation.

"Look at me, darling." His eyes were looking into hers with teasing speculation and, at such close quarters, she didn't stand a chance. The sight of him and the feel of his hands overwhelmed her.

"God, I want you. Christmas was endless without you. Are you expecting any visitors in the next half hour?"

"Amanda's bringing some papers."

"In that case, I suppose we'd better stick to business."

"In that case, you'd better be at a safe distance. Sit in that chair the other side of the desk." Poppy said shakily. "I can't guarantee sensible answers while your hands are just exactly where they are at the moment."

With a last caressing stroke he reluctantly unhanded her and went to sit on the chair that Francis had so recently vacated.

For a moment the two of them just sat, looking at each other; the tension was so great that there might have been strings stretched taut between them.

"So where did you spend Christmas?"

"Duty visit in Bracknell," he said, without further explanation.

"Home of the Met. Office!" The piece of useless information came floating back from a game of Trivial Pursuit.

He gave her an impenetrable look.

Today he was wearing a charcoal suit. Underneath it the pale blue Turnbull & Asser shirt was cuffed with pigeon's blood rubies, carved with the seal of a Persian emperor; you could drown in their depths. Poppy smiled, remembering Sarah's little fox-masks; cabochon rubies were in another league.

"Giles, there's something I have to tell you." She steeled herself. "I talked to Daddy over Christmas. He's decided to hang on to the Hoarde." She held her breath. If Francis were right, he would sack her on the spot; but Giles's face was unfathomable.

"I'm glad he can manage without having to sell."

"It's part of Winchendon. I'm glad too."

"One day it'll be yours, have you thought of that?"

"Not necessarily." She explained about Henry and Lorraine getting married.

He looked thoughtful.

"And you don't mind?"

"It takes the burden of responsibility off my shoulders. Besides, I like Lorraine."

"An ex-bunny girl?" He made it sound like a crime.

"That was a long time ago. She makes Daddy happy, that's the important thing." Giles's look told her he thought plenty of other things were more important.

"I've just had Francis in here," she went on, "flourishing a balance sheet. Have you seen it?" Giles shook his head. "He's saying that any actual money not in doesn't count. That's not the arrangement as I understood it."

"Darling, you know Francis, he's just trying to unsettle you."

"Good. I'm glad, because I've got another absolute plum."

She told him about adding the Jervis Collection to her total of sales.

Giles gave her an odd look. "There are going to be great changes at Trenton's in the New Year," he began.

"You've settled on the new partner?"

"Something like that. But all will be unveiled on January 1st. We're calling a small meeting of key staff to put them in the picture before the rest of the workforce gets back in on the 2nd. Don't forget to come into the office that day, will you?" he teased.

"I'll try to remember."

"Are you free on New Year's Eve?"

"Of course." She'd had a couple of invitations, but nothing that couldn't be scratched.

"Good. I've just finished building the Orangery in my garden. Will you come to my Orangery-warming party?"

"Wonderful."

"Nine o'clock, I think. Wear your dancing shoes and," his expression changed to the frankly lascivious, "do you still have that dress you wore to model for the jewellery sale?"

Of course she did.

"That was the first time I realized what I had sitting behind the door marked Books, Prints and Pictures. Wear it, will you?"

"Maybe." She smiled enigmatically.

It looked as if he might reach across the desk to punish her for teasing but the telephone went and it was an important call so, while she spoke of shipping crates and customs forms, he slipped out of her office, leaving on her neck a lingering kiss, and on the air an atmosphere charged with promise of things to come.

It was a lovely surprise to find the Earl and Countess of Ilchester in the flat when she got home.

"It didn't stop raining for three whole days," Suzie explained, "we couldn't possibly stay a moment longer."

"So you're honeymooning in Redcliffe Gardens?"

"Such a romantic spot," said Freddy,

"We think it will catch on."

"Darling, why don't you go to your club or something? I've got so much to talk about with Poppy."

"Not wanted already." He looked like a mournful bloodhound. "They told me young wives were heartless. I should have listened."

Suzie consoled him with a kiss. He brightened immediately.

"What if I had a bath?" he suggested. "A long one? You could do all the catching up that's confidential, and then after the secrets session I could take you both out to dinner."

"Now," Suzie was businesslike, "did you go and see Alan Jervis like I told you to?"

"Yes, Nanny."

"I'll ignore that." Suzie was forbearing. "And?"

"And he's a sweetie. I can't think why the entire county of Devon is up in arms against him; he couldn't be nicer or have better taste."

"That wasn't what I meant, exasperating girl. How did you get on?"

"Terrific. Marvellous pictures — we could

make world prices with our hands tied behind our backs. Thanks, Suze, it'll be a real contribution to Trenton's figures next year."

"And?"

"That's all really, about Alan Jervis. Far more important, I want to tell you about Francis. He came into my office, gloating and preening. As good as admitted he was behind the Boudin fraud, *and* he blocked the Millington Rubens, Suzie, but there's absolutely nothing I can do about it."

"Why not?"

"He'd deny it all and I've no concrete proof."

"There must be some way."

"Tell me if I'm grasping at straws, but I think I've found it. He slipped up and incriminated himself about the break-in at home."

Poppy told her about Francis dropping the intruder's name.

"There was no way he could have known that. The Police still haven't released his name."

"But you must do something about it, Poppy! You should go to the police."

"Not yet. I read all the papers I could

lay my hands on in the office but they don't have every single publication. He just might have seen a later edition with a special newsflash, you know how they change."

"The police could check."

"And what if the name *was* in a paper and I'd accused Francis falsely? It wouldn't do me any good to be making wild allegations about my business rival, and it certainly wouldn't thrill Giles to have Trenton's staff dragged through the popular press. It's stalemate." Poppy could have cried, with the frustration of it.

Freddy had emerged now, scrubbed and resplendent.

"How's Nick?" he asked. "Hero of the shining hour."

"Being fussed over at home." Suddenly she longed to be alone to telephone him and talk to him for ages and ages.

"It was sweet of you to ask me to join you," she said, "but I'd really rather stay here this evening. Suddenly I'm terrifically tired."

"I should think you are." Suzie was solicitous. She bustled about the kitchen with her customary efficiency and would not leave until she had put a club sandwich of tremendous proportions in front of Poppy.

"You're to eat every mouthful!" she commanded. "I shall inspect the bin in the morning."

"Freddy's right," Poppy tilted her head to contemplate her friend, "you know, you could win awards for bossiness."

"Poppy," Suzie was serious, "what we were talking about before. May I ask Freddy's advice? He's not a complete fool, my husband," Freddy beamed, "and this is too important to give up on."

Alone, Poppy collapsed. Suddenly she felt completely drained; she longed for a bath but seriously wondered if she'd have the energy. Bed was the answer, with the skyscraper sandwich and the cordless telephone: she must ring Winchendon before she flaked out utterly.

The phone rang for a long time and then she heard Lorraine's voice. Whenever she rang home, she was fated to speak to her.

"Poppy, we've been so worried about you. We're sure you shouldn't have gone back to work so quickly."

"I'm absolutely fine, really. I couldn't possibly have stayed at home anyway," she'd try to make Lorraine laugh, "that little shark Francis circles the waters. Take a day off and I'd be likely to have my job snapped up in one greedy gollop."

"I don't know how you can cope with someone like that. I've always thought I was tough but I couldn't begin to."

"It's just a game," Poppy soothed, and was pleased that Lorraine did not know the extent of it. "How's Nick?"

"He's all right in his body," Lorraine responded. "The doctor came to look at him and his pulse and things are doing everything they ought. I made him spend most of the day in bed. He didn't want to but I think he was grateful really. He's weak, of course, from losing so much blood."

Poppy felt queasy at the thought of Nick's blood. Lorraine seemed unconcerned.

"He still looks white as a sheet and it'll take a bit of time for things to mend; the ribs still hurt when he laughs. It seems quite difficult to make him laugh at the moment."

"I suppose there's no chance of speaking to him?"

"He's asleep now, I'd hate to wake him up. Didn't he ring you this afternoon? He was making calls."

"No."

Why hadn't he? If their night together meant what she had thought it meant, he should have rung her before he rang anybody else in the whole world. She'd been perfectly reachable all day to anyone who knew her office number.

"Do you love him, Poppy?"

"No way." Right now she hated him. Why hadn't he rung?

"Don't sacrifice your happiness to your career, Poppy. You're luckier than you know having Nick in your life; if I'd had someone like that in love with me when I was your age, it might have spared me a lot of heartache."

"He's not in love with me, Lorraine." Suddenly she wanted to cry.

"That's not the message I get. Maybe he's backing off because you're so high-powered. Men like to be the bread winner, you know."

The last thing she wanted was Lorraine's

advice. "Look, I know that when people get engaged themselves the first thing they want to do is to marry everybody else off but Nick and I are just friends, okay?"

"Sorry, Poppy."

"Okay."

It was not only Nick and Lorraine she was cross with. Lying in bed, furious with herself, she started to cry and simply couldn't stop.

18

NICK stayed at Winchendon the short days between Christmas and the New Year, leaving Poppy in an exasperating limbo.

As she dressed for Giles's New Year's Eve party her emotions told her she was betraying Nick by even thinking of going. Her mind told her not to be silly, you didn't refuse the boss's invitation to a party, ever. Besides, the silence from Nick's end remained deafening. Every time she rang home he managed to be out or asleep; it couldn't be a coincidence. Once she had got through to him and they had an illuminating discussion on the current depth of Devon snowdrifts and the absolute deliciousness of Lorraine's homecooked hams. All very well in its way but far from the nitty-gritty. She imagined that the impersonal futility of that conversation had to do with Nick not being alone in the room at the time but as the hours passed by and he did not ring back, she wondered.

Poppy knew that Lorraine, in her guilt over Jo's attack, had the deepest suspicion that Nick would probably die if left alone for one whole minute at a time and it would be entirely her fault, but surely he could escape long enough to manage a solo effort on the telephone if he really wanted to?

Uncertain of his feelings, Poppy was in defiant mood. Tonight she would dress for Giles and see what the New Year brought.

Her hand wandered along the magical creations of chiffon, lace, sequins, satin, velvet and wicked draping that comprised the couture collection. Her hand reached for a sugar pink pearl-embroidered Balenciaga, but then she changed her mind. Giles had specified the strapless silk satin sheath. Giles should have what he wanted.

"Next time, Monsieur Balenciaga," she murmured apologetically as she returned the pink.

What to do for jewellery? Her throat looked naked without the flawless diamond *rivière* necklace. She rummaged. Eventually she decided on a piece she'd picked up for a very few pounds second-hand. Indian and chunky, the thick multi-stranded pearl collar was threaded with occasional garnet beads and each end of the pearls terminated in a fabulous serpent's head of gold with wicked garnet eyes. Studying herself in the mirror, she ran her hand across her throat and twisted her head back and forth to catch the harshest light. Even her critical eye found no trace of bruising.

She looked out of the kitchen window to check the weather. White flakes were falling lazily against the backdrop of the London roofscape. She called up Charley the cab and was treated to a cheerful stream of his opinions on Christmas, with special reference to his mother-in-law and the extreme meanness of tips bestowed by the customers at Harrods' sale.

As they drew up to the Spitalfields house, there was an air of bustle. The streets were clogged, and Charley advised Poppy to get out and walk the last twenty yards.

"You'll get there a lot quicker and I won't 'ave no bovver wiv these drivers in flat 'ats and no steering locks to speak of."

Chauffeur-driven limos were jockeying for position, red Porsches were growling to be noticed, the mêlée around the brightly lit entrance was prodigious.

Once inside, she gave care and custom of her coat to one of many waiting footmen and received in return a little mother of pearl fish engraved with a number. Part of her Fine Arts-trained brain recognised the fish as an eighteenth-century gambler's token. Not for Giles the humble cloakroom ticket!

The crowd of guests was moving through the hall which was lit solely by big wax candles in silver sconces. There were also candles in the large central Georgian 'lustre' or, to give its modern name, chandelier. The dancing flames gave sparkling, shimmering rainbow colours to the jewel-like cut crystal drops; light gave off radiant light like diamonds.

Poppy let herself be carried along with the crowd. The movement took her through the downstairs Morning Room: a fleeting impression of a deliciously domed ceiling painted to imitate the sky, scagliola columns with silvered capitals, and quietly restrained walls of a soft grey-blue.

Still the human stream moved on, chattering, gossiping, kissing in greeting and being handed champagne flutes by

488

Georgian-liveried footmen amongst whom Poppy recognised one or two Trenton's porters.

"Hi, Paul. The wig suits you a treat!"

The sometime porter gave a very unGeorgian grin.

"It's ever so hot and itchy," he confided.

At last she reached the door which led to the courtyard at the back of the house. The enclosed space still retained its original granite cobblestones, worn with the footprints of time. Two marble statues stood, whiter still than the sparkling of snowflakes that swirled and fell about them with the wilful wafts of wind. And across the courtyard stood the new Orangery, painstakingly constructed to match the original which had stood here two hundred years before. A pretty little building, it was perfectly symmetrical. Large round-headed windows stretching to the ground took up the façade, and through the glass Poppy saw orange trees, strictly and spherically clipped to echo the shape of their own vivid fruit which shone with a bright waxy gleam on the bough. Once inside the door, the air was heavy with the scent of orange blossom and busy with the chatter of friends. On a little daïs a string quintet played mostly Mozart.

Giles received his guests within the doorway. Many of them had come masked or in fancy dress but he stood out as only he could: magnificent, dark, and completely confident. He didn't need fancy dress to mark him out in a crowd. As host he wore white tie tonight and his shirt sparkled with Fabergé studs of diamond and black South Sea pearls; larger versions of the same were in his cuffs

"Poppaea." He drew out the melody of her name as though he were singing it in opera. "I want to find some time alone with you. Don't disappear, will you?"

He only had time for a long look before the next guest had to be greeted, the next hand shaken.

Poppy looked about her, there were many faces she recognised: Trenton's best clients were here, but only a few of the staff. She saw Maurice across the room. He kissed his hand to her with a gallant flourish and indicated in eloquent mime how impossible it would be for him to reach her just then across the crowd. Poppy was pleased to see that he had his little matelot beside him.

Francis was squiring the bulk of Phyllida Box: he wore sky blue satin and the lady wore quantities of feathers. The Hon Sarah was here and had trotted out her best and safest Hunt Ball navy blue, flouncy and bouncy in a bulky taffeta. She looked like a human festoon blind and was being awfully gracious at Giles's side, which must irritate him considerably since a secretary should know when to draw the line. If Sarah was here, so must her young man be. Poppy craned but couldn't spot a pinstriper.

"You're Poppy Palmer, I've heard a lot about you."

She looked round to meet the eyes and outstretched hand of Ian Agen.

"I know who you are," she said, "but how on earth did you know me?"

"Dear girl," he put his head back to laugh, "can you really ask an advertising man that question when you've been plastered over every publication and hoarding for the last three months?"

"Oh, yes. I somehow never think of those photographs being me. Listen," she felt brave, "I'm glad you said hello. There's something important I want to talk to you about. Can I monopolise you for a minute?"

"Five would be better." The Iron Man of advertising seemed much more approachable than the press gave one to believe.

"It's Nick Coles," she started.

"Best art director I ever had."

"Why on earth did you sack him, then?"

"Rules. He broke his contract."

"Can't you give him his job back? He lost it because of me, you see."

"We seem to be between the crowd and its Vintage Clicquot. Shall we get out of the mainstream?"

Ian Agen managed to find a way between the press of the crowd. He led her to a little garden seat, tucked out of the milling bodies and secure behind an orange tree in a Versailles tub. A man with an impeccable flair for organisation, he had also somehow managed to pick up two flutes of the Widow on the way.

"Let me explain," he said. "You did both me and Nick a great service in getting him sacked. Me because, as I said, he was a great art director and, when push came to shove, I would have kept him on for the sake of the business even though I knew his talent was wasted there."

Poppy took a sip of her champagne and kept her eyes fixed on his face.

"You did Nick a great favour," he went on, "because what he really needed was to be kicked out of his comfy job. Nobody but a saint or a lunatic is going voluntarily to give up a big fat salary to go away and try his hand at painting. Nick's neither saint nor lunatic. He needed a push out of that job and you, I'm afraid, provided it."

"How did you hear that he was working on the Trenton's campaign?" She wondered if this were another of Francis's sabotage jobs.

"Oh, your Chairman and I coincided in Los Angeles. I was on a shopping spree: Hockneys and some lesser knowns. Giles was looking for capital."

Poppy frowned. Giles had known the moonlighting could cost Nick his job.

"I don't want to put my eight-and-a-half where its not wanted so stop me if I'm overstepping," Ian Agen said. "Rumour has it that there's more between you and Nick than just an advertising campaign." She opened her mouth to object but laughingly he held up his hand. "Hear me out, for what it's worth! I'm a great fan of Nick's paintings; he doesn't know this yet, and I don't want you to tell him either, but the Agen Gallery is going to have a major collection of Nick Coles's. Leonid has already spotted the talent; we're not going to be outbid by a creep like him. *That's* how good I think Nick is.

"In case you're not as bright as you seem to be, I'll spell it out for you: Nick's not going to starve because you lost him his job. In fact, I would feel quite safe in predicting that your young man will be earning more in three years' time by his paintbrush than he would by staying in the commercial world."

Another person referring to him as her young man.

"You're a sweetie." She reached over to kiss his cheek. "Thanks."

Here was more food for thought but not enough time to digest it. She saw Suzie and Freddy deep in conversation with Alan Jervis. Suzie beckoned her over.

"There's no need to introduce you," she beamed.

Poppy wondered if it would be bad

form to talk shop but Alan, as usual, was principally interested in shop and had no such scruples.

"It's going well," she answered his queries. "I've got the whole sale schedule roughed out. We only need your approval to go ahead."

"A week early." He raised his eyebrows. "Well done."

"It's nearly midnight," Suzie interrupted, "and it looks as if Giles is about to organise us."

He had gone to the little podium that held the string quintet and, such was his natural authority, had simply to stand there and wait for the laughter and the chatter to die down, and all eyes in the room to focus on him.

He consulted the Patek Philippe. "Midnight! Happy New Year everybody."

The hubbub of people wishing each other Happy New Year rose immediately but was quelled by Giles's attitude. Clearly he had more to say.

"Tomorrow I'll be announcing great changes for my company, but if you want to know about that you'd better read the papers; not even I can give you a sneak preview without getting into hot water with my lawyers. So watch the front page on January 2nd."

Again the murmur arose; again he had not finished.

"My second announcement, just as important, has something to do with Trenton's as well. London is about to lose one of her most eligible bachelors, if the gossip columns are to be believed. I am about to be delivered up into the jaws of matrimony!" Theatrical groans. "I have had the good fortune to work with my fiancée over the past year or so, and her performance at Trenton's has only added to my love and respect for her."

Poppy held her breath and felt the hot colour flooding her cheeks. Trust Giles for the unexpected!

"Sarah Cavendish has consented to marry me. Wish me joy."

Poppy heard scattered applause and congratulations and saw Sarah materialise beside Giles and lift, from the capacious skirts of the matronly dress, a sapphire of staggering dimensions.

Shock prevented her hearing any more. She had to be alone. When she got out into the cold air of the courtyard she ran across it and into the house, now mercifully free of flunkeys who had moved to other duties amongst the guests.

She ran up the nobly proportioned staircase, tore open doors to look for her coat but couldn't find the cloakroom. One of the doors led to a guest room with a little bed. She flung herself down on the quilted chintz cover. She desperately needed time alone to sort out her feelings.

Poppy did not know how long she lay there in the dark, crying, puzzling, and berating herself for an imbecile.

She was brought out of her reverie by the soft touch of a hand stroking her hair and caressing the back of her neck. She turned to sit up, and there was Giles!

"Crying?" He wiped away the tears. "For me?" He looked pleased.

She must sit up and get herself organised but she'd not brought a king sized handkerchief, where did you put one in a strapless dress and, besides, how was she to know she'd need one?

Giles produced an immaculate cream silk confection with hand-rolled edges. "I want you to stay the night." With a light push, he kept her horizontal and looking up at him as he bent over her on the bed.

She couldn't believe her ears. "Sarah?" she faltered.

"She won't find out. She always goes home to Mummy and Daddy, I think they sit up and wait. She won't sleep with me until she's got a wedding ring on her finger." The contempt in his voice astounded Poppy.

"But, Giles, I don't understand," she raised herself up on one elbow, "did I just hear you announce your engagement to her or did I dream it?"

"Certainly I'm going to marry her but that needn't change anything between you and me, Poppy, my sweet." Giles's hand trailed lightly over her bare shoulders in the way that had always made her shiver. "Say you'll stay, darling, it's a perfect chance for us."

She was dumbstruck.

He started to kiss her passionately on her face and neck, and suddenly he was on top of her and trying to undo her dress so he could kiss her breasts. Poppy struggled and her dress helped. Thank God for a million satin buttons! A zip would have yielded her up to him in no time at all.

"Come on now, don't be coy." Giles's breathing was ragged. "It's exciting when you struggle but there's a time and a place. Can't you see, Poppy, I want you now?"

There was only one thing to do and she did it. She was perfectly placed for a strategic kick and my, was it an effective tactic. When he had recovered the power of speech he asked her with genuine puzzlement, "Why did you do that? It damn well hurt!"

"It damn well hurts your getting married to Sarah when all the time I thought it was me you loved! Why do you want to get married to that idiotic . . . " she searched for a word damning enough " . . . nincompoop of a woman?"

"Are you still young enough to think that people marry for love?" he asked, with a world of weariness in his voice. "Poppy darling, even you can't be that naïve."

"I am, actually." Her chin went up.

"Sarah's going to be the perfect wife for me: very rich, well-connected, compliant, not too bright."

"And efficient," Poppy interrupted, "she'll run your life like clockwork." She was recovering fast, her voice was steady.

Giles had noticed the recovery too and put his own interpretation upon it.

"Let's not waste time talking about Sarah. Come here," he sank his voice to its most seductive murmur, "I need you."

Poppy could play this scene too. She looked at him with smouldering eyes, parted her lips and said in a voice husky with pretended passion: "Giles darling, you may need me but I don't need you any more."

She blew him a kiss and left, pleased with her exit line. It might even be true. Later there could be tears and regrets, certainly there'd be embarrassment. For the moment his amazed expression was balm to her fury. How could she ever have been taken in by him? Poppy went in a businesslike fashion to collect her coat and made her way downstairs to leave. Suddenly the inclination for tears had left her, in its place only a soldierly stiffening for battle.

A smaller crowd was centred on the front door now, people making their goodbyes to Sarah in their host's unexplained absence. Poppy did the conventional thing and lined up to shake hands.

"Lovely party, and congratulations, Sarah. I never realised it was Giles you were talking about."

"You weren't meant to," Sarah smirked. "Do you know," her blue eyes narrowed appraisingly, "I always thought you had your claws out for him. Of course, I couldn't blame you. He must be the best catch in London."

"Sarah darling, you deserve each other!" Poppy gave her a sweet smile.

Giles would lead her a merry dance, and Sarah would give him absolute sour-faced hell. Poppy decided she must be irredeemably wicked to take such pleasure in the thought.

"Darling?" Suzie had spotted her across the room. "Can we give you a lift? It's all right now," she put her arm about Poppy, "we're well away from the crowds. You can cry, Freddy won't mind."

"But, Suzie darling, what if I don't want to cry?"

She took a long and speculative look at her friend. "I don't understand at all but, oh, the relief! I thought you'd be heartbroken over Giles."

"Giles de Vere Trenton," Poppy said slowly and deliberately, "is a lowly worm."

"May I quote you?" Freddy grinned.

Heaven not to have to hit the office till twelve!

Poppy lay and luxuriated and thought about last night. She was quite surprised how unemotional she felt. Looking back over the last months, so many clues fell into place. She'd been foolishly trusting, blinded by her own feelings for Giles. He'd never said he loved her, never pretended that. Maybe he assumed she was playing the same sophisticated game he was himself? Maybe everyone in his world played by such rules?

There was one great consolation. Giles's passion for secrecy meant that very few people had even guessed at the affair. Amanda might have surmised that there was more than a game behind her boss's theatrical worship of the Chairman, but Poppy had not confided even in her. So people would not be looking at her with pitying eyes. She could go into the office today and no-one would treat her with kid gloves.

There was Giles, of course. She wondered if, after last night, he'd give her the sack? Then Francis would be cosily installed as his number two. The thought of Francis made Poppy think of the attack on Nick.

Now she was truly overwhelmed with shame. How could she have wasted all that time mooning over Giles when Nick was there and wanting her? She remembered Ireland and how she had rejected him then; she thought of Nick and some unnamed girl learning to tango in Sloane Street. Damn, damn, damn!

It looked as if she'd lost Nick, and now she'd lose her job too. Heigh ho, how did one dress for the big exit scene?

"Ready?" Suzie called through the bedroom door.

"Just about," Poppy lied.

"A fiver says you're not even out of bed. You'd be late for your own funeral, Poppaea Palmer. We're leaving in ten minutes if you want a lift."

"Are you coming in, too?" she asked, as

Freddy parked the car outside Trenton's. She'd expected to be dropped.

"Thought we'd just look in," he said.

"Thank Giles for the party," Suzie put in. She caught her husband's eye and both of them started to giggle.

"Is this some exclusive family joke or may I share it?"

"Exclusive, I'm afraid."

"You'll be sharing it quite soon." Freddy gave the girls each an arm with his usual courtesy, and ushered them into Trenton's.

There were quite a few people in the Boardroom: some journalists, some photographers, the dry Trenton's lawyer whom Poppy remembered all too well, and all the saleroom Directors. Alan Jervis was there which made Poppy check her watch; he was really much too early for his appointment with her, maybe he could wait in her office. Most surprisingly, Nick was there too.

She looked across at him and, without meaning it to be so, her heart was in her eyes. Nick saw their message clearly and took a step towards her. Had they been alone she felt it might have been more than a step. He had a heavy scar now, above the eyebrow where the bandage had been; a scar he'd wear forever and she would never stroke it, never smooth the hair away from his forehead to kiss it. Oh, what she had wasted!

"I think we're all here now, ladies and gentlemen."

Unexpectedly it was Alan Jervis who made the announcement. It wasn't his place to open the meeting and his statement was not correct; there were two notable omissions from the gathering: Sarah and Giles.

"You'll be surprised to find me here and not Mr de Vere Trenton," the flashbulbs had started popping, "but I am here in my capacity as new owner of Trenton's, having bought out the whole of the previous Chairman's holding which gives me, as you may know, well over fifty per cent of the stock in the company. I have several changes to announce both in staff and in policy at Trenton's for the coming year.

"My business interests have hitherto been chiefly in the property world and I would no more assume that I could run a saleroom unaided than win an Olympic medal for iceskating.

Poppy was pleased that he did not stop for sycophantic laughter.

"But," he went on, "I have, as you can imagine, spent some considerable time looking into the commercial potential of an auction house. Ladies and gentlemen, the fact was forcibly borne in upon me that Trenton's is a goldmine. I'd have been foolish not to buy it, given half a chance. I'd also be foolish not to have it managed by efficient professionals. In the last year of his chairmanship, Mr de Vere Trenton found it hard to choose between the merits of two of his best staff but I find no difficulty at all in taking the decision as to who is to run the business on a day to day basis: Poppy Palmer has shown great initiative, commercial good sense, and clearly has the knowledge and experience needed for the job."

She was not quite sure that she was hearing right but she certainly liked what she heard.

"Miss Palmer is, I know, unusually young for a job of such magnitude and, to help her through treacherous waters in the early days, she might appreciate some wise counsel. Maurice Blessingham has consented to give us a little of his time on a regular basis and he will act as Miss Palmer's adviser for at least the first year."

Poppy and Maurice smiled at each other.

"I am surprised to see Francis Dernholm at this meeting," Alan Jervis went on relentlessly. "In view of some of his activities over the past year, I feel that he is not of sufficiently high moral character to represent Trenton's Auction House and herewith sever any connection with him. I believe the police want to interview Mr Dernholm on several matters concerning fraud and incitement to burglary."

Alan Jervis might be small in stature but he certainly packed a punch. He raised his eyebrows and looked directly at Francis who did his best to become invisible and slunk crab-like towards the door, a sale catalogue over his face against the clicking cameras. Poppy thought she'd be blinded by the flashlights.

"Two new Directors are to be appointed to the board: the Earl and Countess of

Ilchester have kindly accepted to open an Irish arm of the company: Trenton's will be the first of the internationals to open in Dublin, and I look forward to a new and healthy source of income from across the Irish Sea."

Poppy looked at Suzie. Freddy's little job indeed!

"Lastly, and forgive me for so trying your patience, it was brought forcibly upon me how very successful the advertising campaign had been in boosting actual volume of sales during the last quarter of the past year. If Trenton's is to become a modern, commercial saleroom on an equal footing with the best, publicity must not be ignored. Nick Coles was the mastermind behind the autumn campaign and he will now play a more central part in the structure of the company as Director for Contemporary Art. I feel very strongly that living artists should have an opportunity to sell competitively in the auction world. As a talented painter himself, this is a cause dear to Nick Coles's heart. Thank you, ladies and gentlemen."

Poppy could not reach Nick, she couldn't even catch his eye; the surging tide of pressmen was engulfing her.

"Look this way, Poppy."

"Give us a smile!"

"What d'you think of your new job then?"

"Well done the Trenton's girl!"

"Chin to the right a bit, love."

Poppy was dazed with the battery of blue lights and commands. She and Alan Jervis gave a short impromptu press conference then Alan, with customary authority, drove the journalists away so he could speak privately to her.

"I have two confessions," he began. "Firstly I have absolutely no intention at all of selling my collection of paintings, I love them far too much. I'm afraid I played an unforgivable trick on you but I could think of no other way to gauge firsthand your business ability. Forgive me?"

She shook his outstretched hand.

"Secondly I'm sorry for springing news of the appointment on you in this way. It would have been polite to ask you first."

"Polite, but unnecessary."

"I must explain. As soon as I became interested in buying Trenton's it was clear to me that my ideas were so diametrically opposed to Giles's that his departure must be a condition of sale. He has left quite happily, by the way, and is starting a fine arts investment consultancy, backed by the Cavendish money and with his fiancée as the sleeping partner."

She made no comment.

"Until recently," Alan continued, "I had thought I would continue Giles's system of running you and Francis in competition until I had made up my mind for myself which one of you I would prefer to take over. However," he looked grave, "last night I was told of some very disturbing suspicions about Francis Dernholm's conduct."

Hence the huddle with Suzie at the party!

"First thing this morning I spoke to my friend the Chief Constable and he confirmed those suspicions. The burglar has admitted that he was acting on Mr Dernholm's instructions to break in and steal the Hoarde." Poppy held her breath. "Clearly it had to be my first act as Chairman to sack Mr Dernholm. He must not work for the new administration for even one second: our reputation is our greatest asset."

She smiled to hear the old familiar First Commandment.

"You've not yet said if you'll accept."

Her grin broadened. "Certainly I will, and thank you."

Alan Jervis put out his hand in a businesslike fashion and she was glad beyond measure to have a Chairman who shook hands. She'd had enough of Chairmen's kisses.

"Oh, and thanks for giving me Maurice," she said, "I'll need a nanny for the first year."

She hit the street in a nimbus of elation. Had she been barefoot and coatless in the snow she would not have noticed. She could afford a car now on her new salary. Maybe she'd stop short of a Trenton's green Bentley, they were rather large to park. She could think about buying her own flat too. Suzie and Freddy couldn't be sweeter, they hadn't even mentioned it, but they couldn't *really* want to start married life with a lodger. She grinned at the thought of the two of them running the

Dublin saleroom. She'd have to keep on her toes lest Suzie in Dublin outperform Poppy in London. The coming year was not going to be dull.

Where would she get her flat? Not far from Trenton's . . . Kensington? Chelsea? She saw herself in a perfect flat, immaculately decorated like the pictures in *Interiors.* It looked very pretty in her mind. Pretty and empty.

Suddenly she knew that she didn't want empty perfection; there was actually only one place she wanted to live in London, and one person she very much wanted to live with. Her steps had been taking her there of their own accord. She found herself turning into Tite Street. She stopped at the door to Nick's building, suddenly overwhelmed by nerves.

Ringing his doorbell felt like the bravest thing she'd ever done. When he came to answer it her breathing was so panicky it felt as if a rollercoaster was giving rides inside her chest.

For a moment he stood stock still.

"Can I come in?" she asked in a small voice.

"On two conditions."

She looked up at him enquiringly.

"This time I have you all to myself."

"And?"

"This time you stay forever."

THE END

TO FIGHT THE WILD
Rod Ansell and Rachel Percy

Lost in uncharted Australian bush, Rod Ansell survived by hunting and trapping wild animals, improvising shelter and using all the bushman's skills he knew.

COROMANDEL
Pat Barr

India in the 1830s is a hot, uncomfortable place, where the East India Company still rules. Amelia and her new husband find themselves caught up in the animosities which seethe between the old order and the new.

THE SMALL PARTY
Lillian Beckwith

A frightening journey to safety begins for Ruth and her small party as their island is caught up in the dangers of armed insurrection.

NURSE ALICE IN LOVE
Theresa Charles

Accepting the post of nurse to little Fernie Sherrod, Alice Everton could not guess at the romance, suspense and danger which lay ahead at the Sherrod's isolated estate.

POIROT INVESTIGATES
Agatha Christie

Two things bind these eleven stories together — the brilliance and uncanny skill of the diminutive Belgian detective, and the stupidity of his Watson-like partner, Captain Hastings.

LET LOOSE THE TIGERS
Josephine Cox

Queenie promised to find the long-lost son of the frail, elderly murderess, Hannah Jason. But her enquiries threatened to unlock the cage where crucial secrets had long been held captive.

TIGER TIGER
Frank Ryan

A young man involved in drugs is found murdered. This is the first event which will draw Detective Inspector Sandy Woodings into a whirlpool of murder and deceit.

CAROLINE MINUSCULE
Andrew Taylor

Caroline Minuscule, a medieval script, is the first clue to the whereabouts of a cache of diamonds. The search becomes a deadly kind of fairy story in which several murders have an other-worldly quality.

LONG CHAIN OF DEATH
Sarah Wolf

During the Second World War four American teenagers from the same town join the Army together. Forty-two years later, the son of one of the soldiers realises that someone is systematically wiping out the families of the four men.

BUTTERFLY MONTANE
Dorothy Cork

Parma had come to New Guinea to marry Alec Rivers, but she found him completely disinterested and that overbearing Pierce Adams getting entirely the wrong idea about her.

HONOURABLE FRIENDS
Janet Daley

Priscilla Burford is happily married when she meets Junior Environment Minister Alistair Thurston. Inevitably, sexual obsession and political necessity collide.

WANDERING MINSTRELS
Mary Delorme

Stella Wade's career as a concert pianist might have been ruined by the rudeness of a famous conductor, so it seemed to her agent and benefactor. Even Sir Nicholas fails to see the possibilities when John Tallis falls deeply in love with Stella.

FATAL RING OF LIGHT
Helen Eastwood

Katy's brother was supposed to have died in 1897 but a scrawled note in his handwriting showed July 1899. What had happened to him in those two years? Katy was determined to help him.

NIGHT ACTION
Alan Evans

Captain David Brent sails at dead of night to the German occupied Normandy town of St. Jean on a mission which will stretch loyalty and ingenuity to its limits, and beyond.

A MURDER TOO MANY
Elizabeth Ferrars

Many, including the murdered man's widow, believed the wrong man had been convicted. The further murder of a key witness in the earlier case convinced Basnett that the seemingly unrelated deaths were linked.

DEAD SPIT
Janet Edmonds

Government vet Linus Rintoul attempts to solve a mystery which plunges him into the esoteric world of pedigree dogs, murder and terrorism, and Crufts Dog Show proves to be far more exciting than he had bargained for . . .

A BARROW IN THE BROADWAY
Pamela Evans

Adopted by the Gordillo family, Rosie Goodson watched their business grow from a street barrow to a chain of supermarkets. But passion, bitterness and her unhappy marriage aliented her from them.

THE GOLD AND THE DROSS
Eleanor Farnes

Lorna found it hard to make ends meet for herself and her mother and then by chance she met two men — one a famous author and one a rich banker. But could she really expect to be happy with either man?

A RARE BENEDICTINE
Ellis Peters

Three vintage tales of medieval intrigue and treachery featuring the author's monastic sleuth Brother Cadfael.

POIROT'S EARLY CASES
Agatha Christie

In this collection of eighteen stories, Hercule Poirot begins his celebrated career in crime.

THE SILVER LINK
– THE SILKEN LIE
Lynn Granger

Elspeth is determined to preserve her Scottish heritage and the Elliot name, but running Everanlea, a large hill farm, presents problems.